SCENTED GARDEN OF DELIGHT

The coolness of the terrace garden after the stifling warmth of the ballroom suddenly made her shiver. Here, the moist, weeping fragrance of wisteria vied with night-blooming jasmine, engulfing them in a wild sweetness. Alone with Merrick in this romantic setting, one she had envisioned in all her fantasies, Adria felt strangely cold, and wildly excited.

When Merrick caught her to him, Adria melted against him, feeling the hard length of his body. She lifted her face to his, her lips slightly parted, waiting, wanting.

"I knew you were beautiful when I first touched you in the darkness," he said gently.

His mouth came down heavily on hers, soft, yet demanding, tasting, then retreating. His big dark hands worked in caressing patterns over her slimness, not ungentle; masterful, experienced hands, warmed with passion. She heard his aroused gasp, felt the weight of her gown drawn from her shoulders.

"No," she murmured without meaning it. Something unknown stirred deep in the hollow of her being, something charged with life, with need. . . .

Other Leisure Books by Lynna Lawton:

UNDER CRIMSON SAILS

LYNNA
LAWTON

LEISURE BOOKS NEW YORK CITY

For Art Jones, a scholar and a gentleman, always

A LEISURE BOOK®

Published by

Dorchester Publishing Co., Inc.
276 Fifth Avenue
New York, NY 10001

Printed in the United States of America.

1992 Edition
Leisure Entertainment Services Co., Inc.

Glory's Mistress

PART I

THE KNOWING

CHAPTER 1

"Now all that is needed tonight is the right sort of persuasion."

Telling herself so, Adria created her most suitable affectation of the evening, the orphaned pose. A touch of the melancholy, a touch of the gamine.

The Sommerfield eyes, tawny and unpredictable like candleflame just weren't soulful enough. The haughty feline slant discouraged innocence, no matter how much Adria practiced the mood.

Everything tonight, of all the crucial nights in her life, hinged on her portrayal of a naive, totally witless female. Being a Confederate general's daughter naturally brought with it a certain acclaim, particularly if that general happened to be Alfred Sidney Johnson. Until tonight, she had basked in its welcome graces. She wouldn't let it all be ruined—war or no, not if it was in her power to forestall it.

Adria shrugged at the lovely pearl-beaded flounce that caressed the slope of her breasts, working it another half inch lower. Her reflection in the Tulip framed mirror glared encouragingly back at her. She drew a full breath, struggling against the corselette stays that were torturing her ribs. Adria exhaled slowly, magnificently, until the creamy upper fullness settled cleverly above the bodice line. She must look vulnerable as well, and that pose, her body could certainly provide.

From the stove grate beside the chimney pillar she could hear the musicians down below in the garden terrace tuning their instruments. The French clavicord with its mellowed throaty tones, used only for Savannah's traditional Yule galas, was echoing a keyboard scale amid the faint scarping of violins. In the hushed moments that awaited the conquering downstroke, Adria heard her heart thrumming desperately in her ears. This once she prayed, just this once, let me have my way.

The "hidey hole" room on the top gallery floor with its tiny powdering alcove must have somehow been overlooked by the other guests seeking the same respite as Adria; it was a place of privacy in Savannah's war-swollen City Hotel. There wasn't a room to be had, what with the influx of Confederate officers and uprooted Southern families retreating from Union General Sherman's "March to the Sea." General Hardee had his regimental headquarters on the second floor, a virtual encampment for the Army of Northern Virginia. At all hours of the day or night the graceful iron-laced stairway teemed with gray-clad officers. They moved quietly with grim dedication among the clusters of guests. No one asked any more how the war was progressing. Everyone knew it was only a matter of weeks now, or, more realistically, days.

Adria smoothed her tortoise-shell handled brush over her sun-glinted hair, then tossing her head, brushed its tumbled length forward, letting the weight settle on her shoulders. At least here, in this forgotten room, a haunt for prominent devotees of *ecarte, vingt-et-un* and "brag" who preferred to gamble outrageous fortunes far beyond what was considered decent by tolerant Southern law, she could be to herself, compose herself for the scene to come. She wouldn't let her life be tampered with any longer. She refused to be some "glory mistress" wedded to Southern pride. She was eighteen years old tonight, surely old enough to decide her own future, and she intended to tell General Hardee as much. Still, it all must be done with utterly believable innocence. The general was proving to be a very difficult man.

In the tarnished light, Adria's *Pensee* satin veloute gown seemed to catch at the waning twilight hues, shuddering a violet cast over the supple cloth with such unexpected magnificence it was breathtaking. A good omen, she decided, snatching up her single strand of amber pearls, a birthday gift from Thressa and the General. The safety catch proved exasperating, slipping beyond her reach a dozen times before she secured it.

She flung a confident glance at the mirror,

paused to steady her mood before leaving the hideaway, then unlatched the door bolt. It wasn't really a stairwell; the dumbwaiter that served the upper floors reaching even to the "hidey hole" had been abandoned when the City Hotel added on an east gallery. The steps down were nothing more than arranged planks staggered atop each other with scarcely enough passage room for one person.

"Oh, damn!" Adria swore, crushing her lovely gown tightly against her and lifting the satin hem over one arm. The darkness in here—why hadn't she remembered this? Two hours ago, when she had climbed this same turreted passageway, the sun had been full, grazing enough light through the downshaft for her to see. It was black as a witch's tail in here now, with only a sliver of light where the second floor converged. She couldn't very well surface there, not amidst the swarm of officers that occupied the general's restricted second floor. Still, the devilish thought amused her. But it would not amuse the general.

If she was just careful enough; a small tear or dust blot on her gown was certainly preferable to spending the evening up in the "hidey hole." How could she have been so thoughtless? Because she *needed* to be alone, she consoled herself—away from Colly Blanchard's pathetic illness, away from Thressa Hardee's companionable tears, from all the mothering, the ceaseless, depressing war talk. Of course she cared, it was just that she felt so suffocated, so stagnant in their mature, benevolent company. Thressa would never allow the alterations that

Adria had just made to her appearance, much less approve. But, there would be *no one* to approve unless she was able to find her way down these black floating steps into the pantry closet on the ground floor.

At the third step her courage revived. Light seeped quickly up from below, outlining the rough underside of the stairwell. It wasn't as far down as she had imagined. A dozen steps, no more, and she was nearly halfway down. As suddenly, the light was gone. There was a brushing, breathy movement, quick determined steps. Someone was inside the stairwell with her.

Frantically, Adria took a step back up, bruising her elbows against the grainy, unplastered wall when she tried to turn her body. Voices overhead now, boisterous, laughing, drifting down from the "hidey hole" room. The room was being used for the night, and its occupants had just locked the bolt.

She felt someone touch her, felt the warm, quick shudder of breath against her naked shoulder.

"You can't come up here," she swallowed.

"And you can't come down," he said.

Adria could feel his smile, the hot strength of his body pressing against her, the languid arrogance in his voice. This wasn't happening. She was dreaming it.

Adria preened her voice. "If you were any kind of a gentleman, sir, you would—"

"Usually, when I am this close to a woman I am making love to her."

British—the crisp timbre in his voice was clearly British. There was no hint of humor in his words, just a flat honesty.

"I—I don't think you understand your position, sir," Adria said smartly.

"I don't think you understand your own, madam."

Adria couldn't see him. There was no hope of light in the swallowing darkness. There was just this hot closeness, this impasse that was suddenly shrinking the space around her.

"Please, I must get—"

Merrick gathered her to him, holding her against a certain fall. He cupped her head gently between his big hands, tilted her face up to his.

Adria felt his hand wander down to the concave between her rib cage, moaning as he pressed his palm deeply into her.

"Christ, no wonder you're suffocating," he husked.

He sounded angry, impatient, yet his hands were cool, strong and soothing, loosening her bodice stays until she gasped with relief. In the sultriness, Adria was intimately aware of him, of his moist masculine scent, knowing that when his fingers freed her, they had lingered, caressing the weighted fullness of her breast, touching confidently over the rigid, upthrust nipple.

"Who are you?" she breathed, her voice humid.

Merrick kissed her once askingly, almost shyly, disarming her. His long finger felt for, found her mouth and parted it. Holding it to his will, his mouth took her then, moving hot and wet on hers. His tongue was rough, thrusting, then silken, dueling her own to enslavement.

Languidly, Merrick released her. His voice was warmly different. "I'll take you back downstairs now."

"You're a *Yankee*!" Adria accused as Merrick leaned away from her.

She heard his laugh, low and insolent, forgotten as she groped after him. She seemed to be floating in a void, led only by instinct. Then, blessedly, the crack of light at the bottom of the stairwell widened to frame a doorway. The rush of waltz music and fresh vibrant air greeted her when Merrick flung open the door. Adria had only a fleeting, dark glimpse of tallness, of wide deep shoulders, a glint of tallow light on his dark over-long hair, and a uniform, blue woolen with captain's epaulettes. She never saw his face.

Dear God, she had really played her role to the hilt tonight. She had even let a Yankee kiss her.

Thressa Hardee looked worn and haggard, not even showing surprise at Adria's thrusted appearance. Her eyes moved tiredly over Adria's hastily altered gown, approved the lone strand of pearls that matched the topaz hue of Adria's overbright eyes, disapproved the hurriedly pinned backknot where Adria's honey-sheened hair was already escaping its pins.

"We won't be staying as long as planned," she said dully to Adria. "The General and I are leaving now for the Blanchard's house. So you won't be deprived of a whole evening, the General will send an escort back for you. You do understand, my dear, don't you?"

"Of course," Adria nodded quickly, her eyes humid. This last night, of all nights, with this senseless gaiety, with the Union Army encamped at Midville—it was madness, a delightful madness. A Jubilee table set among marble urns overbrimming with blue-water hyacinths and grape wisteria, a feast of crayfish souffle and pheasant flamande, daintily sugared ming cakes, and an enormous silver swan punch bowl cooling with cranberry cider. Champagne trays were being circulated, offered sparingly so the hoarded supply would last the evening.

"Major Altree will be your companion in our absence," Thressa was saying above the glorious lilt of violin strings.

But he's so old, Adria thought wiltingly, smiling a courteous acknowledgment to the Major from across the room. He was threading his way over to her when Thressa brushed a lifeless kiss across Adria's flushed cheek.

"You really should wear a capelet with your gown. You don't want to be discussed, dear. I can leave my shawl for you—"

"No, Thressa, my shawl is—" Adria almost said, "upstairs in the gentleman's 'hidey hole' where I left it,"—"in the retiring room," she finished smoothly. She could never explain why she had taken refuge there, or what had happened on her way down. She couldn't even explain it all to herself. "I'll send one of the *nigras* for it."

"The General did wish a word with you tonight. Please see he isn't kept waiting over long," Thressa said tellingly, nodding a greeting to Major Altree as he moved beside Adria.

"Yes, certainly," Adria said distractedly, her gaze struck by the tall, intense man fastly approaching Major Altree from across the ballroom. The man sorted a path through the maze of waltzers, his brooding jade eyes smouldering from beneath thickly fringed dark brows. No one had eyes that color—blended like a restless seascape, arrogant emerald depths stormed with sapphire blue. Eyes that were at this moment slowly impaling her.

He was wearing dun-colored riding breeches with buffed-leather planter's boots. His dress coat appeared almost as an afterthought, blue velvet notched at the waist and worn over a box-pleated white Norfolk shirt. He was tieless, and held a dark Chinese silk ascot in one of his large hands.

"My birthday wishes for you are undoubtedly belated, Miss Adria, but no less sincere," Major Altree was pressing. Adria couldn't return his enthusiasm, not now—she couldn't even look directly at him. The bulge inside his coat where his left arm, severed at Gaines' Mill, was concealed; the limp, tarnished gold braid that encircled his coat sleeves; the war-worn slump of his thin shoulders. It saddened her too much.

"Such a remarkable age, eighteen. More of a promise than an age, wouldn't you have to agree?" Major Altree smiled stiffly, trying to capture Adria's averted glance.

"I have only been eighteen for a day, sir," Adria smiled back.

The man striding across the dance pavilion toward them had suddenly been enclosed by a swarm of Confederate officers. He spoke briefly with them, his expression grave when he shook hands with two of General Hardee's regimental officers whom Adria had recognized.

Without seeming overly interested, Adria said, "Who is that man, there—among the officers?"

Major Altree pivoted, staring a moment across the ballroom.

"I'm not certain I know him. I can make inquiries if his presence concerns you. Perhaps I should, with all this rumor of Yankee infiltrators among us. He is a rough sort, isn't he?"

Yes, Adria thought. He is the most fascinating, the most wildly handsome man I have ever seen. His features weren't truly perfect, not in the accepted sense. His jawline was too angular, the aquiline nose slightly off-centered. His face was darkly bronzed, broody, sun-lined, and she had yet to see him smile.

Major Altree shuffled uncomfortably, debating whether or not to ask Adria for a waltz. There was a certain awkwardness about it all. Most of the Southern ladies, seeing his disability, kindly refused which worked another advantage for him—the garden stroll. Their sympathies spared explanation, and most were content with tasteful conversation which later worked another advantage. General Alfred Sidney Johnson's daughter was an exception to nearly every rule—beautiful, headstrong and unpredictable, or so the ladies' comments about her ranged. Living as she had with the Hardee family after General Johnson's death at Shiloh, blossoming under the careful tutelage of both esteemed Southern ladies, Colly Blanchard and Thressa Hardee, had only fueled Adria's rebelliousness. But, after all, what could these dear Old South ladies expect? Adria was only half-tamed, growing up as she had in the Sabine bayous, left practically without discipline to roam in a wilderness.

True, she looked the accepted lady tonight, except for the low-flung, overburdened bodice of her pansy velvet gown where, in spite of himself, his eyes kept straying. She seemed breathless and somewhat flushed, almost on the verge of quiet rebellion. Her wide-set topaz eyes were clearly following that tall intruder who was now advancing across the room toward them.

"Are you Major James Altree?" the man asked.

Him—his voice—as Adria suspicioned it would be when she first saw him enter the ballroom. A voice tinged with anger now, not husked with softness as it had been with her inside the stairwell, but authoritatively British. And worse, troublesome.

"We are not acquainted, sir," Major Altree said loftily, a trifle sharp, Adria thought, as though he was purposely avoiding an introduction.

"I brought the British blockade runner in at dawn," Merrick gritted shortly.

"Oh, yes, we thought they, meaning of course the Yankees, were only practice warming their Columbiads down at Fort Pulaski. The reports said your ship's fire decommissioned two enemy cannons. Quite a feat, sir. Accept my congratulations for it, if that is your reason for searching me out."

Merrick looked quietly murderous.

"Ma'am," he bowed deeply to Adria, his hot jade eyes scalding quickly over her. He honestly didn't recognize her, Adria thought sinkingly, or else he had already dismissed their recontre as unimportant.

"What forces me here tonight is the delay over my coal consignment, the coal requisitioned by General Hardee for my ship before I agreed to bring British munitions to Savannah," Merrick said heatedly. "Both my officers, Mr. Barlow and Mr. Ditwell, were refused a meeting with the General this afternoon. I am told that you, Major Altree, as ranking Depot Officer can sign the release order."

James Altree stiffened. "Unfortunately, sir, only the General's signature can release that order for you. And the General has retired for the evening."

"Retired—where?" Merrick demanded.

"Where his privacy will not be molested, Captain."

From somewhere in the charged stillness that followed the hot exchange of words, a melodic chattering of glass silenced the violins. The glass chimes, as if on cue, were announcing dinner.

Merrick turned abruptly to Adria, offering his arm.

"Miss Sommerfield," he urged, ignoring the livid flush that strained across Major Altree's face.

"Captain—" Adria swallowed around the

pulsing in her throat. It was all the name she knew to address this utterly mannerless Englishman.

"I want to talk to you—is there someplace?" Merrick husked, steering Adria away from the crush of people.

"The garden," Adria whispered, smiling innocently at one of Thressa Hardee's stoic friends who swept disapprovingly past her. Undoubtedly, tonight she had committed social suicide. Major Altree was not the kind of man to be bested socially, particularly by someone who had invaded his social premises on a political errand.

The coolness of the terrace garden after the stifling warmth of the ballroom suddenly made her shiver. Here, the moist, weeping fragrance of wisteria vied with night-blooming jasmine, engulfing them in wild sweetness. There wasn't any war here, no rumors of war, there couldn't be, not here, not in all this loveliness. Alone with Merrick in this romantic setting, one she had envisioned in all her fantasies, Adria felt strangely cold, and wildly excited.

When Merrick caught her to him, Adria melted against him, feeling the hard length of his body. She lifted her face to his, her lips slightly parted, waiting, wanting.

"I knew you were beautiful when I first touched you in the darkness," he said gently.

"You know who I am, while I—"

"A man makes it a point to learn the name of a beautiful woman," Merrick smiled. "The same man wearing a blue uniform in a Confederate stronghold has to take certain chances, like the one I intend to take now."

His mouth came down heavily on hers, soft, yet demanding, tasting, then retreating. His big dark hands worked in caressing patterns over her slimness, not ungentle; masterful, experienced hands, warmed with passion. She heard his aroused gasp, felt the weight of her gown drawn from her shoulders.

"No," she murmured without meaning it when his hot mouth searched over her breast, suckling gently with a sort of hungry pride. Something unknown stirred deep in the hollow of her being, something charged with life, with need.

"God, if there was just time!" he rasped along the slender length of her throat. Abruptly then, he lifted his head, capturing her chin between thumb and forefinger, his breath searching against her mouth when he spoke.

"I need one thing from you, Miss Sommerfield, then you can return to your social fairy tale. Making love to you, however tempting the thought is at the moment, requires time, time I can't spare. You are General Hardee's ward. You know where the General is tonight. I want you to tell me. I need the coal for my ship."

"*Your ship*?" Adria gasped. "Is *that* what you were thinking about when—"

"Not altogether," Merrick gritted, roughing her tightly against him. His long warm fingers closed over her mouth, stilling her struggles.

"Listen to me. I was on the river last night. In two days, maybe less, Sherman's armies will cross the Ogeechee into Savannah. The whole Yankee Blockade Fleet intercepted me out of

New Orleans. With any other ship, I couldn't have outrun them. The fireworks that so impressed your Major Altree were the result of my ship running under Yankee cannon fire at Fort Pulaski. Four of my crew were wounded and one killed. I took this risk because the Yankee harbor commander in New Orleans tried to buy me off, first with flattery, then with gold. When I said no, he threatened me with a treason charge which will reach all the way back to London. If I don't get my coal loaded tonight and sail, I'll probably hang when General Sherman marches down Bay Street. I hadn't really considered sides in this back-fence war of yours over slavery. Until tonight, whoever won, I still made a profit. General Hardee has always been a man of his word. So, there has to be something else he wants from me, otherwise he wouldn't have made himself unavailable. I need to find him and ask him."

Adria struggled limply in his arms, her topaz eyes glittery, humid, in moongold shadows.

"If I free you, do I have your word you won't bring a Confederate detachment on the run?" Merrick asked quietly.

Adria nodded, still tasting the salty, warm scent of his hand on her lips. His fingers moved upward along the slope of her jaw, fondling a silken wisp of hair, caressing it behind her ear.

"I think you are truly despicable, using a woman this way," she spat.

"Agreed, but I have little choice."

"I don't think I believe you."

"I think you do," Merrick smiled. "Where is the General?"

Adria hesitated, glorying in a rare moment of superiority over this forceful man. "The General is at the Blanchard's home on Abercorn Street, near Oglethorpe Square. But, I think you—"

Merrick hushed her with a quick kiss, still holding her, his jade-dark eyes momentarily questioning the truth of her words. His smile, arrogant, assured, flashed whitely against his dark face.

"I expected more resistance," he said.

This wasn't what she wanted him to say. There was nothing grateful in his tone, nothing to dignify the intimacy that had just passed between them. She felt suddenly cheated.

"I think the Yankees are right about you," she remarked hotly.

"Don't always assume too much, Adria. The truth may disappoint you."

Merrick left her in the columned shadows of the balustrade, his boots striking the flagstones like a cadenced drumroll.

CHAPTER 2

Corporal Eiloss, with a flair of importance, flicked the reins and guided the General's buggy through a maze of Confederate cavalry. He glanced sideways at Adria, sharing the same emptiness he knew she must be feeling at seeing the sumptuous homes along Abercorn Street standing dark and shuttered. There was still an air of stately defiance about the street, with a few brave lamps muffled behind thick velvet draperies. Some of the populace had decided to stay; not everyone had panicked at the threat of Yankee bootheels trudging Savannah's majestic streets.

"You scairt', ma'am?"

"Yes, I suppose I am," Adria said, startled that she had not, until this moment, realized the enormity of what was happening.

"Me—I was scairt' 'til Atlanta. I seen a lot of dyin' that day. Now, I ain't so much no more," the corporal shrugged. "Major Altree, he says you liv't in Texas. I ain't never been there, but I seen Capt'n McNary's Texas Rifles ride onc't," he drawled. "Pleasin' sight, if a body could stand their hollerin'. Some of them Texas boys can shoot a whisker off'n a flea. I even hear there's cattle down there with humps like a camel. You ever seen one, Miss Sommerfield?"

"No, Corporal," Adria smiled, warmed by his breezy attempt at cheerfulness. Corporal Eiloss was pitifully young, still growing to his hands and feet, strapping and awkward, his language a disgrace. He was serving General Hardee as an orderly, and the one proud stripe sewn on his outgrown preacher's coat might well have been colonel's braid-and-clusters.

"We'll be ready for them thievin' Yankees, you just see. We'll be ready this time. So, you don't be scairt', ma'am," he grinned, drawing rein between the Blanchard's lion-sculpted carriage posts. Adria stared sickeningly at one of the leonine marble-heads that had been toppled from its pillar, the chalky fragments strewn across the walkway.

A picket line of cavalry horses stood in readiness. Two fully loaded field wagons were being hitched to teams in four-point traces. Through the stir of activity, the General's aide, a grizzled, red-bearded Irishman whom Adria knew only as Fenton, approached the buggy and offered his hand to assist her down.

"One of the limbers broke loose this morning," he explained, seeing Adria's distress as she picked her way among the marble shards, lifting the velvet hem of her gown above mud slashes left by wheels of a Confederate sling-cart.

Through the swarm of activity, team masters were bellowing above the complaint of restless horses. Hollow-eyed troopers moved in ragged order around her, all unsmiling, charged with purpose.

"What is happening here? Why all this activity? Are we under siege?" Adria gasped.

"There's been a change of orders, ma'am. General Forrest has withdrawn with the Army of Tennessee south of the river. General Lee has given the retreat order. We're marching north at dawn."

"Retreat? From Savannah?"

"It appears so, ma'am."

"But the army is needed *here*. What will happen to *us* when the Yankees—?"

Sergeant Fenton nodded gravely. "It's regretful, ma'am, for all of us. I am to tell you that General Hardee wishes a word with you before you join the others at the Arnold's home. He is inside with his officers now. I'll inform him you are here."

Adria climbed the familiar stone steps to the verandah, pausing to look at the trellis-covered porch swing snugged among newly budded pink roses. The breeze touched over it, setting it to motion. It seemed for the moment the only certainty in this suddenly eruptive chaos.

Inside, Colly Blanchard's receiving parlour had been transformed into a makeshift command post. Chairs and tables were stacked with field gear; japanned water tins were piled against the Stillman clock; haversacks were overspilling with rations; cartridge boxes, sabers and baldrics were staggered in hasty order down the stair hall. A finger-stained memo sheet was tacked to the far wall to be glanced at, read and forgotten.

Adria scanned the grim faces of the officers in some attempt to memorize their existence. She swallowed around the tears in her throat and braved a smile when General Hardee left the circle of discussion surrounding him and crossed the room to her.

Adria," he acknowledged in a blur of soft emotion, taking her by the arm toward the day parlour. He closed the double doors behind him, nodding an order to Sergeant Fenton that they were not to be disturbed. When he turned to face her, the paternal glow in his tired eyes had hardened.

"I wished to spare you this night, or at best, postpone it," he said searchingly, motioning Adria to Colly Blanchard's needlepoint rocking chair. He moved to the floor length window with his back to her, staring out at the clutter of activity. His words were slow in coming.

"I promised Albert when he brought you to Richmond for schooling that I would see to your care. Guardianship documents were drawn forth before you entered Miss Druary's Seminary in Macon. Perhaps Albert knew, perhaps he had some premonition before the battle of Hornet's Nest. His death was a great loss to the Confederacy, to all of us."

How different, how wearied the General looked now. Could a day, a year of such days, cause so remarkable a contrast, Adria wondered? She thought back to the first time she had ever seen him, the stunned day after General Albert's death at Shiloh when Adria had been summoned to Miss Druary's office with the message that a General Hardee from Savannah was waiting to see her.

Resplendent in Confederate dress gray, an engraved saber slung from a Russian baldric, yellow gilt spurs catching at the sunlight, General William Hardee represented to her all the nobility, the *savoir-vivre*, the compassion of a true Southern general. He was, he explained, her guardian, and was taking her to live with his family in Savannah.

Gradually, in vibrant new surroundings, the numbness and disbelief that had gripped her since General Albert's death began to dissolve. Savannah was alive, sophisticated, spirited. It was home.

Adria sat straighter in her chair. Seeing the hesitation in the General's eyes, she assumed her muchly practiced pose of innocence.

"There is very little time, Adria."

It wasn't working. She needed to concentrate, to convince him. He couldn't just snatch away this newfound happiness. She wouldn't permit it.

"I have arranged for you to leave Savannah and return to China Grove by way of Mexico. The Blanchards will be accompanying you."

There, it was said, the dreaded ultimatum, a command as calloused as the ones he executed to his men. How did one argue with a command?

"I—I had hoped to remain in Savannah, sir," Adria swallowed. "It's been two years since I left China Grove. Nella Lee—we were never really companionable. I think she would object to my living there again without General Albert. I was in hopes I could stay here in Savannah with Thressa until—"

General Hardee shook his head in annoyance. "Thressa is leaving for Charleston with me tonight under military escort. And your concern about Nella Lee's welcome is needless. As you recall, she never liked the isolation of China Grove, nor did she object when Albert deeded the land to you. She writes that she plans to remarry and move to Sacramento."

"But then I would be alone there at China Grove," Adria countered.

"No, my dear. Dickson and Colly Blanchard will make their home with you. The doctors feel a change of location might well benefit Colly. They are gracious people, dear friends. Dickson is a gentleman of some means. You will be well taken care of."

They are strangers, Adria thought miserably, puritan and dull, and Colly is sickly. A week in their morbid company and I'll be as gray and lifeless as they are.

"Perhaps, sir, I could travel to Charleston with Thressa," Adria prompted brightly, secretly praising herself for this flash of ingenuity.

"The matter is decided," the General snapped. His eyes smiled then, warmed with understanding. "You are a Confederate general's daughter, and I can see the question of decision in your eyes. You are also of age today, but without means of support. What monies Albert had were given over to the Confederacy. All that is left is China Grove. This does seem best for you, Adria, despite your misgivings at the moment. Savannah will not be the same when the Yankees come here."

"But I will be the same, sir," Adria said steadily.

General Hardee moved to his desk, fumbled among the stacked clutter for a long bulky envelope.

"This, I would ask of you, Adria," he said, handing the envelope across to her. "These documents are to be given to a Major Kelly in Matamoros, along with a cargo key which is inside. This voyage will be unofficially considered a mission of sorts, the importance of which I cannot divulge to you at the moment. I can only stress the urgency."

"A voyage, sir?"

"Yes," he nodded. "I have made arrangements for your passage with the captain of the British ship that ran the blockade last night."

"But that's a *warship*!" Adria gasped, gaining her feet.

"It is at present the only escape south of Savannah," the General replied. "I was informed by Major Altree of the scene at the hotel. There is some risk, of course, but Merrick will take his ship out of the river. I think you will agree after meeting him that he is a man of intention."

"I—I told him you were here," Adria confessed softly.

"I expected that you would," the General smiled. "Merrick can be quite persuasive. If you hadn't told him, the woman he keeps company with at the hotel, a Miss Leona Delorme, would have obliged Merrick. I understand he has certain informative dealings with her, something in the nature of blockade reports which this woman somehow obtains from a Yankee officer. They rendezvous in the old chimney room of the hotel, and I would suppose," he lowered his voice, "exchange favors there."

Exchanging favors—so that explained their chance meeting in the stairwell. He was going to her—to that Leona woman. The "hidey hole" room was where he had managed a change of clothing to appear less conspicuous when he confronted Major Altree. So, he hadn't needed the pretense with her at all. It was just an *amusement*!

"He was wearing a Yankee uniform," Adria blurted out.

"A British naval uniform, no doubt," General Hardee said, unconcerned. "The Yankees, out of respect for the *Trent* reprisals, have been wary of Merrick; and I do sense his sentiments are wholly with our cause. Merrick is a somewhat complex man, an extraordinary sea captain with a devoted crew. His private life, I am told, is quite another matter. He is considered a *roue*, so I would caution any further association with him. He is not a marriageable sort."

The General watched Adria for a moment, then with slow, ponderous steps walked to the door and opened it, the indication that their discussion was ended.

"Had time only been more pitying for all of us, dear Adria. Someday, perhaps you will understand the obligation of duty to one's convictions." He held the door open for her to pass, brushing a quick kiss on her cheek when he took her hand in his.

"Goodbye, Adria. I will be advised of your safe passage to China Grove."

"Goodbye, sir," Adria mumbled, her thoughts suddenly alive. Duty? Why was he talking about "duty" when her whole future had just crumbled. She wouldn't cry. She wouldn't beg, but she'd find some way out of this nightmare. What in God's name could be worse than an early spinsterhood with the Blanchards at China Grove? There was so much of the world she longed to see, so much she needed to learn. Her life was new, fresh. She wouldn't let it all be ruined. There had to be some way.

Adria brushed determinedly through the confusion of officers, this time without seeing their faces. She heard Sergeant Fenton calling after her and hurried her steps. She didn't want to go to the Arnold's home, not now. She didn't want to be shepherded anywhere, anymore. Tears, hot and angry were misting her vision when she reached the stair hall. *Blast* and *blast* this war and all the lordly politicians who had favored it. It wasn't fair, it wasn't!

"Adria—"

Her eyes fled over him, following a neat row of anchor buttons across a hard blue uniform, lifting to a sun-bronzed face, to the clear jade eyes that halted her. For a moment, neither one moved. Then, wordlessly, Merrick took her arm and escorted her through the busy doorway out onto the side porch. He drew her from the path of activity into the shadows.

"What in the name of hell are you doing here in all this?"

Adria swallowed down a hot rush of tears. "I am often in unexpected places, sir—as you may well recall."

Merrick stared intently down at her, at the defiant lift of her chin, at the rebellious tears glistening in her amber-flecked eyes, and smiled. "You look at this moment almost capable of commanding the Army of Northern Virginia."

He was teasing her, almost forcing a reluctant smile from her.

"And are you as capable a sea captain?" she flared.

Merrick laughed softly. "I would hope, madam, a reliable one." He was near enough for her to see the sun-lined corners of his mouth lift with arrogance. Suddenly she wanted him to kiss her, wanted to be held in that insolent pride, to know him, to believe in him. Merrick's gaze lifted impatiently above her head toward the doorway.

Sergeant Fenton, breathless and haggard, looked roughly relieved. "I'll see you to the Arnold's house now, ma'am," he urged. He eyed Merrick with obvious suspicion. "General Hardee asks that you join him now, Captain Ryland."

Merrick Ryland—the name was certainly British enough. It troubled her tongue to repeat it, whirled in her brain as Adria watched him shoulder his way back through the choked doorway. She'd never been to sea before. Perhaps, just perhaps, things were not as bleak and hopeless as they seemed.

Merrick refused the chair that General Hardee indicated.

"The amont of four hundred pounds is owing for the Enfields, the Armstrong repeaters, two howitzers, and food supplies for your army, General. And I want the coal for my ship."

General Hardee held a long sheet of paper against the oil lamp, glaring above the light at Merrick. "This is the ordnance requisition for your coal," he said tastingly. "All it requires is my signature." He replaced the order atop a raft of papers, squared them neatly together. "There's some Kentucky mash in my saddle pouch. It bites a gentleman's taste some, but we recovered it from Kilpatrick's bummers, which sweetens the flavor somewhat."

Merrick rummaged through the saddle pouch, then held the dark, unlabeled bottle to the light. He uncorked it, tested its scent. The General handed him a glass and brought his own from behind the lamp. Merrick sloshed both glasses full.

"What happened last night on the river? My reports state that your ship artillery demolished two pivotal Columbiads, that the Yankees were caught napping."

Merrick shrugged and set his glass aside, wiping his mouth with the back of his hand. "You should have let the bastards keep that whiskey," he shuddered. "You wouldn't need bullets."

General Hardee labored a smile. "How do you propose to get back downriver, past the guns, past the Yankee blockade fleet?"

"First, General, I propose to get my coal loaded."

The General leaned both fists on the desk. "You can have your coal, Merrick—but there are conditions."

"I suspected there would be," Merrick said. "But there's not room aboard for your whole army."

"There's cargo I want delivered in Mexico. You can refuse, of course, just as I can refuse to release your coal consignment."

Merrick let the threat slide. "Sherman has advanced down the Ogeechee and will take Fort McAllister by the end of the week. Once he connects with the Union fleet, I won't need your coal. I'll need a fast horse."

General Hardee leveled a venomous look at him. "I am well aware of General Sherman's activities. So are the ten thousand troops I am taking north tonight."

"And you expect Sherman to follow you into Carolina with the Yankee fleet in pursuit?" Merrick exploded.

The General slammed his glass down on the desk. "I am inclined at this moment to let the Yankees hang you."

Merrick shrugged the bluff aside as meaningless. "I fly both the Tudor Lions and the Union Jack with Lord Russell's upraised fist guarding the bowsprit," he smiled.

The General settled irritably in his chair, and quietly drained his glass. "There will be passengers," he said finally.

"The *Warlock* is not provisioned for Confederate refugees," Merrick said flatly.

"Passengers, and a guard detachment of

select standing," the General continued strongly. "Your payment in gold will be waiting for you in Matamoros. For that you have my word. The coal will be released and loaded upon your order."

"I could refuse *after* I clear the river," Merrick grated.

General Hardee reached across his desk, lifted his worn chapeau, staring at it as though it were strange to him. He plucked at the gold braid along the brim, his fingers nudging the threads back inside their felt slots. Gently, he laid the chapeau back down on the desk.

"You haven't shown interest in the cargo," he said without glancing at Merrick.

"I am only interested at this point in seeing my coal loaded."

"I don't approve of you, Merrick. Your age disturbs me with the gravity of what is at stake here. Your undisciplined sea games cause me great concern. But, I must trust you in this. There is no other alternative."

"You *could* sail with me," Merrick grinned. "That would either eliminate or fortify your concerns."

The General's weary eyes followed Merrick to the door. "War does press one to extremes. I pray, in this instance, Captain, that you are successful."

"No more than I do, General," Merrick said arrogantly. "This cheap coercion of yours will cost more than we originally agreed upon for this run. One hundred British pounds to be exact." He smiled, slamming the door behind him.

From the Arnold's vestibule window across Abercorn Street, Adria watched Merrick mount his horse and ride cautiously through the bivouac area and down State Street, watching until his tall silhouette was swallowed by distance. A sudden emptiness clutched at her, some frantic impulse that made her want to run into the night after him. Is this how it must feel to love someone, she wondered? Lord, no, it couldn't be, she decided. It shouldn't hurt this much.

CHAPTER 3

A feeble dawn hesitant with the promise of rain lengthened across the river. Kendall Chase held the newsprint against the bleak light and read with dismal interest the *Savannah Republican's* account of the *Warlock's* blockade feat, unimpressed by slanted words that attempted to drum vitality into the South's waning glories.

"Lieutenant Chase, sir," Corporal Eiloss saluted. " 'Bout 'em crates 'at are assigned to the captain's quarters. Do I tell the boys to bring 'em aboard?"

"How are they marked?" Chase snapped.

"They ain't, sir—heavy though like munitions," the corporal snuffed, scratching at his sleeve, a determined twist to his mouth as he squeezed a flea between his thumbnail and forefinger. He grinned an apology. "Camp on Bull Bluff is thick with them little bastards," he muttered, glancing upward toward the coal shute that had emptied the last ton of coal into the *Warlock's* hold.

"This ship here don't seem true somehow," he shrugged, shaking his head. "The men is takin' odds on the outcome downriver. Been hearin' around camp that them Yankees is all bunched for this 'un."

"Possibly, corporal," Kendall Chase said with obvious boredom. "Bring the crates on board. I will sign for them."

"Howsomever, sir," Corporal Eiloss prodded, kneading his cap between his hands, "it's about them water casks. I done asked Sergeant Fenton about the order and he didn't know. He says to ask you."

Chase sighed impatiently, turning his back to him and walking to the deck railing. His gaze skimmed over the canvas-bulked cotton bales, a hundred or more lined in neat order along the docks, Southern cotton awaiting the torch of destruction.

Corporal Eiloss fumbled along behind him, craning his neck over the railing. "General Hardee give orders to do what the ship's captain say, and that British mister say all 'em water casks be scoured and freshened. Some is still full, but he ordered—"

"Bring the fresh ones on board and fill the others at the tank on York Street." Chase spoke curtly without turning around.

"There's eighty-one of 'em, sir," Corporal Eiloss groaned.

"Then you should have started before now, corporal."

"Not to argue, sir, but there's a 'yella fever' rumor at the prisoner's tank on York. Ain't nobody taking water from 'em wells."

Kendall Chase stomped his anger and rounded on the corporal.

"There seems to be a confusion of command here. Since we are all that is left of this segment of the war, we will share the responsibility for this particular order."

"Y—Yes sir," Corporal Eiloss stammered. "I was only thinkin'—"

"Don't think, corporal." Kendall Chase smiled without humor. "The time for that is past."

The *Republican's* description of the *Warlock* had read honestly, Lieutenant Chase admitted to himself. He studied the long deck, meeting the suspicious eyes of the British crewmen who glanced pointedly away from him. The Union Jack snapped arrogantly in the upriver wind above the jib-boom, classifying her registry. Her length, a sweeping two hundred and twenty feet with a beam that measured twenty-three feet, a sleek weight of six hundred tons, a novel steel cutwater that made the "runner" uniquely impressive. As for the *Warlock's* captain, the test of his uniqueness lay eighteen miles upriver. Major Altree expressed a ready dislike for the man, General Hardee had been noncommittal, the populace of Savannah was too war-numbed to comment. This mission, like recent others that floated on the whim of a defeated general, was riddled with skepticism.

"Lieutenant, sir," Corporal Eiloss complained from behind him. "That British First Officer won't allow us below with 'em crates. "He sez' the ranking Confederate officer has to accompany the men."

"Where is he?" Chase demanded.

"Here, sir," Hillary Barlow replied crisply, approaching Chase. "Captain Ryland permits no one except officers or assigned crew personnel below in his quarters."

"And how then do you suppose to deliver them below?"

"The British crew will take them below, sir," Barlow said steadily. "You may assist their order if you so wish."

Kendall Chase dusted his Kossuth hat against his knee, his dark eyes pinpoints of fury. "*Where* is your captain?"

Hillary Barlow straightened and said coolly, "The captain has not yet reported aboard ship."

Chase sneered and nodded to Corporal Eiloss. "Does he plan to come aboard before we clear the river?"

"I assume the captain has some duties to attend on shore," Barlow said stiffly.

"Perhaps the Yankees have dissuaded him," Chase smiled dryly.

"I would doubt that possibility," Hillary Barlow bristled, "but I shall inform the captain of your concern."

Chase didn't smile back. "Leave the crates on deck, corporal, and see to the water casks," he ordered with a glaring secondary command that silenced the worried question in Corporal Eiloss' eyes.

Kendall Chase wandered back down the passageway, inhaling the blended scents of pitch and rosin, easing his hand along the newly varnished timbers, purposely delaying until

Hillary Barlow, occupied with other matters, left him. Quietly, he backstepped to the captain's door and slipped inside, closing the door behind him.

The crates, five of them, were pyramided against the far wall, oddly sealed in chain mortar and each drop-latched against opening. The tops were unstenciled, painted over from the previous C.S.A. artillery labels. He kicked at the siding. Nothing inside yielded.

The captain's room was orderly, even elaborate for a ship's cabin. A cedar armoire with oval-tilted mirrors lined one wall, scrolled cupboards bulging with volumes of Chateaubriand, Voltaire, Rosseau, and Hugo ran the wall's length to an overlong berth. A cherrywood French Revival desk bolted to the planking sat in the middle of the room in an attitude of refined arrogance. Only the clutter of map crayons and crumpled pieces of paper strewn across the desk top spoiled its haughtiness.

He seated himself at the desk, running his fingers across the elegant wood rays, caressing a memory. Four years before, riding in grandoise regard beside Georgia's General Howell Cobb, saluting the guidon of the Fifteenth Georgia Infantry, the ostrich plume of his Jeff Davis hat nodding with pride, his cover portrait had been sketched for *Civil War Times Illustrated*. And later in the bloody chasm of battle, listening to the pitching screams of the undead, he had unrolled the muddied sketch of himself and decided.

He left the war, left John Pemberton's flank unit at Big Black River and survived by hiding in a backwater cave, his only companion the Quaker log propped beside him, hewn to resemble enemy cannon, as impotent and useless that day as he chose to be.

A sound decision between desertion and death, a decision no one questioned when he rejoined a Rebel battalion near the Yazoo River. His appointment to General Hardee's adjutant staff in Savannah was complimentary to his knowledge of the Spanish language, perfected, he recalled slyly, in crude conversation with a mulatto slave in one of the river shacks that bordered his Virginia home. A memorable home where prizes of prosperity, such as this one he sat before now, gleamed beneath his fingers.

Kendall Chase opened one drawer, then another, fondling through their contents, lifting for inspection a small oil miniature portrait set in a weighted gold frame—an older, starkly beautiful face, clouded in wavy dark hair, wide-set eyes that shadowed emotion, a warm, sensuous mouth that invited passion.

A sudden wind draft shuffled the papers across the desk top. The door slammed shut, vibrating the wall planking.

With a fast glance, Merrick took in the scene, his dark jade eyes hardening with disgust.

"From a Yankee I might expect such clumsy pilfering. From a Confederate officer whose chivalrous word built the South, I am amazed."

Kendall Chase hurried to his feet, stretching a smile as he rose and extended his hand, a gesture that met only empty space.

"I was admiring your lady, sir," he said smoothly, turning the miniature in his hand.

Merrick leaned against the door and folded his arms. "My lady is this ship," he said coldly.

"I have already admired your 'iron lady,' sir. A stately choice, I might infer."

"In what capacity do you function on this ship other than common meddling?" Merrick said harshly, watching the Rebel officer grow rigid, his smile a frozen grimace.

"You might presume such from my position when you entered, Captain; however, I assure you your accusation is grossly overstated, for which I must seek an apology from you," Chase said heatedly.

For an incredulous moment, Merrick stared at him, then threw back his head and laughed, ignoring the stammered flush that spread over Chase's taut face.

"Since you obviously command the forgotten brigade above decks, I'll caution my crew to secure what miserly goods they do possess and remember to lock my own door," Merrick said, the lightness gone now from his voice. "For now, I'll spare you the awkwardness of spilling your pockets and tell you to get the hell out of my quarters."

Kendall Chase faltered past the desk, holding Merrick's gaze until he reached the door. Merrick straightened slowly, stepped to one side and flung the door open.

"This is a British ship—my ship. My orders apply to everyone aboard."

Chase's dark eyes narrowed. "My name is Kendall Chase. Lieutenant Kendall Chase. I want you to remember it."

Merrick moved across to the desk, retrieved

Chase's hat from the desk top and sailed it across the cabin to him.

"Get out, Lieutenant Chase."

Cara's miniature portrait smiled up at Merrick with the same innocent, subtle smile that always belied her motives. The slender ivory column of her throat arched seductively, and graceful shoulders thrust squarely forward accenting perfect breasts that overspilled the artist's careful drapings.

It had begun as a game of wits between them, a game without rules when the enfeebled Comte Louis Breaux had, in the cause of royal sentiment for the Southern states, purchased the newly launched *Warlock* and, in a downstroke of senility, made a gift of the blockade ship to his young wife.

The Comtesse Cara Breaux had insisted on an inspection of her expensive possession and appeared oblivious to Merrick's rudeness as he dutifully explained to her the *Warlock's* engine installation, the ship's awesome speed, and lastly, the anticipated profits of her blockade ventures.

"You do not approve of me, do you, Captain Ryland?" Cara had asked suddenly as Merrick assisted her from the passageway.

"I find your pretense of interest in a remarkable ship a waste of my time," Merrick said sullenly, leaving her, calling for Hillary Barlow to escort the Comtesse to her carriage.

After two days an invitation had arrived for Merrick, a dinner request at the Comte Breaux's home on Cheyne Walk, reinforced by a polite suggestion that sailing schedules would be cancelled unless the invitation was honored.

Merrick endured the lengthy, lavish dinner, responding with sympathy to the Comte's lame attempts to question the durability of his enterprise until the Comte sagged with weariness and Cara rang for the servants to assist him to his rooms upstairs.

Cara's voice was soft with no note of apology. "Usually, the Comte prefers his dinner served in bed. Tonight, he made an appearance because I asked it."

Merrick let his eyes wander appraisingly over her, from her perfectly coiffured hair, fashionably upswept with an aigrette of star-sapphires, down across her blood-red satin gown inset with a transparent bodice aglitter with tiny prismed stones. Her fingers curled climbingly along the stem of her wine glass and Merrick noticed a slight tremble to their otherwise composed motion. When Cara lifted dark hungry eyes to him, he read her mood and nodded an acceptance.

Later, as Merrick lay in her sumptuous, gondola-shaped bed, staring overhead at gilded cherubs floating sensuously in an Aegean Sea, the rules of their game became more complex.

"What do you want of me, Comtesse—only this?"

Cara took a delicate sip of her wine, caressing her tongue thoughtfully over the rim of the goblet.

"This for now, *capitaine*," she smiled. "I have learned much of you, perhaps more than you know of yourself. The son of a woman felon who died slumped across her machine at Padiah Ryland's convict mills in Manchester with a filthy ragtot chained beside her, a pitiful child with eyes the color of the Irish Sea. A destiny, perhaps, for you," Cara paused, taunting.

"Limms is still a servant at your home in Aylesmere Quay, and he remembers well the day Padiah Ryland brought you there. He even recalls the wooden *dhow* you clutched to your heart, your only possession beyond the rags you wore."

Cara's fingernails tapped nervously against the delicate crystal of her wine glass. "I know of your rebellious youthful adventures as a narrowboat captain on the Thames canals, your time at Cambridge, your excellence in preliminary medical studies, your explusion and your return to the sea, the shipwreck at Cala Cadolar which nearly devoured you—I know all this. Yet, I find no woman, no love for any woman, in your history."

Merrick stuffed a pillow beneath his shoulders and propped himself up on one elbow. "And why, Comtesse, should that be of such interest to you?"

Cara forced her melodic laugh. "I must be discreet, *amant*; Louis is generous to a point. I think he purchased you for me along with your ship."

Cara stood above him, a slow, shuddering tremor gripping her as Merrick reached for her and pulled her down beside him. Sensing her need, he kissed her languidly without frenzy or passion, feeling her desperate response to tenderness.

"Perhaps you did not know of your birth," Cara murmured against his mouth. "Perhaps I have been cruel with you."

Merrick's dark jade eyes became crystal as they leveled down at her. "I have always known. I still have the *dhow*, Comtesse," he said quietly, touching her fingertips to his mouth. "You will never own me, or have more of me than I am willing to give. I command when I make love to a woman the same way I command aboard my ship. For this night, we play by my rules."

Merrick replaced Cara's miniature portrait inside the drawer, closing the drawer with a finality, pushing her from his thoughts. He turned to the aft-port window, watching the burnished ripples of sundown slant across the river. Encounter strategy was fixed in his mind; the inland fog charts from Fort Jackson had arrived by courier an hour before he came aboard. General Hardee had removed his garrison of ten thousand men north to the Carolina border sometime before dawn. It was the tenth of December, and a new risk lay eighteen miles downriver.

Hillary Barlow rapped once, then squeezed the door open. His gaze fell instantly on the mysterious crates stacked along the inside wall. "What do they contain, sir?" he asked, moving across to them.

"I don't even know who has a key," Merrick frowned, "or why they are in here instead of in cargo."

"Confederate general's orders, his adjutant officer informed me. I can consult Major

Altree."

Merrick shook his head. "That can wait. How many civilian passengers on board?"

"Three, sir—Dickson Blanchard and his wife who appears ill, and the general's ward, a Miss Sommerfield. All of them are quartered and instructed."

"How are we provisioned?"

"Adequate for three weeks, with only one fuel port in Matanzas."

"And the water casks, were they freshened?" Merrick demanded.

"A Lieutenant Chase managed that order, sir."

Merrick's mouth tightened with disgust. "Was it done?"

"To my knowledge it was, captain. The freight dray brought the last of them aboard two hours ago."

"Then secure for sail at tide speed until we reach Fort Jackson. I want no one except you and Ditwell with me on the bridge when we determine our run sequence. Instruct the Rebel brigade and all the crew, excepting gunners, that they are ordered below decks until we clear the river or I order otherwise—that includes the passengers."

"The passengers have been told, sir."

Merrick paused, frowning deeply at Barlow. "And, use nothing that reflects light. Cover the deck with night tarps. And no conversation—none—not even breathing."

"Aye, sir," Barlow replied heavily, weighing a salute, his face grim with apprehension as he left Merrick's cabin.

CHAPTER 4

The *Warlock's* engines dulled to a murmur, then stopped.

Adria flounced across the berth, stretched up to the porthole, and looked out. The sameness, the darkness, reflected only a tinge of light where the Savannah River lapped at its banks.

Where was everyone? Why this infuriating series of impotent halts downriver? There were no sounds of activity now above decks, just this lagging hush. This wasn't at all the fast, brilliant escape she had expected, a race through the blockade to open seas. After the departing fanfare with her glittery sweep between the handsome files of a Confederate escort, and the welcoming aboard by a debonair lieutenant whose manner hinted at nothing more than an excursion to Tybee Island, she felt abandoned.

No, this wasn't the way she had imagined it.

So far, there had been no sign of the *Warlock's* captain. The British crew was sternly remote, obviously duty bound, hardly glancing at her when she stepped aboard. Colly Blanchard commanded much more attention than she had. Dickson hovered over her, two of General Hardee's regimental officers had even assisted with the Blanchard's trunks, and even the Confederate lieutenant, Kendall Chase, had deserted Adria's side when he saw the alarming expression on Colly's colorless face. The Blanchards had retired immediately to their cabin. A crew officer, Mr. Barlow, who looked to Adria like a leprechaun in a sailor suit, had dutifully escorted her to a clean, sparse cabin. That had been three hours ago, three desolate hours ago.

I'm just homesick, Adria thought drearily. A meal, any kind of refreshment, would have lightened the boredom, but nothing had been presented. The Delftware ewer held fresh water; a compote with a drinking cup on a wicker tray sat beside it on the small table. The milk porcelain chamber pot was unadorned, placed expectedly on a curtained floor shelf at the end of the berth. There were three heavy brass hooks for her dresses, as yet unpacked, a task she was saving to do. The oil lamp swung tauntingly overhead, reminding her she couldn't light it. Mr. Barlow's orders had been very explicit.

"You are instructed to please stay to your cabins until you are told otherwise," he had said. "We regret this dark welcome, but it is positively necessary that no lamps be used until we have cleared the river."

At this pace, it could take weeks, Adria groaned to herself. She fondled the locket chain around her neck while she recited for the hundredth time the words of General Hardee's written message to her:

> *The role we must fulfill on the field of honor is often burdensome and perilous, yet we obey. So, my dear Adria, bear well this burden of honor laid to your care. This key entrusted to you will be matched by one in the possession of Major John Kelly who awaits you in Matamoros. Major Kelly carries my final orders and will accompany you to China Grove.*

December 8, 1864—presumably the day General Hardee retreated north to Charleston with his hungry, broken regiments.

"Blast this horrid war!" Adria said aloud. What were they battling about anyway—over who had slaves and who didn't? Why did it matter so much? The only *nigras* she'd ever seen were fat and sassy, certainly clean and well cared for. Uncle Albert owned one or two at China Grove and there hadn't been any quarrel over them. They worked and in return were given a decent home and food. All this nonsense about whips and overseers and chains was just invented by some ignorant Yankee firebrands. That's what Miss Druary had said about it all, and Miss Druary was remarkably correct about everything.

If it weren't for this hideous war she'd still be in Savannah, still enclosed in gentle graciousness—high tea and four o'clock callers, garden strolls with the languid fragrance of night lilies and grape wisteria, the madly blooming azaleas crowding her skirts as she breezed along the walkways. If she could just go back. . .

There might still be time. They hadn't moved that far downriver, not more than a few miles. How could she do it?

Adria stretched across the berth, propped herself up on her elbows and concentrated. The fair lieutenant, Kendall Chase, seemed gallant and certainly a gentleman, a Virginian if she defined his drawl correctly. When she told him, what would he think?

"*You* can understand, sir—I've had this change of heart. Any old body can take this silly little key to Major Kelly. China Grove? Why, no, I haven't lived there in years. The bayous have probably claimed it by now anyway, so you see, I wouldn't really have any true home left. What will I do in Savannah with all those dreadful Yankees there? Well, I'll write to Miss Druary. She'll know of someone I can stay with, she knows everyone in the whole of Georgia. I do know how to paint and sketch a little. I could give lessons and earn something for my keep until—"

It sounded almost convincing enough with a tear or two for good measure. The orphaned plea—it rarely failed her. Now to find this lieutenant. She hadn't the faintest idea of where to start searching.

The passage door opened noiselessly. The ship rocked in sullen blackness; only the sharp planes and angles of its smokestack and the fore and main masts rising like charred spires in the moonless night distinguished the deck.

Momentarily disoriented when she cleared the updeck stairs, Adria leaned against the railing, sorting her position. The bridge was to her right, the crew's quarters somewhere on a lower deck—or was that the cargo hold? The stern—was that forward or behind her? Carefully now, she groped her way around the bottle-shaped hardness of a Dahlgren cannon to a box-like structure with a thin metal ladder at one side. Near the middle rung her fingers located a small wire-meshed lantern.

Adria toyed unthinkingly with the knob, startled, then horrified when a thick bluish flame reeking of mercury flared to brilliance. Frantically, she tried to smother it, searing her fingertips in the sudden flame.

Instantly, shadows came alive all around her. The lantern was doused and snatched from her hand. When she opened her mouth, a rough hand clamped hard over it. She was being heaved along the deck, her feet dangling midair, locked in steel hard arms that were crushing the breath from her. After a few long, remarkably silent strides, they were in the passageway. It was another moment before she was certain where she was—and who he was.

His anger slashed across the darkness at her. "*One* thing I will not tolerate aboard my ship is disobedience of my orders, not any degree of disobedience. No half-witted bitch will cost me my ship and the lives of those aboard including your own. *What* in the bloody god-damned hell were you doing up there?"

Adria gathered herself, choking down hot

tears that swelled in her throat.

"I don't want to go with you. I want to go back to Savannah."

"You are a day late with that decision," Merrick said hotly, grasping her against him as he forced her to the porthole window.

"Look out there. What do you see?"

Adria shook her head.

"I'll tell you what you don't see. Yankee cannons primed for range two leagues beyond our drift zone. They're waiting for us. That camphene torch you just waved in their face just found us."

Merrick felt her slowly stiffen against him, felt the quick shudder that pulsed through her. He turned her roughly in his arms, his long fingers closing to a fist; then, gently he tilted her face up to him.

"If you were a man, I'd have you whipped for this."

"Y—You would—do that?" Adria murmured against his hand.

She felt him brush away from her, across the darkness of the cabin to the door. The door closed softly, emphatically, behind him.

Adria sagged down on the edge of the berth, her heart loping in her breast, and quite stupidly, began to cry.

Hillary Barlow glanced once at Merrick when he took his position beside him at the helm, his expression stoney when he detected the perfumed scent on Merrick's coat.

"Did she give reason, sir?" he asked quietly.

"Reasons that women usually give are meaningless," Merrick said off-handedly, swinging his head up to the scurry of sea wind that alerted a strange acrid scent.

"Is the auxiliary fired?"

"No, sir. Main engine is at lap speed as ordered."

"Then where is that smoke coming from?" Merrick demanded irritably.

Hillary Barlow scanned the cloud-sunken sky, testing the wind scent. The wind quieted suddenly and he lost the trace of scent.

"A drift in all probability from the bivouac fires at the fort."

"It's too heavy for camp smoke," Merrick argued tensely, watching Joel Ditwell's practiced climb to the bridge.

"Your fog as ordered, captain." he smiled tightly at Merrick, then motioned upriver to the vague silvered wisps that gathered at the sea channel.

"Do we go, sir?"

Merrick looked hard at the dark sullen river, taking as he invariably did this one last measured moment of caution. The tide was up, surging, the shoreline fog willowy and thickening in swirls across the river. He clocked the helm, the ready signal to fire the *Warlock's* engines.

"One point twelve to the fort line, captain," Ditwell reported from behind his sea glass.

Scabrous embankments of Fort Pulaski rose slowly into focus, bottle-nosed cannons dark, tight within their arched hulls. The Stars and Stripes twitched in a shallow wind high above the silent river fortifications.

Hillary Barlow cast a determining glance at the unfurled flag traveller. "It's too bloody quiet," he muttered.

Merrick nodded, threshing the reasons. Sherman could have advanced south and east before entering Savannah. That would explain the apparent abandonment of the river fort. But the logic was wrong, and Yankee logic was always stubbornly predictable.

Merrick's order for engine press was never uttered. The darkness exploded brilliantly, suddenly, blinding him. The cannon fort line was illumined, the ugly Columbiads slimed and glittering as they leveled their contact degrees and held.

Blocking the channel, her massive deck lights glaring, her vast iron hulk sluggish and arrogant in battle regard, the U.S.S. *Sandusky* waited.

Merrick heard or imagined the fort cannon wheels pivot on their tracks. The smoke trace he had detected was engine spill from the half-idled Yankee warship. The cumbersome bastard of the Union Fleet, slow and ugly as she rode the tide race with a bloat of importance, ranging on her prey.

"Show our lights." Merrick gritted the command and heard Barlow's rough gasp.

"Lights—to surrender?" Barlow mumbled unbelievingly.

The command was echoed as Merrick trimmed the helm, tightening the distance between the two warships. The next moment, Drummond lamps blazed across the *Warlock's* polished decks, haloing across the dark channel.

"Fire a rocket astern. Stand all engines full to run," Merrick said swiftly.

Barlow gulped a protest, then smiled hugely. "Aye," he nodded with confidence.

The *Sandusky* slowed her engines accordingly. On the bridge her commander, Stanley Orrendale, plucked nervously at his beard, momentarily baffled by the alternate stand-to-defend flare and a surrender signal. So this was the troublesome blockade runner that had become an embedded thorn in the South Atlantic Federal Blockade reports, the very ship whose capture would surely earn him an admiralty. It appeared at the moment absurdly simple.

"Escort launches signal for orders, sir."

Stanley Orrendale shrugged an acknowledgement, watching as the British ship veered eastward toward the sand narrows. "He's running her into the shoals," he thought to himself, "to save his cargo." There was something ethereal, graceful, almost mermeric about the ship's sleek tracking patterns.

"Roll the alert flag to commence warning fire from the fort," Orrendale said dazedly, "and be quick, man! She's moving like an eel in the water." He glanced up desperately at the signal flag limply obscured in the fog-swirled air, the afore agreed signal command between himself and the fort commander at Fort Pulaski. Already, his few seconds hesitation were proving fatal.

"The *Warlock's* heeled, sir! We'll ram her!"

As quickly, the *Warlock* burned dark, disappearing soundlessly, closing leeward in the darkness.

Orrendale went rigid, poised for the iron

impact. Somehow, the *Warlock* had kicked her track beating southeasterly, bringing her broadside into a funnel between the fort's cannons and the *Sandusky's* prow.

"*Jesus—God*—halt that fort cannonade," Orrendale swore, cuffing at the fog. "They'll blow us to kingdom come!"

The first hoarse rumble of heavy Columbiads from the river fortifications belched across the river, sparking the sullen water in molten light.

"*Fools*! *Fools*!" Orrendale was shouting, his voice piercingly lost in a confusion of cannon shots.

Merrick smiled, grimly amused by the *Sandusky's* broach-to back into the channel. Flares flickered helplessly from her decks, then were swallowed by chalky smoke blasts. An obvious confusion of signals between the two Yankee commanders was made worse by the fog shift. He graduated the helm, narrowing the distance a near league portside. His risk was surprisingly on key. The river cannons were ranged on the wrong ship. It gave him the crucial moments he needed.

Merrick turned suddenly from the helm, expecting to see Hillary Barlow beside him. James Altree was in his stead, grasping urgently at Merrick's arm.

"I *demand* that you halt this madness at once!" he screeched. "You know this mission is not ordered for battle!"

"You demand nothing on my ship, Altree. Now get below!"

James Altree bunched forward, confronting

Merrick from across the helm. His hand locked tightly over Merrick's closed fist.

"You want to kill us all, don't you? Just to prove yourself a hero—the daredevil captain of his ship who died in honor with all hands lost!"

The helm clocked a full revolution as Merrick released it, sawing the decks with spill. River water geysered along the prow, sloshed above rails by a near cannon blast. Merrick shook the water from his eyes, focusing first on Ditwell, then on the blurred form of Hillary Barlow and a crewman who were wrestling James Altree from the bridge. Grappling for the helm, he steadied it, shouting the all-speed order to the engine room.

"They found us, sir. The *Sandusky's* cannons are scored for range," Ditwell croaked.

Merrick scanned the deepwater channel ahead. Four minutes to open sea—four timeless minutes.

A tattoo of a ship's artillery gutted the battle sounds around him, distant, then oncoming. An iron hull, squatty and low in the water, was beating a furrow toward the *Sandusky*, its port turret cannons ablaze from steel window-eyes. Rebel Bars and Stars lashed brilliantly from her flagmast; the rusted green lettering read tiredly, C.S.N. *Tennessee*.

A passing salute was shouted, was muffled and then drowned in the swift charging motions of both ships. Merrick charged the helm canting near enough to recognize the Confederate ram-clad captain, his arm waving a path for Merrick to the open horizon. A joining, a separating of extremes, then it was gone.

Merrick wiped his face in the crook of his coat sleeve, needing the moment to down the leaden ache in his throat. General Hardee knew Merrick's distinction, knew that Merrick would at all risks run for the open sea rather than surrender his ship. Hardee had known the odds and sacrificed the last Rebel ironclad in existence, a rusted core with an aged Barcelona cannon mounted in a carcass turret—an order bearing the stamp of polite desperation.

"They'll take it, captain. It hasn't the speed to outdistance the fort guns," Barlow said thickly.

Merrick nodded, surrendered the helm to Barlow. He drew a long rough breath of salt air.

"I am thinking," he said slowly, "that we are all at this moment gallant lunatics."

CHAPTER 5

The sea was silky and turgid, a tumble of hues: mud-colored, green, gray and silver frothed like unblended paints on a floating palate. December sky was gaunt and cheerless with a drum and mutter of thunder from cavernous clouds banked on the horizon. Sails were bellied, straining to an ever-freshening southwesterly gust. A gale before dawn, Mr. Barlow had prounounced during dinner.

Nothing could be worse than the night just passed, Adria decided, watching the softening shift of hues color the sea. At least up here on deck with salt sting and vibrant wind for companions, she was free from the morbid sounds of Dickson Blanchard's pathetic, droning voice, from Colly's ceaseless retchings, from the churn and pitch of steel cargo lashings in the hold. What she had been able to see of the escape run from the porthole had been plainly terrifying: fire tracers hissing and dyeing the waters black, the entire sky chalked in a brittle glow, the sickening zigzag surge up the channel, and afterwards, the relentless sounds of sand buckets scraped on the deck above her head, shouts, running, then silence, frightening silence.

She hadn't slept, not even when she knew it was over, not until a ship's bell consoled her at daybreak. It was well into the afternoon before she awakened to the heading pitch of the ship and tried to recount the lost hours.

Surprisingly, dinner had been announced long before twilight. Uncertain of her reception after her foolishness of the night before, wondering how best to explain should anyone be crass enough to mention it, she chose carefully among her meager collection of dresses. The cerise one with pale lace ruching spilling from clever Pagoda sleeves seemed the most forgiving, and it fit her well; perhaps a bit too well. But there was nothing she could do now without benefit of a seamstress about the low, overblown bodice. The choice had obviously been a wrong one by the look of brooding disapproval of Merrick's eyes.

He stood imposingly at the head of the table while the passenger guests were seated, looking tall and commanding and curiously bored. The meal was a dismal one, frugal fare served in thick, hair-cracked sea china plates. The only point of grace had been a Bordeaux vintage wine consumed in brisk order by gentlemen who ordinarily sipped its flavor by degrees.

Major Altree was slovenly intoxicated by the time a watery chowder was served, and he dabbed awkwardly at a wine spill on his gray tunic which looked horribly like a bloodstain. His dueling scowls at Merrick had finally erupted into a hot exchange.

"It would appear, Captain Ryland, that your ordered support of a Confederate ramclad was merely some heroic afterthought on your part. Have you news of its fate, or does its fate concern you?"

"The ironclad's appearance was inconsequential to the outcome. It possessed neither the speed nor the artillery to be of benefit," Merrick flared back.

"So it was merely sacrificed on your behalf. A pity such an order was ever allowed," Altree taunted.

"*I* saw it," Dickson Blanchard spoke excitedly. "It looked to be a sister-ship to the *Virginia*. She was scuttled at Norfolk by our own valiant men, I believe."

Kendall Chase scratched his chair forward, reaching for the tall green wine bottle already claimed by James Altree. He smiled retreatingly and turned to Adria.

"You schooled at Miss Druary's Seminary near Macon, I am told," he said questioningly. "Perhaps you were acquainted with a Miss Sally Bently?"

"No, I don't believe I knew her," Adria lied coolly, flinching at the recollection of Sally Bently huddled among her select friends from Georgia's landed families, excluding all outsiders, and particularly Adria who refused to be concerned. The Spring Cotillion, she remembered now; Sally Bently's escort *had* been this same flaxen-haired Confederate officer who was, at the moment, running his eyes hotly over the cleavage of her gown. The Lancer's rhythm, the applause, the gush of popularity with all the nauseous flutterings of dour-faced matrons who warmed at his attentions. It was him.

"Do you have Tennessee walkers at your stables in Texas, or, more nearly, China Grove?" he pressed familiarly. "Excellent horseflesh. In Virginia they are considered admirable surrey pacers—or is that a bit too civilized a sport for your more essential needs in the backlands?"

Adria straigthened in her chair. "We had, Lieutenant Chase, some military ponies that General Albert bartered for with the Creeks, and some mustangs that roam the bayous. Our stables are pasture corrals. We are *quite* uncivilized, you see. It was only when I came to Richmond that I forsook my buckskins and animal pelts for a more conventional mode of dress."

Kendall Chase reddened sheepishly. He glanced across at Major Altree for support, then at Merrick whose insolent expression offered nothing.

"I—I must apologize for presuming, Miss Sommerfield," he conceded from over the rim of his wine glass.

There, Adria thought exultantly. That should stiffle any further attempts on his part to impress her. And it should have convinced the *Warlock's* captain that she was quite capable in a social melee of handling herself. But it hadn't. The captain was at the moment seriously engaged in conversation with his first officer, Mr. Barlow. He was being incorrigibly rude to his dinner guests, making it clear that his invitation was a mere formality, not an occasion. He hadn't glanced her way once all evening.

Merrick tossed his dinner napkin aside, gained his feet in one long motion. He strode from the galley without apology, followed quickly by Hillary Barlow.

"The British captain mentioned he had a curative for Colly's seasickness," Dickson said vacantly, invading the morbid silence that lingered after Merrick's exit. "He was a student of the Medical Arts, I understand, some years ago."

"And of other, more disreputable things, if rumors about him serve the truth," James Altree slurred with a scolding look in Adria's direction.

What rumors? Adria wanted desperately to ask, but instead she demurely finished her cup of pale, tasteless custard.

"I would be most honored to accompany you for a stroll above decks," Kendall Chase said suddenly, bringing all eyes to rapt focus on her.

"I'm truly certain you would, sir," Adria smiled, almost flattered by his persistence. "I think tonight, however, I will retire directly after dinner."

"Isn't it a trifle early for even a Southern lady to entertain thoughts of slumber?" Chase argued smoothly, touching his fingers along her arm.

Adria caught the full scent of him—clover tonic meshed with rifle oil and soured wine. An oily crust of dark gravy clung to the fine blonde hairs on his upper lip, and when he smiled, a pale, seductive smile, he repulsed her.

"I may entertain other thoughts tonight, very private ones," Adria said stiffly, watching the play in his dark eyes wither.

"Allow me to see you safely to your cabin then."

Adria leaned against the door, listening while the lieutenant's footsteps left the passageway. The tidy emptiness of the cabin was oppressive, prison-like; so different, so forlornly different from her room at Thressa's home. A heart-shaped pillow tossed on a tulip pink counterpane, satin pulls on a tester bed, a gold-rimmed ewer and basin with pastel robins—comforts that she had forgotten until this moment. How she missed them!

"I won't stay in here. I'll go mad if I do," Adria thought wildly, glancing around her for some distraction. She could watch the sea as she had most of the long night past, the monotonous roiling wall of water that surged and surged. The emptiness, the stillness—how did sailors stand it?

She could always visit Colly and Dickson, but the dreary suggestion only depressed her more. She could pace the cabin, count the nails heads in the planks again, forty-two at last count, multiplied by twelve on each plank with four planks under the berth. Miss Druary would be astounded at her calculations, truly astounded.

Adria opened the door and peered into the

quiet corridor. A candle-lamp washed weedy shadows along the varnished red timbers. The ship was heading again, low in the water now with that peculiar surge of motion that made her feel giddy. She stumbled her way up the stairs, leaning hard on the cold brass railing. The sea wind felt chilled, vital and clean and *magnificent*!

The weighted warmth of a sea coat was dropped on her shoulders. Adria knew without turning that he had come to stand near her.

"That was a hideous meal," she said.

"I intended for it to be. It discourages familiarity," Merrick smiled.

She felt his smile and snugged deeper in the swallowing warmth of his coat, drawing the collar up about her neck.

"That's Sirius, the comet star beckoning in the east. The red one there," Merrick pointed, "is Betelgeuse. Pleiades is nearly overhead."

"I can scarcely see them," Adria murmured. "How are you certain they are even there?"

"If they weren't, we'd be off course, ma'am," Merrick said abruptly, moving a space from her.

"Your coat—" Adria called after him. "Won't you be needing it?"

"I have more than one, Miss Sommerfield."

Before midnight, the gale Mr. Barlow had predicted came. Rain in brief fits thrashed at the porthole and, for the first time, the screech of wind drowned the mutter and churn of the *Warlock's* engines.

Adria sat up sleepily, then lunged for the berth railing when the ship yawed suddenly windward. Quickly, she wrestled her arms into the sleeves of Merrick's oversized coat, drew her knees up protectively to her breasts and huddled within it. She warmed her cheek against the soft fleece lining, drinking in his scent that hovered in the thick dark folds, a salt-fresh male scent, one she remembered from their first encounter on the stairwell beneath the "hidey hole" room.

"I love him," Adria thought simply. "I don't know him. I will never really know him, but I love him."

No, this wasn't the way it was supposed to happen at all. There should be a proper courtship, a gradual knowing of someone, the shared situations where the best and worst sides of character are exposed. You just simply don't love without knowing, except perhaps in fairy tales. And they were so much nonsense—or at least that was what Miss Druary had said.

The mating comes appropriately after the vows, after a respectful year of courtship. That was the rule without exception. A year, dear God, a year!

The cherry-varnished oak door at the end of the passageway with its gold-hammered plaque designating "Captain's Quarters" was closed. A puddle of light from underneath haloed a space in the dim corridor, offering enough light for Adria to guess that Merrick was still awake. The sounds of the ship were different here, muted and mellowed with the thrum of engine vibration like a gentle heartbeat.

Adria brushed her hair from her face, gathered a long breath, and turned the cold porcelain doorknob.

Naked to the waist, his sun-dark arms braced on either side his desk, Merrick slowly straightened while a play of coppery shadows from the tall Argand lamp washed over him.

"You are late," he said steadily, watching the flicker of hesitation in Adria's tawny eyes.

Adria swallowed her heart. "I was frightened —with the storm and—"

Ignoring her, Merrick stared back down at his work and reset the gauge-rule needle on the colored map blocks. His long fingers tapped impatiently with the results. Then, with a harsh snap, he shut the map case, and smiled. "Are you wearing anything under that coat?"

Adria shook her head.

She caught his smile, a brief flash of white against the darkly shadowed features of a gaunt, handsomely chiseled face, moments before Merrick blew out the lamp. Still, it was his eyes, pools of warm jade that held her, and held her.

Adria gasped when his mouth took hers, remembering the touch, the pulse of wanting. The liquid lash of his tongue prodded deeper over the smooth ridge of her teeth until he was sucking the breath from her.

His big hands were warm, possessive within the fleecy length of the coat, caressing deliberately the slope of her spine, his strong sinewy palms kneading her buttocks against him.

Words—but she couldn't understand them—passion-heavy, intoxicating words. He was asking her . . . something. He was lifting her in his arms, cradling her there for a moment, his breath stirring the fine sensitive hairs along her nape.

Floating moments then while Merrick laid her on his berth and began unworking each of the anchor buttons on his coat with a maddening slowness. His finger teased a line from the gently throbbing hollow of her throat, down between her breasts to her navel, pausing before his hand closed over the quivery softness of her womanhood.

His fingers opened, his tongue searched nudgingly between them. Adria flinched. "No—" she murmured, alarmed.

Merrick moved to lie alongside her and folded her in his arms. The storm-bent mood of the sea this night was his mood. He lived above it, he knew it, the lilt and spume, the rut and rage. The creatrix, the provider, womb and place of pleasure. The vilest whore and the most faithless—of subtle mood or brave and energetic. Cruel at times and friendless, frothed now to passion by a force beyond itself.

He lowered his head and found her mouth again. She tasted moist and sweet and innocent. When he lifted over her, the jeweled amber glitter of her eyes flashed a challenge. His lips grazed her breast, then claimed the upthrust nipple, gently at first, soon with a crazed, furious hunger, sucking deeply until she writhed from him.

Feverishly, Adria fought the long fingers that were searching downward, violating her. Then, with forgiveness she guided his hand to continue. More gently, he inserted, then lingeringly withdrew, each clean thrust more determined until she became the instructress, glorying in each molten sensation that was flaming through her.

As suddenly, he grasped her upward to him and embedded himself, kissing away her outraged moans. His mouth bathed over her face, tracing her mouth, her eyelids, loving her, urging her to his own swollen rhythm.

Merrick held her fast during the conquering spasms that trembled her, laboring exquisitely within her. When the hot rush of semen erupted from him he lengthened and deepened, and seconds later, still gushing, finished.

The sting of wind pebbled the brass porthole above them. Rain sequins waltzed, glittered across the darkened pane in a bravado of elements. The sacrifice had been made; the fickle sea should be appeased. The thought made Merrick smile.

Adria flexed contently against him, feeling for the first time his impressive strength upon her. Merrick flung onto his back and roughly gathered a blanket over them both.

The mellowed aftermath slowly dissolved. The strangeness that always came after lovemaking, the commitments that argued somewhere in the reaches of conscience were unexplainably harder this time to ignore. Merrick waited the few decent moments, then swung his long legs over the edge of the berth and shrugged on his breeches. He reached to the table shelf, retrieved his half-full wine cup and took a thirsty sip. He glanced at Adria and smiled.

"Come hurricane, drink your wine.
Here's to the Wind that Blows,
To the ship that goes
And to the lass who loves a sailor. . ."

Adria smiled at his recitation, taking a sip of the wine that Merrick offered her.

"Are—Are you a married gentleman?" she breathed.

"No, to both questions," Merrick said impatiently. He stared a moment at her, watching the play of riddled light over her hair.

"This key you're wearing," he said, fondling the chain between her breasts, "does it fit the crates that were cargoed in Savannah?"

Adria could only stare blankly up at the wide silhouette that shadowed her. Why was he asking her this now, of all times, when they had just made love, when he should be as humbled as she felt and so fulfilled that he could think of nothing but the moments just spent?

"I truly don't know," she swallowed, stunned.

Merrick leaned over her, and, for an instant, Adria thought he would kiss her and was ready to forgive him. Instead, he fumbled for the clasp and slid the chain and key from around her neck.

"I'll see if it does, later." He shrugged to his feet and stood looking down at her. "Why is it a woman always expects some reward after she has let a man make love to her?" he said brutally.

Adria sat up and furiously began a groping search for Merrick's coat, for something, anything, to cover herself with. With dignity she swayed to her feet and snatched at the coat Merrick held politely out for her.

A wash of nausea threatened, and for a moment she was terrified that she would faint.

He didn't touch her, not then, not when he walked with her to the door of her cabin. Now and again through the lagging night hours she could hear his voice raised in command above the swell of wind.

CHAPTER 6

Pan de Matanzas, the harbor landmark, lifted a gray stone finger from the sea and pointed to land refuge. Above the fanged shoreline on tufted yew-green hills, a smattering of lights winked a timid welcome. The colors of dusk, a patina of breaking gray far to the west, and beneath that an ocher rimmed with lavender cast a molten pallor over the sea.

"He's bringing her in too hard," James Altree fumed, drawing Adria back from the ship's railing. Too late, a thick spume peppered across the deck, flecking them heavily with sea water.

Adria snugged her cashmere shawl closer about her, refusing the handkerchief that Major Altree offered her. He mopped irritably over his uniform with it, over the wine stain from a few nights ago. She was enjoying herself—the spindrift, the lovely harbor view, the salted dusk where a first inquisitive star had appeared on the horizon.

Merrick was above her on the bridge. Maybe he was watching her (she prayed he was), but she stubbornly refused to glance up there with the others in an attitude of praise. Whatever his moods, his mastery of his ship and the sea approached perfection. The storm two nights ago had been a trying one. The ship wore and heaved on somersault waves. The rain had been cold, relentless, and the wind unforgettable.

"The coaling is expected to last until midnight," Dickson Blanchard spoke quietly from behind her. "The captain has granted us all a brief stretch ashore. It will be good to be on solid footing again, don't you agree, Adria?"

"Yes." Adria nodded. "Only I wish it were daylight. There's so much now I won't see."

Dickson stepped up beside her. His thin shoulders hardened, then fell with a sigh.

"Colly isn't stout enough for a walk ashore. I was wondering. . ." He paused to clear his throat. "She would like to have a trinket of some sort, something rather native. I grieve so to leave her by herself. Would you mind—"

Adria touched his arm. "I'll find something lovely for Colly, I promise," she smiled. When she withdrew her hand, Dickson had pressed a twenty dollar gold piece into it.

"So much, Dickson—"

"Whatever your choice for Colly, purchase something of equal worth for yourself," he said rather sadly, blinking up at the bridge above them. "These Englishmen are a callous lot, and quiet men, too. I always believed them to be a wordy sort."

"Perhaps ashore they change," Adria remarked wistfully. Dickson must be feeling it, too—Merrick's towering presence above where they stood. She looked up then to soothe her curiosity. Merrick's wide back was to her, his large hands fisted behind him, graceful sun-dark fingers clenching and unclenching with each bolting surge of the cutwater. His hands—beautiful, square and sensuous, warm and pleasure giving—she couldn't stop staring at them, or remembering how they had claimed her. When Merrick turned to Hillary Barlow with the anchor command, she glanced quickly away, her face aflame with the raw vibrant memory.

Outright seduction, that's what it had been, the surrendering of her virginity that should have won him. Her willingness, fresh innocence, however inexperienced, should have conquered him, or at least made him feel guilty or responsible, or *something*. Thus far since that night, there had been nothing more—no visits to her cabin or his, no searching her out, only a chance glimpse of him, and then only when he was in the company of his crew. At times, it was hard to believe it *had* happened, that it hadn't been some delirious fantasy. But when she saw him now, as she just had, it was again warm reality.

"Miss Sommerfield." Kendall Chase bowed, touching his gray chapeau. "Since Mr. Blanchard is unable to accompany you to shore, perhaps you would accept my escort."

Adria hadn't even noticed him until now, but he must have been nearby, eavesdropping on Dickson's conversation with her. He looked somewhat better now, his uniform pressed and clean, his boots sheened, his slight blonde beard trimmed and waxed. His manner still annoyed her for some reason; still, his invitation seemed timely. If it accomplished nothing more than a disturbed glance from Merrick, she could well endure the lieutenant's company for an hour or more.

"I would be charmed, Lieutenant Chase," Adria said sweetly, accepting his arm, praying on the hope that Merrick was watching.

Merrick smiled to himself. Adria was beautiful in a reckless way—slim, naive, almost coltish except for the impudent jut of her breasts. Her hair, tawny and untamed, was mate to the topaz depths of her eyes. When, and if, she ever did grow to her ambitions, she would be an awesome challenge for any man.

He had ignored her, and if she hated him for it, as he expected she would, it would simplify the remainder of the voyage. She had offered herself to him in innocence, and in a lost moment when passion overcame reason, he took the advantage. That first conquering kiss should have frightened her into reconsidering, and it should have sobered him. Instead, it made him forget the rules, that he was first and foremost captain of a ship, not a pleasure vessel but a British warship. Duty above all, forgotten in a few feverish moments with a trembling virgin. It was the one rare time aboard ship that he had strayed from his responsibility, and the only time he had ever made love to a woman on his own ship.

Hillary Barlow stood to as Merrick stalked up the bridgeway toward him. It looked a little ridiculous at the moment, Merrick thought, with just the two of them on the bridge.

"Sancho will be drunk by now," Merrick said, pulling a playing card from his pocket. He examined it for a moment, then handed it to Barlow. "When you give him this, tell him I need two loading crews, and I will pay double wages for a night loading." Merrick started to walk away, then remembered. "For Christ's sake, tell him to wash before he comes on board. The last time my cabin reeked of his sheep for a month."

"Aye, captain," Barlow said, watching as Merrick stormed off. The girl, the Confederate general's daughter, she had to be the reason for Merrick's latest show of temper.

Moonlight spangled the Paseo de Marti, highlighting the vast rows of *corojo* palms in a chalky glow. Adria eased back against the worn leather squabs of the rented phaeton, thinking this had to be the most magic night of her whole life. A breeze, cooling and sensuous with fragrance, a night that was pale day, a moonscape night complete with all the alien shadows, a night studded with bright stars. Happily, she fondled the sunstone gems of her new necklace.

"The storekeeper thought you wished to purchase a broom," Kendall Chase teased pleasantly—"*una escoba*, made of dyed beargrass, four *pesos*."

"Was he as angry as he seemed? You argued

so with him."

"A game they play tediously well. He was pleased, in fact, with such a generous purchase from his humble shop."

"Oh," Adria said vaguely. "I truly hope Colly will be pleased with the ear baubles. They're the same stones, only in a smaller setting."

"I'm certain she will be," Chase soothed, watching for the loop of side road the storekeeper had told him about, an isolated place to take a lady. Ah, the Latins, they understood common lust very well.

"Are you certain we'll be back by sailing time?" Adria fretted suddenly, glancing back at the white expanse of road behind them. The shore lights of Matanzas were hardly visible now, no more than a disappearing blur. She was having some very uncomfortable thoughts just now in realizing that she shouldn't have let herself become so enraptured with a candlelight dinner, mellow guitars and a soft Virginian drawl that fed on the nostalgia of Savannah. She should have returned to the ship with the others.

"The word of a Southern gentleman is quite reliable, Miss Sommerfield," he smiled.

When he reined to a halt beside the moon-blazed statue of Ferdinand VII, the magic reappeared.

"Ah, to be so sculptured for eternity!" Chase said passionately, grasping Adria's hand. "To know this man breathed, he walked this same soil as you and I and is now carved in immortality. How I have yearned for such!"

When he turned to face her there was a

peculiar, almost fanatical gleam in his dark eyes that worried her.

"He watches us here below from his marble eyes, and perhaps he envies us our mortal passion," he rasped.

Adria smiled convincingly, warned by the uneasy shudder that was pulsing through her. Now she *knew* she shouldn't have come up here alone with him.

"Shall we walk awhile, Lieutenant Chase," she said with a strained confidence that bordered on panic. Kendall Chase didn't move. He just sat staring up at the moon-silvered statue.

"Are you a believer in greatness?" he asked intensely as he closed an arm about her.

Adria squirmed free of him. "The stroll now, if you please, sir, then we really must be returning to the ship." She tried to sound composed, but her voice trembled.

Chase outpaced her and took her by the arm. "I will be that great—no, far greater. *I will be remembered*!"

Adria backed a step from him. The cold marble boot of the Cuban monarch prodded painfully against her spine. She flinched to one side and he trapped her. His breath was heavy, rasping along her throat. He was forcing her backward, holding her face in a vise between his hands. His mouth, urgent and wet, locked over hers and sucked at her lips.

"Treat a lady like a whore," he grated feverishly, fumbling with his own clothing. He ripped at the delicate buttons on her dress, groped for her nipple and pierced it with his thumbnail.

"Women like the pain—it prepares them for *later*—"

Adria gasped in agony, so struck with the suddenness of what was happening she couldn't react quickly enough. He pinioned her against the marble base of the statue and ran his hand up her thigh, probing, squeezing, until she screamed.

Chase locked one knee across her hips, positioning her. He lifted her then and brought her down on him, impaling her. She was above him, over him, tangled to him. He bit at her nipple until that was the lesser pain. In a half-faint she felt him tense, and the long deep pain that came when he climaxed freed her.

Chase staggered sideways then lunged suddenly, missing her. Adria fell once as her feet stung the ground. The salty, metallic taste of blood filled her mouth and she retched. She ran, her legs caving, and reached the phaeton seconds ahead of him. She only had time to slip the reins and lash the pony forward. The empty phaeton clattered down the hard sand road, trailing enough dust to hide her while she ran for a grove of silk cotton trees.

Chase stumbled in the same place where she had. He walked the road and returned to the spot where he had stopped the phaeton.

"If you can hear me, Miss Sommerfield, I suggest you compromise. It is a long walk back to Matanzas."

His words fell to echoes in the soft warm night. A *paroquiet* nesting above Adria complained, a cricket symphony answered. She didn't dare breathe.

Chase seemed undecided. "I don't believe your trick with the phaeton. You didn't have the time." Now when he spoke, he sounded closer somehow. "There will be questions when I return to the ship alone. I can give any number of plausible reasons for your behavior. The storekeeper was ogling you, along with the waiters and a crew of French sailors. Men can always scent out a whore, and you are one, you know. Did you think your night with the captain in his quarters went unobserved? I heard all your little anguished moans of delight."

Adria gritted her teeth, determined to remain motionless while he baited her. "I'll kill him," she raged silently, "someday, I swear I will kill him." Whatever story he told couldn't be worse than the truth. She listened while his boots crunched in a wandering circle near her, then paused, waiting at intervals for some tiny sound from her.

"As you will then, Miss Sommerfield. These hills are infested with *jutias*. Be careful you are not bitten."

Adria strained, listening to the faded sound of his boots as he walked back down the road. She blotted at her swollen eyes with the hem of her gown, tried to massage away the raw pain in her left breast. She was bleeding there, and the dark splotches on the lap of her gown told her she was bleeding from inside as well. Tears burned her face, tears of rage and helplessness. She cradled her face in her arms, gathered her knees to her, and wept.

The moon had set when Adria wakened. Achingly, she struggled loose from a moist pasty vine that had coiled over her ankle. She scratched at the fiery welt it left on her skin and slowly sat up. Night sounds had lessened in the hesitant way they sometimes do before dawn. She couldn't even hear the crush of sea anymore.

Thankfully, with light she could find the road and follow it, and pray every step of the way that the *Warlock* hadn't sailed without her. The thought made her suddenly and desperately thirsty.

A sudden scrambling sound like a pebble-slide made her forget her thirst. The quick needle of pain in her foot brought her surging to her feet. She stamped at the ground, sick with horror when her heel crunched down on a live, furred thing that emitted a high raw shriek. She stepped on one, then another, falling over herself. She shook them from her foot, lashed at them with the skirt of her gown, and still they came.

She was running before her legs were ready, clawing through a maze of foliage so dense she was suffocating. The hot twinge in her side slowed her, and, for a dizzying moment, the shadows around her reeled with sunspots. The slight hill above her was clothed in straying bluish mist. She must be near the sea now, please, *God, she must be*.

The scurried sound was moving, swarming from somewhere in the trees behind her. She looked there and froze. A single eye, red like a cinder, was climbing the hill after her. The wild scream building in her throat stayed, and stayed.

Adria lifted herself to run again, and quietly fainted.

CHAPTER 7

Near the sheep pens a freckle-feathered rooster crowed a lusty greeting to the oncoming day. Shivering, Sancho Pelagra slapped his arms inside his *chaleco* to warm them, still hunkering before the grayed-out ashes of a withered fire.

Today, the smell of the sea was strong in his nostrils. Today would not be another monotonous sun-scorched day for him. Today would be different. Merrick Ryland was in port.

Sancho felt inside his pocket for the worn King of Diamonds that Hillary Barlow had brought to him last night, smiling again at the tender memory. A steamy cantina in Havana, the Biloxi gambler with fast smooth hands whose temper had ignited as swiftly as the shot from his pepper-box pistol when Sancho caught the slick shuffle of a pair of kings in the dealing box.

Jesus, if he could just remember it all, the way it happened. Merrick told him, others told him, but *he* wanted to remember it. A misaimed shot that would have been fatal but for Merrick's quick ministrations. The wound had left one arm paralyzed, but Sancho had lived. Now he tended sheep instead of sail, yet he could remember the old times. Merrick and he had tasted the brine and lemon before they downed their tequila, each reliving the treachery of Cape winds, each vehement in their differing versions until the tequila numbed their thoughts and quieted their recollections. Sancho rarely thought of the sea anymore. Only Merrick could remind him.

A sheep dog growled near his feet, another bristled and joined in the warning. Quickly, Sancho grabbed a reed torch and swung it along the path to his hut, nudging at the frightened sheep that bunched in his way. The dogs circled the path, barking dangerously now, a sound that pained Sancho's rum-sogged head.

"Sancho! Call off your bitches!" Merrick shouted above the curdling growls that enclosed him. Sancho hurried through the door pens, a huge grin spreading across his granite-leathered face. *Chenga*, the curse of age that made him deaf to Merrick's footsteps, ones which he usually recognized, for Merrick did not simply walk, he marched.

"*Bueno*, Merrick," he called. "I wait for you after the loading. Your men say there is trouble. *Que es*?" Shushing the dogs, he rounded the path, waving the reed torch in Merrick's direction.

"Two steps up, you remember, eh, *marinero*?" Sancho chuckled, a chuckle that died to a gasp when he saw Merrick approach carrying a woman in his arms. Sancho crossed himself.

"She is dead, or only sleeps?"

"She's alive," Merrick said grimly. "I found her in the hills west of the Paseo de Marti. We've searched the night for her. What do you have for medicine in the hut?"

Sancho hurried after Merrick. "A little Bacardi, some cowslip you leave from the last time," he muttered, worried.

"Bring all of it and some blankets, clean ones."

"I boil for you what you need," Sancho nodded, following Merrick over to the straw cot and kicking to one side the clutter of carding implements that littered his way.

"The *obreros*, they want more money for the night loading. They complain. I tell them to wait, talk to you," Sancho rambled, flinching when Merrick tested along the length of Adria's legs with fingers remarkably gentle as he felt for dislocated bones.

"Stir the fire and boil these," Merrick said, loosening Adria's petticoat and tossing it to Sancho.

"The marks on her, Merrick—*por que*?"

"She ran from me when I came up the hill after her," Merrick said, still leaning across Adria. "I saw what she was running from. There must have been a nest of them." He lifted Adria's foot and traced a jagged cut with his fingertip. "This one was made by a stone—the others are rat bites."

"*Dios*, the *jutias*," Sancho groaned, finding

the chair that was suddenly under him. "Is bad, Merrick—they have the rabies. From my sheep I know this."

With a long stick, Merrick fished the steaming muslin strips from the kettle, waving them to cool. "Where is the Bacardi?" he grumbled, then saw it and swilled it in a cup. "Goat's milk, do you have any?"

Woodenly, Sancho pulled a stone crock from beneath the table, still shaking his head as he handed it up to Merrick.

"I tell you, Merrick—is bad, very bad. Sometimes, the sheep, they die."

Merrick dropped the hot cloth, swearing under his breath while he blew on his scorched fingers. "Help me hold her while I make her swallow this."

"There is no medicine for the *rabia*," Sancho moaned.

"There is no medicine for many things, yet people survive," Merrick said irritably while he prodded Adria into his arms.

Adria fought the first swallow, her head slumping leadenly in Merrick's big hand. The second effort, she managed an obedient trickle.

"Try to take a little more," Merrick coaxed her.

Adria pushed his hand away, upsetting the warm liquid over his fingers. She covered her eyes with her hand to shut out the glare of daylight.

"I lost my shawl," she whimpered incoherently.

"I will buy you another one," Merrick said gently, lifting the cup to her mouth again then removing it when she slipped from consciousness.

Sancho stumbled back across the earthern floor and returned in short order with a sheepskin flask. He offered it first to Merrick. Merrick leaned against the cross post at the foot of the cot, wiped his mouth with his sleeve and lifted the flask.

"Your 'varnish' needs more time in the barrel," he shuddered, swallowing it.

"No, Merrick, it is the cowslip wine. She ferments two times," Sancho grinned up at him.

Expertly, Merrick measured the muslin strips, cut their length with shears, soaked the warm cloth in Barcardi and gently lifted Adria's foot against his chest.

Quietly fascinated, Sancho watched Merrick apply the compress, wincing when Adria winced, outsighing her sighs, his tongue laboring with Merrick's work.

"Why did you not be the doctor you study to be?"

Merrick located a button of tallow soap and scrubbed his hands with it. He splashed the rest of the clear water over his face.

"I was a better sailor," he said at length, toweling his hands in the same way Sancho had seen the *medicos* in Havana do.

"I think I wonder why the girl was alone in the hills," Sancho frowned.

"I'll ask her that when she revives," Merrick said shortly, reaching again for the sheepskin flask that Sancho cradled to him.

"And your ship—I see the Confederates aboard."

"An arrangement I had to make with a desperate Confederate general. It was the only way I could take the ship out of the Savannah River," Merrick yawned, pausing to look down at Adria.

Sancho shrugged, confused. "You answer me nothing."

"I don't like prisons," Merrick started to explain, then noticing the first shivers that overtook Adria, he snatched up an armful of blankets.

Sancho was already slipping out of his *chaleco* and handing it to him. "This is body warm, Merrick," he urged.

"And reeks of sheep," Merrick complained, stripping out of his sea coat and snugging it over Adria. He turned to Sancho and began unholstering his LeMat. "Fire three shots, two in succession, one delayed. It will tell the men she is found."

Sancho nodded, holding the LeMat with reverence. He ducked through the doorway out of Merrick's sight before his eyes filled with tears of awesome praise.

James Altree stabbed an accusing finger at Merrick. "By *whose* order has Lieutenant Chase been confined below decks?"

Merrick reached for the curl of his cup handle, halting its yawing slant across the galley table. He tilted back in his chair and leveled a sullen glare at the major while he took another long thoughtful sip of his coffee.

"Until we port in Matamoros, there will be only one voice of command. Mine," he said coldly.

Major Altree reddened. "You are committing a deliberate breach of orders from the Confederate States General Command. The Confederate detachment assigned to this mission is responsible under my sole command."

"Which resulted in the entire regiment being lost all day on the Yumuri, a delay which cost another day's sail," Merrick gritted back.

"You refer, possibly, to an accountable search for Miss Sommerfield. It was my duty to investigate the story of a *peon* who swore he had seen her wandering about there."

"Only she wasn't," Merrick added.

"She might have been," James Altree hissed, his voice thin with rage. "Lieutenant Chase reported to me the entirety of the incident. I am satisfied with his report. I demand he be released."

"No," Merrick said flatly.

"Then I demand to question Miss Sommerfield myself and get to the truth of this matter. The guard at the door of your cabin refused me admittance."

Merrick stood suddenly and spread his bronzed hands out across the table. "You reminded me once, Major Altree, in a different setting, that my demands were without authority. I am telling you now that your demands are wasted here on my ship. If necessary, I will strip your whole regiment of weapons and confine all of you below decks."

James Altree sneered across at him. "Could it be, Captain Ryland, that Miss Sommerfield is being kept in your quarters for some convenience other than her health? It was reported to me that four nights ago she—"

Merrick advanced on him in one stride, heaving him upright by the collar, his words close to the major's flushed face.

"The passengers aboard my ship were assigned to my protection. That includes protection from their own kind when called for."

The major struggled to swallow. "Protection from everyone excepting yourself," he rasped, "that is the true case, isn't it, Captain?"

Merrick let him slide from his grasp. "There are no exceptions to my orders," he said quietly.

James Altree wrenched his tunic back into place, then bent behind him to retrieve his hat from the floor. He flicked imaginary dust from the brim, grunting as Hillary Barlow slammed the door into his backside.

Barlow assessed the scene and moved wide aside for the major to exit.

"Another disagreement, Captain?" Barlow smiled thinly.

Merrick shook his head. "The same one, a rich man's war, a poor man's fight."

Barlow nodded. "There is a matter, sir, of some gravity."

Merrick frowned up at him above the rim of his coffee cup. "Undoubtedly. Which passenger is it this time?"

"It's Mr. Blanchard's wife. She seems to be failing severely. He has asked that you come to their cabin."

Merrick nodded and reached for his sea coat. "And the five crewmen on sick report?"

"There is no improvement, sir."

"The tincture of sulphur did not help?"

"Very little, sir."

Merrick waited while Hillary Barlow fished in his right coat pocket. "Sancho Pelagra asked me to return this to you," Barlow said. "He said to tell you something like—" he hesitated, remembering, "like, '*vaya come vit—vito—*' "

"*Vaya con vientos,*" Merrick smiled. "Go with the winds." He glanced down at the faded King of Diamonds and turned it in his hand.

"Some private joke, Captain?"

"A promise, Mr. Barlow."

Dickson Blanchard watched Merrick's gentle examination, sighing with relief as Merrick laid Colly's wrist back across her chest.

"Mr. Barlow confided that you were a student of medicine," he said with hope, paling when he saw the answer in Merrick's steady green eyes. Leadenly, he followed Merrick out into the passageway.

"I regret, sir, that my skills do not extend to the seriousness of your wife's ailment," Merrick said gently. "Perhaps, when we port in Matamoros there will be a surgeon who—"

Dickson waved him to silence. "Our last hope was a Creole physician in New Orleans. I wrote a letter to General Banks begging permission for Colly and me to cross Union lines so she could be treated. Naturally, there was no reply. Doctor Arnold knew of a specialist in San Francisco, one whom he thought treated these rare diseases of the blood that eat away at a person. When we told General Hardee, he suggested the voyage with you. I had to try, Captain."

"You knew then that your wife's illness was advanced to this stage when you came aboard ship?" Merrick said, amazed.

"I did, sir," Dickson admitted softly. "She wished to make the voyage. I could scarce deny her."

Merrick felt a dark weariness settle over him. "I will send Mr. Barlow with another dram of laudanum," he said with compassion, knowing that Dickson Blanchard's gaze paced each of his steps down the long passageway.

Merrick kicked the door to his quarters shut, peeled out of rainslicker and coat in stride and stalked over to his desk.

With a hurried show of modesty Adria smoothed a coverlet over herself, then relaxed, resting her cheek on her arm while she pretended to nap. Merrick slammed through the cupboards, leaving the doors to groan on their hinges while he combed through the shelves. Adria started once at the clash of glassware, wondering what she had done now, other than just being here, that had provoked him. A measured slosh of Irish whiskey, followed by a long disgusted sigh, and the cabin grew still again.

"Do you know *why* sea captains become notable drunkards?" he stormed at her, banging his glass down on a table shelf above the berth.

Adria stared innocently up at him. It was coming—the rage she had been expecting. She might as well forget her nap for now and simply deal with it.

"I'm certain you will tell me," she sighed.

Merrick almost smiled. "At least the sea is honest—brutal, beautiful, illusive, but *honest*. Unlike the men who trample it." He leaned an arm on the shelf and stood looking down at her. "You haven't eaten—why?" he nodded to the untouched tray of potato biscuits and still full teapot placed on a stool beside the berth.

Adria sat up and shrugged into the sleeves of her dotted blue wrapper which Merrick held open across her shoulders for her. She tied the eyelet streamers, winding and unwinding them nervously over her fingers until Merrick stilled the play with his hand.

"You can't remain here in my quarters, and your cabin is unsuited for my needs. I command the ship from this cubicle, and I can't do it effectively with you in here."

"I distract you, I suppose," Adria sulked up at him.

"You remind me," Merrick said steadily, "that there is nothing sane about this voyage."

"I am *not* to blame for that!" Adria gritted back.

"Then I would suppose that your little overnight jaunt into the hills with one of your gallants was just—coincidence."

"Yes!" Adria defended hotly. Surely he wasn't going to drag her through the whole hideous episode again just to satisfy some latent male curiosity. What did he want from her—an apology or a confession?

At the moment he seemed preoccupied; still angry, but the hot jade depths of his eyes were softening a little.

"I want you to dress. Then I want you to visit

for awhile with Dickson Blanchard," he said quietly.

"Well, for how long?" Adria demanded irritably.

"For as long as it is necessary." Merrick flung the coverlet back, swung her legs over the edge of the berth and settled to his heels facing her. Gently then, he lifted her foot between his hands, frowned over the mottled, purplish bruises. He probed along her instep watching the report of pain in her amber-flecked eyes. His mouth bracketed as he straightened and let her foot slide to the floor.

"The other bruise—there." he motioned close to but did not touch her breast. The warm prickling sensation that suddenly engulfed her made her want, desperately, that withheld touch. She started to unfasten her wrapper but Merrick drew it firmly together and shook his head.

"Just tell me," he husked.

"H—He said—" Adria choked, "that I was a whore, your whore."

"So you assured him otherwise and set about to prove it," Merrick smiled tightly.

"And I suppose that amuses you?" Adria spat. "Or perhaps it flatters you."

Merrick touched his hand over her hair, crushing, smoothing it between his fingers. Adria closed her eyes, gentled by the caressing sensation. When she opened them, a monstrous sponge from the ewer basin was slopped in her hands. The weight tripped her arms and the sponge lumped to the floor.

Merrick picked it up and handed it to her.

"Wear something cheerful, not gaudy, just cheerful."

"Merrick—"

He turned slowly on heel and walked back to her.

"You won't faint. You may feel like you're going to, but you won't." He wrung out the sponge for her, soaped it, and lathered it along her arms. "I'll fetch a dress for you," he said.

"Colly is worse, then?"

"Mrs. Blanchard is dying."

"Oh—" Adria swallowed. "I don't want to watch her die."

"Neither does her husband," Merrick spoke impatiently. He slammed out the cabin then, and Adria just sat for a time staring at the door while she debated her strength.

Cheerful—she felt anything but cheerful. She bathed around her wrapper, then finally removed it. The water, sea water by the fleck in it, was tepid and fragrant with the same clean pungent scent that clung to Merrick. It tingled her nostrils and only slightly lathered when she kneaded the sponge. It certainly wasn't the Scottish hyacinth savon she had used so sparingly at Thressa Hardee's home, which remembering now brought a tremor of homesickness. She was toweling herself when Merrick returned.

Stiffly, Adria accepted the chemise and pantalettes that Merrick draped over her arm without even turning to look at him.

"My underdress," she demanded next, smiling to herself at what must be a pained expression on his dark face.

Merrick dropped the petticoat over her head, letting it float to her waist, then spun her around to him and fastened the ribbons. The horsehair weights sewn in the hem swung gracefully at a proper rise above the floor.

She was about to say, very sarcastically, how practiced he was at this when the folds of her deep russet gown engulfed her, nearly suffocating her. She flailed for air, and flushed with exertion, faced him.

Tauntingly, Merrick held out the hairbrush to her. Adria snatched for it, and when she did, the cabin began an upended tilt. She felt his arms go around her, seeing starshine and brillance until a soft darkness smothered it.

Now she swallowed something that outraged her throat, felt Merrick bathe damp ringlets from her forehead. He was saying those words to her—no, to someone else. She didn't want to hear the other voices. Why were they arguing? Leave us alone, she was trying to say.

"Miss Sommerfield—"

It wasn't Merrick. Adria's eyes blinked open. Joel Ditwell, his face swimmingly distorted, looked gravely down at her.

"I am to stay with you," he said reservedly. "The captain has asked that when you are recovered sufficiently, he wishes you to come to the Blanchard's cabin."

CHAPTER 8

Soft blowing wind caught at Merrick's epaulettes, teasing them over the slope of his shoulder, fluttering the pages of India parchment he read from. With an impatient touch, he smoothed down the page, his voice quietly dedicated to the words he quoted aloud.

Adria refused to look again at the hideous lump of canvas shroud, refused to pray anymore, wishing she could silence Merrick's complex ramblings about a far off resurrection, a better faith that was prepared to commend Colly Blanchard's soul to the deep. At best, it was still horribly barbaric.

The burial sled was tilted. Sea water flooded over the shroud, ingesting it until it disappeared. A rifle salute shattered the air. Dickson was accepting a thrice-folded Rebel Battle Flag. He blinked vacantly down at it as though its weight pained his hand. Awkwardly then, he shifted the tribute to his other hand, pausing to use a corner of the red silk to wipe at his eyes.

The regiment was ordered dismissed. The long deck seemed to shrink to the spot where they all gathered. It was over. It had all been finished last night when Colly, in her quiet agony, had died. Ditwell and four of the British crew disengaged the winch, rewinding the sled ropes in a calm attitude of duty, as unfeeling, Adria thought, as when she had watched them hoist cargo into the hold.

Dickson moved to the deck railing, his face glazed with grief, unaware that he stood within a thorn of molten sundown shadows. How sweetly pathetic he looked, standing inside the shadowed halo of graying light. Adria started toward him, then hesitated when she saw Merrick cross over to him. Merrick said something to him that gained a weak smile from Dickson. His hand tightened on Dickson's shoulder while, gently, he led him away from the railing, nodding a prearranged command to Hillary Barlow above Dickson's notice.

Adria shivered suddenly with some late reaction, reaching along her arms for a shawl that was no longer there, not realizing the exact moment when Merrick had come to stand beside her. He took her arm and led her out of the wind's reaches. Opening her stiff fingers, he dropped the pair of sunstone earrings into her hand.

"Mr. Blanchard asked that these be given to you."

"I bought them for Colly. She never even saw them," Adria said hollowly.

"They were not her type of stones," Merrick

said unthinkingly, then seeing the hurt in Adria's golden eyes, he wished he hadn't opened his mouth. He wanted very suddenly to hold her, comfort her, but damn his pride. She wouldn't have that satisfaction.

"Are you always so unfeeling?" she asked tartly.

"You know what feelings I am capable of," he snapped at her.

"No, Captain, I don't," Adria said with a defiant lift of her chin that brought a flash of jade ice to Merrick's eyes.

"Haven't you another shawl to wear?" he stormed.

Adria almost laughed. He was furious with her again. How easily his quicksilver moods ran their course. She could almost believe she was winning. She turned to walk away, but he halted her.

"Dinner will be served in the galley within the hour. My officers and I will expect you."

"I doubt that my appetite could cooperate with your invitation tonight," Adria smiled narrowly. "Please issue my regrets to Mr. Barlow and Mr. Ditwell."

She left him watching her, her thoughts reeling with success at besting him. She could almost convince herself at the moment that he cared.

Confined below decks for four days in the disciplinary hold, his thoughts rampant with revenge, Kendall Chase paced the length of his cabin, envisioning every form of barbaric torture with Merrick Ryland as his victim.

Ryland, with agonized sweat on his face, his words broken with pain, begging, pleading for death. A time, he vowed, very soon.

Major Altree had accepted his account of that night in Matanzas without question. After all, a Confederate officer rarely questioned the integrity of one of his brother officers. Miss Sommerfield had, unfortunately, suffered some impulsive emotional disorder, caused, no doubt, by the anxieties of the escape. A type of war shock, temporary, but unexplainable. Hadn't her reaction, fleeing into the hills as she had, proved itself?

Certainly, he regretted it. Had he known her vulnerability to such a serene setting, he would never have honored her suggestion that he take her there. He had tried to reason with her, coax her back to safety, and even spent serious time searching for her himself before returning alone to seek help in finding her. True, she had appeared withdrawn, clearly disturbed over the purchase of Colly Blanchard's gift. Perhaps that morbid chore had contributed to her sudden, erratic behavior. The facts were so tight, so credible, he could almost believe them himself.

An hour later, when he faced Merrick Ryland over the same glaringly remindful desk as he had on their first encounter, Ryland alone appeared unconvinced.

"Major Altree waived the provision consignment in Savannah to your command," Merrick stated flatly, his words somewhere between fact and the question.

Chase bristled, missing the probe. "*That* matter is unimportant at the moment. Unjust imprisonment of a Confederate officer against a senior officer's order takes priority."

"Why do you think it is unjust?" Merrick snapped.

Chase ran a grimed fist over his three day beard while he baited Merrick. "More importantly, *why* do you think your role of jailor is just?"

"You were ordered to return aboard ship an hour before sailing time," Merrick said coldly, watching the smoulder of anger in Chase's wary eyes.

"I do not serve British command."

"Nor your own Confederate command if the answers reported to me by your men are accurate," Merrick said.

Chase paled slightly. Could Ryland know about his desertion at Big Black River? No, that was impossible. Only he had survived that senseless rout. It was something else—but what?

"My service account and conduct are recorded as impeccable," he said, unmoved.

Merrick laid the provision list on the desk before Chase.

"Other than the ready stores I brought from Nassau, Mr. Barlow's list shows molasses, cotton and food stocks cargoed in Savannah."

"Your provisions or lack of them are your concern, Captain," Chase retorted.

"Eighty-one water casks were also cargoed in Savannah, and were your concern," Merrick gritted.

Chase drew a sharp breath. "That order was reassigned to a Corporal Eiloss."

"Who reports that in following your orders, he filled the casks where an outbreak of yellow fever had been rumored."

Chase smiled blandly. "Rumors are rumors in time of war, simply that. The location was left to the corporal's own discretion."

"Five crewmen have advanced symptoms of either yellow fever or typhoid. Six others fell ill today," Merrick stated harshly.

"Again, Captain, that appears to fall under the jurisdiction of *your* responsibility."

"Are you aware of the penalty for disobeying military orders in wartime?" Merrick asked quietly.

Chase felt a lurch of heartbeats. "The orders were obeyed and completed to maintain your forced sailing schedule."

Merrick was on his feet. "*Where* were the casks filled?"

"That information should be on Corporal Eiloss' report," Chase replied heatedly.

"Corporal Eiloss cannot write, Lieutenant Chase. The consignment order bears *your* signature."

"That was for those!" Chase exploded, pointing to the five crates stacked against the far wall.

"The order was in duplicate," Merrick pressed. "Eight-one water casks freshened to specifications. Five unlabeled munition crates assigned to Captain's Quarters." He shoved the order at Chase.

The order bearing his own careful signature trembled in Chase's hands. He read it quickly. There was no mistake.

"You can't hold me responsible for an illiterate corporal's bungling!"

"I do, Lieutenant. Just as I hold you responsible for what occurred with Miss Sommerfield," Merrick said evenly.

"*That*!" Chase shouted. "That's the reason for this idiotic interrogation! It's not the goddamned water you care about. You want the details, how it was, how she was. Well, I'll tell you. Her tits are a good mouthful, with nipples like little acorns, but she's a cheap teasin' 'cunny.' I've had better nigger 'poon any day of the—"

Chase never saw the ram-hard fist that struck him full in the face. He doubled and slid bonelessly, unconsciously, down the length of wall.

Ditwell stomped the door open and burst into Merrick's quarters, followed by Major Altree who, inopportunely, drew his saber.

"Take the lieutenant back to confinement," Merrick ordered, straightening. "His army can deal with him."

"*Now you hear me, suh*! His army will deal with you now!" Altree blared, shoving his way past Ditwell and reinforced by a heavily armed Confederate platoon. "We have all had a bellyful of your British discipline!"

Merrick jerked his LeMat from its holster and heard a successive round of firing hammers click to ready position and aim.

"I will shoot the first trooper who moves," Merrick said, steadying his aim at Major Altree. The passageway outside the door was filling with British crewmen. Barlow's voice was certain, deadly, as he gave the order to hold.

"Just how effective is your word of command?" Merrick snapped the question to Altree.

"This display should be evidence enough," Altree hissed back.

"Then I suggest you order your men to listen to me."

James Altree wavered for a moment, then nodded the order. Sullenly, the Rebel troopers cradled their carbines.

"Lieutenant Chase disobeyed my orders in Savannah. As a result, some of the water casks on board carry yellow fever virus. When they were loaded, they were all set in the same section of cargo so it is impossible to determine which are contaminated. Five of the British crew have obvious symptoms, which means that all are susceptible," Merrick paused, allowing the impact to settle.

"If it is a mutiny you are considering, I remind you that this particular ship requires a fully trained crew of one hundred and eighty-two men who obey only British command. I further remind you of navigational technology and Yankee controlled gulf waters. If you, Major Altree, or any of your men feel equal to the responsibility of my command, so state yourself!"

Stunned murmurs translating indecision and near panic spread among the troopers. Major Altree turned to them, glaring them to silence. He faced Merrick with a notable tremor in his voice.

"Considering this unwelcome, and supposedly truthful report, no further action will be ordered at this time. However, be assured that General Hardee will be sent a full accounting of your conduct during this mission, with particular reference to the abusive assault on Lieutenant Chase. No sea captain with your unstable temperment should be given such responsibilities."

Merrick lowered his LeMat. Let Altree take a few swipes at him if it averted some bloody exchange between factions. As aroused as both sides were at the moment, it was more than he had hoped for.

"We port in Matamoros day after tomorrow," he said assertively. "Until then, I recommend that your men stay above decks as much as weather permits, and not drink any water that has not been properly boiled."

Major Altree sheathed his saber and pushed his way among his men, ignoring the condemning looks that preceded him. With a stern threat, Barlow swung the door wide, hurrying the crush of troopers through it, and bolted it closed. He slumped against it, dazed.

"I believe I understand, sir, why they have had difficulty in winning their war," he said dryly. He muffled a yawn and asked, "When do we sleep?"

"In two more days," Merrick snarled back.

Barlow gathered himself, remembering then what had brought him to Merrick's cabin in the first place. He lost heart in telling him when he saw the wearied disgust in Merrick's green eyes.

"Well, what else needs attending?" Merrick demanded.

"It appears rather unimportant at the moment, sir. I believe it can wait."

It was only important to Adria that Juno kept her wine glass filled. Only important that she collect the wine corks and arrange them around her untouched plate. *Poulet Gruyere*, Juno had christened his dish of excellence as he encouraged her to sample it, fetchy words that rhymed over her tongue until she couldn't remember which word came first. After several glasses of the captain's *mousseux*, the bleak galley became a fairyland. The dinner cloth was a rippled expanse of new-fallen snow, the wine goblets crystal towers sparkled by rainbow prisms. The ship's bell sounded a clear wind song chant that sung through the galley. The hum of the *Warlock's* engines became a lullaby for a floating cradle. Whatever other tasty delights were being offered, the wine had certainly brightened her world.

Poor Colly, poor dear thing, floating and floating like a gray dove in that dark eternity. And, Dickson—what would he do now without her? Why did she have to die? Why does anyone have to die? Oh, Adria whimpered to herself, feeling again that deep dry pain that seemed to suffocate her.

"I pray no one will ever watch me die," she said aloud, snatching at the wine bottle that Juno held undecidedly above her.

"*Quoi*?" Juno smiled. "*Je ne comprends pas*."

"I said," Adria sighed, annoyed, "where is your foul-mannered captain and his officers who invited me to dinner? I almost didn't accept, you know, but I decided—" The words were almost musical now in keeping with the wind chant that was sweeping through her brain. Both Mr. Barlow and Mr. Ditwell had made an earlier, very brief appearance, then left abruptly without explanation, forgetting their manners, and forgetting her.

Adria was contemplating the rising whorl of wine bubbles in her glass when Hillary Barlow, with a censuring look at Juno, seated himself beside her.

"I didn't hear you knock," she giggled, then caught herself and tried to appear prim.

"Have you dined as yet, Miss Sommerfield?" he asked tightly, avoiding a look at her full plate.

Adria felt suddenly, peculiarly sad. "Have you been with Dickson?"

"I have," Barlow nodded. "He and Mr. Ditwell are quite intrigued in a game of whist."

"Whist?" Adria cried. No, she must have misunderstood. Nothing was in focus this night, not words, not sounds, not even reason.

Juno moved deftly between their chairs, carrying Hillary Barlow's plate and a fresh bottle of *mousseux*. Barlow glared him into retreat, nodding to the wine bottle.

"I should like another glass of wine," Adria said indignantly, her elbow stabbing the table edge. "Would you join me, Mr. Barlow?"

Hillary Barlow hooked a finger inside his dress collar and loosened it. "Another time, Miss Sommerfield, and I should be honored. Tonight, I regret, I am duty officer on the evening watch."

Adria digested his refusal, then manfully drained her glass, setting it stoutly before her. "Duties," she said sullenly, "everyone has *duties*. I am *so* weary of duties. You have to go here and do this and so. I think the only duty we should have is to perform a *waltz*!" She laughed wildly, entertained thoroughly by her own cleverness.

Hillary Barlow sprung to his feet. "I had best see you to your cabin now," he said sternly, helping Adria to her feet. Adria clutched at his arm as her chair slid away. She took one step, then balked, wrenching herself free from Barlow's restraint.

"No, not until we waltz." She sang the words to him, attempting an awkward curtsy. Juno smiled blankly at her while Barlow half-carried, half-walked Adria down the corridor and up to the deck. Near the mainmast Adria pulled free of him.

"Have you ever climbed up there," Adria asked weavingly, pointing up to the dark top-gallants.

"Upon occasion, yes. Most sailors have," Barlow grimaced.

"I could climb to the winds and dance on the clouds," Adria said sweepingly. "We can waltz up there!" She grasped hold of the mainmast and reeled around it. "A *schottische*, Mr. Barlow? Or would you prefer the 'lancer's', or a Southern reel like the Virginia reel?" Adria swung around to face him, sidestepping the rope lattices that threatened to entangle her.

"Oh, don't be such a proper old leprechaun," she scolded, making a face at him. She rounded the mast, still laughing at herself, dodging the play of shadows that reached out for her.

"A choppy sea, sir," Barlow was saying to someone. "It's my fault. I should have informed you earlier. I thought I could manage her safely to her cabin. She's quite a bit—"

One tall shadow was advancing sternly on her, and try as she would, she couldn't outmaneuver it. Merrick caught Adria to him in one long reach and swept her up in his arms.

"She wanted to waltz, sir, up there on the gallants," Barlow spoke seriously, "with me," he added, hoping that the laugh he heard from Merrick was a kind one.

Merrick turned the lantern wick low, gathered his map charts under his arm, and started for the door. Adria stirred from the berth, arched to her knees, and with a groan collapsed again.

"Stay with me, Merrick. I—I'm seasick," she moaned.

Merrick smiled to himself. "No, love. You're drunk, quite so."

"Don't you have some medicine or something?"

"I have some ginger-root for seasickness. For what ails you there is only one cure. It's called sleep."

Adria groaned again and stretched to a sitting position, curling her slim legs beneath her. She tossed her hair from her face, wishing Merrick's long image would settle and stop slithering up and down the door.

"I don't want to be drunk anymore. I never

want to be drunk again," Adria moaned, swallowing back another lurch of nausea. "And, I don't want to be here on this ship anymore that just sails on and on across all this emptiness. I'm going to die just like Colly did, and be tossed into the sea like a dead fish." The room staggered again and Adria grasped a pillow to her, burying her sobs in the softness.

Merrick closed the door. He crossed the cabin to the berth, his dark hands gentle as he tugged the pillow from her. He traced a long finger along the curve of her cheek, feeling the moistness there. Adria's tear-stormed eyes searched sadly over him.

"You are such a child, Adria," he murmured. "You're rebellious, free, and helplessly beautiful. Hasn't anyone ever taught you discipline?"

Adria lifted her mouth to him, tasting the naturalness of him again, like a nectar that swayed her beyond herself to some wild yielding, to something wonderfully vibrant and alive. Some raw joining that surged to ripeness needing only the nourishment of passion. She buried her face in the V of his shirt, kissing the damp crispness there; then pressing his hand against her cheek, she touched her lips along the ridge of bronzed knuckles.

Merrick flinched and pulled roughly away from her. Seeing the gathering shock in her eyes, he smiled.

"No—not for that reason. It's bruised. Now be a good girl and go to sleep."

Adria heard the door close behind him and lay staring up at the solitary shadows that paraded along the wall. Faces and forms mingling and separating like ripples on a deep pool. The wind chant, she could hear it again now, a dark melody that blessedly soothed her to sleep.

CHAPTER 9

Hot Mexican sunlight yawned through the adobe-sod archway, warming the branny stones, cornering the only angle of shade into retreat. Kelly stretched his long arms across the low archway, determined to focus on a bead of water that oozed from the cistern spout. Heat waves shuddered from the stack-stoned cistern, lines that merged, then wobbled into oblivion.

Kelly tried to count them, matching numbers with the tin drum cadence in his brain. He was approaching some degree of sobriety, he realized, when he saw the drop of water drool from the spout. He wasn't blind after all, just crazed from drinking Melio's home-brewed pulque.

With effort he ran his tongue over his lips, over teeth which felt peculiarly soft, and squinted across the brightness of the tiny courtyard where Ignacio was squatting on the ground. Ignacio stabbed a yucca root into the loose sand, skewering a scorpion to the ground, his eyes lighted with fiendish purpose now while red *diablo* ants swarmed their victim. He dropped the stick, his lips twisted with disappointment when the scorpion ceased to struggle.

A lonely game in a lonely land, Kelly thought with disgust, watching him. His own belly lurched as the gorging swarm of killer ants gnawed at the scabrous, wine-colored scorpion.

"Ignacio! *Viengase*!" Kelly shouted at him.

Ignacio blinked across at him with a satisfied smile on his small face.

"Eh, Kelly, you see it? The *escorpion* does not die brave like the bulls at Monterrey."

Kelly braced his boot against the side of the archway to steady himself. He pulled a cheroot from his shirt pocket and chewed loose the leaf-bound end. The tobacco mash made him feel sick.

"The bulls fight matadores, not killer ants," Kelly said sourly, clamping the new cheroot into Ignacio's greedy hand. "Sell it—don't smoke it like the last time."

"*Si*, Kelly, I do that," Ignacio nodded in mock innocence. "Father Amyas, he says only the devil needs the smoke."

Kelly smiled without emotion. "Go tell your sister that I am here."

Ignacio lifted dark worshipful eyes to Kelly, vowing to someday reach Kelly's tallness, to be brave like this *norteamericano* with storm-cast eyes, eyes that reminded him of silver church plates, as cold and hard. Kelly did not wear the same battered gray longcoats of the other soldiers who crossed the Rio Grande into Matamoros. Kelly did not slump in his saddle like the others after a long march north. He did not salute the solitary star-flag of the *tejanos*, or the cross-flag of his own war. But, Kelly was a *caudillo*, a leader.

And Kelly slept with Ignacio's sister. To Ignacio this was a prideful matter, not the sin Father Amyas said it was. How could the coins Kelly gave to them be sinful? Sin was bad, like Father Amyas preached, but the gold was praised when Erlinda left coins in the door plate, so it must be good. Where was the sin in this?

"Did you watch the river today?" Kelly asked in Spanish.

Ignacio shrugged, scuffing his bare brown feet in lumps of sand, finally kicking it at the cistern. He raised troubled eyes to Kelly.

"I worry for sin," he said.

"Do you sin, Ignacio, or does Father Amyas tell you that you do?"

"Father Amyas says that you do sin with my sister."

Kelly nodded his head. "You tell that meddling soul saver for me that I will come and confess up one of these days."

"Erlinda, she weeps for you. I hear it sometimes."

"All women weep," Kelly said impatiently.

"We men do not weep," Ignacio boasted, feeling much encouraged.

"Only in our guts," Kelly smiled. "Now go tell Erlinda that I am here to sin."

With unsteady fingers, Kelly unclasped the

metal tongue in his horsehair gunbelt, dreading the heat-drenched hours ahead that would pass in torturous boredom. Too soon, still too soon. One fuel stop in Matanzas, a day, maybe two, before the British runner made the gulf straights. General Hardee's glory ship, his last triumph over the Yankee grasp of Confederate gold. If the ship wasn't wreckage floating in the Savannah River by now.

An hour with Erlinda, no more, and that only because his conscience demanded it. Another dull night of three card monte at Melio's, scraping the trooper's pay from their frayed pockets. Noisy, tedious card playing without a decent talent among them, and more of Delano's watered beer. But not even boredom would drive him to drink pulque again anytime soon. He didn't need the nightmares it brought. He had already lived through too many real ones.

Kelly picked up Erlinda's *camisa* from the floor and tossed it across the room at her. Her habits were worse than his own.

"I remember when you owned one *blusa*, one *pollera*, and no shoes," he said caustically, stripping out of his shirt. "Now you're so god-damned rich you can leave them on the floor and step all over them."

Erlinda was braiding her waist-long hair, occasionally dipping her fingers in a jar of citronella and smoothing the oil over her neatly parted hair. The *camisa* hit her shoulder and slid off.

The odor of citronella forced Kelly to the only window. He settled himself on the stone sill, watching Erlinda pout at her reflection in the age-cracked mirror.

"Don't braid your hair. It makes you look decent," he griped.

Erlinda spun around on the bench. "You come to complain or make love, John Kelly?"

Kelly stomped his foot back inside his boot. "Whatever I came up here for, I've just changed my mind."

Erlinda was on her feet, snapping her fingers at him, her mouth curled with fury.

"Two days you are back! The *soldadoes* at Fortin Paredes, they tell me this. "Where is your American?" they ask me. I tell them what you say—at Port Lavaca. They laugh, tell me, 'no,' Kelly is at Melio's with the cards."

"And the pulque," Kelly added, his eyes wandering over Erlinda's swollen breasts. "You're getting plump, like old Flavia."

Erlinda's eyes misted with anger. "You do this lie and make me for a fool. Why you do this, Kelly?"

"I've told you before. I go my own way. I don't like questions." Kelly studied her for a moment, his silvered eyes noting every inch of her nakedness, a body as nearly familiar to him as his own, lithe, perfect, with a tawny hint of her Tolteca blood. Four months ago, when he had watched her dance at Melio's, watched the sweat of exertion trickle down the length of her dark legs, watched her feet caress the sensuous hot rhythm of the dance, he had wanted her. Feverish nights, so many of them, too many. Now all he felt was cold boredom.

Erlinda moved close to him, taking his hand

and placing it on her stomach. "You know then, Kelly. You see that our passion makes for you a son."

"I knew before I rode to Lavaca," Kelly said quietly, running his hand over her rounded, taut belly. The nauseous lump in his gut slowly turned.

"I tell Father Amyas the child is yours when I go to confession," Erlinda said shyly.

Kelly couldn't look at her. "Mine, or any one of the *soldadoes* or *rurales* at Fortin Parades."

Erlinda laughed brokenly. "I dance for them, they pay. That is all I do. With you, Kelly, I love. My heart loves."

"Well now, I see it all different," Kelly said slowly. "It won't work for us, Erlinda. We're a special breed of trash, you and I. Maybe we could justify what we are if we tried real hard, but it would always come out the same. Somewhere along the way we just started livin' wrong and never figured out what to do to make it better. You can't stay away from the cantinas any more than I can leave off wearin' a gun. When I started screwin' you, givin' you money to behave, I think I was trying to buy some good for us. But it didn't work out. We can't reform, either of us."

Erlinda was staring at him, just staring.

"What is this you say to me, Kelly?" she asked finally.

"There was some nights when I thought about giving up my soldiering after being with you. Nights when I was so god-damned whipped I even thought I was ready for some kind of future. Then when I sobered up, it all went back to feelin' the same way it was before."

"The child is yours, Kelly. I swear it. I count the times. I know."

The lurch inside him floated free, deadened. It was said now, all confessed.

"There's some money here in this pouch," Kelly said, handing her a worn rawhide money pouch. "It will be enough to take care of you and your kid if you are careful with it. I told you when we started I wasn't one for marryin'. I meant that."

Erlinda licked at her lips, snuffing at the tears that overflowed her eyes. She grasped the rawhide pouch to her breast, fingering over the coins inside she couldn't see.

"*Bastardo,*" she gritted out softly. "You lie, Kelly. You always lie."

Kelly reached for his shirt. "It was never that good between us, Erlinda," he said, "but for the sake of your reputation, I'll say it was."

She screamed at him from the depths of her throat, clawing at him, scratching and kicking him as he left her. She was still screaming obscenities at him when he cleared the last step down into the courtyard.

Cicadas wailed their reedy crescendo from runted mesquite trees overhead, a deafening swell that clouded the air, that hushed suddenly to a droning hum when Kelly dismounted. His legs still felt watery as he picked his way among the low flung branches trailing the riverbank to the edge.

The air came easier here. The river looked hot, muddy, and rebellious when Kelly settled to his heels, bracing himself suddenly with one arm when he reeled sideways. A brassy sun hung in a swallowing blue sky, a molten speck when Kelly looked away, stretched himself belly down to the water, and vomited.

River water lapped at his cheek, causing him to open one eye to reassure himself he was still alive. He groaned deeply, flung onto his back, and kneaded at the pointed pain in his belly.

General Hardee's mission. The dispatches that had brought him to Matamoros four months ago. Confederate scouts that had found him riding south from the New Mexico territory after Colonel Canby's rout of Sibley's Mounted Texas Volunteers at Glorieta Pass, an almost brilliant defeat with the Rebel command deaf to Kelly's warning them to protect the crucial Confederate supply camp at Johnson's ranch. Two hundred and fifty dead, buried in an open field near Valle's farm, an impotent battle to conquer the land of the Apaches; and that was another war, a long bloody war.

Hardee's ordered words were contained in a mud-stained packet:

> *A favor if you will, Major Kelly, which excuses you from Confederate uniform for the present, and places you as a civilian mercenary who holds the balance of this essential mission in your capable hands.*

A flag he no longer saluted, battered shreds of the Bars and Stars that hung limply in the minds of his men, breezed only by vague new direction. What was left of his regiment had followed him south in mute obedience. Some still trembled with the ragged trumpet of cause, fortified only by the sketchy promise he offered them, the last mission of a fast closing war.

A tabled cause, a mission Kelly had declined until General Hardee's offer of payment in gold enticed him. The runner, the *Warlock*, would bring Hardee's agent from Savannah with the exchange keys to the Confederate gold vaults in Matamoros. Months of preventing Juan Cortina's unpredictable *revolutionarios* from storming the vaults would be ended. The gold had a new destination now. Home.

Kelly sat up, his head suddenly clear. A week, no more than two, Hardee had indicated after the British runner cleared the Savannah River. "Ryland will not fail our cause," Hardee had concluded in his coded dispatch to him.

The General now, he was another one, another blindly confident, chivalrous Southern officer immune to defeat even when it stared him in the eye. Like Colonel Adrian Sommerfield had been, the same iron-gutted breed, bolstered with idiotic optimism, their stubbornness as genteel, as graceful as the manners that labeled their orders.

Honorable men even in death. Honorable, sprawled in some unnamed blood-splattered Mexican *arroyo* where Adrian Sommerfield had led an artillery charge, his naive amber eyes stormed with astonishment only moments before bullets took him; his words, "Gentlemen, the day is ours!" had been his last ones.

Kelly swallowed the rawness in his throat. Ten years, a long time, too long a time to still feel the gut wrench of the only death that had ever moved him. Adrian Sommerfield, the only thoroughly decent, honorable man Kelly had ever known.

The dust tail along the riverbank brought Kelly to his feet. The improvement in standing was slight, but steady now.

Delano reined too short, torturing his horse with a spurred side-rear, powdering the air with dust. He grinned broadly, spit appropriately, his dark eyes noting Kelly's bent stance and the pallor that tinged Kelly's sun-dark face.

"Eh, Kelly—you sick?"

Kelly fanned weakly at the settling dust. "You'll kill that horse with your goddam clowning," he spat, wiping his mouth on his sleeve.

"The pulque last night—I think Melio brews it with alkalai water."

"Or rat poison," Kelly groaned, straightening.

Delano backed his horse near Kelly's and swooped down to gather the reins. Smiling, he handed them to Kelly.

"Only a trader from Veracruz comes today to Port Isabel. I ask the trawlers, they say they see nothing of your ship."

"Where is Cortina?" Kelly husked, mounting heavily, still gripping at his belly.

"Ah, Kelly, you know Juan. He comes, he goes."

"But where does he go with my horses?"

"Juan, he say not enough gold. They are his horses."

"That greedy bastard," Kelly grumbled with a smile. "How many did he take across the border?"

"He take some to Fort Ringgold, maybe thirty head, Ricco tell me."

"Did he take my *cargas* mules?" Kelly frowned, running his hand across his eyes.

"No, and Ricco say it is only for a loan to the army with the horses. They bring them back in time. Where do you ride to now, Fort Brown?"

Kelly thought for a minute, snugging the brim of his Stetson down over his eyes. "Juan, have any new girls stabled across the river?"

Delano chuckled. "You know the ones—Lupe, Hortensia, and Flavia," he said enormously, making cups with both his hands. He smiled at Kelly's smile, chewed nervously on the tail of his moustache, then said, "You see Erlinda since you are back from Fort Lavaca?"

"I saw her," Kelly snapped.

"She tell you then, she is *encinta*?"

"I knew it before she told me."

Delano shrugged piously, avoiding Kelly's hard eyes. "You know, Kelly, with war or women, a man has pain."

Kelly threw back his head and laughed. "You tell Juan my horses had better not be saddle-spent when I need them," he said, touching his spurs to his horse.

"I tell him what you say, Kelly," Delano called after him. "I tell him but he listens only to you," he muttered to himself, watching Kelly's horse clear the jump over the rotted footbridge.

CHAPTER 10

The pinpoint smudge on the horizon moved.

Ignacio backed away from the lighthouse railing, away from the heights that dizzied him, unbelieving of what his eyes told him. The blur crept another degree, then disappeared.

Stubbornly he dared it to reappear. The horizon line beyond the crystalline waters of the Laguna Madre was empty, clear like always. Satisfied, Ignacio started for the down stairwell.

"*Madre Dios, perdona,*" he swore, looking back. It was there again. He covered his eyes, sucked in a breath and waited. Through his fingers he watched the blur reforming, and in a flutter of a second, vanish again. He rubbed his eyes with his fist, squinting against the noon-blaze glare. It was a ghost or he was crazy. He rounded the stairs, colliding full impact with Kelly.

"*Cuidado*!" Kelly growled, setting Ignacio from him.

Ignacio tossed his hair from his now wide-opened eyes.

"*Mira*, Kelly. You tell me if I see or not see," he gasped, pointing across the railing.

Kelly's frown tightened. He glanced quickly, following where Ignacio pointed across the water.

"Go below and send Delano up with my field glasses. *Andale, pues*!"

For three days Kelly had delayed, three days of hearing the hot grumblings from his men who pressed him for the order to ride on to the Confederate garrison at San Antonio. Three stagnant days of trusting his own decision to outwait Hardee's deadline. Juan Cortina had laughed and said, weighing the Confederate gold in his pockets for the horses, "Horses you not need now, Kelly." But Hardee was a careful general, one of Lee's best, and there was considerable at stake. Only he and Hardee knew how much. He could wait.

Delano labored up the last few steps to the watch railing, untangling Kelly's field glasses from around his neck.

"*Perdicion*, Kelly," he heaved. "Already I climb up here six times today."

Kelly snatched the glasses from him, tensing as he lined up the range distance across the gulf. A pinpoint of mast entered the focus, a shape followed—sleek, swift, bearing hard southwest. A pulsebeat hammered somewhere in his brain.

"She's fast, damn fast," Kelly murmured.

"Many ships are fast," Delano complained, lounging against the railing with his back to the sun.

"Not like this one," Kelly replied, amazed. Impatiently, he reset the focus. A red blur with enough wind play to catch the red and gold lions against one blue square of British Royal Standard filled the lens. Its companion flag, the Union Jack, snapped below it.

Ryland, if it was him, just might be peacocky enough to fly the Queen's colors, Kelly thought, able now to distinguish the full scope of the fast-coming ship. Slowly, while he watched, a third flag climbed the traveller, whipping hesitantly in the new wind. Kelly's mouth went dry.

"Shit." Kelly choked, his eyes misted.

Infantry size, star-blazed blue saltiers tossed from a blood-red background on a flag he had almost forgotten. Memories rushed past while a quiver of pride arose in his gut.

Delano moved beside him. "*Que dice*, Kelly? Is it the one?"

"Yes," Kelly nodded grimly. "Tell the men."

Sounds exploded from below, a long mad careening high-pitched yell that landed in triumph, only to be taken up again and again. Sad, melancholy, pride-ridden, dreaded, beloved—a sound that echoed fiercely in Kelly's mind, his guts, his heart.

The sound spread into cheers. One called, another answered, matching cheer for cheer with an uncertain answering hail from across the water.

The *Warlock* pressed the deep gulf current, plowing the azure waters in a majestic spectacle that applauded her mastery of the sea. Ryland was a showman, there was no disputing that, Kelly thought, feeling Ignacio tug hard at his sleeve.

"Your ship, Kelly? The one you wait so long for?" he asked.

"Very long, Ignacio—a lifetime," Kelly said heavily, ruffling his hand over Ignacio's hair. A wash of regret came over him. The waiting had ended. It changed everything.

It could have been the hated blue of Ryland's sea coat that prejudiced him, Kelly thought later, even before he had an honest look at the Englishman. The uniform and the man wearing it dwarfed the swarm of gray-clad figures that rushed to the dock bridge of the *Warlock*.

Kelly let the crush of cheering men precede him, taking his time to walk the distance from the lighthouse to the dock. The months and days of waiting had ended too suddenly for him. Maybe he never really expected the ship to clear the mission. Maybe he resented Ryland's chancy success, and maybe he was just sick of the whole goddam war.

A Confederate major, one armless sleeve pinned neatly above the elbow, confronted Kelly. He saluted snappily with his one hand.

"Your men directed me to you, suh. I am Major James Altree, Acting Regimental Officer who carries the Confederate States Communique from General Hardee in Savannah."

Kelly didn't return the salute. He reached instead for the leather envelope in Major Altree's hand.

"My commission was forfeited, Major Altree," Kelly said casually. "As of now this mission becomes a civilian matter."

Altree was taken back. "You are John

Kelly—the same Major Kelly, or am I in error?"

"I am Kelly."

"Your men are wearing Confederate States gray, and I did observe rank elevations among them," Altree insisted.

"It's a different war here in Texas. We wear what we have," Kelly said, reading over General Hardee's hastily scrawled notes. He lifted crystal eyes to James Altree.

"The civilian passengers that came from Savannah—are they aboard?"

"One died at sea, a most unfortunate incident," Major Altree said vigorously. "There are other incidents that I intend to report in full when we—"

"Which passenger?" Kelly demanded, interrupting Altree.

Major Altree cocked one brow at him. "Why, a Mrs. Blanchard," he said curiously. "Were the two of you previously acquainted, Major Kelly?"

"No, and it's Kelly," Kelly said shortly. "I want to talk to the British captain now," he added, shoving his way past James Altree. He sidestepped the celebrating troopers, shook his head when his name was called.

Clarence Leitman juggled the quid of tobacco to his other cheek, then said to Kelly, "There's some sickness aboard your 'glory ship', sir." He spat a stream of tobacco juice over one shoulder and thumbed in the direction of the *Warlock's* dock bridge.

"That runty fella', there," he nodded conspicuously toward Hillary Barlow, "he just gave me an order to ride to Fort Brown for the

Post Surgeon."

"What kind of sickness?"

"Well, he don't say what kind," Leitman drawled. "There's a woman aboard, too. I seen her."

Kelly raised his voice above the twangy mouth harp and lusty chorus that had taken up strains of a song he'd never heard before.

Sittin' by the roadside on a summery day,
Lyin' in the shadders' a'neath the trees,
Wearin' out your grinders eatin' goober peas—

"Tell the captain," Kelly began, turning then on heel toward the troopers. "Will you shut that up?" he yelled above the singing.

"Aw, let 'em celebrate, Kelly," Leitman drawled. "It's been a rotten ass war."

"Get Pendergrast and have him ride to Fort Brown for what passes as a surgeon there. Get him sobered up first before you bring him down here."

"Why Pendergrast?" Leitman grinned.

"Because he doesn't argue an order," Kelly said, already near the dock bridge before he remembered. "Tell Delano to cut our horses from Cortina's remuda and empty out the wagon shed."

Leitman touched his cap to the order, mimicking a few playful steps of the Texas reel, refusing to be crowded into the circle of troopers when he was grabbed by one of them.

Hillary Barlow extended his hand, supporting Kelly's leap across the gaping distance between the makeshift dock bridge and the *Warlock's* looming deck.

"An inconvenience, sir, until the planks can be set," he explained, clearly startled by the tall, coarse man who faced him.

"I am Kelly," Kelly said, glancing over Barlow's head to where Merrick Ryland stood.

"We were informed, sir. Welcome aboard the *Warlock*. It was necessary that we deny your men permission to board at this time, under the circumstances."

Kelly nodded at the same moment that Merrick turned around. He was younger than Kelly had expected, a whole lot younger. And of all the damned things, he was armed, on his own ship.

Their handclasp was firm, cautious, as the two men judged each other. Barlow smoothed through the introductions, forgetting his own and Ditwell's, more concerned about the sudden competitive crackle in the air.

"You're four days late, Ryland," Kelly said unsmilingly, watching Merrick's eyes lift and harden.

Merrick chose at the moment to ignore the jibe. This rude backwoods type probably wouldn't get the facts right in his mind even if he did take the time to explain. The drawl said enough about a slow brain.

"I have eleven men quarantined below decks. I gave orders to one of your sergeants to bring the Post Surgeon from Fort Brown to attend them. Also, there is the matter of this—" Merrick said, handing General Hardee's payment certificate to Kelly. "Can you read it, or shall I do it for you?"

Kelly stiffened. "You are well paid, Ryland, as a matter of fact, overpaid," he said, reading over the voucher. "Charles Wellman has an office in Brownsville. Anyone can direct you there."

"Tomorrow, then," Merrick said coolly. "I expect to sail for London at the end of the week. See that all your cargo is offloaded by then."

"Well now, just what cargo would you be referring to?"

Merrick tensed impatiently. "There are five crates stacked below in my quarters, designated for this port. The rest of the cargo I brought from Savannah is standing over there by the port rail."

Kelly frowned into the sun, turning full around, his gaze locating Adria. The "woman" Leitman had mentioned was hardly more than a girl.

"It should have made for a very interesting voyage," Kelly said with a hint of sarcasm.

"There is one other passenger, a Mr. Blanchard. His wife died during the gulf crossing. If you could arrange some kind of lodging for him for the next few days until his plans are made stable, you would be doing him a kindness."

Kelly couldn't drag his gaze from the girl. When Adria turned around from the railing, tossing her windblown hair from her face, her eyes searching and troubled, Kelly felt an odd quiver in his belly.

Hillary Barlow stepped between the two men, his voice worried.

"The crew is bringing Lieutenant Chase updeck, sir. He is in need of restraint."

A scuffling erupted from the passageway as

Kendall Chase wrenched himself free from the British crewmen who held his arms, his face a mask of bloodied torn flesh, his jaw sagging brokenly, his left eye swollen shut. He bolted in one direction, then another, his eyes glazed and wild. He saw Adria then, and lunged stumblingly across the deck towards her.

"*You scheming slut*!" He spat out a clot of fresh blood and clawed at her skirt, smearing his bloodied face in the softness.

"*Look* at my face, you slut! Look and remember!"

"*Oh, God—*" Adria whimpered, covering her face with her hands.

As suddenly, her skirt was ripped from his hands in a grappling tangle of arms that were separating her from Chase. Ditwell's locked fists came down hard behind Chase's neck. Chase slumped into her, slid to his knees and sprawled in a disjointed heap at her feet.

Kelly outpaced Merrick and reached Adria first. He spun her to one side, his arms tightening around her as he pressed her face against his shoulder.

"Oh my God, did you see his face?" she sobbed, "What happened to his face?"

A man, a stranger, looked quietly down at her. He didn't let her go when she looked up at him. His touch was soft and cool as he brushed her hair back from her face, guiding one pale strand into place behind her ear.

"I'm Kelly," he said.

Weakly, Adria reached again for him when she reeled forward.

"Don't turn around, not yet," Kelly said

gently, still cupping her head against his shoulder.

"I cleaved him a bit hard, Captain," Ditwell was saying.

"Just get him off this ship!" Merrick stormed back. "Barlow!" "Find Major Altree and dispose of this man!"

Kelly grinned to himself, watching the orderly precision of the British crew as they neatly carried Chase from the deck. His men would have dragged him off by the heels.

Adria shuddered and stood free of Kelly. "Major Kelly," she smiled thinly. "I am Adria Sommerfield."

Kelly swallowed his shock at hearing the name. That's what had intrigued him. The resemblance.

"You're Adrian Sommerfield's daughter," he said, smiling at her.

"You knew my father?" Adria asked, her eyes a sudden brilliant amber.

"Yes, I did. I served under his command."

"I have General Hardee's letter in my trunk. I haven't read it because your name was on the envelope. I thought it might contain some private message to you from him. He did tell me to expect you when we reached Matamoros. I think I expected—"

Kelly wasn't listening to her polite sweet words. What in the hell was Hardee thinking of sending this flit of a girl with something as important as the master keys to the vaults in Mexico? Hardee had said the owner of China Grove would be on board the *Warlock*. Surely it wasn't her, not Adrian Sommerfield's forgotten offspring, the fruit of his military wanderings, her mother a petite French Quarter beauty who had followed Adrian to Fort Ringgold. There had been talk, like there always was about a not so righteous officer who shunned marriage, but lived as man and wife with the wronged woman. After Adrian was killed in the battle of Resaca de la Palma, some Texas general had taken the child to his home on the Sabine bottomlands.

The details clicked. The general had been Alfred Sidney Johnson who owned China Grove before the war. The girl, Adria, must have inherited it. She would be the one to guide them there. It was just hard to swallow at the moment.

"Did General Hardee give you anything else?" Kelly managed to ask, wondering at the evasive glint in her topaz eyes.

"He gave her this," Merrick said, holding to length the chain locket and key he had taken from Adria.

Kelly almost snatched it from him. His silvered eyes blazed down at Adria.

"Maybe you could explain to me why *he* has this key," he said tightly.

"For safekeeping," Merrick said offhandedly.

Kelly laughed roughly. "You probably thought it fit those crates you were talking about. They were just draw cards, fool's gold. Hardee had to make the mission look authentic, even to you."

"I was paid well enough for it," Merrick shrugged, his eyes smouldering over Adria. He walked casually over to her, lifting her hair from the nape of her neck, smoothing into place the chain locket and key, fastening it.

Adria's throat ached, was so dry she couldn't swallow when Merrick walked away from her. Kelly took her by the arm, his drawl soft and reassuring as they walked toward the dock bridge.

CHAPTER 11

Juan Cortina, dressed in a parrot-green Napoleon coat studded with Zacatecas silver, calmly savored his tequila, immune to the hostility that greeted him. Let the *norte-americano* populace of the Rio Grande delta spurn him, what did he care? Had he not risen from the miserable *jacales*, the hungry son of stupid *campesinos* to become a grandee of cause? Who among *them* could match his courage, his cunning, his genius in leading a peasant army? Let them tolerate him now as he and the river breeds before him had tolerated the encroaching thievery of their given land. He stood this moment among them tonight and smiled with disgust.

Fort Brown, abandoned, reoccupied more times than it was worth remembering, and once the site of his own camp, glittered again tonight with life. The runted fort had been built on an alluvial bog which still seeped, even in dry weather, an elysium for the curlews, sandpipers, purple gallinules, St. Domingo grebes and sandhill cranes that nested among march marigolds and delicate monkshoods. A beauteous terrain that flourished proportionably to the fabled beanstalk.

The Fort Pavilion gleamed now, and no one noticed the flame-gutted hulls where barracks had stood a year before. Confederate soldiers, most of them weary remnants of once proud regiments camped along the charred adobe ruins, determined to outlast another upheaval in the forgotten patch of territory that concerned only the *tejanos*. Kelly's men camped among them, sullen, disillusioned men who, like Kelly, smiled rarely and spoke little.

The rumors had been true. The Confederate runner had docked at Port Isabel. Kelly had sent Delano Reyes for the remuda and the wagons. This news was enough to bring him, Juan Cortina, to *their* side of the river. For this, he could endure their slights.

Delano nodded to him above the crowd, the usual communication that each understood. Delano was of generous talent, swinging between armies, favoring whichever side supplied a better mount, a better meal, more whiskey, and more leisure. A good soldier whose allegiance at this moment stood with Kelly. Cortina understood. It was the way of his people.

And Kelly, had he been able to persuade him, would have been his field general. With Kelly, the whole of the stolen Rio Grande delta would have been his, perhaps even all of Texas. But

Kelly was parched of emotion. He rode, he marched, he stood, he killed. Tall and fair, he moved through the land like the hungry, hot spring wind, touching, changing, and quietly disappearing. A *mercenario* who had no heart, no fire for causes.

Umberto was shouldering his guitar, picking timidly over the chords. Juan Cortina set his glass of warm tequila down. The celebration had begun to bore him.

Polite applause preceded Eunice Stewart to the melodeon in the center of the Pavilion. A swishing conflict of starched taffeta and jangling glass beads whispered past Cortina and he bowed generously, amused by the plump, severely coiffured woman whose graying hair bounced in piglet curls around her face.

Eunice Stewart nudged Umberto aside and seated herself at the melodeon. In a gathering attack, she pumped forth the strains of "Bonnie Blue Flag," swelling the refrain to a viscious crescendo as throaty cheers joined the melody.

Juan Cortina edged toward the flag-draped hall, locked among the swaying, singing guests who suddenly separated into partners as Eunice trilled forth a waltz.

The air was close and sweet with the scent of swamp lilies. Cortina rocked on his heels, side-stepping Charles and Elizabeth Wellman, nodding an unreturned greeting to the Kings and Kenedys who swept coldly past him. He glanced back across the room and saw Kelly. But it wasn't Kelly who held his attention. It was the girl standing beside him.

Her pale, tumbled hair had slipped its pins, as though freshly mussed from lovemaking. The haughty tilt of her chin as she smiled at something Kelly said defined her breeding. Her cerise gown was whorish, too bold for her youth. Juan Cortina smiled. It was the way of anxious youth.

Adria glittered with excitement, even encouraged the feel of Kelly's hand at the curve of her back. He was noticeably silent tonight, even stern in his dark-vested cutaway suit. She hadn't seen him since the hot afternoon when he had taken her to the Wellman's home the day the *Warlock* docked. And all evening she had wanted to ask him why.

Three days before, dusty and exhausted, miserably distraught at leaving the security of the *Warlock*, Adria had waited outside the Wellman's portentous home in Brownsville, feeling the tired rejection of an unwanted waif.

"Mrs. Wellman asks that you come inside," Kelly had said, snugging his Stetson back from his forehead. His eyes were teasing her. "It's no hotter here than in Savannah," he smiled, assisting her down from the wagon.

"Well, it certainly is dirtier," Adria complained, fanning the dust from her skirt, gazing nervously at the serene home. "I don't think I want to stay here, Major Kelly," she murmured. "These people are strangers to me. I'd much rather stay at the Miller Hotel where you took Dickson."

Kelly shook his head. "The Wellmans knew your father. It's best you stay here with them in decent surroundings. It won't be for long, just until the gold can be readied for transport."

Near the brick steps, Adria balked again. She lifted wide, troubled eyes to Kelly.

"There is something else," she confessed, watching a spark of cold interest flash in Kelly's eyes.

"And that would be, Miss Sommerfield?"

There was really no other way to say it. "I haven't any money," she blurted out.

Kelly smiled down at her, almost convinced. Her mauve cotton dress, travel-worn and salted with dust, her wilted poke bonnet of deeper rose, framed her in helplessness, some innocence that suddenly made him want to take her in his arms.

"And just what would you be needin', ma'am? A new bonnet, maybe a pair of them silk slippers?" Kelly drawled, feeding her distress.

"No, Major Kelly, nothing so frivolous," Adria replied hotly. "It was ill-mannered of me to ask a stranger for honest funds." She started past him, her face flaming with shame. How could she have ever thought—

Kelly reached for her arm. "We are hardly strangers, ma'am."

"Truly, sir!" Adria flared. "And *why* would you presume otherwise?"

Kelly was laughing at her. "Well, you don't ask a stranger, right off, for money, not here in Texas. And, when an unmarried lady asks a man for money, he generally expects something in return."

Adria paled slightly. "Then I suppose I would be in your debt should I accept a small loan from you," Adria swallowed.

"I suppose you would," Kelly agreed, watching the defiant gleam in her topaz eyes. "To keep it all proper, I'll leave some money for you with Charles Wellman. Maybe he can keep you honest in the spending of it."

From that moment, Adria was welcomed into an atmosphere of cordial affluence where war was something merely discussed, not lived. Elizabeth Wellman was tall, queenly, given to the kindness that flourished with prosperity. Adria's room was furnished with a square-canopied Victorian bed, ornamented with blush-stained rosebuds. A companion night chest and dry bath held a pink crystal basin and ewer. Sandwich-glass hurricane lamps with teardrop pendants stood on each side of a lyre-based writing table near the corner of the room that overlooked a small garden. Sunlight dazzled through silk-pane curtains, almost blinding her. It was the loveliest room Adria had ever seen.

In turn, Adria had been introduced to the Wellman family, to Charles Wellman, a tall, imposing man, gravely sincere when he spoke of his admiration for her father, Colonel Sommerfield. Elizabeth Wellman's spinster sister, Eunice Stewart, was plump and bustling, her hair fashion and mannerisms almost comical until she sat before the melodeon, her fingers working beautiful strains from the ivory keys. James Wellman, only two years younger than Adria, already bore the handsome stamp of esteemed parentage. He teased her, correcting her Old South vowels, imitating her, then craving forgiveness in his simple boyish way which charmed her.

There were disapproving glances and reluctant conversation when Adria mentioned Kelly's name. Invariably, the subject was switched. Yet it was Adria who fell utterly silent when Merrick's name monopolized the conversation. James, in particular, suffered from an acute case of hero worship.

"It's said that the *Warlock* is the fastest ship in the world," James prodded. "Captain Ryland, himself, designed the auxiliary engine. Some French count named Breaux owns the ship. Did you know, Adria, that you sailed on the gem of the seas?"

Adria smiled demurely, thinking not of the ship, but of its captain. Knowing that the *Warlock* was still at Port Isabel, wondering how she could manage a discreet visit to see Merrick only made her miss him that much more. Somehow, she had to see him again before he sailed for London.

The waltz ended. Adria plucked at her gown, rearranging its sweep to the floor, a gesture to entice an invitation from Kelly to dance. How commanding he looked tonight, his gray eyes hard and determined. At times, she almost felt afraid of him. His arm tightened then around her waist, causing her to turn and look up at him.

With an arrogant bow, Juan Cortina was smiling down at her, his tongue licking quickly over the length of his moustache.

"*Buenos tardes*," he said twitchingly. "I am General Cortina, a man who humbly begs the pleasure of an introduction."

Unthinkingly, Adria offered her hand to him, feeling a surge of attraction when the general's lips grazed her fingertips.

Kelly brought her hand back. "Miss Sommerfield is from Savannah," he snapped.

General Cortina smiled knowingly. "So your blockade ship brings you this lovely bounty. It was well worth the waiting for, eh, Kelly?"

Kelly's jaw tightened. "Tomorrow, Juan, just like we planned it, *comprende*?"

Sadly, Cortina smiled at him. "Ah, Kelly, I am a lonely man. Perhaps the beautiful lady will honor me with a waltz."

"No, Juan, she won't," Kelly said evenly.

With devouring slowness, Juan Cortina's eyes raked over Adria, like glowing coals, Adria thought, fascinated.

He shrugged, cocked his head to one side. "As you say, this time, Kelly, but there will be other times, always another time." He bowed again smoothly, his bootheels clicking angrily across the pavilion as he crossed it, causing heads to turn in his direction.

Adria whirled on Kelly. "That was insufferably rude of you! I wanted to dance with General Cortina."

"And I said *no*," Kelly spoke flatly. "In Savannah, you have your rules about slaves, the 'niggers,' you call them. We Texans have our own rules about Mexicans. Being a general doesn't change it none, and Juan knows that."

Abruptly, Kelly took her by the arm and steered her toward the circle of ladies. "Stay with the women for awhile. I'll be back for you later."

Swallowing a threat of tears, Adria stared at him, watching while he disappeared within a knot of steel-gray uniforms. Elizabeth Wellman patted the empty chair next to her, only briefly distracted while she listened to Mattie Harris elaborate on her most recent childbirth. Adria tried not to listen to the gruesome whisperings, tried to smile with admiration when the other ladies did. She didn't want to sit here with them like some ugly old prude. She squirmed miserably in her chair, counting how many steps it would take to run to the door. Another second of this and she would scream with boredom.

Then suddenly, Eunice Stewart took up the strains of "Chivalrous C.S.A."

"I'll sing you a song of the South's
sunny clime,
Aye, in Chivalrous C.S.A.,
Like heroes and princes they lived
for a time,
In Chivalrous, C.S.A."

Stomping cheers burst from the pavillion. Cadenced applause joined in one long welcome. Adria stood with the others, caught up in the sweeping mood, applauding what she couldn't see because of the crowd. Who, she wondered, would command such a welcome.

"He did come!" Elizabeth Wellman gasped, supporting Mattie Harris while she heaved herself up on a chair for a better view.

"Why, he looks almost angry," Mattie whispered down to Elizabeth. "Charles is toasting him—if Eunice wouldn't play so loud, I could hear. He's shaking hands with Charles. No, he doesn't want to say a few words. Oh, dear! I wish he hadn't worn that *horrid* blue uniform!"

Adria sank back down in her chair. The room had become a warm wavery blur of colored strings and garish light. Of course the social would be in Merrick's honor. Of course, he was a hero now, everyone's hero.

The corner of the pavilion became softly hushed as candles and lamps were snuffed for the late hour dancing. Umberto's guitar strummed demandingly, sensuously amid the quiet shuffling, vibrant above the waning conversation, a melody that pleaded from the warm Mexican loveheart.

Merrick listened impatiently while Charles Wellman's questions about the *Warlock* mounted.

"With that noteworthy speed, and she takes only eleven feet of spill. I find that damned amazing. I believe the British have outclassed us with this invention, or should I say, "innovation?" he laughed at his own remark. He grew serious then and said, "My partners, Mr. King and Mr. Kenedy, and I have a lucrative proposal for you, Captain Ryland. Since you plan a few leisure days at Port Isabel, perhaps you would give us an hour or so of your time to discuss it?"

Merrick handed his glass of Scotch whiskey to him.

"Your office then, at eight tomorrow morning—when the bank opens," Merrick smiled.

"Done," Charles beamed, glancing smartly around him. Noting Merrick's restlessness he suggested, "Elizabeth will be glad to introduce you to some of the young ladies, to say nothing of how honored the ladies themselves would be."

Merrick had already found Adria. "If you gentlemen will excuse me," he said in leaving the group. He angled his way through the circle of waltzers toward the corner of the pavilion where Adria was sitting.

Warm bronzed hands reached down for the nervous ones Adria held in her lap. Gently, Merrick loosened her fingers and lifted her to her feet. Wordlessly then, he gathered her to him.

The hard strength she remembered, the salt-cool scent of him, all wonderfully familiar as Merrick caught her to his rhythm, sweeping her out across the dance pavilion.

Merrick held her close, feeling the quiet passion of her heart against his. The stirrings of possessiveness surfaced.

"I expected you to have a new gown tonight, or are you finding Major Kelly to be rather ungenerous?"

Adria's feet stopped. Merrick lifted her smoothly against him, recovering their rhythm. With studied arrogance he watched the topaz fire in her eyes.

"Waltz with me, lass," he taunted, "the way you wanted to do on the topgallants that night."

Adria smiled brilliantly up at him through clenched teeth.

"That's better now," Merrick coaxed, "you're supposed to look honored waltzing with the man of the hour."

"Then I shouldn't be waltzing with *you*," Adria gritted with a smile. "Just why would you presume that Major Kelly would be less than gallant?"

"The sum of money he left for you with Charles Wellman seemed less than 'gallant.' It looked meager."

Adria flushed with humiliation. How would he know such a thing anyway? Who could have told him? Oh, how she hated him at this moment.

"It is you, sir, who are ungallant when you make reference to a lady's private affairs," she seethed.

"Loans have to be repaid, one way or another, or didn't you think of that?" Merrick said, angry now.

"My business affairs are no concern of yours, Captain Ryland. Your responsibility for me, if you could call it such, ended when I left the *Warlock*."

"Ever the offended lady," Merrick laughed dryly. "I've missed you, Adria," he murmured, waltzing with her to the edge of the pavilion. "Hillary Barlow will call for you at the Wellman's home tomorrow evening. And wear something else. I don't like that dress."

Stunned, Adria waited beside him while he exchanged a brief farewell with Charles Wellman and Lester King.

"Must you be leaving us so early, Captain?" Charles pressed, winking at Adria.

"I confess to heeding a ship's bell, sir," Merrick smiled. "The London watch has already sounded."

Adria watched him walk away, watched him pause in stride to bid goodnight to several of the guests who detained him. The music sounded wearied now, the room suddenly cavernous and empty without him.

Across the pavilion, Kelly leaned against the wall, seeing Merrick leave. He almost had to admire Ryland, the confidence he used like a weapon, the experience that brought the gentlemen to heel and the ladies to heat. Adria was taken with him, there was no mistaking that. The look on her face had been plain as day. But she was young, too goddamned young.

Slowly, he strolled back across the pavilion, taking his time while Adria worried, searched the shadows for him. She'd be sulky, maybe even hurt that he'd neglected her all evening.

Damn, it hadn't been easy either. The honeyed words, soothing as silk, that perfumed softness, an innocence that tore at him. It was still there, the dark sweetness of her gnawing inside of him, just like it had been that first day he'd seen her on the deck of the *Warlock*. Or the day he'd taken her to the Wellman's and watched the defiant pride in those swallowing amber eyes. Tonight, he had even backed Juan off to protect her, and he and Juan had always had an understanding about shared women. The cost of that insult to Juan still lay undecided.

Quietly then, Kelly moved to stand beside Adria. It was a few moments before she noticed him.

"Where have *you* been all evening, Major Kelly?" she demanded scathingly.

"Army business, Miss Sommerfield," Kelly drawled. "Come, I'll take you home now." Home—the word had a strange ring to it tonight.

CHAPTER 12

Perspiration beaded Eunice Stewart's face, fattening into occasional drops that dribbled down on her ample bosom.

"Lord, such heat!" she complained, sponging her handkerchief along her neck. "Charles always says it's the harbinger of spring storms. Seems to me they are surely slow in coming."

Adria nodded listlessly, too drowzy to feed the conversation. The lazy rumble of the Wellman's calash, the thickening clouds of dust that darkened the air made her sleepy.

Eunice glanced irritably at her, then resumed her fanning.

"I don't understand why Elizabeth insisted that I come with you today with all this handsome cavalry to escort you," she sighed, puffing at a lifeless curl plastered to her damp forehead. "All this nonsense and secrecy has me fair exhausted. And all that gossip about what happened after the social last night, if I let myself believe such vile things—"

Adria opened her eyes and looked out the slit of curtain, reassured by the mounted line of Kelly's men who were spaced every few feet on either side of the calash.

"What happened after the social?" she asked lazily, smiling at one the horses that danced in stride.

"It's the man of it, I suppose," Eunice said, ruffling her sweat-damp skirts, her fan floating to a gradual repose. "That Captain Ryland seemed quite the gentleman to me. That just shows you how easily character can be misjudged."

Adria stretched forward in the seat, thoroughly awake now.

"When was this, Eunice?"

Eunice dabbed her handkerchief around her mouth. "We women shouldn't even be discussing such vulgarity," she said, wanting to be encouraged. When Adria didn't respond, she lowered her voice. "Having a little celebration of their own, even at a pesthole like that Melio's is one thing. Charles was invited, of course, but he declined like any 'gentleman' would. It lasted until dawn, James said, and how he knows such things, I do wonder. It was the usual cards and liquor and that sort of thing until—"

"The men have been at sea a long while," Adria yawned, disinterested.

"Well, that may be, but I can't think," Eunice sputtered, "why that Captain employed that vile Mateos girl to dance for them, and her completely unclothed!"

Adria flinched inwardly. Eunice thrived on gossip. Maybe it was just that, gossip.

"With the evils of liquor there's just no telling what men are capable of. I overheard James tell his father that Captain Ryland even danced with that filthy girl, and her in such a disreputable state. And afterwards, they," Eunice fidgeted, almost losing her courage, "the Englishman took liberties there with her right on top of the bar in front of everyone!" Eunice let the words go in a rush, covering her face with her handkerchief.

Adria felt sick. Maybe she was going to have a baby, Merrick's baby. She certainly had all the symptoms today that Mattie Harris had described with such relish last night: the queasiness, the headaches. And she hadn't even been able to swallow any breakfast this morning. If she could just tell someone, but it couldn't be Eunice. Eunice was as ignorant as she was about such things. Maybe she was just imagining things, and hearing all this horrid gossip about Merrick made her worry needlessly.

Eunice was patting her hand. "Of course, you're much too young to know about such seamy things. I think that's why I never married. I just couldn't see making a barnyard out of a bedroom. And that's what happens, you know, with men," Eunice prattled. "Now that nice Mattie Harris with six little children of her own was positively smitten with that Englishman. And the King twins were on the verge of a swoon when he smiled at them. But you, Adria, dear, were the only one he waltzed with the entire evening."

"You're forgetting the Mexican whore," Adria

said sullenly.

"We don't *use* that word," Eunice replied stoutly. "And this ugly little tidbit of gossip is not to be repeated. Why, if Elizabeth knew that James and his father discussed such filthiness, she'd disown both of them."

"Why did you tell me all this, Eunice?" Adria asked suddenly.

Eunice turned maternal eyes to her. "To warn you, my dear, against the vileness of men."

Adria cupped her hand over her mouth, thinking that the moment was upon her. She swallowed it back in time to see Kelly leaving the column and riding back toward the calash. He threw one leg across the saddle and swung down from his horse into the door of the calash. He settled next to her, inching his Stetson back from his forehead, giving her a long hard look.

"You're lookin' a little unhealthy," he commented. "Are you all right?"

Adria ignored him, staring beyond Eunice to the serene Mexican countryside. Doll-like *jacales* thatched with broom corn and reeds dotted the landscape, roughhewn adobe huts devoid of chimneys, their doorways painted in shades of blue. Crinkled strands of red chiles hung from the front and sides of them, a colorful adornment for contented poverty.

"Adria and I were just talking about the social last night," Eunice said, her plump hands fluttery in her lap.

"We enjoyed your music, Miss Stewart," Kelly said, "didn't we, Miss Sommerfield?"

Adria shrugged an answer, refusing to be drawn into another senseless conversation with

Eunice. Kelly smelled of steamy horseflesh and hot leather and there were dark circles of sweat under his arms. He hadn't shaved since last night. He looked dirty, and he stank.

Kelly lowered his Stetson back down over his eyes, folded his arms across his chest. So she was still sulky-pretty, just the way he had left her at the Wellman's door last night. Her type was used to being coddled and made over, and damn if he'd follow suit. The money he'd given her had been well spent, he had to admit. A prim spoon bonnet with rose velvet 'follow-me-lads' ribbons, a simple yellow-sprigged muslin dress, dollette boots, and a careful accounting from Raphael's Dry Goods, presented to him this morning with a cold smile. "Necessities," Adria had called them. Damn expensive ones to his way of thinking.

"Oh, my goodness, who are those men?" Eunice gasped, holding her heart, straining to see through the dust cloud.

Kelly glanced up. "They're just advance scouts sent by General Cortina to escort us beyond the Avenida Rosas."

Eunice patted her drooping bosom. "But, they are so fierce looking. They look like bandits."

"They're a type of bandit, so some people say," Kelly spoke lazily. "They are well paid to be on our side today." He looked over at Adria. "You're very quiet today, *chica,*" he said, taking one of the velvet ribbons from her bonnet and winding it over his fist.

"You're mussing my skirt and ruining the velvet," Adria snapped at him.

Kelly tossed the ribbon back into her lap. "My apologies, ma'am. I was just fondling my investment."

Of all the rank remarks to make, Adria thought furiously. If Eunice wasn't sitting over there like a fat sow she'd level a barrage at Kelly he'd never recover from. Who did he think he was, her keeper? He must have told everyone. Merrick certainly knew and now Eunice was sure to suspect the arrangement between them, innocent at the moment as it was. How in the world was she going to tolerate this coarse, ignorant man over the long weeks ahead?

El Banco Federacion de Tamaulipas had been erected first as a chantry by Spanish friars intent on chrisitanizing the cannibalistic Seri Indians, a formidable chore that had ended in disaster. A despondent dwelling now, its plaster and whitewash were pocked and splotchy with time, exposing in places the ribs of the foundation walls.

Umberto drew rein, then flicked another command to the horses, bringing the calash to rest beneath the huge pointed leaves of a giant maguey plant. Adria preened herself, glancing again into the tiny ivory hand mirror attached to the bracelet on her wrist.

Annoyed, Kelly assisted Eunice down from the calash, then turned back to Adria, his long arm barring her steps down.

"When we go inside you won't understand what's being said, so I'm going to tell you right now. The interlocking keys will be exchanged in the vaults below. I don't want you to react, no questions, no flirty little smiles, nothing—not until this is finished. Do you understand?" Kelly demanded, his hand closing hard over her arm.

Adria winced in pain. "You're hurting me," she said.

"This is not Savannah. These men are not gentlemen, they're greasy cutthroats. You stay close to me, real close, only give room for my gun arm if I have to use it."

Adria glared at him. "I didn't want to come here, anyway. You didn't tell me there would be any danger. And I'm thirsty, I want some water or something."

"And I'm telling you right now how it is," Kelly exploded. "You quit acting like a brat and do what I say, exactly as I say or none of us will leave here alive." He pulled her roughly along with him to the carved front entrance of the bank.

Adria glanced back at Eunice who stood surrounded by Kelly's men. Umberto had hailed a vendor and Eunice had already half-eaten a fruit mush she held in one hand.

The massive wooden doors to the bank were sculptured in some Egyptian vision of Creation; birds, beasts and fish were oddly positioned above the arch where the Garden of Eden with the fabled serpent, his head downward to represent the defeat of evil, was carved. The granite slab door hinged with brass and iron appointments showed a sickle design that looked like an anchor laid on its side. The anchor made her think of Merrick, and she wished to heaven he was here with her this moment.

Kelly shut the door, stiffling the sunlight. A dank, vinegary smell choked her throat. Dungeon-like stones, perfectly fitted together, a mossy growth sprouting between them, loomed on all sides, broken only by a caged alcove at the far end of the building.

"There's no one here," Adria shuddered, feeling relieved.

"They're here," Kelly said, guiding her toward the alcove.

Juan Cortina rose suddenly from the cover of shadow, his smile starkly white in the dimness.

"*Si*, Kelly. We are all come here. Did you think I would forget this day?"

"Where are the *oficiales*?"

Cortina clucked his tongue reprovingly. "Today, I tell them the bank in Matamoros is closed. I order it closed."

Kelly's arm moved outward, nudging Adria aside.

"Bring them in here, Juan, if you and your boys are done with scaring the hell out of them."

"Ah, Kelly, you worry. And so much worry is bad for the liver. I do not worry until is time for the worry. You worry, you make your lovely *gringa* lady worry, too." He smiled complacently at Adria, then shrugged, his fingers snapping a brief command.

The alcove filled suddenly with soldiers, all dressed in the same sand-drab uniform Juan Cortina wore. One approached with a lantern. Behind him, a small bespeckled man in a somber black coat mopped constantly at the sweat on his face. He bowed nervously to Adria, then to Kelly, motioning with his finger for them to follow him.

The circle of lantern light pointed upward then down along the low-beamed corridor. Moist, smooth stones topped another lower level which reeked heavily of sump water. Here the walls seeped, and thickening clumps of lichen oozed from the crevices.

Adria clung to Kelly, her body sandwiched between both he and General Cortina. The passageway down to the *catacombas* grew progressively narrower as their steps took them deeper into the earth. Cortina's Spanish sounded softly indulgent, Kelly's curt and harsh, words that were rapid and not understood by Adria.

The corridor ended abruptly in a chamber vault of iron-banked earth. A shuddering brilliance ringed the chamber, flecking dusky light over the metal walls, a sight so unnerving, so unexpected that Adria turned away from it.

"No!" Kelly demanded, grabbing for her. "Take a good long look. It's why you're here, why General Hardee sent you here. You're looking at the dream of Southern generals, a new Confederacy built on that dream."

Adria looked then, and kept looking at the layers of gold ingots that stretched the length of the vault, square, gleaming shapes that appeared newly cast. She wanted to touch them to see if they really were real.

"I didn't know." She swallowed hard. "I honestly didn't know about this, any of it."

Kelly gave her a suspicious look. "No, I guess he wouldn't have told you," he said, convinced.

"Only six men knew of this plan. Most were officers of the Confederate General Command, the rest were investors who started to worry after the First Bull Run scare. One of them was an abolitionist with heavy investments in Mississippi and Louisiana. He persuaded Johnson and Hardee to safeguard the gold here, just in case."

"That—" Kelly said, pointing to the grilled doors that protected the vault, "is the master locking system that only two keys will unlock. Mine, and the one you brought from Savannah with you."

Adria felt a wash of weakness. "Oh, so much could have gone wrong," she murmured, thinking back.

"Hardee figured on all that. The key I have unlocks only the first series of bolts and activates a dynamite trap that will bring the whole chantry down and bury the gold for eternity. Your key disengages the explosives and unlocks the last dual bolts. The system was planned by the same abolitionist I just told you about, who owned an explosives foundry."

"The only hitch that had me stewin' were the deeds to China Grove which arrived by courier from New Orleans two days ago. Hardee had the deeds transferred to your name after General Johnson's death at Shiloh. Only I didn't know who was comin' from Savannah with the key. And, I didn't know how I was goin' to find that blasted place in the swamps without someone to guide me there."

Adria thought for a moment. "Why can't you just leave the gold here where it's safe until after the war?"

Kelly nodded in Juan's direction. "General Cortina could explain that better than me. We can't do that, lady, because the *revolutionarios* know the gold is here."

Adria looked at Juan Cortina, confused. "But isn't the general a—?"

"A *revolutionario*," Kelly finished for her. "No, Juan is only interested in reclaiming all of Texas, not the whole of Mexico. His army is what we *tejanos* call, 'conservative.' We have word from Vera Cruz that some *Juaristas* have banded together with a force that outnumbers both Cortina's army and mine. They smell this gold and they want to get their hands on it."

"And they're coming here?" Adria gasped.

"They're already here. They're camped at Monelova, which explains why we're taking the gold out. Once they storm this museum and start messin' with those grills they'll blow the gold to powder. Juan is taking it out by donkey cart a few bricks at a time so as not to get anybody overanxious. We started a few days ago breaking a trail across the river."

"But after we get to China Grove, how will the investors know that?"

Kelly touched a finger to her lips. "That, *chica*, is my worry, all mine. It's what General Hardee pays me to do. When the war ends, and my dispatches from Richmond tell me that day isn't long in coming, they will come to the bayous for the gold. It's a long careful plan that was a long time in the doing."

Adria looked at Kelly with newfound respect. "And I thought all this time I was being punished for something by being sent back to China Grove," she said softly. Her gaze swept the vault again when she took Kelly's arm and started for the steps.

"You probably were," Kelly smiled. "It's still a long way to China Grove."

Thoughtfully, Juan Cortina watched them step out in the sunlight, his eyes caressing the eager motion of Adria's slim hips. He reached in his coat for a Berina cigar. Instantly, his man, Rocco, touched a match to it.

"The gringo still waits for you, General. The one with the broken face. His name is Chase. He says he leaves his gray army to fight beside us. He says he has a revenge for an Englishman."

Juan Cortina pulled deeply on his cigar. "We all have a 'revenge.' It is what fires the heart." He stayed a moment longer to watch Adria as she walked across the small plaza to where Eunice Stewart was waiting.

CHAPTER 13

Merrick struggled the second story window open and leaned out across the sill along with the sun-faded curtains lashed outward by the wind. He gulped deep breaths of the rain-scented air, seeing his hands still at a tremble, though his brain was slowly clearing. The "sick fancies" brought on by the *agave*, the honey-water, had, blessedly, finally ceased.

Lightning scarred across bloated lavender clouds groaning with thunder. The wind, rampant and sharp, licked at the ground rioting the trees in the hotel stableyard below. An inland storm, pure and savage, probably born at sea, was rocking the *Warlock* in her moors tonight at Port Isabel.

Merrick let the sting of the first raindrops caress over him, feeling almost revived. He leaned into the wind, into the eerie whiteness that flashed all around him and felt a moment of peace, of oneness with the elements.

The military social at Fort Brown last night, he remembered. What had happened in the night long celebration at Melio's was still hazy to memory. Cavernous sounds, melting faces, applause that had sickened him, his drunken crew, a dance—a long tediously complex dance—a woman, another woman, the same woman, then the dawn with its coppery disc of new sun that never climbed the sky. This day, when the exploding nightmares had left him alone.

The Mexican girl, Erlinda, was still asleep belly down in his bed, her leathery buttocks twitching in some dreamy rhythm. Her dancing was better than her lovemaking despite all of a whore's pretended ecstasies, the filthy words hissed in his ear, her feverish writhings that bordered on insanity, and her mouth, big and swallowing that engorged him, depleted him over and over again until he had to make her stop. He was remembering more than he thought he would.

The Rochester lamp on the window table trembled from a vicious thunderclap, setting a jangle to the glass teardrops. The sound, still echoing, muffled the patient knocking at the door.

Hillary Barlow bristled inside the door, his woolen uniform plastered wetly to his body, his visor cap dripping rainwater from both edges. If he was startled at Merrick's nakedness, or at the shivers that raced over him, he concealed it well.

"I was of the impression that it rarely rains in this country," he muttered while he shrugged out of his wet coat. He started to toss it on the bed when, frozen in motion, he saw Erlinda curled there between the sheets.

Merrick grinned at him. "Where is the box from Pepitpain's?"

Barlow found his voice. "I left it below, sir. The—uh—wine is with it, packed in sawdust, wet sawdust at this hour."

"I assume that Miss Sommerfield is also waiting downstairs along with the wine," Merrick prompted.

Still distracted, Barlow shook his head. "No, sir, she is not. I took the hackney myself for her after the driver quit the post, some bloody superstition about the storm or such rubbish. I was told by the younger Mr. Wellman that Miss Sommerfield had retired for the night."

Merrick rocked the bed with his foot, provoking a sleepy groan from Erlinda. Hillary Barlow watched, open-mouthed and reddening, reaching almost desperately for a near-full bottle on the table.

"That's rum," Merrick said. "The lady and I drank all the pulque last night." He smiled to himself as Barlow rotated the label and sniffed its contents with a suspicious nose.

"These local brews can be quite treacherous," he spoke solemnly, glancing again toward the bed when Erlinda stirred complainingly.

"So I found out when I thought I was being chased by a man-eating flamenco dancer with claws for feet," Merrick smiled, remembering more of the night just spent. "Tell me, did you see the crew?"

"I did, sir. All are improved and can sail for London within a fortnight." Hillary Barlow sat the rum bottle down on the table and paced to the door. "There were two gentlemen, a Mr. King and a Mr. Kenedy, aboard ship today inspecting the storage hold."

"They are partners with Charles Wellman," Merrick frowned.

"Yes, they mentioned that. They also mentioned that Miss Sommerfield and a Miss Stewart had gone to Matamoros for the day."

"With Major Kelly," Merrick guessed. "Did they say for what reason?"

Barlow swallowed dryly, staring at Erlinda while she uncoiled herself and teased a sheet over her breasts.

"To visit a Mexican bank of some sort. A General Cortina was supposedly thereabouts with that troublemaker, Lieutenant Chase. It's rumored he has deserted his commission to join with the general's peasant army."

Merrick took a new white shirt from the armoire drawer, snapped the tailor's bands on the collar with his teeth. He worked his long arms into the sleeves and selected a pair of gold cuff studs from a small enameled box.

Erlinda smiled sleepily, watching him.

"We dance some more, eh, Captain?" she purred.

"No more," Merrick smiled.

"You pay me good like you want more," Erlinda pouted. "I like a big eager man like you. You make it good for me, too. I like that."

Hillary Barlow broke for the door and was down in the hallway before Merrick caught up to him.

"Can't you hold a damn minute while I fetch my boots?" he snarled.

His First Officer faced him squarely. "I am a God-fearing man, sir, not hardened to a complete lack of decency in one's life. I admit to having my toddies, and admit to being a ready man. But, I cannot admit to being a bystander to what I have just seen."

"Then, I apologize for it," Merrick managed to say, quietly amazed at Barlow's sudden display of conscience. This man he thought he knew, a tidy drinker who had, on occasion, outdistanced him with a bottle, was still morally pure in regard to women. The realization was sobering.

"Accepted sir," Barlow nodded once. "Do you still intend to call upon Miss Sommerfield?"

"Yes," Merrick said. "To tell her goodbye, which may require the whole evening."

Awestruck, young James Wellman ushered Merrick and Hillary Barlow into the stairhall, fumbling an apology for his parents' absence, adding chatter about the rainstorm, the groundkeeper's lodge at the new cemetery, finally exhausting himself and just staring openly, worshipfully, up at Merrick.

"I have come for Miss Sommerfield," Merrick smiled, seeing a point of his own ragged youth in James Wellman's gangling confusion.

"Yes, sir, well, sir, I explained to your officer that Adria has—"

"He told me. Which room is hers?"

Barlow planted his feet along the scroll of Brussels carpet while the silence lengthened. James, still gawking at Merrick, upset a chair then righted it, staying well ahead of Merrick's fast strides through the adjoining rooms to the upper hallway.

"Have you ever been to sea, James?"

"No, sir, Captain Ryland, sir. That is to say, not as you know it, sir."

Merrick watched the leap of excitement in James' adoring eyes and smiled. "If your father will permit it, I will take you with me on the *Warlock* when we sail to Vera Cruz."

James merely croaked, "Thank you, sir," as he knocked softly on Adria's door.

Merrick outwaited James, who, at a nod from him, left Merrick in the hallway. When there was no reply, Merrick opened Adria's door. She lay at the foot of the bed, still fully dressed with an afghan clutched over her. Her spoon bonnet was neatly tied on the bedpost above her head. Her worn brocade reticule she hugged closely to her.

For a time Merrick stared down at her, at the sleeping childlike expression on her face. The next moment he was shaking her.

"It is very wet outside. I suggest you dress warmly."

Adria flung to the other side of the bed, scrambled to her knees, her eyes wild with fright.

"*How did you get in here?*"

"Through the door," Merrick said, pointing back to it.

"Well, you can just leave through it," Adria gasped. "I told James to tell you—"

"He did so, but just not convincingly enough. Now get dressed."

"I'm not leaving this room," Adria spat.

Merrick reached across the bed and caught her by the wrists. "I am not giving you a choice, Miss Sommerfield," he said before snatching up her capelet and shoes, his grip none too gentle as he prodded her toward the door.

Dark and rainswept, Boca Chica road lay north of the town, a glutted stretch of pocky road that jounced Hillary Barlow from one side of the driver's perch on the *jehus* to the other. He swore at the mules, swore at Merrick's folly, swearing that favors or no, the captain could drive his lady back to the Wellman's. He refused.

Having made her own sullen vow to provide Merrick with the most miserable evening of his life, Adria sat stiffly in the corner of the *jehus*, flinching only once when a raindrop seeped through the rotted leather overhead and winked on her shoulder.

Merrick braced a long leg across the seat, imprisoning Adria in her chosen corner, almost amused at her mood. Let her shiver; better yet, let that hot venomous armor she was hiding behind thaw her out. Still, when he heard the tight chatter of her teeth, he suffered a little.

"You need a cloak," he muttered, remembering the sable and emerald velvet one he had seen at Pepitpain's Emporium.

Adria endured another crawling shiver. "I came with you only to spare James from further embarrassment," she managed to say.

"Did you now?" Merrick smiled, relieved that she was beginning to thaw even a fraction.

"James is not accustomed to some ill-bred

sailor barging into his home and forcing his way into a lady guest's bedroom."

"I don't recall that it took that much forcing," Merrick said straightly, smiling to himself.

Oh, such arrogance! Adria seethed. How could she have ever let this horrid, pompous satyr make love to her? She hated his voice, that accent that sounded so dominating, so proper. And worse, how could she have *ever* thought she was in love with him? She was the fool, the utterly witless fool.

The *jehus* bogged when Hillary Barlow pulled rein before a pair of stacked-stone pillars. The gate was swung apart by a Mexican lad who trotted along beside the *jehus*, pointing directions and chattering in Spanish to Merrick.

Tarnished light spilled from the cave-like windows of the *casita*. Merrick flung open the door of the *jehus* to be greeted by a circle of dripping umbrellas. He reached hesitantly for Adria who slunk deeper back into the corner of the *jehus*.

"You can walk through this muck or let me carry you."

"I didn't want to come here with you," Adria choked, close to tears now.

Merrick felt her tense as he lifted her, caught the humid fragrance of her when he shielded her against him. The dark studded door of the *casita* swung hard behind them. Merrick set Adria on her feet and impatiently drew the capelet from her shoulders. He flung it in disgust to one of the servants.

"Why haven't you bought another shawl?

That pitiful shred belongs with the ragpickers."

"It belongs to Eunice," Adria said bitingly.

"I have seen its better in Shadwell," Merrick flared, walking ahead of her across the stone-tiled patio.

Firelight created a patchwork of brightness and shadow over the rough high walls, and a warmth that drew Adria to the clever beehive fireplace. Her fingers ached, tingled with the rush of sudden warmth as she kneeled on the hearth bench. The cold sound of Merrick's boot-heels crossing the stone floor made her remember another night at the City Hotel in Savannah—so far, so long ago.

He handed a goblet over her shoulder to her. It was not the wine she expected to taste, but rather brandy, dark and fiery.

"It isn't a night for wine," she heard him say. At least he didn't sound quite as angry now, only more resigned. She would find *some* way to humble that infuriating arrogance of his before the night was out. She hadn't forgotten or forgiven him for the rude aftermath of that night in his cabin on the *Warlock*. She'd never forget it, or let him forget.

Rain silvered the thick rounded windows of the *casita* in a serpentine dance of candled shadows. Juno, the *Warlock's* chef, served an elegant dinner of small exquisitely seasoned dishes which appeared in miniature beneath imposing silver candlesticks.

Merrick sat facing her in a tall grandeza chair, his white dinner coat in vivid contrast to the scarlet velvet of the chair. He appeared strangely at ease in the luxurious attitude of the room. He ate little, spoke even less, his remarks to Juno all in excluding French. Juno frowned once at what Merrick said, with a questioning glance at Adria.

They were talking about her. Merrick was probably telling him how bored he was with her company. Well, she certainly intended to bore him, punish him into taking her back to the Wellman's home, and obviously she was succeeding.

"I know you must be most anxious to sail for London," she remarked when she could no longer abide the silence between them. The smile was wasted. He hadn't even glanced up at her.

"Why were you in Matamoros today?" The sullen question hurled at her caught her off-guard.

She returned the same insolent glare. "It was Confederate business, sir, which should be of no more interest to you than my activities should."

"That is very uncompanionable country for a lady. I trust you know this."

"I trust Major Kelly," Adria said coolly.

Merrick smiled evenly at her as though saying without voicing it, "No, you don't."

He reached then behind his chair for a long box with an immense pink velvet bow and placed it before her. The box was enormous, wrapped in brocade, the wrappings a gift in themselves. For a treasured moment, Adria's fingers trembled over the lovely new velvet bow.

She stiffened, quieted her hands, and shoved the box aside.

"There is no occasion for your gift, Captain Ryland," she said steadily.

Merrick straightened in his chair, then lifted to his feet. He tore at the wrappings on the box, grappled the box lid open and shook to length yards of shimmery cream satin. He flung the gown back across the table at her.

"You are quite correct, madam. "There is no occasion."

Adria swallowed thickly, flinching at the furious sound of his bootheels down the stone hallway, a sound so horribly final, so empty and cold. She smoothed the cool pastel satin and started to refold it in the box. The gown was of lovely, memorable design—Dolman sleeves that tapered to a square bodice which backswept to an outrageous bustle of satin rosettes.

In a separate compartment of the box she found the shoes, caged satin slippers stitched with tiny seed pearls. They were, in truth, the loveliest pair of waltz slippers she'd ever seen.

Perhaps she could at least apologize for her rudeness in refusing the gift. It must have cost—how did you measure the cost when you had never before in your life owned anything of such elegance? There was a certain pride in just caressing the fabric, and it looked to be a perfect fit. How in the world would Merrick know such a thing?

Adria slipped off one of her shoes and snugged her foot into the new supple satin. The saucy heels wobbled just slightly when she stood up, wearing both of them. Oh, such magnificent shoes for waltzing. And the gown—she couldn't resist trying it on just once. But she was being silly again, and greedy as well.

Couldn't she just admit to herself that she wanted to keep his gift, that she had purposely behaved like a sullen, nasty shrew all evening to hurt him? Oh, he deserved it, and the gown and matching shoes were obviously a bribe of sorts, only—

She found Merrick lounged on the stone window casement, his knees drawn close to his belt, a brandy snifter tilted in his palm, staring out at the rainswept night. He took a rough swallow from the snifter, then said, "Barlow will see you home. Keep the gown or destroy it. I don't want to see it on anyone else."

Her reflection shimmered over the window, coloring the blackness. Still, he didn't look at her. Adria teased the folds of the gown, fascinated with the starry glimmer of the fabric.

"I—I have never been given anything so beautiful before," she spoke softly.

Still, Merrick was silent. He sipped his brandy slowly, watching the dark liquid curl with motion. It seemed a long agonizing time before he reached a bronzed hand out to her and drew Adria to him.

Sometime during the night, the rain quieted to a sterling drizzle, then ceased. The room was still dark, the candles lumped in congealed tallow. Adria stretched up on her elbow, fumbling for the blanket Merrick claimed. He lay face down beside her, arms flung out, embracing both pillows.

"Are you awake?" Adria teased, cradling her cheek in the hollow of his spine, her fingers tracing the firm ridge of bone.

"No," Merrick groaned.

"I want you to be," she pouted, still aglow from the awesome hours just spent. The way Merrick made love, the simple, assertive, and glorious way he made love to her. An innocent tenderness when his lips touched over, healed the welts on the underside of her foot, the same reverent kiss when his hands and mouth possessed her breasts. Like an unfed hunger, glowing and wanting.

Remembering, Adria snatched the pillows from beneath him, evading the hand that grabbed for her, still laughing when Merrick flung onto his back and trapped her in his arms. His head came forward, his mouth groping for, then suckling hard over her erect nipple.

He lifted his head. "I'm awake now," he warned.

"We can't again so soon, Merrick," Adria breathed. "We just, you just—"

"This ill-bred sailor never keeps a tally. He just wants and takes," he kissed her softly, "and takes again." He held her mouth with his, kissing her deeply, harshly now while he brought her over him.

"Merrick, can't we just stay here, this way, forever and ever," Adria husked between breaths.

"Merrick—" she gasped as he thrust upward into her, knowing only a small moment of doubt before wonder engulfed her.

CHAPTER 14

Dull, uncomprehending eyes stared back at her.

"*Lo siento, no Ingles,*" the Mexican gardner repeated.

Adria felt another sickening jolt. "The captain," she insisted, "do you know where the captain is?"

"*El Capitan, si,*" he grinned displaying awesome gaps between his teeth.

It was like an idiot's game, the same question, the same answer over and over again. At dawn she had awakened alone in the massive bed she and Merrick had shared, finding the *casita* quiet and empty. The stone-ovened kitchen was dark, the grates swept clean of ashes, crockery and kettles scoured and hung in a brick cupboard. Only the Parisienne ballgown draped over a chair told her that the night had been real and not some lurid illusion.

They couldn't have just left, Adria told herself, trying to assure herself that Merrick or

Hillary Barlow would surely return for her. She haunted through the kitchen with some wifely intent, stoking enough kindling for a fire, boiling some water left in an enormous amphora. She searched about for a tin of coffee or tea and found nothing. No stores or rations, only freshly swept shelves.

After an hour or two, she decided to face the situation. She was here, miles from nowhere and she was alone. When you accepted the worst, it didn't seem so hopeless. The bitterness brought her back to the moment.

"Horses," she gritted, her hands shaping the imaginary form of one. "Are there any horses?"

The gardner whom she had found poking about the shrubbery nodded his head. "*Caballos, si*!" he kept nodding.

Adria felt limp with success. What was the word she had heard Kelly use? "*A donde*?" she gasped.

With an afflicted gesture, the man pointed due east down the mud-glutted road that trailed over a low empty rise. Adria saw nothing, no stables or corrals, not even fences.

"I don't see—" she murmured, turning around in time to see the gardner, his back stooped low to the ground, disappear among the bulbous foliage. She started after him, furious enough to drag him with her and show her where he pointed. Such ignorance, such infuriating ignorance! How could anyone be so simple-minded? He must have understood what she needed. Anyone with an ounce of intelligence could understand.

She walked slowly back to the door of the

casita. Merrick had left her here, abandoned her to this extreme, but he hadn't defeated her. Anything would be better than this senseless waiting. He had said to her, "I am not giving you a choice, Miss Sommerfield." The words, honed with hate now, were enough to motivate her to action.

The first few miles she walked in her new satin slippers almost made her return to the *casita*. Somehow, wearing them, watching their deterioration fortified her enough to forget the painful steps. Every hard-won step added to her hatred for Merrick. There wasn't any way, no possible way he could ever explain aside or apologize enough for leaving her like this. She'd get even, somehow, she would. And never, ever would he make a fool of her again.

At the splintered, nail-gouged sign, "Boca Chica Road," she paused to straighten it, leaning across the weathered wood, afraid to sit down to rest for fear she'd never get up again. The ride last night to the *casita* had been a long one. Or perhaps, with Merrick, it had just seemed that way. The rutted wheel prints of the *jehus* were still here along the withered seed grass.

There was only one road. How long it stretched, or how far to the Wellman's home, Adria refused to guess.

The sun broached the noon mark, a colorless, tormenting disc that frowned in and out of swollen thunderheads. The ground steamed in shimmers beneath her feet, bringing a parched ache to her throat. The miles, the time, became unimportant. The road behind her looked as far as the one they lay ahead, and after a time, it was only important that she was still walking, somewhere.

The sound rushed by her and was lost. A faint thunder that quieted as suddenly as it had arisen. Adria turned to listen, bewildered when it failed to repeat. The dank ground at her feet floated dizzily for an instant. Her gaze focused and she noticed that her toes had ruptured through the delicate fabric of her waltz slippers. Another mile would find her shoeless.

There was no warning dust with the approaching sound. It was as though the riders had been suddenly dropped on the jutting rise in front of her. They rode swiftly, recklessly through mud wallows in a zigzag chase, swearing at the horses when their hooves balled in the muck. Swarthy riders, outfitted in batwig chaps, their steerhide jackets spliced with *bandoliers*. They wore their hats low on their faces, showing only an expressionless leer. They came down the rise toward her in a single line.

Adria turned to run, forced aside by a reaching lariat that shrunk above her head. The riders circled wild didoes around her, cramping her into a pocket of space between them. She shielded her face in her arms as one of the horses charged her, only to be brought up short, inches from where she stood. The horse pranced, blowing out his nostrils, his sweat-hot fleck running down over her neck and arms.

Lewd catcalls, playfully dangerous, passed among them, a Spanish game. They seemed to be waiting, amused at the naked terror in her eyes. When she moved, they moved, pressing their horses in closer. Their horsemanship was daring, controlled, each one besting the other.

Adria fought down the panic. "Is there some-one, any one of you who speaks English?" She waited while the innocent headshaking spread from one rider to the next. Angry then, she shoved at the horse nearest her, clearing enough space to confront one of them.

"You, sir—if you will allow me to loan of your horse to return to the Wellman's home in Brownsville, I will see that you are well paid," she said, holding the quiver from her voice.

The words hung empty for a time. Then, with arrogant slowness, one of the riders unfastened the *barbequejo* strap beneath his chin, unslung the dark kerchief from across his face. He swept off his high-peaked hat and leaned across the saddle, speaking down to her.

"*Si*, I know, Miss Sommerfield," Delano Reyes grinned. "Tell me what you do here alone on Boca Chica road?"

"*You*!" her mouth formed the word, her topaz eyes brilliant with fury.

"Juan's riders, they only play. They are curious, but harmless."

"I could have been trampled to death!" Adria stormed. "Why didn't you tell them you knew who I was? If you have finished with this—this *game* of yours, I—"

Delano stopped her with a wave of his hand. "I am not leader here, just a rider. I cannot say what we do or not do. Maybeso it is better they not know who you are. I will take you to Rocco. He can say."

Weak with relief when Delano pulled her up

into the saddle with him, ignoring the rapid argument that spread among the other riders, Adria locked both arms around his waist, sharing the too-long stirrups with him, caring only that for now she wouldn't have to walk any farther.

An assortment of carriages, their wheels caked and doughy with mud, ringed the Wellman's home. Horses snorted, twitched in their traces, perking their ears in the direction of the house.

Kelly's men were listless and silent, prowling the length of spear-ironed fence, pausing occasionally to grumble over the delay.

"I hear one of them Savannah Rebs say she done the same fool thing down in Cuba. Got herself lost there, too."

"Aw, Christ, Leitman," the tall sergeant drawled. "What better'n you got to do than chase down women what is lost?"

Leitman guffawed, heeling the mud from his boot. "I'd most like to be doin' some serious drinkin' 'afore the chasin'."

"Hear tell they got Yankee beer down at Melio's now. It 'jes fizzes up and vanishes."

"Long as it ain't fizzin' blue," Leitman grumbled, a remark that brought coarse laughter from the men. The laughter choked to silence when Kelly moved out across the porch and walked toward them.

"Do we ride, Kelly?" Leitman shouted.

Kelly nodded, waving them into a circle, his voice dark with anger. "Wellman says she left with Ryland sometime after eight last night.

Ryland has the old Vasquez place on Chica Road, rented it yesterday or so Wellman tells me. There's no one on the property now except some ass-brained Mexican. The place intersects with King's pastures to the north where Juan has been raiding his beef."

Kelly paused, drawing a jagged line in the mud with his boot toe. "There's Chica Road," he said, drawing another square beside it. "There's where Juan goes borrowin'." He looked around at the men. "She may be with Ryland on his ship. Wellman says no, he already sent a rider to Port Isabel, but those damn fool Englishmen are making for sail and won't let anyone aboard."

"They'll let me aboard," Leitman spat sourly.

Kelly shook his head. "I'll go there. You scout over Chica Road. Do you know it?"

"Well enough to know it's flat and lonely. What was the lady wearin'?"

Kelly nudged off his hat and ran his fingers through his hair. "A dress, Leitman, if Juan's bastards haven't found her."

Delano stamped the mud from his boots, eyeing Juan Cortina's *caudillo.* He and Rocco had disagreed before over less, often to the point of outfacing each other over pistols before Juan intervened.

"I say she spoils our raid. What do you say, Delano?"

"I say give her a horse or let me take her back. She says she will pay."

Adria glanced desperately at one, then the other, trying to read the argument.

"So how does she pay for a herd of best cattle?" Rocco demanded.

"The cattle are still there. Tomorrow, we take them," Delano argued.

"No!" Rocco bellowed. "Tomorrow, King takes his cattle to the ready pasture. The raid is lost. Do you have the courage to tell this to Juan?"

Delano stood his ground. "I have the courage to tell Juan that you take Kelly's woman."

Rocco sucked on his thumbnail, studying Delano. "You do not say this before about the woman, that she is Kelly's," he groused, pacing a few steps. He whirled suddenly back to Delano.

"Do you lie about this thing with Kelly?"

Adria flinched at the sound of Kelly's name, wanting to interrupt and ask Delano what was being said. The ugly glitter in the bandit's eyes made her reconsider.

"We go and ask Kelly," Delano said shruggingly, taking Adria by the arm and leading her back to his horse.

Leitman recognized the fierce restraint that kept Kelly loose in the saddle, his wrists dangling over the saddle gullet. The hollow ping of raindrops beaded his slicker, the only sound in the strained stillness. Kelly's hands were calm, controlled, straying purposely from his holster. His stoney expression said nothing.

Rocco propped his boot in the latigo strap and leaned across the saddle. "You soothe Juan, I let the girl go without, what you say, 'ransom.' She make the trouble, distract my men. I lose the raid and this angers Juan. When the army goes in hunger, Juan kills men for little obedience."

From beneath the curled, dripping brim of his Stetson, Kelly looked steadily at Adria, still astride the same horse with Delano, her pale hair dark and wet, plastered close about her face. Her topaz eyes no longer pleaded with him, but gazed disinterestedly back at him. The expression in them was almost enough to make him change his mind. Her only words, "I can explain it all, Kelly, if you will just listen," and he had replied, "I haven't asked you to, yet—" still hung in his thoughts.

She sure as hell looked the part of Ryland's whore. The neck of her gown, fastened so primly yesterday when he had taken her to Matamoros, now hung rudely open, the shell buttons missing, her breasts showing almost to the full. Her bare, tawny legs glistened with raindrops where she had drawn her skirt up beneath her. She seemed almost passive to the show of justice that was before her.

Rocco spat profusely, kneeing his horse closer to Kelly's.

"You talk to Juan. Pay him a little for the cattle. We make even, no?"

Kelly straightened in the saddle, shrugging his rainslicker closer about him. "Could be I'll tell Juan the truth," he said heavily. "That you were too drunk to sit your horse, that you led the men to the wrong pasture where King keeps his breeders. That *you* botched the raid, not the girl. She was just an easy excuse."

Rocco glared murderously at Delano. His

finger snapped loose the rawhide strap holding his hat, then stabbed across at Kelly.

"You make a lie, Kelly—a big lie. Lies make for killing."

Kelly nodded slowly. "I am taking the girl with me now. The killing can come later."

Rocco backed his horse away from Kelly, his voice a slurred threat. "It will come, Kelly."

"You say the time, Rocco," Kelly smiled tellingly. "When you are sober enough to square the odds."

They rode sullenly in a misting waxen twilight, a gaunt line of riders slouched against the rain. A dying grumble of thunder haunted along the horizon, groaning to a feeble echo. Leitman's horse stumbled with weariness and limped to a halt. Kelly reined up and dismounted.

He sloshed across to Leitman's horse, rummaging through the pommel pouch for a cavalry talma. Leitman bit through a corner of his quid, watching Kelly.

"You gonna' stand-to with the Mexican?"

"Probably," Kelly nodded, turning to look at Adria. She had fallen asleep in the saddle a few miles back, and leaned bonelessly now against Delano, her cheek sawing against his back. Delano stretched his arms to the air, then grabbed quickly for Adria when she started to topple from the saddle.

"*Chenga*, Kelly," he groaned. "Already I ride too long before you come. Why we not rest for awhile?"

Kelly shrugged the cavarly cloak over his shoulder and crossed over to Delano.

"You said you were birthed in a saddle," he snarled, reaching up for Adria.

"*Si*, Kelly, is true," Delano grinned, holding onto Adria while Kelly wrapped the cloak over her. "Gentle, Kelly, you pull hard at her when she sleeps you hurt her. She have already enough hurt today."

Kelly lifted Adria in his arms, knowing then how chilled through she was. He battled down a stir of concern at seeing the bluish smudges beneath her eyes, the whitened outline of her mouth. She felt frail, like a child against his heart.

Delano held Kelly's horse while he mounted with Adria.

"You know, Kelly, I think maybeso she is sorry now that she go away with the Englishman."

"And I think, *maybeso*, I could give a damn," Kelly said with bitterness, hoping his words carried more conviction than he felt in his heart.

CHAPTER 15

Church walls smelling of market hay, a grainy scent blended with stale tallow. Somberly, Adria tried to shut out the scene before her, a scene that was torturing her already overplayed emotions.

Eunice Stewart and Dickson Blanchard were dwarfed in the quietly bowed setting, each submissive as they exchanged their vows. Their courtship, Adria thought, had been appalling. Eunice was disgusting in her overblown coyness, her flushed responses to Dickson's wearisome recountings of ante-bellum Savannah. And, in spite of all Adria's pleadings that he wait in reverence to Colly's memory a decent interval before taking Eunice as his new wife, Dickson proved immovable.

She had seen Kelly only once since the day he had taken her to the Miller Hotel after rescuing her from General Cortina's *banditti*. He had brought Eunice there as a companion for her—a trying arrangement that, at best, shielded her from the more vicious gossip and saved her from empty explanations. The arrangement had proved to be the warming ground for a courtship between Eunice and Dickson. It revolted her. She blamed Kelly and told him so.

"They are unsuited!" Adria stormed at him. "Dickson is a confused, grief-stricken old man being outwitted by a fat spinster."

Kelly was indifferent. "He's alone and troubled. Let them alone, Adria."

She refused to let the matter rest. "Dickson is a *true* gentleman. His family is landed Old South gentry of Savannah. He has entertained Braxton Bragg, John Hood, Hunt Morgan—all the Confederate generals of note. And, Colly was related to the Telfairs. Dickson is—*quality*!"

"This is Texas. It's different here."

"Different?" Adria raged. "And just how is quality ever defined in this cloddish backwoods? You made it oh so convenient for them by bringing Eunice here to the hotel."

"I made it convenient, as you call it, to keep you here away from social punishment," Kelly said sternly. "It appears that the Wellmans no longer welcome a '*lady*' fallen from her '*quality ways*' sleeping under their backwoods roof."

Adria had said no more. From Dickson she learned that Merrick had sailed, not to London as planned, but to Vera Cruz with Charles Wellman's cargo. Dickson had treated her with a patient tolerance without the censure she expected, the way one forgives a child after disciplining him.

Eunice adored Kelly and included his name, or some obvious mention of his activities, in all her florid conversations with a pointed emphasis on Kelly's bachelorhood.

"He *did* serve your father's command," she would say, boring the point home. Never once, Adria noticed, did Eunice mention Merrick's name again; quite the reverse of her former conversations when she played so admiringly on Merrick's fame.

Church benches creaked as they were emptied in a huddled shuffling that moved quietly past her. Dickson and Eunice left through a side door, leaving the altar deserted. An altar boy ceremoniously doused the tapers, stretching on tiptoe to reach the graduated heights, then in a burst of frustration, leaped up and blew the tallest candles out.

Numbly Adria glanced around her at the emptiness, the chill that made her wonder how such a supposedly blessed occasion could sour into such despair. Dickson was family, her one link to the only normal order of things she had known since leaving Savannah. She felt betrayed.

"The reception is at the Wellman's house," Kelly said quietly from behind her.

"I was not invited," Adria snapped back.

Kelly shifted his chapeau to the other arm and leaned over her. "I am inviting you."

She couldn't meet his eyes, not yet, and concentrated instead on the solitary gilt star and horizontal bar attached to his standup collar. Kelly had been Dickson's only attendant, his tall bronzed ruggedness complimenting the Confederate major's uniform that he was wearing.

That he should own, or even have been able to borrow, such an elaborate uniform was cause for wonderment.

"I prefer to return to the hotel," Adria said stiffly after a time.

"I think that's called 'cowardice,'" Kelly said, "or maybe 'selfish' is a better word for it. It's expected of you to be there. Dickson expects it and so do I."

His words rekindled the ugly scene between them. "Well, I don't want or expect him to be happy with *her,*" Adria blazed, meeting Kelly's slaty eyes. "You don't know Eunice. She's vile and she's hateful and—"

Kelly jerked her roughly to her feet. "Stop it, Adria! You just can't take your licks, can you? It's being here in church, seeing it all done proper that has you skulking around like a beaten pup. It's where you expected to be after that one night with Ryland in his bed. Your captain is a seafaring man who takes his women where he finds them." Kelly hesitated, watching her topaz eyes mist over and spill. "Dickson deserves whatever happiness Eunice can offer him. You're going to their wedding dinner for the sake of their happiness, not your own. Call it obligation, or honor as it may be. I know you Southern ladies are well acquainted with that lonely word."

Throughout the evening Kelly was protective, unassuming, drinking little and determined to outlast the frigid attitude that enclosed Adria. James Wellman approached Adria once before he was frowned aside by his father, the painful bewilderment still lingering in his young eyes as he walked on past her.

Bravely, Adria kissed Dickson's cheek, murmuring unfelt congratulations, suffering a sweaty embrace from Eunice who reeled affectedly when Kelly took her plump hand and raised it to his mouth.

"You will come to call when we are 'homed,' won't you Major Kelly?" Eunice panted, nudging Dickson to animation.

"Most certainly," Kelly said; then noting the sickened expression on Adria's face, he led her away from the receiving line.

Fragments of conversation hummed around her, retchy laughter from the women who were secretly indulging the brandy punch, stern and assertive opinions from the men who were smoothly segregating themselves from the women. Adria recognized Merrick's name in one of the conversations.

"Now I hear tell that Ryland has the Mexican *oficiales* hot on his heels in Vera Cruz. Seems he overbid Wellman's silver cargo above its rate then pleaded unfamiliarity with the currency translation."

"Intentionally?" someone laughed. "You should take him into the partnership and retire."

"Charles swears up and down that Ryland is wealthy enough in his own right, only he prefers his fox hunts on the high seas." The mimicked brogue brought gruff laughter from the audience of men who then drifted into the same timeworn discourse about Maximilian's defeat in Mexico.

Adria listened, hoping they would discuss

Merrick again, but they didn't. Kelly came to her with a crystal cup held awkwardly in his big hand.

"What is it?" she asked, taking a cautious sip.

"Mexican champagne. You'll like it." Kelly smiled down at her. For the first time Adria noticed his smile. The insolent quirk was missing from his hardened features, and when the smile reached his eyes, the depths colored from a stormy hue to an indefinable blue.

"You are staring at me, Miss Sommerfield," he said.

"Truly, Major Kelly? I wasn't aware before that you knew how to smile," Adria replied with a saucy *moue* as she handed the champagne cup to him and walked toward the door.

The hotel was barren and oppressive, the air hung with stale cigar smoke. The red carpet was threadbare to the wood and scarred with rowel prints. A squat spittoon near the door still dribbled with berry-dark tobacco juice from the last passerby. Had it been this grim a place all along, or did it just seem worse tonight with the drunken, throaty laughter from Melio's cantina a few doors away? Maybe it was just the time of evening that depressed her—this gaunt, colorless twilight.

Kelly drew Adria's room key from an unlettered slot, then glanced down at the pages of the register book and thumbed through them.

"Some of the guests can't write," he remarked, showing the page to her. "Now this one was from '63—a Spaniard named Barnardo from Torreon."

Adria tried to smile. In another moment or

two, Kelly would say goodnight and leave her. Somehow, with Dickson and Eunice both gone the hotel had assumed a sinister, almost frightening aspect. She felt suddenly, hopelessly terrified.

The Mexican clerk stepped from between the curtain behind the counter, still wiping at his mouth with a butter-stained napkin. He eyed Kelly, grinned at him, then leveled a hot look at Adria.

"We have rules, *senor,*" he said, smearing his thick hands over the front of his shirt.

"I know, golden rules," Kelly shrugged, tossing a gold piece to him and watching with disgust while the clerk snatched it from its spin and bit down on the edge of the coin.

He grinned apologetically at Kelly. "For you, *Senor* Kelly, always there is, how do you say, 'the exception'?"

Adria stiffened. They were playing a game for her benefit, a game that couldn't hide the practiced routine between Kelly and this man who obviously knew him. It was all planned, like it had been all the countless times before when Kelly brought some woman to the hotel for the night. She felt horribly sick and ashamed and dirty. She was across the lobby and almost to the street before Kelly caught her.

"What in hell did you want? A rainstorm and a borrowed farmhouse?" he spat.

Adria struck him with all the fury she could muster. His head jerked back. He slapped her harder than he meant to, more from reflex than anger. He wrestled her to him then and kissed her, a savage grinding kiss that hurt her, drove the breath from her. When he felt her go slack against him, he relented.

"I've been saving up for that for a long goddamned time. I should take you right now here in the street," he heaved, his fingers tangling in her hair and snapping her head back.

Adria bit her lip, determined not to cry out against the pain that was swelling to tears she couldn't hold back. Kelly raged tall above her with a cold anger that was more brutal than anything she'd ever known.

Slowly, almost gently, his fingers slid from her hair. It wasn't the first time he'd ever slapped a woman, and none of them ever more deserving than this cool-eyed beautiful bitch who wore her arrogance like a halo. So why this lump of regret in his belly, this knot of conscience that at the moment hurt like hell?

"I'm sorry, Adria," he husked, unexpectedly.

Speechless, Adria watched Kelly square his shoulders and walk away from her down the unlighted street. Her mouth felt dry, bruised, her face glowingly numb where he had struck her. There were worried voices around her. Someone was asking her a question she answered mindlessly. A round of drunken laughter erupted from Melio's. From the darkness beyond a puddle of thin yellow light that spilled from an open doorway, a dog was baying.

She just stood there, stunned, while the world went on living all around her.

Kelly stopped at Melio's. The blast of odors—sweet smells, a sweaty smell only more rank, something to do with the pure corn diet, a fleshy smell of a woman in rut, odors that defined the place and enabled a blind crawling drunk to find his way there.

Damn it all, with Erlinda it was different. She battled him on his own level. She was his kind, coarse and lusty, and demanded only endurance from him which left his emotions kindly unscarred. The fury she spat at him he could understand.

Adria could infuriate him with her silent haughtiness, the accepted barrier between gentility and commonness. He couldn't go up, around, or over it. It just loomed there and made him feel worthless. The taste of her was still in his mouth, her fragrance like wild honey still clung to his hands. She was the first, the only woman who had ever won an apology from him.

Kelly glanced quickly over his shoulder down the bleak rutted street, not really expecting to see her there.

Adria stood straight, proud and alone, a silhouette shadowed in waxen light. He took the first hesitant step, then fell into a run when he saw Adria start towards him. They met middistance in the street. Kelly swung her against him, crushing her in a violent embrace, each murmuring frantic forgiveness. Kelly buried his face in the tumbled fragrance of her hair and husked softly, "I love you, Adria."

Water-leached roots from the overhung black willow trees groaned against the river current, the only sound in the otherwise gaunt stillness.

Kelly fumbled tiredly for his coat, finding it

in a mass of clump grass where he'd tossed it off. It felt heavy, cumbersome when he covered Adria with it.

"I hurt you, didn't I?" he said, knowing that he had when she didn't answer him. "I triggered too fast. Usually, I don't." Now why in hell was he apologizing when she probably didn't even know how it was supposed to be? She hadn't been exactly passive like he expected, far from it, but he hadn't satisfied her, not yet anyway. There was some consolation in thinking that maybe Ryland hadn't succeeded there, either.

Adria lay limp, uncaring in Kelly's arms, surprised that she felt . . . nothing. Kelly had hurt her. He was big, thrusting like Merrick, but without Merrick's considerate restraint. The ache for him, for Merrick, still lay deep within her. How quickly she could call him to thought—sea blue eyes that caressed or scorned her, a smile, rare and disarming, the clean salt-scent of him, his languid, instinctive love-making with its violent energy that he gave or withheld.

I love him, God help me, I do, Adria thought, feeling suddenly adulterous. But Merrick was gone, he was lost to her, and Kelly was here. He was now. "I love you, Adria," he had told her. It had to be right, it just had to be.

"The last time I took a woman on a riverbank I was sixteen and she confessed to being thirty," Kelly yawned. "She was older though, and just as hungry as I was." He poised above Adria, roughing his jaw over her naked shoulder, remembering the insatiable raven-haired widow whose name had been April.

"You loved her?"

"No, not love, something different," Kelly smiled. "I used her and she used me."

Adria shrugged away from him onto her side. Merrick had used her that same way—without love, a sea-roving man who took his women where he found them for a night, perhaps two, always without the entanglements that should follow. How incredibly stupid she had been. She winced, trembling.

"You're cold," Kelly rasped, turning her back to him. "The hotel would have been better. Beds make for an easier night of it."

It surfaced again, his coarseness and the shame that accompanied it. She had never felt this way, never felt ashamed with Merrick. The memory brought a slip of tears. Kelly was kissing her gently, thoughtfully, his tongue blotting over the wetness on her cheeks.

"I want to make love to you again, Adria, tonight, all night, but not here, not this way. I hurt you because I was impatient. Maybe I was a stud and sixteen again on a riverbank with a woman. Maybe I never knew a lady who demanded better. I'll have to learn."

Adria choked down a hard sob while Kelly folded her against him.

"No, sweetheart, I don't want you to cry. I want you to listen. I'm not an honorable sort. I kill and take money for it. There's a whore in Matamoros who swears her belly is swollen with my son and I'm not even honorable enough to care. There's nothing noble in my background. I didn't run away from that stinking backwater shack on Caddo Lake, I walked away. My father had a fondness for using the strap. The 'justice strap' he called it, said it would cleanse me of sin. I saw his 'saving strap' make a feebleminded mute out of my brother. One day he beat me to my knees and when I could get up, I started walking. I can still remember the way his eyes looked when he went for that strap. It's the same kind of hate I see when I face a man over a gun."

"I stole, I begged, and walked all the way to the Mexican border. I met your father when he was recruiting volunteers for his Mexican campaign. He didn't ask me any questions, he just accepted me for what I was. I wasn't much then, just a half-starved kid playing at being a man. He made me try. The harder I tried, the more he demanded. In three years I was an officer, and Colonel Sommerfield kept right on demanding. He saw better of me than I ever could see of myself."

Adria's fingers trembled over Kelly's mouth, hushing him.

"Please, Kelly, I don't need to hear any more."

"There isn't any more to know," Kelly said quietly. "When I saw you that first day on the *Warlock*, even before I knew you were Adrian Sommerfield's daughter, something inside me began to want. It was a thing I couldn't feed until tonight. Most likely, the only honorable thing I will ever do in my life is ask you to marry me. I'm not a man for promises, so I won't make any. but I'm honest in wanting you, Adria. That will have to be enough."

Kelly kissed her then, not gentle any longer,

but with need, with passion, proving his words. And, after a time, Adria didn't try to think beyond the moment.

CHAPTER 16

"Yankees!" "Yankees comin'!" "Yankees on Chica Road, Yah-ho!" "Yankees comin'!"

Kelly jarred upright in bed, disentangling himself from Adria's arms. He touched the slope of her shoulder with his lips before drawing the blanket over her.

"Kelly—what?"

"I don't know, sweetheart," Kelly husked, flinging the covers back. He was to his feet when he heard the second call.

Fevered shouting now, joined by a gathering jangle of horses and wagons outside the hotel window. Someone was battering against the door, heavy enough to dislodge the doorknob and send it rolling across the floor.

Kelly was halfway into his breeches when the door gave way and Delano plunged into the room, his eyes wild with excitement.

"*Ees* bad, Kelly," he heaved. "Umberto, he count two *battallones*, much horse with cannon, big ones on carriage beds."

Adria clutched Kelly's shirt to her, refusing to surrender it when he reached down for it. "Never mind, put it on," he muttered to her as he shrugged into his coat. "How far down the Chica?" he snarled at Delano.

"The artillery, it slows them—maybeso ten miles north of the Resaca."

"Where is Juan?"

"He come with me and have the wagons outside. The gold is loaded yesterday, but Juan, he say the blue soldiers will ride first for Fort Brown so he bring it here," Delano panted.

Kelly nodded, snatching up both his Dance revolvers.

"How many men with Juan?"

"All his horses, but is still not enough for battle, Kelly. Too many Yankees with field mortars."

Kelly stomped into his boots, grabbing up a tangle of clothes and handing them to Adria. "Put on the breeches and field coat, and tie your hair up under the hat," he said, frowning over his shoulder at her. "I'll be downstairs."

Delano snatched the ewer from the table and drank heavily from it, his eyes darting curiously over Adria. He wiped his mouth with his hand and followed Kelly out into the hall.

"What we do now, Kelly?"

Kelly bolted down the stairs, fastening his holster around his waist. "What ships are docked at Port Isabel?"

Delano grinned, nodding his head. "*Si*, Kelly, it is there. The Confederate ship is back from Vera Cruz *anoche*,"

Kelly's eyes hardened. "No mistakes, *amigo*.

There isn't time."

"No mistake, Kelly. I see it dock."

"Leitman!" Kelly shouted, stepping into the street and threading his way between the wagons.

Leitman hurried from behind the lead wagon, bringing Kelly's horse. "We runnin' or fightin', Major?" he grinned crookedly.

"Some of both," Kelly snapped back. "Send a flank column up to the Resaca. I want a report of their position and march speed. You and Henry scout the beach trail. I'm taking the wagons over it to Port Isabel."

Leitman swallowed roughly. "You gamblin' on that British ship to take the gold out?"

Kelly scanned the wagons and smiled grimly. "Find Cortina and tell him I need his horses, all of them." He swung into the saddle and leaned down to Leitman. "Bring up that roan and put the Mexican bit on him."

"We takin' the lady with us?" Leitman gulped.

"That's two damn fool questions, Leitman," Kelly growled. "Now see if you can remember the orders that went with them."

Merrick snapped the razor back inside its pearl-inlaid handle and rinsed the last of the shaving soap from his jaw. Thoughtfully, while he toweled over his chest with a monogrammed linen, he kept turning the razor case in his hand until the tiny scrolled engraving, "*Mon Amor*, Cara", glared up at him.

He looked hard at his reflection in the nautical mirror. A gaunt, deeply bronzed face scorned back at him. Two nights ago in Vera Cruz, being interrogated by Mexican harbor officials who threatened him in faulty English with imprisonment, the same repetitious questions over and over throughout the long night had taken its toll. He looked exhausted.

Strange that during the ordeal when his brain was groping for distractions, he should think of the things that he did. He thought about Mallorca in a molten twilight, the sea aflame with blood-dark hues, a rain nest that hovered above the landfall at Dieppe, a poetic wind that whispered its salty chants until he found his own words in its murmurings and could no longer distinguish between the two.

And he thought about Adria. She seemed to invade his thoughts, her face blurring in and out of them, topaz eyes full of hurt and bewilderment, caressing him, hating him. With something akin to amazement, he realized he missed her.

Hillary Barlow had appeared at dawn with a translator from the French embassy who explained to Merrick that the Mexican officials requested a "convenience fee" for the use of their nonexistent harbor facilities, in addition to the *Warlock's* docking fees. The fee was staggering, even in Federal currency and it absorbed his profit from Wellman's cargo shipment.

It had been a more complicated game with the silver exchange agent. Merrick had assumed the international silver rate would be standard in Vera Cruz, a technicality that Charles Wellman had neglected to explain before he sailed.

Merrick had demanded full cargo value rate. It was given, then recalled. Merrick had refused to return the difference, bringing an onslaught of related problems, this time with the Mexican and French exchange officials who couldn't decide between them which popular revolution they were currently favoring. He had both won and lost against a flexible Mexican law that recognized only one value—greed.

One thing he had vowed after pacifying the Mexican officials, which amounted to nothing more than polite extortion in agreeing to their payments, he would learn to speak their language, read and write it as well. His French was passable due to Cara's efforts, and learning was simply a matter of interest. It was something he should have done a long time ago.

Merrick reached for his boots, choosing the pair of "bottle boots" he had bought at Pepitpain's Emporium. The leather was still coarse and noisy, but after a wearing today to Charles Wellman's office they should be seasoned. The cargo account would be settled, the crew was due for release from the Post Hospital at Fort Brown, the *Warlock* was provisioned for sail again, and Hardee's mission was history, all neat and tidy, except for Adria. She was too trusting, and too young, too impossibly young for him. At least thinking so made it easier to battle the throes of conscience afterwards.

He glanced routinely out the port window, then took a longer look. The dock was deserted. The Mexican crews of the shrimp trawlers were gone, two river barges still flat-loaded with cargo stood abandoned. The French bark moored in the adjacent dock berth only last night was headed for the seafall, its high gallants diminishing along the horizon line.

"Barlow!" Merrick thundered, stalking through the updeck passage and meeting him on the stairs.

"Quickly, sir," Barlow heaved. "There's a Confederate column in a bloody run towards the harbor. It's Major Kelly, I believe."

Merrick was on deck in fast strides, frowning into the bitter sunlight, watching the fanning column of wagons and soldiers approach, the horses whipped to full gait as they labored up the long incline to the dock.

Kelly circled the lead wagon and motioned the column on to the dock. He dismounted at a run, pulling his Tarpley carbine from the saddle holster, whisking the saddle pouches from behind the cantle in one grasp. He didn't look up at the *Warlock*, he just ran towards it. He faced Merrick suddenly, his stone-gray eyes dark and grave.

"I can ask or demand, Ryland. The choice is yours."

Merrick stiffened. "What are you asking or demanding?"

"I need your ship," Kelly said tightly.

"The answer is no. The *Warlock* is not for hire at any price." Merrick turned on heel, his reflexes primed as he heard the gun hammer on Kelly's gun snap a quiet release. He rounded on Kelly.

"I am demanding now," Kelly said.

Rifle shots stuttered through the air, a rapid succession of four shots. Leitman was shouting hoarse orders from the rear wagon. Confederate troopers scattered from the wagons, knotting at the foot of the dock bridge.

"The Yankees won't care whether or not you agreed when they level their howitzers. Make your choice," Kelly gritted. He waved a signal to Leitman, then turned back to Merrick.

Immediately, two riders left the front column. Merrick recognized one of them as General Cortina, the other one—her pale hair slipping from beneath a Rebel forage cap, wearing a butternut shirt and breeches, her feet unshod, was Adria.

"What in the name of hell brought Yankees *here*?" Merrick demanded, watching Adria and the Mexican general dismount.

"They are five miles west of us," Kelly heaved. "The shots were from my flank column. There's a reason for all of this. Hardee could explain it better. I haven't the damn time."

Merrick took one long step then ran to the deck shouting orders. "Barlow!" "Full engines, gunners advance!"

Kelly pivoted, staring in disbelief as the *Warlock's* crew sprung to action. Dahlgren cannons on port and starboard creaked forward in their deck carriages, readied for loading. Quickly then, he climbed over the side of the dock bridge and lifted Adria to him, carrying her and reaching at the same time for Juan Cortina's outstretched hand.

"The last wagon is yours, Juan, whatever the outcome. *Con Dios*, General."

Cortina smiled lazily. "Only one wagon of gold for me, eh, Kelly? And I be your watchdog all these times. Well," he shrugged, "is *guerra*, no?" His dark eyes flicked over Adria. "Your woman, Kelly, she do you honor. I think, in time, you give up much for her. *Con Dios, amigo.*" He disappeared within the ranks of his men, holding his hand to the air. "*Vamanos*!" Kelly heard him say.

He swung Adria across the dock bridge to the port deck.

"Where are your boots?" he asked, holding her feet up a few inches from touching the deck.

"I lost them miles back when—" Adria froze, staring up at Merrick. Kelly set her roughly on her feet.

Merrick looked past her to Kelly. "What's in the wagons?"

"Gold," Kelly snapped, "as if it was any of your damn business."

"It is my business if I'm going to fight off the Yankees for it to take my ship out," Merrick flared back. He was still glaring at Kelly when he shouted again for Barlow. "Order ready crew to assist with unloading the wagons."

"Aye, sir," Barlow saluted hurriedly.

"Have the wagons backed to the dock bridge, two at a time. Drop the coal shute and oncargo with it and reset the coil winches for the tonnage." He nodded to Kelly. "How is the gold crated?"

"In bullion packs of twenty-five, nine wagon loads," Kelly said.

"I counted ten wagons."

"I just paid off the Confederacy's debt to Juan Cortina with one wagon load," Kelly gritted.

Merrick looked at Adria, his eyes cold. "It will

be safer for you below in my quarters until we are under way. I suggest this time you stay there. Barlow will see you below."

Adria looked imploring at Kelly who only nodded his head.

"He's right, Adria. Do what he says."

"You'll be here, on deck, with Merrick?" she asked desperately, clutching at Kelly's arm.

Kelly drew her to one side, knowing that Merrick could still hear every word he said to her. There just wasn't time for the sweet privacy he needed.

"Yesterday, last night, was all a man could ask from a woman. I'm not sorry, Adria. I guess I expected to be when daylight came. It's a beginning for us, a long one. If we can outdistance the Yankees and clear the border I'll join you at China Grove."

"Oh, no, Kelly," Adria pleaded, backing away from him. "Promise me—" she swallowed, "promise me you'll stay on board. The men don't need you now. The gold is more important, you told me that. The war will be over soon. *I need you. You promised*!" She was still pleading with him when Hillary Barlow took firm hold of her and led her below to Merrick's cabin.

Merrick was about to ask Kelly just what he had promised Adria when Leitman bounded up the dock bridge and nudged his way across to Kelly.

"Yankee advance cavalry, less than two miles back, and there's a rig on the side fork road with a man and woman in it."

Kelly made two strides to the railing before

Merrick halted him. "You're outnumbered. Forty six men won't hold off Yankee cavalry and mortars long enough for me to cargo the gold."

"You think I don't know that?" Kelly said roughly. "We've been outnumbered before. These are good men."

"Get them on board. We can defend from the deck with my guns," Merrick ordered.

Kelly swallowed once. "You'd take my rangers, all forty-six of them?"

"Rather than see them blown to hell, yes," Merrick said fiercely.

The coal shute rumbled above their heads, the case swaying in mid air while the winches reversed. Merrick leaned to the port rail watching the dust tail in the distance.

"Barlow, disengage dock loaders! Load the rest of the crates into the shute. All hands stand clear below!"

Kelly pointed to the road. The flimsy rig careened wildly up the incline to the dock, the slender red spokes a whirring blur as they churned the dust.

Merrick grabbed his sea glass, tossing a quick glance up at the upended coal shute that hovered above them.

"Release it on deck," he ordered. "Drive that last wagon aboard."

Delano laid his whip on the horses. The front wheel jammed in the rope brackets, causing the lead horse to stumble as the weight shifted. Kelly leaped over the railing and shoved the wheel free. The horses balked, reared when their hooves touched the deck vibration, backing the wheels a revolution. Kelly jerked at the curb reins, swearing at the horses, tugging them aboard.

Delano jumped down from the wagon seat, wiping his face in the crook of his sleeve. "I go this time with Juan," he said tiredly, extending his hand to Kelly. "You know the way of us *revolutionarios*. Juan's war I understand. Your war is too hard, Kelly. You come to Mexico. I be with Juan. *Con Dios*, friend."

"*Cuidado, amigo*," Kelly called after him, watching as Delano ran for the gaping dock loader.

Merrick handed his sea glass to Kelly. "Dickson Blanchard is driving that rig."

Kelly nodded. "He's going to overturn the damn thing if he doesn't slow it at the steep."

On instinct, Merrick backed from the railing, pulling Kelly with him. As quickly, heavy canister shot from short range repeaters scarred the planks near his feet.

Kelly crouched down beside Merrick. "Yankee advance, not more than two or three of them," he husked, peering over the railing.

Dickson Blanchard was inching the rig along the dock, craning his neck to see Merrick.

"Christ," Kelly swore. "Eunice is with him."

"Mr. Blanchard!" Merrick shouted down at him. "Leave the rig and crawl to the bridge!"

There was no sign that Dickson had heard him. Merrick moved low to the deck toward the dock bridge. "We're going to have to go after them," he muttered as Kelly settled next to him.

Kelly shouldered his carbine and sighted it. "I have one near the lighthouse spotted. The other one is flanking his right, the third one is behind him."

Merrick lifted his head, straining for a glimpse of Barlow. Barlow raised carefully from cover.

"Fire the port cannon, point succession one hundred yards, full clock."

"Aye, captain," Barlow shouted.

Merrick heard the thrust chain on the Dahlgren slide in the trunnion. The fuse sizzled in the load eye. He waited.

Cannon blast shocked the air, furrowing the ground beyond the rig. Merrick sprinted down the dock bridge, leaped the drift distance to the wharf and ran to Dickson's rig. Kelly shadowed him, his movements close to Merrick's.

Merrick reached inside the rig for Eunice. "I'm going to help you to the ship, Miss Stewart—but you must hurry."

Eunice nodded rigidly, clinging to Dickson.

"We were caught in a cross pursuit. We had no choice," Dickson panted, his short legs buckling under him as he climbed down from the rig. Kelly crept towards him, pulling Dickson down behind the cover of the rig.

Yankee cavalry had positioned on the rise above the dock now. A steady hail of grapeshot and canister sparked the dust near the wheels of the rig. Merrick hesitated, motioning to Kelly, waiting for the Dahlgren's second range. His gunners were ahead of their timing. The next minute, the cannons fired.

"*Now*!" Merrick shouted, running with Eunice toward the ship.

Barlow and Leitman reached across the

stretching dock loader to them, heaving Eunice aboard. Dickson stumbled after them, his feet missing the jump distance. Merrick grappled for him, dragging him up by the cuff of his collar. Kelly's carbine was firing steadily in smooth retreat. As suddenly then, it ceased.

Merrick glanced behind him, stiffening as he saw Kelly slump forward only a few feet from the widening dock bridge, a spreading circle of blood staining his coat front.

Barlow uncoiled a rope line and flung it across the water to Kelly. Kelly lifted his face from the ground, trying to focus, his fingers clawing for the knotted rope. He stretched forward once, then was still.

"He can't see the goddamned rope," Merrick swore, hurrying along the length of the port rail. "Draw anchor, let her drift," he said to Barlow. "I'm going after him."

The Dahlgrens thundered again from fire-hot barrels, a longer unordered round that trembled the *Warlock*, scattering through Yankee field positions. Merrick's feet touched the dock. He reached Kelly with the coil of rope in both hands. He quickly prodded Kelly onto his back, tying the rope over Kelly's shoulders. Somewhere, deep in his brain, he heard the cool hiss of canister shot, then nothing.

Cold sea water shocked Merrick awake. He plunged backwards into the slit of distance between the *Warlock* and the dangling dock bridge. He shook the water from his eyes, feeling a strange numbness in his head. The ship was a sudden looming blur that was moving sluggishly away from him.

Barlow was shouting at him, garbled words that sounded like applause screaming across his brain. His arms felt weighted, unconnected. The life rope curled, floated to him again. Merrick splashed the water for it, feeling the prickles of wet rope in his hand. The sea became a dark cradle, weightless and silent as it rocked him in murmurous, swallowing blackness.

CHAPTER 17

The *Warlock* had been hurt. Carcass shells gashed her plate timbers, tangling across her cutwater beam. Two British gunners were dead, blown overboard when a Yankee field howitzer positioned near the lighthouse slope had lowered its range. The *Warlock* sagged in the water, her list to port unresponding to demands from the helm. The ship limped from Port Isabel with five gaping holes astern, her pumps displacing sea water for the first time in the runner's remarkable history.

An apathetic confusion had descended over the British crew. Response to Barlow's commands was slow and bewildered. Leitman, with some of Kelly's men, prowled the length of the scarred deck, their leaden gaze trained dismally back across the gulf. The frenzy of battle had subsided. Only the wearying shock remained.

Adria stared unseeingly down at the map Hillary Barlow spread before her. At first she had tried to concentrate. Calcasieu Lake and Sabine Lake merged together, making one lake. Lines and curves with unreadable nautical symbols swarmed the map. It was useless to try to understand it.

In desperation Barlow placed her forefinger on the outstretched map. "Please, Miss Sommerfield—rather, Mrs. Kelly—please, show me this port, China Grove."

Even being called by her proper new name failed to penetrate the leaden numbness that gnawed through her and glistened her eyes with tears.

"I'm sorry," Adria shrugged. "Nothing looks familiar."

Hillary Barlow straightened beside her. He rolled the map carefully and tied it, then laid it down across his knees. There was little that one could say at this time, but he knew what must be done.

"You are the only one who can direct us to this place, China Grove," he said quietly.

Adria gave a hard sigh. "Did you see what happened, I mean, everything as it happened? You—someone must tell me. Someone must have seen whether or not Kelly was—"

Barlow shook his head, his eyes grave. "Major Kelly fell as Captain Ryland secured the Blanchards on board. The captain went back for him. It was then that the Yankees brought their primary artillery onto the slope. It was a difficult cross fire. The captain—" Barlow's voice roughened, "we were able to pull him from the water."

"And Kelly?" Adria swallowed.

Hillary Barlow looked down at his hands. "At the time we cleared the harbor the Yankees were already in command of the dock. I could no longer see Major Kelly." Painfully then, he watched the limpid glitter in Adria's topaz eyes. "I am sorry, Mrs. Kelly, deeply so."

"Merrick left him there," Adria murmured vacantly.

Barlow got to his feet. "The captain was wounded and unconscious," he said emphatically. "It is by a miracle of God that we were able to save *him* aboard. I can understand your grief, Mrs. Kelly, but not your resentment."

Adria watched Barlow walk angrily away. Perhaps anger *was* preferable to sadness, she thought miserably. Surely some kind of feeling was better than this deadened ache she held so closely within her.

Merrick groaned terribly. He flung his arms wide, tasting brine water, his legs working quickly to keep himself afloat in a bed of imaginary waves. A jaundiced sky blazed down on him, a sun with a blood-red rim fevered over him. He burned, he ached, he vomited sea water until his body screamed in rebellion. Lifeless bodies floated around him. He called out to them above the tide lash.

"A captain's error," he laughed deliriously at one discolored victim, slapping aside the stiff chalky fingers that reached out for him. "*Fool*! He vaulted sail when he should have tacked," Merrick screamed at the crush of waves. Upmast rigging tangled his arms, his neck, suffocating him. The French schooner plowed the humpbacked offshore rocks, its sharp youthful lines crashed to splinters against the saw-toothed shore.

A young forgotten summer, a night in the shipwrecked deep off Cala Cadolar, his first voyage in apprenticeship. The night had been long and windless. With dawn, a slow coming of light, beautiful and soft. He had to outwait the darkness, the blind darkness where he floated mindless and limbless in a watery eternity. The rope he held was life—find it—hold it, hold.

Adria leaned against the door inside Merrick's cabin, her gaze roaming the quick-silver light for the berth where he lay. His demented, fever-thick sounds had awakened her, an inhuman sound of pain that no amount of consolation from either Eunice or Juno had been able to silence.

Eunice sat half sprawled in a chair near Merrick, her plump chin drooped on one shoulder. A basin of water sloshed innocently in her lap. Heavy, exhausted snores fluttered from her sagging mouth. She twitched once, then re-settled.

Adria tiptoed across the cabin and took the basin from Eunice, soundlessly placing it on top of Merrick's desk.

"Eunice," she whispered, nudging her.

Eunice jerked awake, fumbling for the basin that Adria had taken from her. "Oh, it's you Adria. I must have dozed. The captain only now became quiet."

Adria nodded, helping Eunice to her feet. "I will stay with Merrick. Dickson needs you."

Eunice shook her head. "No, dear. Let me call

Juno to stay with him. He just stepped out to go to the galley to see about some tea," Eunice said, her voice trembling. "We had to restrain the captain some time ago. He thinks he is still in the water and keeps raving about a shipwreck. It's the shock and all, you know. And the fever, too. He can't—he hasn't been able to see. I don't understand—"

"I know, Eunice. Dickson told me. It's all right. I know what to do," Adria said gently.

"Poor Dickson blames himself," Eunice sniffled back her copious tears. "If we hadn't come to the dock both Major Kelly and the captain would be—"

Adria steered Eunice to the door. "You're overtired, that's all. I'll stay until morning."

Mindlessly, Eunice reached for Adria's hand and patted it. "You're a good girl, Adria. And I know you were a good wife to Major Kelly, bless his courageous soul. But you can't stay here with the captain. Mr. Ditwell will come soon to change the dressings on the wound. You mustn't see anything like this. They have to hold the captain down to do it. Even with all my years of sickroom experience, I feel a faint coming on. And I don't think Captain Ryland would want you to see him in such circumstance."

"Mr. Ditwell is needed on the bridge if they are to see the *Warlock* to harbor at Sabine Lake," Adria said with a flare of impatience. "Juno can dress the wound when Merrick wakens. Now please, Eunice, get some rest."

Eunice paused inside the door. "He must recover, dear. We must do all in our power to see that he does."

Adria closed the door, feeling a warm tingle of possessiveness at being alone with Merrick. She righted an overturned bench, smoothed the stack of flannel bandages, counting through them. The oily scent of laudanum reached through the cabin, camphor vapors from the kettle steamed over the porthole glass. A soapy smell of scrubbed wood hung over all the scents. It smelled like a sickroom.

It took a few moments before Adria could approach Merrick's berth. He looked clean and immaculate in the flannel swaths. Rope tarps were bound over his chest and arms to prevent movement. A thicker dressing covered his eyes. The wound in his left hip was left unbound, only a square of cloth covered the lip of the still-seeping bullet welt.

Merrick's bronzed fingers curled, uncurled before hardening to a fist. The knuckles were strained, whitened when he lifted his fist.

"God damn all you bloody bastards!" Merrick swore, rasping the words. The next moment Adria thought she heard him sob.

"Merrick," she whispered. "Please, you must be still."

"Let me up," Merrick husked, gritting into the pain. He fell back, exhausted. "By damn, I'll kill every one of you for this!"

"If I loosen you, Merrick," Adria humored him, "where will you go? What will you do?"

He was quiet for endless moments, his dark fist gradually unclenching. A long hurtful sigh breathed from his mouth.

"I can't see you, Adria."

Adria felt a bite of tears behind her eyes. No, she couldn't let herself pity him. Others would do that. Merrick needed strength from someone now, even angried strength, the strength that came from hating her or himself.

"You left Kelly to die," she said heartlessly, watching while a rigid shudder overtook him. Her heart wrenched in her breast, a pain so huge she thought it would suffocate her. She forced the words, "How fortunate for you that you were the first one to the dock bridge. And how fortunate for you that you had Kelly to stand off the Yankee bullets for you while you ran to safety."

The impotent struggling beneath the leather restraints began again. Merrick groped his fingers along the edges of the berth searching for her hand. Adria moved away, flicking at the hot tears streaming down her cheeks, all the while steadying her voice.

"You left him there to die. That's a habit with you, isn't it, Merrick, leaving people behind to fend for themselves? Let me see, how long ago was it that you left me at the *casita*? Oh, I was lucky, I suppose. No one was shooting at me. All I had to worry me was the long trek back to the Wellmans, and General Cortina's renegades. Only Kelly cared enough to come searching for me. Perhaps I should have warned him about you, about your kind of heroics. It might have saved his life."

Merrick tried to shake his head and groaned in pain.

"I don't believe you, not any of this you're telling me."

"Oh, but it's all true," Adria rasped, swallowing back a surge of emotion. She strolled over to the porthole to watch the dawn-washed sea, the mellowy amber disc that was stretching brilliantly through pink-hulled clouds. Her voice no longer resembled her own.

"Kelly and I were married two nights ago, the night before the Yankees came," she said more slowly. The words had a dreamlike quality to them, as though she were talking about someone else, not herself. "It wasn't the sort of wedding I always thought I'd have someday. You would have probably been amused by it all. The chapel was quite old, so old it was crumbling down on us. I think only the vines held it together. The priest, a Father Amyas, was furious with Kelly about something. They argued for a long time," her words trailed to silence. Remembering it all only made it seem more unbelievable.

"My maid of honor was a whore named Flavia. Delano Reyes stood with Kelly—I should say tried to stand with him after Kelly dragged him from Melio's. Did you know, Merrick, that no one spoke any English that night? I learned the only word I needed to know. It meant, 'yes'."

The stillness seemed to scream at her. She had gone too far, said too much. She couldn't help herself, she couldn't. The bitterness and hurt just kept welling and welling within her until she had said all the things she never intended to. She shouldn't have attacked him when he lay here helpless, slashing with words at him with a knife honed in bitterness. But there was no turning back now. It was done.

"You bitch," Merrick grated, "you lying bitch. Get out, Adria."

"Merrick, I didn't mean—"

Merrick never heard her. His tortured breaths told her that he had slipped from reality and the nightmarish agonies had begun all over again.

CHAPTER 18

It was another two days before Adria saw Merrick again. A polite conspiracy had been formed to protect Merrick from her visits. Hillary Barlow was aloof and preoccupied; Joel Ditwell was gruffly courteous though immune to her questions; even Juno, the ship's chef, reverted to speaking French when Adria cornered him in the galley with questions about Merrick. There was a different crewman outside Merrick's door each time Adria tried to see him, each with the reply, "The captain is resting, ma'am." As a whole the crew was detached, devoted to their duties, their tasks doubled by the awesome list of the damaged ship.

Eunice and Dickson estranged themselves in their cabin, appearing infrequently for meals in the galley, then gradually asking that they be served below. When Adria did see Dickson he seemed spaced between events, his childish ramblings about Savannah more and more incoherent. Eunice mothered him, encouraging his rare lucid spells, her face set in forbearance when listening to the same recountings over and over again. Dickson did not mention Brownsville, nor make any reference to Colly again. It was as though she had never existed.

Kelly's men regarded Adria with a grim tolerance. They talked among themselves, the conversations invariably quieting when Adria approached them. Leitman still removed his outsize Stetson to her, but his eyes were grave and disapproving when they touched over her.

Finally, the force of guilt drove her to the solitude of her own cabin. Everyone was blaming her for something, some openly, some more subtly. Suddenly she seemed responsible for everything that had gone wrong. Kelly was presumably dead because of her, Merrick was blind and suffering horribly from the pain, Dickson was on the doorstep of lunacy, and all the British crew and all of Kelly's men hated her. It was the most alone she had ever felt in her whole life. Tears hadn't helped, and it was too late for anything else.

At the noon watch, Clarence Leitman called at her cabin.

"Not to disturb you, ma'am," he said self-consciously, staring down at his scuffed boots. "But I just been with Captain Ryland," he said, lifting his eyes to her with a show of pride that indicated a transference of loyalties.

"How is he?" Adria asked gratefully.

"He's admirably improved, ma'am," Leitman drawled. "He give me these here maps to show to you. They ain't like the ones Kelly had. These got all messed up with scratchings and such. I can't hardly make out what's what. I thought to ask you, bein' as how you know that bayou land."

"I'll try again," Adria smiled, stepping out into the passageway with him at the same moment that Hillary Barlow came stiffly down the updeck stairway.

Leitman began to smile, a long smile that spread to a deep chuckle. "We're goin' to find that place for you, that Sabine Lake since you sailors is lost."

Barlow reddened. "I believe, sir, our port destination has already been located."

"What'd you do, send out a dove to look for land?" Leitman laughed outright.

Adria glanced from one to the other, sensing a teasing undercurrent of humor between the two. The contrast of mannerisms was dearly amusing.

Mr. Barlow looked very tired. "Captain Ryland would like to see you, Mrs. Kelly, before we port."

For an instant Adria felt a flutter of hope. "Will he see me, Mr. Barlow?"

"Rather," Barlow said solemnly, "he wishes to speak with you."

Adria stood outside Merrick's door, praying for the strength to open it. An eternity ago she had stood here before this same door ready to offer all she could give as a woman to him. The *Warlock* breathed of these memories. Merrick was everywhere in the shadows, tall and commanding. He strode the decks with an eye trained to every detail, the men braced with respect when he passed them. It was hard to believe that had all changed.

The porthole was thrown open to the brisk salty air that stirred desk papers to a heap on the floor. Side curtains and bedding fluttered softly in its wake, drenching the room in freshness. The medicine smells were blessedly gone.

Merrick was propped upright in his berth. He flinched once as Adria closed the door. How handsome he still looked, thinner, much thinner, his body dark against the glaring whiteness of the bed linen. His over-long hair grazed over his forehead, over the thick white dressing that covered his eyes. How much she wanted to smooth it aside, to touch him, to tell him—

"Mrs. Kelly," he said clearly, turning toward the door. He blanched with pain, his dark fingers wandering briefly to his eyes, over the cloth that covered them.

"Yes, Merrick," Adria said holding the emotion from her voice.

He turned his head slightly following her voice. "If you will sit down here, please, beside the berth, I have some questions regarding this mission that General Hardee and Major Kelly devised."

Adria chose the desk chair and moved it close to the edge of the berth, far enough to keep her from touching him. Merrick seemed to sense when she was settled near him.

"Did Major Kelly discuss with you a plan for taking the gold to your home in the bayous?"

"Only a simple one. It was his plan to build

enough swamp barges or borrow johnboats from the fishermen to float the gold through the bayous."

Merrick frowned, his hand flicking impatiently along the berth railing. "These barges, is the wood available there for their construction?"

"There's cypresswood and pine," Adria said hollowly, wondering how she could be sitting here beside Merrick this way and talking to him in business-like tones as though they were complete strangers. It all had a ring of absurdity.

She tossed her head, determined to play out the scene.

"Cypresswood rafts might be too light for the weight of the gold on shallow bayou waters. Pine or birchwood might serve better."

"I am well aware of the laws of physics, Mrs. Kelly," Merrick snapped. "What is required at this point is a reliable map of the bayous themselves."

Adria stifled a smile. He seemed to be taking some cruel delight in calling her *Mrs. Kelly*. The way it was said sounded only a notch above what he had called her on her last visit to his cabin.

"There aren't any maps of the bayous," she said tartly. "The only map makers are the swamp Indians who live there. The waters shift into new channels before the maps can be completed. The only map of the *chenier* I have ever seen was sketched by a Creek Indian. General Alfred sketched his own when he needed one."

"*Chenier*—that's a French word. What does it

mean?" Merrick asked, suddenly interested.

"It's a silt island anchored by the roots of live oaks," Adria replied with a stir of impatience. "China Grove is built on Fausse Chenier, one of the larger, more stable ones."

"Can you guide the men there without a map?"

Adria lifted to her feet. This whole discussion had taken on an air of boredom. Merrick didn't want to talk about what would happen now to them, to their relationship now that Kelly was lost. And that seemed for the moment the only thing she needed to know.

"If that is all the questions, Captain Ryland, to which you presumably already know the answers, I have other things to do to occupy my time," Adria said loftily. "Not everyone requires a map for each place they go."

Slowly, painfully, Merrick straigthened in the berth.

"Apparently, you needed one in Matanzas," he said.

Adria rounded on him, almost forgetting for the moment how defenseless he was. "I would expect you to remember that and to remind me of it. You should have left a map for me at the *casita* so the walk back to Brownsville would have been more scenic."

Merrick was thoughtful for long moments. "Clarence Leitman has convinced me he is capable of taking the gold into the bayous with you as guide. Mr. Barlow will undertake the repairs on the ship until we can get to London and have a new hull refitted. Just lying here I can feel the strain on her list to port. It's a ballast list that even retiming the pumps can't correct. If I could see the slant of the damage—" Merrick shrugged, turned his head toward the porthole.

Adria's heart twisted in her breast. The strain of conflict was written plainly on his face. It was all she could do to keep from touching him, comforting him. She moved quietly towards the door.

"You married Kelly. Why?" Merrick demanded suddenly.

"He loved me," Adria said simply, turning back to him.

"That isn't reason enough," Merrick husked.

"It was, at the time."

"What did he promise you, Adria? A mud soddy somewhere in the outback? A passle of hungry mouths to feed from the rock-hard ground you plowed yourself while Kelly kept promising that things would get better?"

"It wouldn't have been like that," Adria said fiercely, defending Kelly.

"Then how would it have been?" Merrick taunted.

"I never had an opportunity to find that out," Adria said, her hand on the doorknob.

"Wait, Adria," Merrick said softly, relenting. He struggled up on one elbow, his mouth whitened with pain. He reached a hand out to her.

"Come here, close to me, and tell me that it was reason enough," he gritted.

With a lazy obedience Adria walked over to him, letting his fingers close over her hand, if only to prove to herself that she could hold her own ground with him, that she wouldn't crumble with passion when she was near him.

Merrick drew her down to him and kissed her, a hot, insolent kiss that pounded at her defenses until she felt limp against him. He didn't have this power over her, she wouldn't let him have it. Primly, she struggled free from him.

"I am John Kelly's wife. You're forgetting that."

"No, *you're* forgetting it," Merrick said languidly. His fingers smoothed the hair from her face, lingering down across her shoulders to her breast. Adria felt herself being swept into a storm of sensation, wondering why she couldn't stop him, why she couldn't stop herself. He was unfastening the buttons on Kelly's shirt and she was letting him do this to her.

The door to the cabin creaked open and slammed shut. Adria wrenched herself from Merrick and stood up, quickly fastening up the buttons Merrick had freed. She walked calmly to the door and opened it.

Hillary Barlow was shaken. His eyes held a peculiar sadness, but his mouth was set in a pencil line of disapproval.

"The captain needs rest, Mrs. Kelly," he said steadily.

"Yes," Adria nodded, "you're quite right. He does," she said numbly, wondering what would have happened between Merrick and herself if Hillary Barlow hadn't interrupted them. She was very indebted to him at the moment.

A sickly mist hovered over Sabine Lake. Thin

opaline clouds catching at the last ashen rainbow of dusk retreated beyond the ridge of loblolly pines in the distance. Their fragrance owned the air, a drift of home that Adria had almost forgotton.

Clarence Leitman removed his Stetson to her when she came to stand beside him at the deck railing. He twirled the brim over his fingers, standing in silence a long while, respectful of her mood.

"This is still Texas, but it ain't mean land," he said thoughtfully. "Me and Kelly, we rode a lot of mean land together."

Adria pocketed her handkerchief for the hundredth time it seemed that day. She had, for the moment, a firm rein on her emotions.

"It ain't you, ma'am; ain't none of us that Captain Ryland don't holler at. He's just healin'. People do that when they're healin'."

Adria clutched Kelly's overlong field coat about her shoulders, feeling the sudden chill of sundown over the lake.

"He's blind, Mr. Leitman," she murmured. "I don't know how that heals."

"Me and the men, we ain't fancy on words, ma'am, but Kelly handpicked every one of us for this mission. We been talkin' around this here plan about what's best. All is agreed to stay on at China Grove and see you comfortable there, least ways until after the war. It ain't the same as havin' Kelly, we all know that for a truth." he hesitated, watching Adria from the corner of his eye.

"Now that there gentleman from Savannah, Mr. Blanchard, he ain't right in his mind since he come on board. And that spinster woman what he married with, she ain't spent no time in the wilderness. The men can build and do for them, too. Some knows farmin'."

Adria was reaching again in her pocket for the discarded handkerchief. Simple words from a simple man, a gruff kindness that touched her to her soul.

"Thank you, Mr. Leitman," she managed to say.

"The other thing we pondered on was how to talk that mule-headed Englishman out of goin' into the bayous with us. He was firm decided to go, so we planned it over how to do it. That Ditwell feller, he volunteered to care along for him without the captain knowin' he was being looked out for. It's bad for someone like that captain to be coddled after. He's used to givin' orders, so we just let him, only he's goin' to need someone to tell him without him knowin' he's being told since he can't see."

"Merrick can't go there," Adria gasped. "Why, he can't even see to walk, and he's not strong yet. The whole plan is ridiculous!"

"I know it, ma'am. But, like I say, the captain was firm decided. We won't none of us be changin' his mind. You didn't change nothin' with him when you was in there visitin', did you?"

"No," Adria admitted, shaking her head slowly. "But, he never told me about this."

"Kelly and Captain Ryland is some alike," Leitman said, reaching across her thoughts. "It's a special kind of stubbornness there ain't no cure for."

"And who is going to be his 'eyes,' and see for him, tell him what he isn't able to see?" Adria asked limply.

"I was thinkin' you could do that, ma'am, real gentle like," Leitman smiled down at her, cheeking his tobacco quid to the other side until he could spit in private.

CHAPTER 19

The day was softly misted and warm when the rafts, ten of them, eased into the hushed bayou waters. Clogged masses of water hyacinths parted sullenly, their coffeeweed stems tangling around river poles, convulsing into ripples a carpet of emerald duckweed. Teakwood floats attached to the heavy rafts padded between lazy blossoms, creaking a protest at the resistance, the only sound from beneath a ubiquitous swarm of sickly moss that overhung the floating land.

Merrick stood straighter now, though he still favored his left leg. He still flinched at the slightest sound: the stab of river poles, the outraged bird calls, the swag of loud words. How well Adria could read his blindness now from the frown of pain that signaled a crippling headache, the strain of weariness that made him turn around for her. She knew when to approach him, and when to let him fumble about on his own for some object. It was, at times, heartbreaking.

In the beginning, Merrick had refused to use the cane that Clarence Lietman made for him. Leitman had persisted. "I thought all you British fellers carried a cane whether you were needin' one or not," he would say drawlingly, "then again, maybe it was an umbrelly I was thinkin' of."

Adria watched Merrick reach for it, her own eyes so full of tears she couldn't notice the ones in Leitman's weathered eyes.

"I even made one for me, Captain. I figure to poke first with it so as I'll know whether I'm standin' on air or water."

During the time the rafts were being constructed, Hillary Barlow and Leitman had agreed upon a truce. Their rambling arguments had begun to play on everyone's nerves. They argued, they shouted at each other, then went for days without speaking, each complaining in turn to Merrick.

"Hell, capt'n," Leitman growled. "The way he's doin' it, them cypress logs is split too deep. Them rafts is too long anyhows. They'll buckle up in the middle and leak a river."

Barlow was adamant. "I have carefully calculated the weight of the bullion against the shallow depth of the swamp waters. Six rafts equally loaded should displace the weight. The ones used for our gear have been as correctly distributed and should not be in question."

"How come Barlow jus' sits there with a pencil scratching his head when I can tell you the same thing by jus' puttin' my foot on the raft?" Leitman grumbled to Merrick.

"It is the same principle as ballast on a ship," Barlow fumed back.

Merrick had solved the dispute with the use of teakwood cork floats. At this, Leitman groaned in disgust.

"Now tell me, Captain, sir, just where in the hell do we get some cork?"

"From fishermen with fishing nets," Merrick smiled.

It was Joel Ditwell who brought the circuit doctor from Houston, a small, vile man who reeked of tidewater gin. He wore red suspenders over a soiled, moth-chewed undershirt and sported a dust-streaked Homburg over his carrot-colored hair. His name was Ephriam Parmalee. Adria refused to let him examine Merrick, and, over this, she and Hillary Barlow had disagreed.

"He will have some type of medicine for the pain, Mrs. Kelly," Barlow insisted. "Perhaps he can at least examine the captain's eye wound. He will let no one of us tend it."

"But the man is *filthy*!" Adria raged. "Merrick, if he could see him, would never consent to being treated by him."

"Let the captain decide the matter," Barlow had said.

Doc Parmalee, as he preferred to be called, was a coarse, good-natured man, as fond of Merrick's Canadian Scotch as he was his own tidewater gin. He stayed for three days aboard the *Warlock*. During that time, he bathed, shaved, wore one of Merrick's Norfolk shirts, brushed his Homburg to frayed newness, and sternly treated Merrick.

For the first time since the ship had left Port Isabel, Adria heard Merrick laugh. She also heard his outbursts of rage and despair; but the moods, not the words, told her he was responding. Whatever was being discussed, Merrick's raw, vulgar words in the salty language of a sailor were matched by rougher verse from Doc Parmalee. Hillary Barlow had left the cabin once, his face aflame, and even Leitman was subdued after a few visits with Merrick and the backwoods doctor.

Doc Parmalee had sought her out after three days, his revered Homburg held between freckled hands, his manner gruffly respectful when he spoke with her.

"It's time I'm leavin', ma'am," he told her. "The captain and me, we had us a good big drunk, sorta' bared our souls clean. I know it ain't the kind of 'doctoring' that's in the medical books, but sometimes it works better."

He squinted across at her, plopped his Homburg on his head and carefully tilted it to an angle.

"The captain now, he's some kind of doctor himself. He up and left it all one day for the sea. He told me all about that, too. Had to do with some young girl who up and died on him. He's been carryin' that guilt for a long spell."

"Will he be able to see again?" Adria asked impatiently.

"I'm comin' to that. I know you aren't approvin' of me. I can see it in those pretty gold eyes of yourn'. But, one thing, he don't feel cryin' sorry for *hisself* no more. You taken care of that for him. Made him madder than a hornet what you said, but it started him thinkin' again."

"I said some very cruel things," Adria confessed softly.

"It's hard for a man to admit a woman beyond her place, especially for a man like the captain. That took some courage from you. Maybe it even saved him."

"He hates me for it," Adria said.

Doc Parmalee grinned, shook his head. "He may act like he does, but he don't. He just ain't goin' to let you boss him. I seen his kind of condition before with some boys that were wounded down way of Sabine Pass when them Yankees thought to take Texas one day. Wasn't never a day like that one in September, '63. Our boys captured two Union steamers and took three hundred prisoners in one blessed hour. I treated boys on both sides of the flag that day, and I seen this same peculiar sickness. Makes some of them mutes, some deaf, some not seein' when they can. Usually, it don't last."

"But Merrick was shot," Adria argued.

"That he was," Doc Parmalee nodded. "Canister nicked over his eye and scraped some. He's got pin scars above both eyes, but it ain't deep. His hurt come later from fallin' in the water."

Adria shook her head, confused. "We are talking around my question," she said sharply.

"No, we ain't. I'm answerin' it," Doc Parmalee snarled. "I can't see a mind like I can see flesh. Like that Mr. Blanchard feller, for instance. He just up and picked a time somewhere in memory where he can live without hurt. He don't trouble nobody, and he don't suffer anymore. It's a kind of blindness, too. It's the same like a widow woman down at Beaumont what got rattlesnakes under her house. One night they all come up free through cracks in the floor. She hollered for hours but nobody ever come. She wasn't bitten, wasn't hurt nowhere, but she never uttered another sound for the rest of her days. So, I'm sayin', Mrs. Kelly, the captain's mind is likely tricking his eyes. He'll see again, just give him time to sort things out."

"Time," Adria thought later. There was so little of it left before Merrick took the *Warlock* home to London. She watched the crusty doctor leave the ship, still wearing Merrick's shirt, and somehow she hadn't the heart to ask him to return it. What he had told her about Merrick's blindness was the most senseless thing she had ever heard of.

Emerald shadows, flecked with sunlight, hid the wandering patch of sky overhead, deepening the stillness of the bayous where cypress knees rose like embedded spears along the spongy banks. Adria moved closer to Merrick and touched his arm.

"We altered direction a half mile back," he said twitchingly.

"Yes, to the east," Adria said quietly.

"There was a maze of circles. Are you certain we are not making sternway?"

"No, Merrick," Adria smiled, not certain at all of what he meant by 'sternway.' "The post point is Genet Chenier, another two miles beyond.

We've been circling the cypress knees. The rafts are too wide to float between them."

"This *chenier*, is it above water?" Merrick frowned.

"Yes," Adria sighed, suddenly weary of his questions. She looked tiredly at Ditwell who nodded to her.

"It looks to be a good place for camp, sir," he suggested. "We need to recheck the rafts to make sure the weight hasn't shifted."

Merrick swung his head in Ditwell's direction. "Are you finding a swamp pole so much heavier than an oar, Mr. Ditwell?"

Ditwell grinned back at him. "The pole's lighter. It's the ship that's heavier, sir."

The bayou overflowed the southern length of Genet Chenier, encroaching a timeworn stand of loblolly pines and wild black cherry trees. They braved above the water with white leached trunks, like foliage in a carved vase. Weedy scents of swamp azaleas and cherry blossoms mingled with the buttery fragrance of new pine cones. Merrick took a deep breath, his senses keen to the colliding scents. Before any of the others noticed, he knew that the birds sounds had changed from flight trills to a rustling retreat, then to silence.

"It's going to storm," he said suddenly. "Are all of the rafts beached?"

"Leitman is bringing up the last one, sir," Ditwell said. "He swung off course a while back and had to look for the tidemaker we left for him."

"Are the Blanchards with him?" Merrick demanded.

"Aye, sir. Everyone is accounted for."

Adria lifted her eyes to the weighty stillness. The bayou steamed narrow and airless beyond the *chenier*. Bruised clouds were lowering in the fickle sky overhead where only wisps of sunlight were visible.

"I think we should go on, Merrick. The rain will flood the bayous."

"One of the larger tributaries crosses the access to China Grove. It's impassable at high-water tide."

Merrick swung to his feet, steadying his cane beside him.

"This ground," he said, stabbing it with his cane, "will it stay above floodtide?"

"This section back-crosses the silt range. It's at a higher level now than I can ever remember," Adria replied hurriedly. "But bayou storms are savage, Merrick. No one can predict them."

"How far is it to China Grove?"

Adria bit her lip worriedly. "Another twenty or so miles if the channel hasn't shifted. But there's no shelter here and I have seen—"

Leitman grumbled up beside her and dumped a camp pack at Merrick's feet. "I can sure understand why them Confederate brass chose this spot to hide the gold in. A Yankee'd have to be part muskrat to find it." He lifted his nose to the air. "Sure do smell that rain comin', don't you, captain?"

Merrick smiled. "Storms don't frighten sailors, especially one in a creek flow. We'll camp here for the night and wait the storm out. If the water gets above our heads we can always take to the rafts."

The play of arrogance was still there, the practiced logic of his command that reached above objections. Adria looked at the circle of weary faces around her. Leitman bit off a corner of his tobacco and winked at her. Ditwell leaned tiredly on his river pole, then straightened when he saw her watching him. Dickson was mumbling to himself again, shrugging off the coat that Eunice was trying to make him wear. Eunice looked bedraggled, her piggish curls straggling over her ears, her face puffy with exhaustion. The rest of them, volunteers from the *Warlock*, and Kelly's entire command, stood or sat near the rafts, awaiting orders. They all looked different here in the bayous, like a lost brigade, doomed. She was glad for the moment that Merrick couldn't see the despair around him.

The *chenier* was quickly transformed into a makeshift camp. The rafts were heaved onto the ridge in the center and anchored between sack pines. Sail canvas was stretched to length and pegged down to make a canopied tent. Axes sung in the stillness as the men hacked dry wood and stacked it beneath the shelter of the tarps. Eunice took command of the kitchen duties with a dedication that amazed everyone. The social fragrance of brewing coffee brought smiles of relief.

Adria handed a steaming cup to Merrick, her fingers testing with his own for the thick handle. When it was firm in his grasp, she loosened hers.

"It's coffee, not tea," she said unthinkingly,

then bit her words when she saw Merrick's jaw tighten.

"I do know the difference," he said sullenly.

The first vicious gusts of wind brought the odor of swamp broth. Still, the rain delayed. Merrick felt along his coat, buttoning the anchor buttons in fumbling succession while Adria watched him. He was getting more adept at it. She didn't know why it infuriated her so to watch him do something as simple as buttoning his coat. There had been few moments alone with him, such as now, moments when Ditwell or Leitman or one of the other men weren't within a hand's reach of him. Everyone watched him, every moment. He was never alone. They were never alone.

"Where are Eunice and Dickson?" Merrick asked, stretching his long legs over two up-ended crates.

"Dickson is asleep. Eunice is pouring coffee for the men," Adria said moodily.

"They shouldn't have come," Merrick grumbled, lifting the rim of his cup to his mouth.

You shouldn't have come either, Adria thought to herself, watching him dribble coffee over his hand. He should be someplace where he was safe and being cared for by doctors.

"They didn't have any place else to go. Dickson talks about Savannah all the time. He even confuses Eunice with Colly and calls her that. Eunice starts to cry when he does."

"After the war they can go back to Brownsville," Merrick said. "Eunice's family is there. Dickson is lost. It won't matter to him."

Adria swallowed the nagging ache in her throat. She stared at Merrick with hollow eyes, noting the bitter, gaunt lines of his face shadowed in firelight. He seemed to be following the play of flames. Maybe she was just imagining it.

"Can you see the firelight, Merrick?"

Merrick stiffened slowly, turning to the sound of her voice. His fingers fumbled up to his eyes, wandering over them. With a rough jerk, he stripped the bandage off. He stared coldly, unseeingly back at her.

"This is what you had to know, isn't it, how I look behind that bandage? Well, look long and hard at me, then tell me. Do I still have eyes or are there just empty holes there? What expression am I wearing? Love, or hate, maybe defeat? It's all there somewhere beneath the surface."

"Y—You look the same, Merrick," Adria choked, taking his hand and turning the dark palm close to her lips. His fingers tightened, searching over her face.

"You're still wearing those earrings," he husked, cupping her face between his hands. "And Kelly's coat," he murmured, his hands trembling over her shoulders.

"It's all I have. Eunice and I have only what we were wearing the day the Yankees came."

Merrick flinched, remembering. "Since you are in a believing mood there is something I want to tell you. I asked Leitman about what you said. He was with Kelly when they took you from General Cortina's men so I know he's being honest. I sailed for Vera Cruz thinking that you'd be there at the *casita* waiting for me when I got back. I left the *jehus* for you to use with a driver, the Mexican caretaker whom I thought was trustworthy. I had rented the *casita* for a week with all the trappings, servants, plenty of food. I even left money for you in the candle dish by the bed. There was a note there, too, which I suppose you never read. I *was* coming back to you, Adria."

"The *casita* was empty of everything and you were gone," Adria said numbly.

"I know the details. There wasn't much time for explaining that day at Port Isabel. Kelly and Leitman found the Mexican across the border selling the *jehus* and the team. He had your gown and his pockets were full of my money."

"Oh, Merrick, none of this should have happened," Adria moaned, "not the part with Kelly, not with you, not with any of us."

Merrick drew her into his arms. "I didn't know then about the marriage. If I had, I would have kept Kelly with you on the ship at gunpoint, if necessary. There's a chance, a small one, he may still be alive. General Cortina will know. So will others. Kelly had a number of friends—and enemies. When the war ends, I can make inquiries."

"I'm so weary of running from the Yankees. We ran from them in Savannah and they came here where we were. I'm so tired of all the killing and all the grief," Adria cried softly.

"Hush, lass," Merrick soothed, wrapping his blanket over her shoulders. The rain began to fall slowly along the curtain of tarp, dripping, hissing into the fire. Adria fell asleep in his arms and when she whimpered, he clutched her to him and kissed her.

CHAPTER 20

Adria trekked on ahead of the others, needing these few minutes alone to collect herself. She and Merrick hadn't made love last night at the camp, not in the complete sense anyway, there hadn't been privacy enough for it. But the desire, the intention was there, just as it always had been with them, as though the weeks between their first time on the *Warlock* together and last night had never interferred.

What Merrick had said about Kelly being alive had troubled her more than she cared to admit. There was no way of knowing for certain, at least for now. She had already accepted the fact that Kelly was dead. The undoing of all that grief confused her, and worse, it complicated everything now that she and Merrick were together again. She didn't wish Kelly dead, no, not in honesty, she just wished that night on the riverbank with him hadn't happened. She had married him because of it.

China Grove stood in mournful grandeur before her. Roofline met crumbling chimney stones in staggering grace. Galliers sagged over pocked colonettes, splintered and broken like ageing bones. Gilt finials dangled at pathetic angles from warped spindles. The glassless windows yawned at her through a film of swamp mold. Here it was, her home, stumbled in the grimness of time.

She could hear the disappointed murmurs as the men approached. Dickson pushed his way through the knot of men, shuffling after Merrick and tugging at his coat.

"Are we home now, captain? Is this Adria's home? Will General Hardee be greeting us?"

"This was Adria's home," Merrick said patiently, moving instinctively to stand beside her. He took her hand and closed it within his. "It couldn't look the same. You should have known this," he spoke quietly. "I'm going to order the rafts be unloaded. Is there a dry place under the foundation to store the gold?"

Adria pointed beyond a row of hackberry trees. "There's an orchard cellar beneath the jerry-shack over there," she said to Leitman. "The steps leading down are very old, and I remember at times there were snakes down there."

Merrick tensed. "Leitman?"

"I heard, captain. Me and some of the men will take a poke around and see what's habitable for now. If the house ain't, there's some sheds around back what look sturdy for a night or two until we can get the house livable again."

Merrick nodded, tuned to the sounds around him. He could envision the great house, its glory and warmth moldering into neglect. The banjo frogs Adria had described to him, their deep-throated notes like a loose string on a banjo, were sounding their objections at being invaded; a woodpecker's smart assault on a wind-bent tupelo tree competed with the lusty caws of blue herons that circled the bayou, brushing their wings on the surface of the water. It was a strange land, this compromise of land and sea.

"Did you have a well for fresh water?" he asked suddenly.

Adria dragged her gaze from the house and looked toward the slope of Fausse Chenier. "There are some freshwater springs on the far side of the *chenier*. The Creeks, at one time, came and carried the water to their camps. They thought it had healing powers. Uncle Alfred built trestles to carry it over the ridge to the house. There used to be a pump for it in the cook house, but I don't think it would be working now."

"We can fix the pump if the springs are still pure," Merrick said decidedly. "I want you to go with me there and see."

Adria slumped down on an oak stump, remembering from somewhere in her past, to check for termite tracks in the wood. The wood was leached white and brittle. She picked at the loose chips while Merrick paced around her.

"It's a hard walk to the slope, Merrick. Leitman can go," she said half-heartedly.

"Leitman has enough to do. I want to see the springs." He corrected himself then, "You can tell me if they are still there."

A graying sky cast with a peculiar brightness brooded above the slope, a swollen light that hurt Adria's eyes. Even in the stillness there was a foreboding sound, a silence that gasped for some breeze. A single bloated cloud front lay like a darkening sail over the sky with a strangeness that sent a shiver through her.

"What is it, Adria?" Merrick asked, sensing her concern.

"I don't know. The sky looks different."

"It's probably that storm we didn't have last night," Merrick shrugged, scratching his cane over the ground in front of him. The isolated sound in the stillness sent a rasping along her nerves, suddenly infuriating her.

"Do you have to use your cane that way? Like some blind man?" she erupted.

Merrick stood rigid for a moment. He stared past her beyond the thicket of sweet gum trees that enclosed the springs. Slowly then, he started to walk away.

"Oh, Merrick, I'm sorry," Adria gasped, catching him by the arm. "I forget when I shouldn't. It's just all so new to me, seeing you like this."

Merrick's mouth hardened. "I hope to God you won't have time to accustom yourself to it," he gritted out. "As soon as the gold is stored and Barlow makes contact with the investors, my part in this charade is finished. I'm going home, Adria, to London."

"But what about us? I thought—"

"I thought about it, too, all night while I held you. I thought about how our life would be together. I didn't like the way it felt. You just told me you didn't like it either. You're still married to Kelly, whether or not you want to face that. You may be his widow, I don't know. But we are where we are at this moment. We can't change anything for awhile.

"You need someone, Merrick."

"I will find someone, but it will have to be on my terms." He turned away from her toward the height of the slope. "Now, I want you to leave me alone here. When you get back to the house, send Ditwell up the ridge for me."

"You can't stay here alone—"

"I don't need your companionship, Adria. I never needed it," Merrick said feverishly. He brought his cane up between his hands, laid it across his knee and snapped it in two. He tossed the pieces down at his feet.

Adria felt a horrific emptiness tremble through her. She was cold, yet her hands were moist. The air had changed. The sky, which had been a metallic cast, had shifted to livid yellow.

Merrick felt it, too. He lifted his head to the breathless air. He pivoted full about, facing the angry southern sky.

"I'm still here, Merrick," Adria said softly.

"The wind will come and soon," he spoke wonderingly. His boot nudged a tree root, disturbing its anchor. It cracked, quivering in the silence.

Adria took a step towards him, then froze in stride. The words screamed from her lips but no sound came. She could only pray, "Don't move, Merrick, just be still, *be still*!"

Merrick felt the side-slip weight across the top of his boot, heard the scaled rustling that followed it. It coiled to rest between his feet, a careful, fluid gathering poised to strike.

"Wait, be still," Adria was telling him. Seconds pulled by. Sweat was coursing down his face, his chest, trickling to his belly. The salt stung his eyes, filled his mouth with sour bile. He had to move, get the LeMat from its holster and shoot it.

The pressure eased. The hesitant lumpiness protruded over just one of his boots now, lolling in motion as if undecided. Merrick steeled himself, sensing a slow, writhing, advance motion. His legs were stone, numbed. With exquisite dead-still movements he lowered his fingers to his holster. His LeMat wasn't there.

The gunshot was so close he fell to his knees. Brittle pieces of dry rotted bark leaped in the air around him. In a death dance the cottonmouth lunged, stretching its limbless form to recover its severed head. With a majestic shudder, it dropped and was still.

A maelstrom of color exploded behind Merrick's eyes. The sooty taste of gunpowder filled his mouth and nose. The ground marched in muddied whorls before his eyes, molecules of earth like giant beads rioted before him. He dug his fingers in the earth, catching at them to stop them. He swayed to his knees, looking for Adria.

She held his still warm LeMat in her right hand. The trembling began slowly, spreading to her arm, her shoulder, until it consumed her. She wanted to let go of Merrick's pistol, but it stuck fast in her hand. The moment of drawing it from her coat, aiming it, hoping it would fire, played over and over in her brain. She needed to go to Merrick. He was there on his knees, looking so very strangely at her. Her legs wouldn't move.

"When did you take my LeMat?" he husked, his jade-cool eyes taunting over her.

"When we stopped to rest in the orchard," she said woodenly, moments before her legs gave way. Merrick was stumbling on his knees toward her, lifting her against him.

"God, Adria," he heaved, his voice moist. "The things that have happened to me, to us, since we met." He rocked her in his arms, touching his lips over her hair. "No, don't say anything, not yet. Just let me see for a while. Do you know what it's like, the darkness, that void where there is nothing else? You learn to see in other ways. You listen, you touch."

Adria stirred against him. "He told me it would happen like this and I didn't believe him," she murmured, thinking of what Doc Parmalee had told her that day on the *Warlock*.

"What didn't you believe," he rasped, nuzzling the nerve pulse behind her ear. His fingers strayed down across the fastenings on Kelly's field coat with a breath of caress over her breast. Adria leaned away from his hand, watching while he slowly unfastened each one.

"You're as beautiful, as perfect as I remember," he marveled when his mouth fell to one nipple, suckling it hard, shrugging aside her hands, her shocked outcry. Her fingers tangled in his hair, trying to ease his attack.

There was no slowing him. He was devouring her, teasing her, his hands, his mouth reckless, then confident, then savage in turn. She pleaded with him, whimpered, demanded, racing her passion with his own.

He came hard, strong inside her, gripping her within his frenzy. She shattered first, clawing at him while he absorbed the very life from her. He climaxed violently, at the same moment inserting his finger where she was still virgin. She gasped, writhing against a thrust that threatened to split her apart. New spasms were shooting through her, so fast, so many; she gushed again, this time feeling Merrick's scalding mouth take her own.

It seemed a long dark while before she could float back to herself again.

"I never want to close my eyes again," she heard him say, distantly. His wide bronzed back was to her, arms crossed on his knees. He was wearing only his breeches and boots. His hair curled damply along his hairline, tempting her fingers to smooth it.

"You need a haircut, captain," she sighed.

"I always seem to need one," he said, turning to her. He leaned over and kissed her.

"We've got to be getting back, lass. Look at the sky."

Adria looked up at it. The world seemed to have perished. The sky burned golden, streaked with some strange coppery hue. The air that had been silent erupted suddenly in a riot of sound, birds calling all at once, a stampede of swamp creatures seeking shelter. Cat squirrels left the hollows of their sweet gum trees, a family of raccoons fled over the rock nests by the springs. Schools of green trout darted to the safer depths of the pool. Blue geese lifted from the fringes of the slope in disoriented flight. A lone egret paused on tall spindle legs to watch the wing-filled sky, then, sullenly, flapped up to join them.

Merrick reached down for her, drawing her up to her feet. He helped her fasten the buttons on her coat, bent his head down and kissed her soundly.

"I thought you said sailors weren't in awe of storms," she said, recovering her breath.

"I am of this one, now that I can see it."

"It always storms when we make love," she complained, following tiredly along behind him. She stopped then and stared up at the sallow writhing sky overhead. Her footsteps quickened.

The wind came through a stand of sack pines with a vicious whorl that stripped the needles from their branches. The next gust was longer, uprooting foliage close to the ground. The water in the springs frothed over the rocks, sucking at the wind, spilling over to where they stood.

Merrick pulled her close to him, bending into the wind, picking his way through floating, wind-lashed debris.

"We can't go back the way we came," Adria shouted above the shriek of the wind.

Rain salted the ground in a sudden bursting of the tortured sky. Within seconds, their clothes were soaked through to their skin. Adria stumbled into the wind, clutching at Merrick.

"The path is flooded. We'll have to go up to the other side of the slope," she gasped.

"No, there isn't time," Merrick shouted back. "We've got to find cover." He led her toward the water-swollen berm that had been the path to the springs.

The bayou beyond the path became a shapeless dark mass, growing, feeding on the wind. Angry whitecaps hurled over the rim of the berm, swallowing the earth. It was as though the ground was sinking.

"We're going to have to swim it," he told her, stripping out of his shirt and tying a wedge knot with it. He slipped it over Adria's head, tightened it about her waist, and did the same for himself.

"No, leave your shoes on," he grimaced, feeling with his boot along the dissolving edge of the berm. "There're rocks and other things down there we can't see."

He plunged with her into the hurling water, shaking the froth from his eyes when they surfaced. They swam, rising and falling in the brackish water, laboring to stay above the now neck-deep current. Something smashed against Adria's ribs. A searing, gashing pain charged through her. Merrick's arm went about her, lifting her above the water. A wall of darkness swallowed her, crushing out the storm.

Merrick fell once, cushioning Adria in his arms. He crawled up the far side of the berm with her, laid her on the incline, gasping for breath. A land lake blurred across the earth. The wind-snapped row of hackberry trees near the house lay in broken, jagged stumps. These were the trees Adria had described to him. The grand old house was gone.

"Leitman!" Merrick shouted, hearing the name swallowed in a screech of wind. He stared at the wind-strewn debris around him. A clotted mass of dead birds, their bodies tangled, their wings bent double beneath them, was heaped against one stump. A map turtle, its legs stiffened in death, lay overturned at Merrick's feet, bobbing grotesquely in a pool of water. Merrick shouted again for Leitman while he searched out the direction where the house had been.

The wind ended. The calm came suddenly without air, without sound, as though a giant silencing cleaver had fallen across the sky.

Leitman hunched between the row of stumps toward him, swinging a lantern in the near darkness. He broke into a run when he saw Merrick.

"Jesus, God, capt'n." He wept unashamedly, staring at Merrick while Merrick squinted against the harsh lantern light. "We thought for sure you two was lost."

"Something in the water struck Adria," Merrick said, surrendering her to Leitman's arms. "I'll see to her when we get inside. Where are the others?"

"We taken to the cellar when the wind come. It come up so sudden like we didn't have time to come lookin' for you. That Blanchard feller, he lit out runnin' for the bayou, screamin' and swearin' his head off. Took me and Ditwell to get him back to his senses. There've been a lot of peculiar things this day, a lot of them."

Merrick looked past Leitman, past the suddenly naked earth that was floating toward the bayou. China Grove had vanished.

CHAPTER 21

Hillary Barlow arrived at what had been China Grove a few days after the hurricane in a mood of efficiency, accompanied by a Creek Indian who served as guide, and by an imposing man from New Orleans who introduced himself as Cedric Beemis. His amazement at Merrick's recovery was matched by the sight of the massive wooden staircase, suspended in emptiness at the edge of the bayou, where Merrick and Adria sat waiting for him.

"It was a bit of a squall, sir," he said dryly, shaking Merrick's hand. "There was only some surface damage to the ship, nothing, I am pleased to report, of great concern."

Cedric Beemis, his tasteful clothing watermarked and grimed with mud, presented his credentials to Merrick, explaining that he was one of the delegates representing the gold investors, and had come to see to its removal among selected locations in the South until the war ended. He stood patiently by while Merrick examined the dispatches from Richmond.

> *Army of Northern Virginia, strength 30,000, engaged by General Sheridan at Appomattox, Virginia. Confederate General Pickett defeated at Five Forks 1 April. War production center at Selma Foundry in Union hands. President Davis en route from Carolina, from there on west. Expect contact, Cedric Beemis, New Orleans, at Sabine Lake 20 April. Last dispatch to Major Kelly in Brownsville unanswered in code. All precautions.*
>
> *General John B. Gordon CSA*
> *Confederate States Command*
> *April 3, 1865, Richmond, Virginia*

Wordlessly, Merrick refolded the document and handed it back to Cedric Beemis.

"Five Forks was the last rail junction for General Lee's supplies from Montgomery," the man from New Orleans said. "The Yankees have wedged themselves between General Lee and General Joe Johnson. Richmond and Petersburg are doomed."

"It was a long war," Merrick said, shrugging. "This says it's finished, except for the formalities of ending it."

"We Southerners say, Captain Ryland, 'Our armies were not defeated. They were only outnumbered.' "

"I have been, recently, where both extremes were the case," Merrick said, lifting his eyes to Adria. She suffered a smile, wincing at the stitch of pain in her ribs. She moved her hand over along her side and massaged over it.

"I told you not to do that," Merrick said sharply, catching at her hand. "That fracture will never set properly if you keep moving it."

"You have them bandaged so tight it hurts to breathe," Adria pouted back.

"That isn't why they hurt."

Cedric Beemis could only stare at the two of them, incredulous at the way these two were behaving, snipping playfully at each other like lovebirds, wholly disinterested in the grave matters which were being discussed. They seemed as indifferent to the awesome shambles that lay about them. The Englishman was, at the moment, fondling the girl's breast, this girl whom he had understood to be John Kelly's widow.

"There, that should ease it some," Merrick was saying.

"I wish I could take the bandage off," Adria insisted.

"And I said no."

Beemis cleared his throat. "How were you injured, Mrs. Kelly?"

Adria smiled lazily at him and leaned back against Merrick.

"We were swimming down from the slope up there during the storm."

Merrick straightened then, setting her from him. "What has happened in Brownsville? Are the Yankees still there?"

Beemis nodded. "At last report they are garrisoned at Fort Brown. The Rebels that were left there, the ones who did not escape here with you, we presume crossed the Mexican border to safety. We are guessing that there was an informer among them who divulged the plans for the gold shipment. As yet, we do not know his name."

"Have you had any word about Major Kelly?" Merrick asked carefully.

"Only the report from your crew and your First Officer who were the last to see him alive. His final dispatch to us in New Orleans was garbled and uncoded which told us something was afoot. We made all haste to reach Sabine Lake when this was discovered. It is indeed regrettable that Major Kelly is not witness to the success of his mission."

Adria stirred back to the moment. "We haven't much in the way of hospitality to offer you at China Grove now," she said softly. "The kitchen tent is near where the orchard was. You should find some tea ready."

Cedric Beemis tipped his hat to her. He took a step down the rotted staircase, then paused.

"The gold *is* here, safe somewhere, I assume." He smiled.

Merrick motioned to Leitman, waving him over to them.

"Show Mr. Beemis the orchard cellar. It's the only place still intact."

Adria watched Leitman and Cedric Beemis walk away. She sorted through the pieces of Canberra marble that had adorned the fireplace in the parlour, arranging the veined fragments in a wistful design. Dickson had brought them to her, carrying them in his hat, hunting for them at the edge of the bayou the way one hunts for shells on the beach.

"You can't put the pieces of the past back together. They never fit," Merrick said, watching her.

"I don't like Cedric Beemis. He's too pompous," Adria sighed.

"You're too used to generals and diplomats. Beemis is a businessman."

"His mannerisms make this whole nightmare not worth the cost. How much gold was there, Merrick?"

"I never had time to count it." Merrick smiled at her. He leaned back on the steps, watching a white heron flap along the edge of the bayou in search of crawfish.

"Dickson and Eunice are going back to Port Arthur with him. One of Charles Wellman's lumber ships is in port there. They can sail back to Brownsville with it. I offered Lietman a place with my crew, but he said he preferred a horse to ride and land he could see. He's a good man. Kelly's men were all good men." He turned to her then, his jade-dark eyes serious and searching.

"I'm going home to London. Barlow tells me the crew is sea weary and homesick. They signed on for two months in Liverpool. It's been three."

"I see." Adria swallowed. She knew this moment would come, and told herself she would be prepared for it when it did. She couldn't stay here alone at China Grove in a tent by herself. And Merrick hadn't asked her what her plans were, nor had he suggested any alternatives. The decision had just been hanging there for the last few days.

"You can come with me, Adria," he said finally.

Adria threw her arms about his neck, kissing him, loving him for wanting her. She didn't care who was watching, she kept kissing him until he made her stop.

"I've never been a man's mistress before. I don't think I even know what a mistress is, or what she does," she said breathlessly, laughing and crying at the same time.

"You'll be pampered, and naked, and spend all your time in bed," Merrick warned, his eyes wandering over her.

"That sounds *glorious*!" Adria breathed, thinking how long it had been since she had slept in a real bed.

The sea was calm and glittering. Adria watched the lope of waves, then went back to tying the blue velvet ribbon in her hair. The knot was contrary, and her hair a fright. Even the shade of blue ribbon that matched the cornflowers in the calico dress she had bartered for in Port Arthur couldn't improve on her appearance. She looked absolutely homespun.

"Oh, damn!" she swore at the mirror, glancing self-consciously at Merrick's reflection from the side of it. He lifted his head.

"You've been at sea too long in the company of sailors," he said with a censuring look.

"Which, I suppose, makes me unable to tie a decent hair bow," Adria flared back.

"Which makes you forget you are a lady."

"Well, you changed all that," Adria said, taunting him. "Maybe I should wear my hair like Eunice did. Then I wouldn't need ribbons."

Merrick stretched to his feet, feeling suddenly stifled. The charts would have to wait.

"Where are you going, Merrick?" Adria asked sullenly, her eyes following him in the mirror.

"Where I can't smell perfume," he stormed, slamming out of the cabin.

Adria dropped the ribbon. She wanted to cry and couldn't. Nothing she said or did pleased him. Their conversations always ended on an angry note. It wasn't her fault she hadn't any new dresses or any rice powder or nubia cream for her eyelids. She could manage a tint to her cheeks simply by pinching them to color, the same way she could imitate lip rouge by biting at her lips. But there was nothing she could do about her apparel until they reached London.

She strolled over to his desk, rearranging things in the order Merrick usually kept them. The sea sketches she had drawn were shoved beneath a raft of charts. He hadn't liked them, not that he had said he didn't; he just mentioned that he had an artist friend in London and that she needed lessons. They had made love infrequently since the *Warlock* left Port Arthur, much to her surprise. Merrick seemed more aloof and preoccupied these days, almost to the point of ignoring her. It was the way it had been between them when they had first made port in Matanzas and she hated it. Perhaps when they got to London—it wasn't her fault, it wasn't!

Merrick pulled a deep free breath. It had been a mistake to bring Adria with him. He was beginning to feel trapped, the way he always did when an affair lasted too long. He would have to tell her something and soon, make some kind of arrangements for her to go home, back to—where?—for God's sake. She didn't have any family. She had been shuttled between Southern generals' families since she was born. Her father had been one of those 'glory men' with morals only tight enough for respectability among his domain. Adria knew nothing about her mother, only that she had died very young somewhere in the bayou country. She remembered only from the time she had come to live with General Alfred at China Grove. And that hadn't been all that pleasant for her until she went to Richmond with him.

Hillary Barlow handed Merrick his sea glass. "A signal launch off windward, thirty-four degrees. She looks to come from Bermuda. We read a White Ensign with Tudor lions."

"A Queen's emissary?" Merrick said, surprised.

"She is signaling approach permission and requests to board."

"What do you make of her?" Merrick asked him.

"She's British, sir. For whatever reason, it will be bloody good to hear them talk."

Merrick watched the impressive approach of the Royal Navy launch, its officers in crisp white uniforms, already in strident formation for boarding. Merrick lifted a salute, waiting while the stiff-jointed English captain cleared the ladder walk to the *Warlock's* helm deck. He was brushing sea fleck from his spotless uniform, his sharp eyes skimming over the *Warlock's* crew. He saluted Merrick.

"You are two days in advance of my calculations, Captain Ryland," he said jovially. "Your headspeed made us wonder if we could catch you."

"Homeward speed, sir," Merrick smiled, shaking his hand.

"I'm Commander Worthington of the Royal launch, *The Victoria,*" he offered briskly, studying Merrick. Most certainly, this young captain was capable, though perhaps undeserving, of the renown being bestowed on him—a calm intellect braced with reckless impatience, the usual ingredients of heroes.

Merrick was introducing his officers to him.

"My orders are to intercept the *Warlock* and deliver a request to you from Major General Seth Holmes, the Confederate Garrison Commander in St. George. And, with his advance permission, I relate to you that the American Civil War has ended."

Merrick smiled. "Seth is a general now?"

"He is indeed, sir, a most admirable one," Worthington conceded.

"And what was his request?"

"He wishes you to port at St. George for a day or so. He plans some sort of celebration, I believe."

"I intended to port for fuel at Ponta Delgada," Merrick frowned, thinking of the extended time to reach London.

"It's only a few admiralty miles off your course, captain. General Holmes was most insistent that I press you into acceptance."

"Then Seth should have come himself," Merrick said, nodding the helm order to

Barlow.

"Advise our host that the officers from the *Warlock* will be in attendance. And a Mrs. Kelly from Savannah will be accompanying the captain."

"Well, I won't go!" Adria ranted at him when Merrick told her. "You know I haven't anything suitable to wear other than this calico flour-sack."

"Wear your ribbon with it," Merrick said straightly, watching the leap of fury in her topaz eyes.

"How are you going to explain me to your important friends, Captain Ryland?" Adria demanded furiously. "May I introduce Mrs. Kelly? She's a homeless widow, you see. I helped make her so and was so torn with guilt that I asked her to become my mistress. Naturally, out of respect for the crew, we share separate cabins."

Merrick was advancing on her. "Careful, Adria—"

"Please excuse her most inappropriate attire this evening. Calico is *so* in season in the bayou settlements. It is all the poor unfortunate widow owns. She did have one ballgown, a rather lovely dress, which was payment for one very long night."

Merrick caught her roughly to him. "That's enough, Adria."

"Oh, no, I'm just beginning," Adria flaunted back. "He won me with words, not deeds," she said melodically, "this tall brooding captain who quotes a sailor's poetry and sips wine after he makes love to his lass. Then he forgets."

Merrick forced her head back, tilting her mouth close to his.

"Tell me you regret that night at the *casita*. Tell me you came with me because I forced you. Tell me you loved Kelly."

"*I loved him,*" Adria said hotly, seeing her anger reflected in Merrick's smouldering jade eyes. His mouth was close, warm, his breath touching her own. She shouldn't have said that, she shouldn't have said—

Abruptly Merrick released her. He looked at her for a moment with eyes that said nothing beyond anger. He left the cabin without glancing back.

CHAPTER 22

The windows of the shops along Duke of York Street in St. George were all strung with "closed" signs. Merrick pulled Adria along the row of shops with him at a fast walk. He frowned into the darkened shop windows, then paused before a millinery shop. He glanced at the card in his hand and tapped on the door.

"We are closed," a heavy voice behind drawn blinds said.

Merrick knocked again. This time a portly lady scowled around the edge of the blinds and, recognizing Merrick, unlatched the door.

"Oh, dear, Flora will never forgive me for this," the lady fluttered, opening the door. "We both closed early this evening to attend General Holmes' invitation."

"I would hope in time for you ladies to enjoy your nightly sherry together," Merrick smiled, watching her blush. "I need to see Flora, if you will unlock that secret back entrance between your shop and hers."

"She will be overjoyed to see you again, Captain Ryland," the lady twitched, leading the way through towers of colorful unrolled felt to the back of her shop. She gave Adria a quick, measuring look and locked the door after them.

Flora Olmey had already topped off one glass of sherry and was pouring herself another.

"*Merrick*!" she glowed, reaching out both hands to him. While Merrick kissed each hand, she fell to embracing him with a stout, motherly hug. She frowned curiously, then smiled at Adria.

"You're married," she scolded. "And after all the promises you made to me."

"Do I look married?" Merrick asked, tongue in cheek.

"You look—renewed, and somewhat settled," Flora said flatly. She padded over to the wicker table and lifted the bottle of sherry. "Shall we toast to all those long ago promises while you introduce me to your lovely new friend."

Adria wasn't feeling very lovely at the moment. She desperately wanted a bath and some hairpins. She was ravenous for something to eat besides ship's food, and why Merrick had dragged her here to visit some matronly friend of his she couldn't imagine. She wiped her hands on her soiled calico dress and extended one to meet Flora's grasping hand. For some reason, this woman reminded her of Eunice.

"Later perhaps," Merrick was saying. "I need a favor tonight. A very quick one."

"When have you ever come to me, Merrick, when you didn't need a favor?" Flora sighed with a sweeping glance at Adria.

"Mrs. Kelly needs a gown for tonight."

Flora looked politely aghast. She measured Adria with her eyes, seeing the most shocked look on the girl's face, like the announcement had been a complete surprise to her. But then, with Merrick, a woman was never certain of anything.

"You do ask the impossible favor tonight, Merrick. Every gown order I took for this affair was completed over a week ago. I left this spare time for fittings and alterations. All my trims and fabrics are completely exhausted. Lenora and I barely had enough to piece together something for ourselves. I am dearly sorry."

Merrick was charming, and insistent. "I seem to remember a certain trunkful of fabrics that I brought to you through the blockade last time I came to Bermuda. Find something, Flora. It's important to her, and to me."

Flora appeared on the verge of tears. "You do ask such difficult favors," she sniffled, pouring a fresh glass of sherry and downing it. After the long swallow, she faced Merrick and smiled.

"I would be violating a confidence that could be ruinous to my profession, to say nothing of my reputation," she confessed. "I have in mind one gown—no, I simply can't do it."

"What would persuade you?" Merrick said, his jade eyes warm and knowing.

Flora looked appraisingly at Adria. "Mrs. Cleremont is about the same size and height, only not so—endowed there," she said, her hand fanning over her bosom. "The design was pirated away from that insolent Lincolnshire boy, Frederick Worth, who has become so worldly he passes himself off as a Parisian now. He insulted Mrs. Cleremont when she visited his salon in Paris and she brought the pattern sketch to me. The gown is finished, however—"

"It will do fine. Just warn us of where this Mrs. Cleremont will be this evening," Merrick laughed.

"She's in Panama, crossing the isthmus on her way to San Francisco." Flora laughed with him. "This will be costly, Merrick, beyond your promises."

Adria stood dumbfounded, listening to them talk about a gown for her. Merrick had mentioned nothing of this to her until this very moment.

"I—I should bathe first, Miss Olmey," Adria stammered, wandering along behind this woman to a Javanese dressing screen. "It's so impossible to bathe on a ship in a bucket of water."

"I'll call Lenora over to help us while I set the boiler on the stove," Flora crooned. "For now, let's take your measurements and see what miracles are in the stars tonight."

Merrick shucked out of his coat, looping the sleeves over the back of his favorite chair. He had tried to buy it away from Flora but she wouldn't part with the chair, stating that if she weakened, he'd never come to St. George to see her. The sumptuous overstuffed chair sank with his weight when he settled into it and reached at the same time for a bottle of Scotch Flora kept in the cabinet table beside the chair for him. The blinds were drawn against a flaunting tropical sunset, dizzying the room with a pinkish cast. Lazy, slitted patterns of waning light swam between the narrow louvers. He watched them for awhile, hearing Adria's voice, soft and distant and surprisingly happy.

Ever so gently, Flora lifted the glass from Merrick's hand and downed the remainder of his Scotch herself. Her fingers smoothed over the dark wool of his sea coat, testing instinctively for loose buttons. She was near enough to him to notice the faded scars across his forehead. Merrick slept deeply, sprawled in the huge chair, one leg slung over the arm.

Time had a way of crowding these rare visits from him into a smattering of hours, quick, lost hours. She tried to savor every moment of them with him, desperate to make them last. In the three years since his ship had been coming to port at St. George, she kept hoping that she and Merrick could become, she might as well admit it, intimate, despite the vast difference in their ages. She still retained her somewhat svelte figure and could conceal the graying in her hair with a honeyroot ointment. She laughed easily and often, was rich enough to own most of the comforts for respectability, yet she had never reached far enough to entice him to bed with her.

The first time he had come into her shop looking for a special gift for some French Comtesse, whom he laughingly referred to as his employer, she had sold him, from her own Oriental collection, a small enameled hairpin box lined with black pearl coral. She regretted doing so at the time, but his visits thereafter had more than repaid her. He brought her bolts of Pekin point, of Algerine silk with blue threads over gold ones, Levantine folice with Arabasque patterns, and once, a pair of Musquitaire gloves in her favorite shade of burgundy. Merrick had a very instinctive way of knowing what pleased women, and at times she did wonder who his instructress had been. Beyond that, the few kisses of greeting, the lazy dinners for him which she had spent the better part of a day cooking, there had been nothing.

This visit from him was even more frustrating. The young lithesome girl standing patiently on the fitting dias while the hem of Mrs. Cleremont's gown was shortened for her certainly had Merrick's interest for the moment anyway. For anyone other than Merrick she would never have risked such a thing. Perhaps this would be the payment she had been hoping for, a night in his arms.

Merrick stirred awake in his chair. His eyes found Flora and he smiled up at her.

"It will take a lot of silk to repay you for this favor."

The moment was here, and she couldn't seem to capitalize on it. All it would require was some coy suggestion, but what if he refused?

"She's barely more than a child, Merrick. And she tells me she's a widow. For someone like you, she's even younger," Flora said with a shrug.

"Are you saying I'm old?" Merrick said, his eyes flicking warmly over her.

"In experience with women you are ancient," Flora said. "I admit I'm surprised at this new side of you."

Merrick looked curiously at her. "I owe this to Mrs. Kelly," he said, lifting to his feet.

"I probably shouldn't ask you why." Flora blushed suddenly.

"No, you shouldn't, but I'll tell you anyway. Adria hasn't any family, she has no money, and I made her a widow."

"Oh," Flora gasped, turning at the same moment with Merrick as Adria came into the room.

Adria walked regally towards them, her eyes glittered with happiness. The gown of Nakara dawn-satin shimmered with rainbow sequins when Adria moved to the light. A drape of softness joined the jeweled butterfly clasp between her breasts, matching the airy metallic gauze that was threaded through a delicate bracelet loop at Adria's wrist. Adria lifted the silken bracelet to Merrick's gaze and smiled.

Merrick overcame the tightness in his throat and nodded.

"Mrs. Kelly will require a collection of varied essentials suitable for traveling," he said hoarsely. "She tends to remind me constantly of her needs. By sailing time at noonday tomorrow, if you would, Flora."

Woodenly, Flora handed Merrick the matching Carrick cloak of Bishop blue and wobbled forth a smile. She watched Merrick slip the velvet cloak over Adria's smooth shoulders, then move to face her while he slowly fastened the silk Brandenburg on the right side. His hands, Merrick's hands, were always so sensual and strong. How she wished—

"Thank you, Flora," Merrick said fleetingly,

holding the door open for Adria. He brushed a kiss on her cheek, not seeing her any longer. His eyes were following Adria to the Victoria carriage.

Flora closed the door to the shop after them. She watched through the blinds while Merrick handed Adria into the Victoria. Her heart felt leaden in her breast when she turned away, walking dismally through her shop and lowering the lampwicks in the routine loneliness of the night.

In noble moonlight the whitewashed Bermudian rooftops appeared laden with fresh snowfall. Cruciform dwellings with "welcoming arms" stairways were nudged among calabash trees and darkly laquered avenues of towering allspice trees. From the seeded throats of countless Jacobean lilies a gentle fragrance weighted the air. Blooms of every shade—fire-orange poinciana, scarlet hibiscus, blush-pink oleanders, bronze-red acalypha, pigeon berries with feathery lavender blossoms—made unexpected gardens of the coral roads. Adria was enchanted.

The Negro driver of the Victoria, his white uniform offset by a showy flamingo feather in his hatband, crooned a native *gombey* rhythm to the horses, flicking the reins in time to the absent drum. Joel Ditwell and Hillary Barlow sat stiffly facing Adria, and every now and again she noticed that Mr. Barlow's fingers tapped along in some off-rhythm on his knee. He was absorbed in the magic, too.

Merrick had lapsed into one of his brooding

and aloof moods. Efforts to humor him into conversation were fruitless. Finally, Adria fell silent.

The entrance to the Holmes' house on Grape Bay was banked by pink-stone slave walls, topped at intervals by coral pedestals sculpted with longtail birds. Bulging slots near the center of the walls were lighted with festive torches. Frangipani hedges grew wild and untrimmed, adding to the fragrant welcome. The Victoria drew slowly to a halt in the line of carriages.

Seth Holmes was markedly older than when Merrick had seen him last, and walked with a limp Merrick did not remember.

"You arrogant sea dog!" Seth beamed, clasping Merrick's hand. "By God, Merrick, how long has it been?"

"Charleston, I think, two years ago when I was running cotton through the blockade."

"Worthington told you then? God be praised, last week at Appommatox Courthouse, General Lee ended it. A truce between gentlemen, I was told."

Merrick drew Adria to him. "May I present Adria Kelly, Mrs. Kelly, from Savannah."

"Mrs. Kelly," Seth bowed, masking his surprise. "Your gown is quite remarkable, ma'am," he said gallantly with an asking glance at Merrick. "Elise is somewhere about. She left the receiving line for a moment. I'll find her."

Adria felt Merrick tense and looked quickly at him. His expression said nothing.

"I'll find Elise myself later," he shrugged, introducing Hillary Barlow and Joel Ditwell in turn to Seth. Seth presented Adria along the reception line and she found herself swarmed by glossy satin gowns and a brilliant clash of contrasting uniforms, voices that prodded, laughter too shrill, in a sea of swirling, unfamiliar faces. She felt like she was being swallowed, and glanced desperately back down the receiving line for Merrick. He was nowhere in sight.

A room-long table dominated one side of the terrace overlooking Grape Bay, its length spread sumptuously with exotic Bermudian dishes. Uniformed servants passed endless trays of delicacies among the guests, pausing to refill champagne glasses that were rarely emptied beyond the first sip.

Breathless from the exhausting steps of the redow and waltz polka, Adria retreated to the terrace, begging off from the overly attentive young bachelor officers who had suddenly swarmed to her side during the introductions. She had flirted with them to impress Merrick with her glowing popularity, hoping that when he did come back from wherever he was he'd notice. But he hadn't come back for her, and that had been well over an hour ago.

Seth Holmes was flushed with liquor when he found her on the terrace.

"Merrick always did have the most astounding taste in women," he slurred, waving towards her.

Adria leaned out across the marble bannister looking at the moonlit bay. "Have you and Merrick been friends a long while?" she asked routinely.

"A very long while," Seth drawled. "Merrick tells me you sailed with him from Savannah on a mission for General Hardee. That is quite astonishing for someone as young as you, Mrs. Kelly. What I find impossible to believe is that you are Major John Kelly's widow."

Adria turned and smiled at the general. "You knew Kelly?"

"I knew your father, Colonel Sommerfield. He spoke often of one of his officers named John Kelly."

"Oh, I see," Adria said, troubled. "I suppose then that Merrick told you the other part about what happened at Port Isabel."

Seth didn't comment. "How long did you know Major Kelly before you two were married?"

"That's a rather odd question, General Holmes," Adria said with a tinge of indignity.

"Forgive my bad manners, Mrs. Kelly. Would you care to waltz?"

He drew Adria close in his arms without waiting for her refusal. He listed on his heels, fell against her and recovered his steps with a notable stumble.

"You dance with the perfect grace of all the Savannah belles," he was rasping in her ear as he whirled Adria away from the doors of the terrace and back into the ballroom.

Adria caught a quick glimpse of Merrick from over Seth's shoulder. He was standing with Hillary Barlow and a small, darkly beautiful woman whose gown was a startling emerald color, the shade of Merrick's eyes when he was angry. The gown was absurdly simple, and boldly spare across the woman's softly crowded breasts. Her fingers were clutching at Merrick's arm and caressing it. Adria knew without a moment's hesitation that *she* had to be Elise Holmes.

To her horror then, she saw Merrick move toward the doors to the terrace with Mrs. Holmes. They had started to waltz, then separated and walked down the coral steps to the quarry garden.

"I think I'd like very much to see your garden, General Holmes," Adria said quickly.

"They look very much like all gardens," Seth balked, sweeping Adria deeper into the ballroom. "They are much more impressive in the sunlight. But if you wish to see them now I can ask Lieutenant Ames to escort you through them. Our quarry gardens are uniquely Bermudian, I understand." He waltzed another corner with her. "I wonder just where that young lieutenant has wandered off to? If he knew the honor awaiting him he'd be at your side in an instant. I'd be pleased with the honor myself were it not for the duties of a host."

He was purposely stalling, Adria realized, all the while this waltz was ending and another one beginning. He surrendered her much later to one of his eager officers whose name she couldn't even pronounce, knowing then for certain that the general had no intention of allowing her to see the gardens while Merrick was still there with his wife.

Elise led Merrick through the fragrant depths of the garden to a stone bench posed in a niche overgrown with white corallita and trailing jasmine. Merrick sat down and drew Elise into his lap.

"We'll be missed and talked about," she murmured.

"Do you care?" Merrick asked, slipping the edge of her gown off her shoulder, his mouth touching the smoothness there. "You were wanting this the moment I walked through the door."

"It wasn't all that obvious now, was it, except perhaps to you because you know me, Merrick." She caught her breath suddenly when Merrick's mouth tightened over her breast.

"Merrick, you mustn't, not here, certainly not now. There are disbandment speeches and toasts—"

"I hate speeches and I never drink to defeat," Merrick husked, his hands determined as he peeled her gown down past her waist.

"You can't be unfeeling about something as important as this," Elise purred when he took hold of her.

Merrick raised his head. "I am feeling considerably where I am at the present moment."

"Are you this famished that you can't wait for a decent time?" she teased, sobering then when his fingers invaded her.

"I'm very bored with the company of children and frustrated spinsters, which is all I've had access to of late." Merrick smiled.

"You went to see Flora Olmey, didn't you?" Elise accused with a soft laugh. "She let you have Jane Cleremont's 'Worth' gown for that girl you brought here tonight. The gown is absurd on her, Merrick. She should be wearing pinafores and blousettes."

Merrick agreed, but something in the way Elise said it made it rankle. "She has one dress of her own, a cornflower blue calico dress," he said.

Elise lay back against him, working her hands over his on her breasts. "I don't recall that you were ever given to charity before."

"You're sounding very much like a snobbish general's life, Mrs. Holmes."

"Oh, I was just remembering those afternoons in a room at the Red Lion Inn," she sighed, turning to Merrick to kiss him.

"A month of afternoons, when it snowed in London. You'd never seen snow before. You opened the window to catch snowflakes."

"You do remember," Elise pouted. "Then the ice in the Thames melted and you left me, Merrick."

"You were promised to Seth."

"And now I'm married to him," she shrugged. "Seth is away, and often. I've had lovers, Merrick. The first time I felt guilty. After that I was searching. I never found you in any of them."

"What we're doing now to Seth is rotten of both of us," Merrick admitted. "Where did he get the limp I noticed?"

"It wasn't from anything glorious. He fell off of our Andalusian mare one day when he was intoxicated. She stepped on his leg while he was lying there too drunk to get up. He's impotent, did you know that?"

"How in hell would I know something like that?" Merrick spat at her. "Women always say that about the husband they are being unfaithful to. Did you ever think that perhaps it's your fault that he is?"

"That's cruel, Merrick, very cruel of you," Elise mewled. "Now love me quickly and make me remember."

Merrick lifted her down with him on the dark lush grass. With the familiar ease she remembered that was characteristic of Merrick's lovemaking, his mouth brooded over the length of her, touching each warm sensitive place, retreating, assaulting, until she was frantic for him.

He pulsed hard into her, uplifting her to him, working a fine deep path through the maze of sensations that were flooding her until she pitched against him and throbbed forth, bursting on him. When he withdrew she leaned forward and cupped her mouth over him, sapping up the chalky liquid that spewed from him.

"Elise, no," he groaned, shuddering. "Ah, lass,"

"You love me, Merrick. Say that you do."

Merrick jerked free from that wonderous, tormenting mouth. He swayed to his feet and began fastening his uniform, first the seed buttons on his shirt, next the clasp and lacings on his dark breeches, lastly the anchor buttons on his dress coat.

"You always used to kiss me, afterwards," Elise breathed.

"Go to bed like this with Seth," Merrick said coldly, turning on heel and walking back towards the terrace.

CHAPTER 23

Adria struggled out of the Nakara satin ball-gown, swearing at the complicated fastenings that ripped from the gown when she tore at them. She kicked the gown into a heap in the sand at her feet. She walked away from it, glancing back to see the surf rush over it. She trudged back across the sand and bundled the dress up under her arm. It dripped on her as she walked. She stopped and wrung it out.

Perhaps she could sell the gown. But who would buy a water-soaked, clawed to shreds satin gown? She could let it dry in the sun and see if the satin recovered enough to be smoothed. She wasn't thinking sensibly she decided, and set her portmanteaux down in the sand and began sorting through it. She pulled the cornflower blue calico dress from among the remnants of Kelly's cavalry clothes and shook the wrinkles from it. At least this gown was hers, and it wasn't tainted with Merrick's promises. She had bartered for it herself, exchanging a muchly treasured hairbrush and mirror for it. Seeing it, holding it to her, she felt better.

To the east, the sky was milky and silvering. The sea was softly oiled and restive, still hung with darkness. Adria stretched out in the cool, blush-colored sand, feeling the surf mist over her feet. How incredibly beautiful it was here in the Sabbath stillness, this place called Grape Bay. The tide pulsed gently at the nape of the beach, lulling at her anger. From somewhere, she thought she heard a ship's foghorn. There wasn't any fog here. She was imagining the sound.

Merrick had never come back inside after leaving through the terrace doors with Elise Holmes. The general's wife had returned alone, looking high-colored and mussed, her emerald ballgown creased with wrinkles as she was seated at the banquet table beside her husband. She gathered her composure rather quickly, Adria thought, was poised and talkative, her gaze locking once with Adria's hateful one, enough to inform Adria that she was no longer of any competition to her. The look was also understanding of Adria's place in Merrick's affairs, a place as tenuous as her own.

Hillary Barlow, appearing straight and stiff, suffered through some wandering apology for Merrick's absence, accepting the Confederate States of America's commendation for Merrick. Seth Holmes drank progressively throughout the evening, his own speech a slurred jumble of elegant words thin with meaning. The disbandment proclamation dissolving the Confederate garrison at St. George was read by a Lieutenant Ames, who reminded Adria of Kendall Chase, the same feigned mannerisms, the same insincerity. The table-size Confederate flag was lowered and replaced by the Stars and Stripes. No one had applauded. Adria felt slightly sick and excused herself.

Her portmanteaux was under the seat of the carriage where Merrick had shoved it when they left Flora Olmey's shop. She explained to the liveryman that she was staying the night at the Holmes' and would be needing the things inside. When he offered to carry it in for her, she smiled her way through a refusal, hoping he wouldn't follow her or tell anyone that she had come for it.

From where she sat at the edge of the garden close to the beach, she could hear the departing sounds, tables and chairs being cleared away, the grumblings of weary servants, the musicians packing away their instruments. The carriages left in quiet order, their wheels scratching along the smooth coral roads. The house loomed aglow in the stillness; then one by one, the lights were extinguished. She hadn't been missed.

Adria strolled the arm of beach, carrying her shoes and portmanteaux, stopping to rest near the ruffle of surf when she needed to. The water tingled over her feet, cold and invigorating. She walked for hours in trackless moonlight. She still wasn't ready to think about her situation.

Merrick had said she was to be his mistress. It sounded innocent enough at the time, simply because she wasn't sure just what the role of "mistress" meant. Did it commit her to him in the mode of a wife? It obviously committed her, but not him, if Merrick's behavior tonight was any indication of things to come. Perhaps it was just a title of sorts, like the other titles she had suffered—orphan, general's ward, adopted, and more recently, widow. At present, it felt no different. The only difference was that Savannah lay a thousand miles across this moonwashed sea, and she was utterly penniless, a penniless mistress. The thought was grimly amusing.

Wearily then, she made a pillow of the water-sogged ballgown, pulled Kelly's cavalry talma over her and closed her eyes.

Merrick leaned across the saddle and handed his bottle of Scotch to Seth. Seth took a long pull from it, grimaced, and shook his head to clear it.

"You're a son of a bitch, Merrick," he grinned. "How in hell can you be drunker than I am?"

"Nights like last night make me want to stay drunk," Merrick said sullenly, coaxing his horse to a walk in the knee-high surf.

Seth prodded up beside him. "I thought the move here to St. George, the straightness of this place, might cure her. It's very British, you know."

Merrick glanced sideways at him. "It hasn't," he shrugged. "She told me you were impotent."

Seth glared at him a moment, then threw back his head and laughed. "Elise told you *that*? Even for her that's remarkable," he said, amazed. "She still loves you, Merrick, and I still love her enough to forgive her for it. She's terrified of having a baby. She makes very clever excuses for not wanting one."

"If she were my wife I'd rape the hell out of her every night for as long as it took," Merrick said with disgust. "You can't be kind or patient with a woman like Elise. Her sort devours a man."

"Like Cara Breaux," Seth spoke sourly. "How is the Comtesee?"

"She's still the same insatiable bitch she always was. I am hoping that after this run I'll have enough to buy the *Warlock* outright. Every time we agree to a price for it she ups the ante. Once the ship is mine, solely mine, she'll have to find herself another stud."

Seth gave him a tolerant look. "You make it all sound very business-like."

"It is business. She owns the ship I intend to have," Merrick said, reining his horse out near the breakers. He turned in the saddle.

"Remember what I said about Elise." He smiled, extending his hand to Seth.

"I tend to remember everything you say and most of what you do," Seth grinned back. He watched while Merrick charged his horse into the low-rolling breakers, then shouted after him, "You still have our bottle of Scotch!"

Merrick drank the last of it, waved the bottle in the air and tossed it to the sea. Seth turned his horse back toward the beach, kneed it to a gallop, suddenly inflamed with the need to have Elise.

Adria heard the shouting and sat up, thinking for a moment she was back in the hotel room with Kelly, and the shouts were from outside the window, shouts that said the Yankees were on Chica Road. The thudding in her breast slowed when she looked out at the languid sea bathed in rosy hues of daybreak.

Merrick dismounted unsteadily and walked along the sand towards her, leading his horse.

"You can ride back or walk," he said weavingly.

"I'm not going back, not there, not with you, and not to London," Adria announced with a toss of her head.

Merrick let the reins drop. He stalked her, backing her into the curl of surf until it foamed up above her ankles. The rebellious flint in her topaz eyes was dissolving into near panic. He reached for her.

"Don't you touch me!" Adria spat. "You're drunk, and you've been with *her* all night."

"Not all night," Merrick shrugged. "Where are your clothes?"

Adria picked up the sodden ballgown and flung it at him. He caught it with one hand and advanced on her, grappling her to him, carrying her as she struggled and kicked at him. They fell heavily into the crush of surf, tangling and floating against each other.

"You taste like salt and sand," Merrick choked, kissing her roughly, his hands firming over her breasts.

Adria was gasping for air. "Let me go, Merrick."

"No," Merrick teased, rolling over with her in

the swirl. He cupped her face and kissed her again.

Adria felt the fight go out of her. Merrick, him, his mouth, his touch, she hated him, wanted him, all in one delicious torment. There would never be another moment like this one for either of them. It was too perfect, too soon lost.

"Where did you go all night?" she had to ask.

Merrick flung onto his back and let the trill of surf wash over him. "I went to settle accounts."

"With whom?" Adria demanded to know.

Merrick groaned and rose to his knees. "Someone who doesn't ask questions, someone who just lets me get drunk in peace."

"Oh," Adria replied thinly, feeling sweepingly defeated.

Merrick took her hand and shaded his eyes from the sun with it. "I don't think we'll sail today," he yawned.

Flora Olmey opened the upstairs door to her living quarters holding a tea cup and saucer in one hand, a lorgnette in the other. There was a sedate glow in her appearance, her pale blue eyes seemed almost brilliant, her hair curled and plaited among ribbons with daisy centers set in jewels. Her peignoir was immodestly fastened two buttons lower so that the creased fullness of her upper breasts showed. She looked to Adria like an overblown, worn fashion doll. Seeing her this way, Adria knew where Merrick had spent the remainder of last night.

She greeted Adria, but she was only seeing Merrick. The embrace she gave him this morning was far from motherly.

"We're quite wet," Merrick apologized, stripping out of his shirt. "I'll be needing that uniform you keep here for me, and Adria will need the things you have ready for her."

Flora seemed to float through the room. "The bath water is still hot," she breezed, trailing a cloud of green chiffon behind her. She smiled steadily at Merrick. "I know it's Sunday, and you suddenly remembered the Sunday menu."

"I didn't have time to pick any day lilies or sweet peas from your neighbor's garden," Merrick grinned. "As I remember, the last time I raided his flowers he set the hounds on me."

Flora laughed delicately in a way that made Adria bristle. What this blowzy woman, who looked on the verge of drooling out of her peignoir for Merrick's benefit, and Merrick were saying to each other, and the way they were saying it, was excludingly rude. Adria couldn't let herself even imagine Merrick making love to someone this old; she'd be sick if he did.

Flora showed Adria to the powdering alcove where Adria's new dresses and accessories were hung. It was a room larger than a walk-through closet, the walls splashed in mushroom-pink with sashed draperies of amethyst. The dark wicker dressing table in one corner was carefully laid with toiletries.

Adria sorted through the bottles of perfume, unstoppered one and sniffed it. It smelled stale. She could hear Merrick whistling some fiery Scottish tune, the same one she had heard the crew chanting on the *Warlock*; she never had been able to understand the words to it. She knew when Merrick splashed the basin full of water, knew when he paused to shave, and heard him rinse the lather from his face. His words to Flora were too low for eavesdropping.

Adria decided on a pale yellow morning dress with gauzy, puffed organdy sleeves layered over black eyelet. The skirt flared with an apron front, checkered in the same eyelet pattern with a deep hem finished in organdy. The crushed-straw hat, turned upside down, looked like a flower basket. Adria tied the apple-green velvet streamers beneath her chin, fastened her sunstone earrings tightly in place and walked down the hall to the kitchen.

Merrick lifted to his feet and pulled a chair out for her next to him. His jade eyes swept appraisingly over her, and this time the approval was clear.

Flora fawned over him while Merrick devoured two sage omelettes, inch-thick slices of sweet pork and a peach-dish souffle. Flora's biscuits were monstrous and airy, crusted with dole cream. Flora sipped at a solitary cup of tea, her eyes quietly grateful while she watched Merrick. Adria managed a cup of syrupy Swiss chocolate and hoped she could keep it down.

Flora was lingering over the dress boxes, shaking and refolding them a dozen times before she was satisfied that they would arrive without wrinkles in London. The hatboxes required another full hour. Adria strolled through the dress shop, her fingers caressing the varieties of fabrics and trimmings. Bored then with the deliberate wait, she meandered outside to where the Victoria was curbed. She had to decide, and quickly, about a future with Merrick. The prospects, at the moment, appeared hopelessly grim.

It was another hour before Merrick joined her. He looked haggard and brooding.

"I had to thank her," he griped as he settled in the Victoria beside Adria.

"I would have thought you had thanked her enough last night," Adria said tartly.

Merrick took the reins. "I thanked her with British pound notes," he shrugged.

The fury she had been holding at bay began to ferment and finally erupted. "How could you, with *her*?" she stormed at him. "She's stodgy and old enough to be your mother."

"And makes excellent biscuits," Merrick added tersely.

"And horrid hot chocolate," Adria sulked. "It tasted like warm glue." She rode in silence for a few moments, trying to subdue the urge to claw into him.

"I'm surprised you're jealous," Merrick said at length.

"I don't *care* enough to be jealous." She spoke loftily, seeing Merrick turn the horse away from the direction of the docks.

"Where are we going now?" she asked, exasperated.

"To some place I think you'll like," Merrick replied quietly, smiling to himself.

Jeweled water reflected from below the domed roof of a cave aglitter with thousands of diamond-like stalactites, some as slender as flower stems, others with tree trunk thickness. Alabaster tints graduated to pearl-pink and bronzed-yellow hues, lulling to quiet blue then to black where the cave met the sea.

Merrick leaned across a pulpit stalagmite that rose from the mirrored floor of the cave and pointed to a pair of sea horses swimming vertically, their boney armor glowing from yellow to murky violet as they swam toward the sea. Adria took his hand and knelt down to watch them.

"That one is fatter." She smiled up at Merrick.

"That one is the male. He carries the young and gives birth." Seeing Adria's disbelief, he laughed. "It's true. It's the only species I know of that reverses the process."

Merrick led her beyond the cave to a coral sea garden where brain coral grew in massive shapes, and fan coral as delicate as lilac lace spread among sea plumes of mauve and bright rose. Green, blue and red parrot fish darted among the coral, startling aimless schools of silver arrow fish into retreat. Angel fish with rainbow markings haunted through the water in a path of jeweled shimmerings, moving determinedly between waving black sea rods. Adria walked through the fantasy of stone and water with dreamlike steps, her eyes warm with wonder.

"I didn't know any place in the world could be so beautiful," Adria sighed.

"The sea goddesses live here. The pool was filled with their tears for wayward sailors like me," Merrick teased. "It was their magic that made fools of male sea horses."

"Next you'll be saying that these invisible

goddesses eat those beautiful fish down there," Adria smiled.

"I know another place where they serve beautiful Bermudian lobster and chilled champagne," he prompted, taking her arm.

"You couldn't be hungry again after that monstrous breakfast you consumed," Adria said, balking along the path that led out of the garden cave.

Merrick checked his sea watch. "That was almost a day ago. We've been sightseeing in this underground fairyland all afternoon."

With reluctance, Adria followed him through the labyrinthine passages up and out of the cave. The evening air was braced with the taint of rain, and pewter clouds hid the amber disc of moon.

The lobster was served in a crock of hot butter and steamed with *aji*. Though she wasn't particularly fond of lobster, it tasted delicious. The champagne was cooled to perfection in a silver bucket beaded with frost. Merrick had ordered it served in their room at an obscure seventeeth-century inn near Government Hill, overlooking a green where he told her the first colonists had had a burning stake for witches.

"They burned witches for flagrant displays of affection," he remarked, watching her tease the champagne bubbles in her glass.

"The executioner was undoubtedly the man she rejected," Adria said thoughtfully, startled when Merrick laughed.

He undressed her with wonderous hands, touching her only fleetingly as her dress floated to the floor. He drew her down into the sumptuous leather chair with him and draped a bed shawl over her nakedness. They drank from the same glass, sipping between his lazy, searching kisses. His mouth roamed the curve of her throat, down her nape, over the ridge of her shoulder while his fingers slowly freed the pins in her hair.

He inched the shawl from her, his eyes knowing and languid. Still the caress did not come.

"Merrick," Adria pleaded, moving his hand.

"Not until you tell me you want this," he husked.

Adria lay back against him, feeling the sturdy beat of his heart against her cheek. She did want him and he knew it. He was, in some subtle way, asking forgiveness. She raised her mouth and kissed him.

Merrick smoothed wisps of hair from her temple, his lips murmurous over its softness. Gently then, he eased her over him, burying his face in the cleft of her breasts. Her fingers curled in his dark hair, tightening when he nuzzled over the swollen, eager peaks, taking each in turn and suckling it.

She yielded magnificently when he worked into her, moaning ever so slightly at the new raw sensation that brought startled tears to her eyes. Merrick sunk deeper, surging with her while the first clawing tremors raged through her. He cupped her head in the hollow of his shoulder while he churned her over him, savoring each new thrust, prolonging the moment until it mastered him. He groaned into her and burst free, still sorbing the sensations when Adria loosened herself from him.

She slid from him but not before his hands captured her. He laid her across him and forced into her again, soothing, searching. Mindlessly she watched him, beyond decency now, lending herself to his succulent domination. She trembled toward another plateau, and gasped over it.

Merrick was asking her something. She nodded limply in his arms as he carried her to the bed. She slept and wakened in fits of passion, reaching for him, her body new and alive each time Merrick took her. He faded from her and returned, and faded again.

Merrick fumbled tiredly for his sea watch, overturning a full glass of champagne as he did. He sat staring stupidly down at the wandering stain in the pillowcase.

When his eyes could focus in the lavender-hushed darkness of the room, he made his way to the only window and opened it. The clutching fragrance of night lilies sweetened the spring air. Merrick slumped down on the window sill, too punished to stand. The stark, pure, white-washed outline of St. Peter's Church dominated the view below. A vesper bell tolled from somewhere beyond the churchyard, a sound that haunted through him. It was time to forget, again.

PART II

THE RECKONING

CHAPTER 24

A cabriolet waited in the golden afternoon shade of beech trees within sight of the British-Roman ruins of Verulamium. At intervals, the uniformed driver climbed down from the seat and walked to the thick of road where it met the bridge. He cocked his head and listened, then walked back to report.

"I am certain they will pass this way, Comtesse," he said. "Rondelieu always bypasses the chalk scrubs for the scenery of St. Alban's."

"It must look unplanned," Cara Breaux insisted, settling back in the seat. "You did splinter the axle in such a way that it will?"

"I did so, Comtesse. No one but a wheelmaster could tell that it was not the fault of a road stone."

Cara waved him away from the window. She needed her wits about her, she needed to concentrate on a mood of surprise when Merrick told her the news. How, oh, how, could he have *ever* reduced her to this sort of groveling deception? The weeks of impatience, of planning, the long sessions with Her Majesty, the Queen, all for the sake of a paltry decision that was costing her dearly, this small price when she considered the reward. There was no other way to win Merrick's love, as cruel as this method was for the time being. Besides, after his most recent slight, he deserved it.

She could forgive him his infidelities, he had forced her into doing so in the time she had known him. She had her own set of lovers to content her in Merrick's absence. It had become a matter of self-esteem now. She refused to be the brunt of loudly whispered remarks about her one-sided affair with the sea captain in her employ. What was she supposed to do with Comte Louis worsening each day, so heavily sedated now that he failed to recognize her at all? Why didn't he just die and be done with it?

The *Warlock* had docked in the Thames, her crew dismissed three weeks ago and she had yet to see Merrick. He had not answered her notes sent to Aylesmere Quay. Inquiries about him had only infuriated her more. He had spent only a day in London and rented a narrowboat for the trip up the Grand Union Canal to his home in Aylesbury. The man she had sent to Seafarer's Row to locate the ship's officers, Barlow and Ditwell, reported that both men were hopelessly intoxicated and offered nothing to his questions about Merrick's plans. The British Registry office in London related that Captain Ryland had declared his cargo and departed for his home in Buckinghamshire.

And, yes, there was a young woman with him, an American lady.

Perhaps when she saw Merrick again, forgiveness would come easier. She could, in a way, even understand why he had taken a narrowboat up the canal to his home. A carnival boat and the gypsies of the canal were to Merrick some youthful stimulus. A young canal boat captain, already too tall and brutally handsome at sixteen in the magnificent innocence of manhood, his brilliant green eyes alive with adventure as he plied his colliery trade from Manchester to Birmingham to London, all with the tolerant approval of his father, Padish Ryland. Merrick's narrowboat was sold when he entered his studies at Cambridge, yet, he had told her, he never failed to look for it on the Grand Union Canal. Thinking of what he had said made her see the with impatience. It wouldn't be much longer now. She *would* see Merrick this very afternoon. He would, of course, answer a Royal Summons. And, she would, in all probability, forgive him.

"It might help," Merrick grinned, noticing the way Barlow nursed his head against the pitch of the wheels. "Ditwell must feel worse than you do today."

"That is doubtful," Barlow groaned when the coach jolted over a pothole.

Merrick settled back against the seat and closed his eyes. The parting scene with Adria when he left her at Aylesmere Quay was still too vivid. It had shaken him more than he cared to admit and enough to make him almost reconsider and take her to London with him. She had been disappointed when he hurriedly rented a narrowboat without first taking her on a tour of London as he had promised to do. She was sulky and silent just as he had expected her to be. At the end of the first day on the canal, she softened. She laughed easily and asked him countless questions about commonplace things—the towpaths along the edge of the water, the swans that swam in clusters behind the narrowboat, the locks, the other canal boats they passed, the people who waved to them from the canal banks. What was commonplace to him took on a vital freshness with Adria. Since that last afternoon in St. George, Adria had been exerting a subtle dominance over him, something, he reasoned, akin to being married. The hunted, rebellious look he had seen for so long in her topaz eyes was gone. They talked more freely, intimately, about simple experiences, and when the meadow mists darkened over the canal they retreated to each other's arms in the carnival-like trestle bed in the sleeping quarters at the end of the boat.

At times, Adria's immaturity still aggravated the hell out of him. Today had been one of those times.

"I'll be in London for a few days, not more than a week," he had told her.

"I'll have the swans to amuse me," she said acidly.

Merrick paced irritably beside her toward the Sartre-Breaux traveling coach. "I don't know what any of this is about," he said honestly. "Barlow doesn't know either, but I can't disregard the Queen's Summons for an audience."

"Have I asked you to?" Adria said hotly, leaning over to pick a thistle rose which she promptly shredded to bits.

"You don't want for anything here at Aylesmere. Padiah has accepted you into his home, even though he still thinks all Americans are disloyal colonists. You have quarters of your own in the gatehouse, servants to wait on you, horses to ride, a fair collection of dresses to wear. I don't know what in the hell else a woman could want."

"I wanted to go to London," Adria sulked.

Merrick reached for the ornate door handle on the Sartre-Breaux coach. "I told you how it would be when we came here. You can't dominate me, Adria, so quit trying to. This trip to London isn't a social one, it's business."

Adria smoothed her hand over the Sartre-Breaux coat-of-arms on the highly-lacquered door of the coach. She looked evenly at Merrick. "It's for other reasons as well, isn't it, Merrick?"

Merrick leaned down to brush a kiss on her mouth, but she turned her face away. She walked haughtily away from him through the clearing mist looking small and forgotten in a way that wrenched at his belly. Barlow had given him one of his you're-a-bloody-rotten-son-of-a-bitch looks when Merrick settled in the seat opposite him.

He wondered suddenly why he cared that Adria was unhappy. Their life had become almost routine over the last weeks. At dawn they rode the chalky uplands through the

Chilterns, following the staggered length of Roman stones to their origin. Merrick had shown her the windmill near Cotswold bridge where an independent family of black swans paddled silent as a whisper beneath the capstones. The spot had become a lover's place for them: the lush meadow grass, the gentle motion of the windmill breezed from Notus, the south wind he told her. The rich solitude with her, the aloneness, their languid and contented lovemaking—

Merrick sat up with a start. That was what it was. He was becoming domesticated so subtly he hadn't even realized it was happening. The habits, patterns, the expected, this was just the way it could happen to a man if he let it. Thank God for this reprieve that was summoning him to London, whatever the reason for it.

Hillary Barlow stretched upright and yawned. He glanced censuringly at Merrick when Merrick bolted down the remainder of Scotch in his flask.

"We'll be stopping to rest the horses at Verulamium. A walk might do you well, captain. You'll need a clear head when you confront the Queen."

Merrick tossed the empty flask across the seat. "Your Puritan remarks come a little late considering the recent binge you and Ditwell have enjoyed."

Barlow squirmed noticeably. "There was nothing at stake except the inevitable hangover from which I am recovered."

"Are you saying there is something at stake in this matter of the Summons?" Merrick said lazily.

"I am saying, sir, with respect, that it is always advisable to be as sober as possible in the Queen's presence."

Merrick shrugged, quietly annoyed by Barlow's suddenly assertive manner. What the hell did he know about Court? He'd never been closer to Hampton Court than the visitor's wall, and all he had ever seen of royal protocol was the changing of the guard at Buckingham Palace.

The Sartre-Breaux coach slowed at the bridge. Barlow craned his head out of the window and began fastening his coat.

"There's a cabriolet halted on the other side of the bridge," he said. "The driver is walking over here. It looks to be trouble of some sort."

"Where are you going?" Merrick snarled at him.

"To relieve myself, sir, with your permission," Barlow said tightly.

Merrick held the door open with his foot, smiling to himself as Barlow stalked into a clump of beech trees. The drivers of both carriages were exchanging remarks in French. He had begun to listen and translate when one of the uniformed men approached him.

"Captain Ryland," the man questioned.

"I am Merrick Ryland," Merrick said.

"The Comtesse Breaux was en route to Gorhambury House when one of the wheels on her cabriolet failed. With your consent, she would like to accompany you back to London."

"It's her coach," Merrick said offhandedly. "Where is the Comtesse?"

"She's waiting on the other side of the bridge, sir."

Cara extended a perfumed hand to him. "*Comment allez-vous,* Merrick," she said melodiously.

"*Tres bien,* Comtesse," Merrick smiled. "You're a very poor liar and your coachman is a worse one."

"Ah, Merrick, you do forgive me? I was desperate to see you again."

"You're looking very well, Comtesse," Merrick said, assisting her down from the cabriolet. She turned and pirouetted for him, flaunting her kerseymere gown and matching Redingote. "How is the Comte Louis?"

Cara didn't blanch. "He's very close to death. It's only a matter of weeks the physicians say."

"Then why are you here and not with him?"

"Must you ask me that, Merrick, when you already know why? It's been nearly a year since we've been together. I have missed you tremendously."

Merrick bent his head and kissed her. "That is for slighting you on my return. There were reasons."

"One of them was the girl you brought with you, wasn't it?" Cara breathed against his mouth. "I forgive you, Merrick, so much that I won't even ask you about her."

Merrick took her hand and they walked slowly back across the bridge to her coach. "Since you seem to know that gossip, perhaps you can enlighten me as to why the Queen has asked for an audience. Is it something to do with the ship?"

"Oh, Merrick, that's extraordinary!" Cara laughed. "I wasn't even aware of the summons.

She must be planning a knighthood for you, or some delicious honor."

"I hope to God that's all it is," Merrick said heavily, so concerned at the time that he forgot to ask Cara how she had known he would be traveling to London today, or why the Sartre-Breaux coach had been sent to Aylesmere Quay for him.

"Oh, la, what else could it be, *cheri,*" Cara said happily. Her fingers played up the length of his arm to his face and cradled it. "Unless, of course, she intends to chastise you for your wicked respect for women to which I can attest."

Cara snuggled into the seat beside Merrick, ignoring Barlow's glare of disapproval. The Sartre-Breaux coach lumbered onto the stone bridge past the green kilometer sign that announced the remaining miles to London.

Later, in fuzzy recall, Merrick would remember the opulent barrenness of the Receiving Hall at Hampton Court, and the feeling of cold subjection that came over him as he strode its length. Barlow had been right about the need to be sober, and Merrick wasn't feeling entirely sober. Cara had, thoughtfully at the time, produced a wicker full of delicacies including two full flagons of vin Mousseux, his preference. Barlow enjoyed the liver pate and pickled crab served on banket rolls, and even smiled once at Cara's chatty remarks about London's "social velvet." The trip had seemed shorter nursing the wine along with it. It wasn't until the coach stopped and Merrick climbed down that he realized he was mildly drunk.

The Receiving Hall lengthened to a carved walnut chair centered near the floor-length window, its elaborate carvings inset with a porcelain plaque of the Prince Consort. Tudor lions graced with gilt dignified the arms of the chair, the only furnishing made small in comparison by the massive interior of the hall.

Lord Derby gave Merrick a righteous look, one that measured Merrick's height against his own. He held a brief possessively under one arm and had said nothing to Merrick beyond a greeting since Merrick arrived.

Her Majesty, Queen Alexandrina Victoria, regal heir of the House of Coburg and the House of Hanover, moved heavily into the room from a draped curtain, her steps weighted with the grief she still carried. Lord Derby assisted her to her chair. He nodded stiffly to Merrick to step forward.

Merrick kneeled, his head a proper inch from his knee, awaiting acknowledgement. It seemed agonizingly slow in coming. He heard the nervous shuffling of papers in Lord Derby's hand.

"Captain Ryland." The Queen's voice was softly clear.

Merrick lifted his head. Eyes that were quietly sorrowful met his own. Her dark gown trimmed with Royal Stuart Tartan seemed to swallow her. A miniature crown, no larger than a ripe orange, was placed over severely parted hair caught forward in braided loops around her ears. On each finger of her hands she wore a different gem, with her favorite, an enormous blood-red ruby, on her right thumb. She strained forward and took the papers from Lord Derby.

"You are quite young for a sea captain of such prominence," she said, glancing at Merrick.

The room was weaving slightly so Merrick reinforced his stance. Her remark sounded like a reprimand.

She smiled at him without mirth. "Confederate envoys brought me a missive from President Jefferson Davis. A report of your accomplishments and those of your ship was included in its contents."

Merrick's mouth felt dry, his eyes grainy, and the leaden thudding in his belly threatened to crumple him. Whatever it was that was coming was taking a damned long time.

Her Majesty, the Queen was reading over another paper. She folded it and handed it back to Lord Derby.

"This one," he said kindly, handing her another page.

"A British-built ship, launched at Prestwick and brought to Liverpool for engine installation, designed in part with some of your own modifications," she paused in reading and glanced over the top of the page at Merrick.

"Your reports read correctly," Merrick husked finally.

"Your encounters with Northern vessels and your successful blockade feats have earned commendable plaudit from all Southern sympathizers, Captain Ryland. However, the American Civil War has ended, as you know. The disobedience in question here is the exploition of the English flag and our politically neutral government during acts of outright aggression. England was not at war with the Union States, captain. It has only been through careful pacification that we were able to disprove our responsibility for your reckless behavior."

Merrick swallowed dryly. "I captained a British ship and delivered cargo with every intention of remaining neutral," he said strongly. "In some cases, I wasn't given a choice as to the circumstances of encounter."

"Is it true, Captain Ryland, that you undertook a mission for the Confederacy during the last weeks of the war to transport Southern gold to its point of destination?"

"I was forced to do so, Your Majesty. It was the only reasonable way to prevent the destruction of my ship by the Yankees."

"And you can, undoubtedly, prove this," the Queen said sternly.

"I will prove it," Merrick replied.

Her eyes lighted with vague enthusiasm. She seemed to hesitate over a decision. She looked to Lord Derby for support and gained it.

"Private registry of your ship, the *Warlock*, has been relinquished to the Crown at my request by the Comtesse Sartre-Breaux. It is my intention to make an exhibit of it, something in the nature of educational value as well as an appeal to the adventuresome spirit. Plans have been approved for a permanent anchorage for it in the Thames for public viewing."

"The *Warlock* is years away from retirement," Merrick said harshly. "It would be an injustice to maritime achievements to make a museum of it at this point in time."

The Queen's mouth bracketed grimly. "There is no point of argument, Captain Ryland. Parliament has voted the funding and the Transfer of Registry has been completed. This conference was a mere courtesy to the Comtesse Breaux and to your seamanship, however questionable your sentiments are at the moment. It occurs to me that you speak more for yourself than for your ship when you refer to a vital future."

"This is only a small distinction between a ship and her captain," Merrick insisted. "I know her capabilities, what could be an honorable future for such a ship."

"Your sentiments are very admirable, captain. But, I must remind you that the captain of any ship is expendable. Hopefully, I trust in time you will agree to the wisdom of this decision for your 'glory ship' as I believe it was once referred to."

Merrick bowed stiffly to Lord Derby when he went to Her Majesty, the Queen to assist her from her chair and into a side room. The room seemed to shrink around him and his hard breaths echoed in the vastness of the room. It was over and done. A creeping numbness swept through him, making him think for a moment that he'd have to crawl the length of the hall to the doors. He held on until the weakness passed, then turned on heel, hoping his long strides would carry him through the tall doors.

Hillary Barlow was walking towards him with a peculiar smile that deadened in stride. The Sartre-Breaux coach was a weeping blur somewhere in the aimless direction Merrick's feet were taking him. He felt Barlow's arm around him.

"They took my captaincy away from me. They took the ship," Merrick choked out.

"Courage, Merrick," Barlow said, steering him towards the coach. "There will be other ships."

No, Merrick wanted to scream, thinking dazedly that it was the first and only time Barlow had ever called him by his given name.

CHAPTER 25

Adria dusted the last of the wheat chaff from her hands, letting the particles scatter down in the stream below. The swans nosed after it, their shoe-button eyes alert with purpose. She called each swan by name now, and Hugo, the smallest one, a darkish speckled outcast, was tame enough to nibble seeds from her fingers. She shook out the pockets of her apron and found Eunice Blanchard's letter. She'd read it later, when she was in a better frame of mind, she decided.

Merrick had been away from Aylesmere Quay almost two weeks now. In the interim, his artist friend, Emory Marsh, had arrived in a flurry of canvases, palettes, empty luggage and volatile temperment which, in the space of an hour, sent the majority of servants flying to Padiah with complaints. He donned an outlandish African smock and demanded to see Adria's sketches. He scrutinized each one and turned pained eyes to her.

"Dear lady," he sighed sadly, "I do forget what Merrick calls you, Miss—?"

"Most probably he calls me his mistress," Adria said bitingly.

Emory Marsh flung back his head and laughed. When he met her steady amber eyes a second time, it was with new respect.

"The name was Kelly, I believe Merrick told me." He smiled in apology.

"Kelly was, is, my husband's name. My name is Adria."

"Egad, are you married?" Emory chortled.

"I am in all likelihood a widow, Mr. Marsh," Adria said coolly.

"Is that by interpretation or fact, my dear?"

Adria started to walk away from him. He dropped the paintbox he was holding under one arm, fell to his knees and grasped the hem of her dress in both hands. He clutched it beneath his chin and made a clownish gesture of dabbing at his tears with it.

"I beg your humble forgiveness, my cherished child. Show a mite of compassion to this lonely, destitute artist who cringes in your talented presence. Say that you do."

In spite of herself, Adria smiled. "How is Merrick?"

Emory groaned to his feet and squawked back at the cluster of insulted swans that had gathered around them. He buckled with laughter, reached for Adria's hand and kissed it.

"Merrick was as boorish as always. He's vague about this and that. He was dreadfully intoxicated when I met him in Godstow. The Queen's summons was about some difficulty with the registry papers of Merrick's ship. He's seeking some legal intervention in the meantime."

"Did he say when he'd be returning home?" Adria said softly.

"Home to Merrick is that ugly iron hulk of his which is home, hearth, wife and kin to him," Emory shrugged. "Merrick mentioned that you possessed a fair talent, and I, being in dire need of money and country air, agreed to instruct you, until what time your seafaring nobleman decides to return. You will find my passion as unforgiving, my temperament as vile as Merrick's. I drink outrageously and my lovemaking is positively barbaric."

Adria could almost believe him. "I think, Mr. Marsh, that you are more the actor than the artist."

"Ah, such words that wound and devastate one," Emory moaned. "I feel at the moment the most devilish need to make love to you. How much longer must we dally at pretense?"

"Until you teach me to paint as the masters," Adria smiled.

Emory slapped his forehead in agony. "So long? I shall be hopelessly withered by then."

It was impossible to judge Emory's age. Boyishly slender and nearly as tall as Merrick with a shock of undisciplined hair that was routinely in his eyes, he would gnaw at the end of his sable brush while he scolded his canvas. He was endearing or sullen, mischievous or depressed. In one fit of anger, he seized his palette and flung it at the unfinished canvas. With wild strokes he blended the oils, laying one final brush stroke over the length of frame. He bowed to his creation and stalked off and was repentant for days afterwards.

Over dinner with Padiah in the formal dining room, Emory emerged a marked gentleman. He was wordy and clever, attentive to Adria. He even won an indulgent smile from Padiah Ryland when he entertained them with stories about his and Merrick's days together at Cambridge.

"Merrick studied the medical arts and I studied British law. Then, Merrick went to sea, and I went to my canvas. I painted seascapes and Merrick learned French during his long sea voyages, which shows the point of dedication in our lives. The Tarot cards proved of great value in our decisions."

Emory Marsh was the most entertainingly complex man Adria had ever met. Their lesson sessions were a different matter. His brutal criticism of her subject brought on frustrated tears.

"For God's sake!" he raved. "Brighten your style with something more infusive. Warships are damnably grim. Why don't you sketch fruit in yellow bowls, or a tree on a mountaintop?"

"You said to sketch something I knew," Adria said stiffly. "I know how to sketch ships like the *Warlock*."

"You know how to draw the inside of Merrick's cabin. You do not know how to draw a sailing ship in motion, dear lady."

Adria placed her brush in the palette tray and began cleaning her hands with a flannel cloth. She arranged her maulstick at the edge of the canvas, cleaned her spatula, sorted her pastel chalks in the order he had taught her, trying to hold her poise before him. She brushed at her cheek with the back of her hand and closed her paintbox.

Emory coaxed the paint cloth from her fingers. With gentle strokes, he dabbed at a paint smudge on her cheek, then kissed her softly on the mouth. Adria trembled into his arms and let him hold her.

"You are a kitten, Adria, among heartless wolves," he murmured, "and I am a colossal bastard for hurting you. This whole idea of Merrick's was rotten; for me to come here and amuse you while Merrick, well, whatever it is he needs to do, was cruel. I needed the money and I needed to escape the amorous clutches of some ignominious hag who wanted to develop my artistic 'potential.' When I met him that afternoon in Godstow and he suggested it, it seemed a reasonable exchange of favors. As to my genius, I have little. I paint a fair likeness and call it a portrait, but it is rarely an honest one. Merrick is a profoundly better sea captain than I am an artist. He and I have shared most of the things in our lives, our dwindling fortunes, our women, our drunken bouts. I think I expected it to always remain that way. I don't know why Merrick brought you here to his home. Whatever the reasons were for it, they were wrong."

"So all of this, the lessons, everything, was just pretense," Adria said.

"Your talent is average like all pupils. Desire separates that talent from genius. My own desire was never overhwelming enough. There were too many distractions. Perhaps yours will be."

Adria loosened herself from his arms. She reached down for her paintbox and handed it to him. "I believe our lessons are completed, Mr. Marsh. I truly hope you will be able to find some other way to pass the time until you return to London."

"I am thinking of one right now," Emory grinned.

"I was not part of the exchange of favors between friends," Adria said evenly. She left him standing in the shadow of his tall canvases, staring after her.

Adria strolled along the stone quay, almost regretting the scene with Emory that had isolated her from his company. He was spending more time in the greenhouse loft with Padiah, and he was painting with a solitary dedication during the morning hours. He kept a neutral distance from her in passing. They still shared the dinner meal together with Padiah in the awesome dinner room, but the undercurrent of discontent, the restlessness was still there for both of them. Adria still rode through the Chiltern hills at dawn to the place where she and Merrick had made love countless times. The windmill soughed in the ever gentle breeze, the family of black swans had migrated downstream, the cushion of grass was straggly and overgrown in the midsummer heat. After a few more times, Adria couldn't bring herself to go there any more.

Still puzzling over her feelings for Emory,

Adria took Eunice's letter from her apron pocket. The letter was crumpled and water-soaked, the postdate unreadable. There had been other letters, she remembered, several ones written on fragranced vellum from a Comtesse Louis-Breaux in London, and one that Merrick had opened before he left, the one from Elise Holmes in St. George telling him that she and General Holmes were expecting their first child at Christmas time. There had been no reply to the one Adria had written to Thressa Hardee at a Charleston address.

Adria opened the fragile envelope and began to scan Eunice's dutifully chosen words.

By now, my dear, I am certain that Captain Ryland's inquiries have been answered in part so the shock of my news to you will be greatly lessened—

Adria swallowed her breath, knowing almost before she read,

Major Kelly visited us on Sunday last. He is thinner, as one would expect from his long imprisonment at the Yankee garrison at Fort Brown. Otherwise, he appears quite well. He was surprised and concerned for news of your whereabouts. I pray I did the proper thing in relating to him the events following his capture at Port Isabel. He seems to have some difficulty in the use of his right arm.

Dickson remains the same as when you last saw him. He is unable to—

Adria calmly folded the letter and snugged it

back inside her pocket. She took a step, then another, determined to clear the distance back to the gatehouse before her legs caved. She staggered once against the slick and mossy jetty-wall and caught herself in time. She sat down numbly and reached again for Eunice's letter. This time it floated from her hand, leaving her to spin in a grasping dark void where Eunice's words melted into oblivion.

Emory Marsh was bathing her face with a cool cloth, crooning over her, his slender hands busily unfastening her corselette stays. Dreamily, Adria remembered the first time she and Merrick had met on a dark stairwell, and he had done the same for her.

"Merrick," she breathed, lost for a moment.

"I wish to God at this moment, I was," Emory croaked, prodding her upright against his knee and reaching for the brandy toddy that Padiah handed over his shoulder. "Take a tiny sip, Adria," he coaxed, waving aside one of the servants. "Get away from me with those damn smelling salts before I puke," he snarled.

Adria blinked up at the swirl of trees above her, beech trees stirred in afternoon sunlight. Thatch birds scolded raucously through the branches, a chattering that brought her slowly back to her senses.

"I never faint," she said lamely.

"Women always say that." Emory smiled at her. "You picked a devilish place for a swoon. Another foot and we'd have had to get the fishing nets to find you."

"The letter from Eunice said—"

"I know. I read it," Emory shrugged. "It does

rather complicate the lives of three people, doesn't it?"

"I must tell Merrick. I must go to London and tell him. We thought— I thought— we were so sure—"

With concern, Padiah Ryland leaned over her and patted her hand. "Merrick will be told soon enough. Tomorrow will be soon enough when you are feeling stronger."

How strange this man, Merrick's father was, so aloof and reserved and oftentimes so stern. He had treated her as he would any guest that Merrick brought to Aylesmere Quay, until this moment when he seemed suddenly aware of her relationship with Merrick.

Emory became abruptly possessive. "I will go to London and bring Merrick here. Adria need not go."

"I want to go," Adria sobbed suddenly, clutching at Emory's arm. "I wanted to go with him when he left, but he wouldn't let me. Something has happened, I know it has, otherwise he would have come back before now. He'll know what to do. We can talk to Kelly and explain together—"

"Hush now," Emory said gently, lifting Adria in his arms. "We'll find Merrick," he told her, wondering where in the devil to start looking in a city the size of London for a disillusioned sea captain who didn't want to be found. Damn Merrick anyway, he seethed, raging with envy against his friend, and against a man named John Kelly whom he had never even met.

Cara Breaux stepped from her perfumed bath

into the velvety towel that Merrick held ready for her. She frowned sharply at him, hesitant to mention again his slovenly appearance.

"Will you wish to bathe?" she asked prettily, snugging into his arms.

"No," Merrick said, dropping his arms.

"Rene comes today to trim Louis' hair. He can do yours, *mon amour*."

"I don't want that greasy fag touching me," Merrick snarled. "He should be strung up by the balls for taking money to cut one of the two hairs that Louis has managed to grow since the last time he was here."

"Don't be so vile, darling. You know I detest that seaman's talk. Why must you be so difficult, like a schoolboy? You say no to this, and no to that. Your appearance is a disgrace. You care nothing for the way you look. I think you care for nothing except the—"

"The bottle," Merrick finished for her. He reached for a fresh bottle of Scotch and tossed it familiarly in his big palm, flaunting it at her. "When I am drunk, dear Comtesse, I don't feel anything. I don't think anything. And I don't remember."

Cara retreated a step. "Must you forever torture yourself over what is past and done with? There will be other commands, other ships in time. I told you that everything possible is being done to hurry the process."

"I want to know why it was done in the first place."

"You ask the impossible, Merrick. I've told you over and over again that the Queen sometimes has queer ideas about some inconsequential things that mature into decisions of some sort or another. It's a trait of royalty,"

"There is only one ship in the world like the *Warlock*. She knows that."

Cara saw the change in Merrick's eyes when he spoke of his ship, the change from dullness to fierce passion. If he ever should learn of her part in this—she shuddered to think what he would do to her. But he wouldn't know of it. She had been very thorough.

"Don't be glum on such a magnificent summer morning," Cara soothed, touching her fingers over his chest. "We'll breakfast in the orangerie. It always cheers you there." She tied a mandarin dressing coat of apricot silk about her, leaving one full sleeve to fall loosely from her powdered shoulder. She handed Merrick the pot of rouge and bared one breast for him.

"Rouge the nipple for me, *cheri*. I know it's wicked, and only accomplished harlots still resort to this, but I adore the way it makes me feel when you do it."

Merrick obliged her in much the same way he would put salve on a wound. He finished and tucked the bottle of Scotch under his arm.

"Shouldn't you dress before we go downstairs?"

"I never dress before ten, don't you remember? And I won't dress at all today with you here."

Emory Marsh tapped on the glass of the Clarence and instructed the driver to stop at 17 Cheyne Walk. He peaked his tall hat at a jaunty angle, straightened his Harris traveling coat, sprung his silver watchcase open and studied the time. The Comtesse Sartre-Breaux never received callers before ten o'clock of any morning, one of the rules of royalty that allowed her collection of lovers to leave discreetly before the Comte was wheeled downstairs from his third storey apartments. Her habits were particularly well known among members of the social velvet in London. And her insatiable habits of making love and her possessiveness of Merrick were tired jokes even among newcomers. Her address was the last place left for him to inquire about Merrick.

The first place he had searched was the docks. Merrick's ship, the *Warlock*, was webbed over with mooring lines and deserted except for a handful of workmen who were erecting deck benches, some kind of toll booth, and a hideous looking latticed arch strung with lanterns. All this folderol looked grossly out of character on a trim warship, he thought with disgust, except, of course, if Merrick was planning some as yet undiscussed celebration with the ship for a stage. Yet, it didn't have Merrick's stamp of command about it. It was another question that needed answering.

At the Seafarer's he was told that Hillary Barlow had left for Surrey to visit his sister's family. Joel Ditwell had stayed on for another week and disappeared without leaving word-of-address; at Merrick's temporary lodgings in Godstow on Trout Row, the report was the same. The owner showed Emory to Merrick's room, waited while Emory checked Merrick's forlorn possessions—thumb-worn medical books, a pewter shaving mug, an unopened box of silk handkerchiefs from a haberdashery on Bond Street, and a muchly abused riding coat with empty pockets. Emory stood for a moment at the crofter's window overlooking Port Meadow and tried to reason where Merrick would have gone.

"Did he say anything to you about his plans?" he asked the owner of the inn.

"I don't as a rule ask paying tenants their plans," the man grumbled back. "Captain Ryland pays whether he uses the room or not."

Emory frowned at the time again. An hour to wait. There was nothing to be gained sitting here in front of the Sartre-Breaux mansion. Perhaps when he explained his errand. . .

He glanced worriedly at Adria, hesitant to awaken her. She had slipped into a deep sleep snugged into a corner against him when they crossed Bishop's Gate Road. She looked vastly weary, with dark crescents beneath her thickly fringed lashes that alarmed him almost as much as her paleness. She had eaten nothing since that afternoon when he found her on the quay, and what she had tried to eat she had retched up.

He should have come right out with it and asked her if she was carrying Merrick's child. It would have been indelicate of him, but, drat it all, and confound Merrick, anyway. He wasn't about to play nursemaid to one of Merrick's mistresses. How in the name of hell had he ever let himself become entangled in such a mess anyhow? And worse, he himself had nearly succumbed to this child-like one. Those nights at

Aylesmere with a husk of moon over the mirrored quay, when he knew she was as needing as he was, had almost made a rapist out of him. This innocent one, of all Merrick's parade of women over the years, could gut a man without even trying.

He reached over and gently shook Adria awake. "I want you to wait here while I go dicker with the servants for an announcement," he said gruffly. "It may take some doing."

Adria nodded sleepily. "Is this where Comtesse Breaux lives?"

"She's an elusive bitch, and a very wealthy one," Emory muttered.

"Do you know her well?" Adria yawned.

"Well enough to have painted her portrait and warmed her bed on several distasteful occasions," Emory admitted sourly.

"And was your portrait of her an 'honest' one?" Adria smiled, remembering what Emory had told her during one of their stormy lessons at Aylesmere.

"Dear lady, I painted her as she wished to be done, in the same deceptive mien as all the other Sartre-Breaux ancestors before her were portrayed."

Adria fretted as an hour crept past. Her legs were numb from sitting, and the air inside the Clarence became more stiffling as the morning lengthened. The driver strolled down the block of elegant homes and paced back again. The horse fidgeted in his leather, dropped slickish manure, stamped at the sudden swarm of blue flies. The city air steamed with soot and fish smells. Adria swallowed down a rise of nausea.

What could be keeping Emory? This wasn't like him at all. She leaned over the glass partition and called to the driver.

"Would you please step to the door and inquire as to Mr. Marsh's delay?"

He cocked his hat back on his head and nodded. "I'll hav' 'ter go 'round to the proper entrance, 'mum," he said, thumbing in the direction of a sheltered side gate. " 'Ere kind is a mite particular about who be usin' the front way."

"Very good, and please hurry. I'm feeling unwell." Adria almost pleaded.

Adria watched the man close the gate and disappear beneath the arched thickness of cultured shrubbery. She should have waited at Merrick's lodgings in Godstow as Emory suggested. Why must everything take so long when time was so urgent? If she could just *see* Merrick and tell him about Kelly.

After more irritable minutes of waiting, Adria climbed down from the carriage and made her own way towards the servant's gate. A breath of coolness greeted her in the perfumed shade, and from somewhere beyond the maze of formal garden with its countless yew trees and topiary design that resembled a complete set of chessmen, she could hear the whispery ripple of fountains. The vine-covered walls of Flemish brick were guarded on all sides by lofty ironwork that made the mansion appear almost sinister.

Adria found her way among flagstone paths bulging on each side with riotous-blooming flowers. She loosened the satin ties on her

Angouleme hat and removed it. She sat down on the marble lip of the fountain, cupped her hand and drank, splashed the coolness over her face and arms and dabbed them dry with her handkerchief.

Near the fountain a small table with settings for two was arranged with miniature urns of fresh garden flowers. The water goblets were chilled and full alongside a Dutch sailor's stein with an anchor engraving over an elaborate "M." For "Monsieur," she thought cleverly, glancing toward the tall French doors of the house. One of the doors was angled slightly ajar as though someone had forgotten to close it. It looked strangely lush and tropical inside from what she could tell, a faint scent of clove and orange blossoms floated through the doors and out across the terrace. Emory must be inside somewhere.

The tart fragrance grew heavier as Adria approached the doors. She wasn't actually intruding, she just hadn't been invited inside, she told herself. When she explained who she was and her reasons for calling on the Comtesse Breaux. . .

The purplish shade and overpowering foliage inside the doorway startled her for a moment. The room was humid and airless, the scent of oranges so overwhelming she left the door open. The space was sparsely furnished with tiers of blossoming oriental ming trees. Life-sized sculptures of the muses, Adonis and others Adria didn't recognize, formed an arcade down to a solitary Roman couch where two figures were entangled in a suggestive embrace.

A play of light roamed over their nakedness, producing a bizzare, mottled illusion, erotic and suddenly alive. Adria stood still, watching. The figures moved in desperate motion with bodies laboring to conquer lust; thrusting, heaving, the woman groaning with pleasure, the man was doing to this creature the same thing, the same way, that Merrick had done to her.

"Ah, Merrick, *cheri*, my love, again—*now*!" she sighed.

Adria watched until it was ended.

Emory Marsh, infuriated by the long, useless wait for the Comtesse, whom, he was told at length, was in residence at her home in Somerset, found the carriage deserted, the driver nowhere in sight. He demanded to see the Comte Louis Breaux who turned glazed, drugged eyes to him when Emory explained his errand and Adria's disappearance. The servants were questioned in turn, and each one provided carefully rehearsed replies.

No one had seen a Mrs. Kelly. No, there had been no message left for him. Perhaps the driver of the Clarence had wandered across to Bridly Square to the pub there after delivering Mrs. Kelly elsewhere. Of course they would notify the constable if he so desired.

Emory paced the length of Cheyne Walk, stopping at each residence to inquire for Adria. At one, a Madame Wallington told him she thought she had seen a young girl wearing a white dress running to halt the omnibus at King's Road. But she couldn't be certain, her eyesight was failing these days and. . .

A mist from the Thames clouded over rooftops shadowed in twilight. The deep, mournful sound of fog horns along Battersea Park droned their warnings. Emory stopped and sat down on the curbing, staring at mist-washed leaves fluttered to a pile at his feet. Adria wouldn't have returned to Aylesmere Quay. She was unhappy there without Merrick. She wouldn't have gone to Godstow, she knew Merrick wasn't there. He hadn't been able to find Merrick, and for some reason known only to her, Adria had simply left without a word. He couldn't let himself dwell on what might have happened to her. He got slowly to his feet and began walking in the direction of the constable's office.

CHAPTER 26

The trembling began. Merrick faced himself squarely in the bevel-glass mirror, shuddering at the gaunt reflection that challenged back at him. The punishment was exquisite. It told him he was still alive.

He spread his hands on the cool glass watching the long squarish fingers quiver with need. He touched over eyes that haunted back at him, over a bearded face, over the hardened lines of his mouth. He was looking at a man he no longer knew.

The first blow was painless. His fists grew harder as he struck at the mirror, destroying this hated image of himself. The blows became rhythmic, first one fist then the other, slowed only by bloodied fragments of glass piercing his hands. The grinding clash roared like the sea screaming across his dulled brain. He'd kill the voices today, he would, he would.

The sea had reddened, engulfing him. Wave

upon wave of welcome pain washed over him, silencing the voices. He didn't need that drink today, he couldn't hear what they were telling him.

"There is no point of argument, Captain Ryland. Parliament has voted the funding and the Transfer of Registry has been completed. It occurs to me that you speak more for yourself than for your ship when you refer to a vital future—"

Oh, God, the words, she was saying them to him again in her clear queenly voice; precise, torturing words he couldn't shut out.

"Must you forever torture yourself over what is past and done with? There will be other commands, other ships for you in time. . ."

That voice, that insatiable she-fiend, how could Cara or any woman know how a captain felt about his ship, about the sea, about the glut of wind that swelled the sails to life?

Screams, he could hear hers now at the door. He wouldn't open it. She couldn't make him open it. They'd have to break it down first.

"I'll have the swans to amuse me while you're gone, Merrick. It's for other reasons that you're going, isn't it?"

Adria—rebellious, headstrong, innocent lass that you are. How you weaken a man into wanting you, loving you.

"I have one near the lighthouse spotted. The other one is flanking his right, the third one is behind him. . .You'd take my rangers, all forty-six of them aboard?"

Yes. John Kelly. I took all forty-six of them aboard. I went back for you when you fell. You should have lived. You should have lived—

Merrick stared down at his hands without seeing them. He couldn't see them, they weren't there anymore. They were smeared over the sea of glass that lay at his feet.

"Get away from that door, you bitch!" Merrick shouted above Cara's hysterical screams.

"Please, Merrick, open the door. What is happening to you? Have you gone mad?"

Yes, Merrick smiled to himself. I have gone mad, stark, raving, enjoyable *mad*, his last thought before he collapsed.

Hillary Barlow replaced the medicine beaker on the table, wrinkling his nose at the smell. Merrick's room glared of cleanness, a scrubbed whiteness overhung with a vinegary scent. Words were hushed, footsteps subdued with only an occasional sound of ship's horns navigating the Thames to disturb the stillness.

Joel Ditwell slept in one chair, chin propped in his hand, his foot twitching in some walking dream. Emory Marsh flipped his watchcase open again, a habit that grated on Barlow's nerves, then resumed his aimless pacing. The door opened a crack, enough to identify Comtesse Breaux's Irish footman who had come again to inquire about Merrick. His expression was desolate, more so each time.

Emory Marsh tried to close the door. "Tell your employer bitch that I bid her a swift journey to hell," he spat, kicking the door shut. The sound brought Joel Ditwell to his feet.

"You'll bring that dragon of a nurse back in

here," he grumbled, settling back into his chair.

Emory grinned at him. "You should have known Nell Parsons before she came to work here at the Royal Hospital. Her father was a taverner and daughter Nell was—accommodating, let's say. She remembers Merrick from his days as a canalboat captain on the Grand Union. That was before she reformed."

"I find that impossible to believe," Ditwell yawned.

Hillary Barlow glanced across at Merrick. How could someone be so violent before and now so oblivious to his surroundings? How could a man sleep for so many continuous hours? Emory had told him that a month of living with Comtesse Breaux would have buried a lesser man than Merrick. It was said in jest, but the implications were there just the same. She had, in fact, almost devoured Merrick.

The scene had been a lurid one after Emory found Barlow at his sister's home in Surrey and told him that he was desperate to find Merrick, that Adria had disappeared somewhere in London, that Major Kelly was indeed alive, and he didn't know what in the hell to do about it all.

Cara Breaux was hysterical when they arrived at 17 Cheyne Walk. Merrick had locked himself in an attic room and was smashing everything in it to pieces. From where they stood, they could hear Merrick's drunken, outraged shouts and the awesome sounds of shattering wood and glass.

"So he *was* here with you when I came to find him last week," Emory stormed at her. "You incredible bitch! What were you trying to protect him from?"

"Yes, I was trying to protect him!" Cara screamed back. "He didn't want to be found. We were in the orangerie when you came. The servants told me. He *wanted* to be left alone."

"*You* wanted to be left alone with him!" Emory accused. "Dear God, you have the pick of London's gigolos to content you. Why did you have to destroy Merrick this way? You knew what the loss of his ship would do to him."

"How dare you speak to me that way!" Cara screeched.

Merrick was incensed beyond reason when they were finally able to break the rafter door and subdue him. He was breaking every object within reach, hurling them against the wall, his fists bloodied paws that he turned at length on himself, pounding and clawing at his body until Joel Ditwell's precise blow at the nape of his neck slumped him. There were tears in Ditwell's eyes when Merrick dropped to the floor.

Emory used his traveling coat to cover Merrick's nakedness, fastening it over Merrick with a brusque tenderness that hid his own pain at seeing Merrick like this. They carried Merrick down the maze of tiered staircases to the street, past hushed rows of shocked servants to the carriage.

Cara was screaming after them. "You can't take him! Where are you taking Merrick? I want to go with you!" She hung onto Emory's arm, slowing him. "I did it for him! We were going to have a child, a son to inherit the fourteenth generation Sartre-Breaux title."

Emory Marsh shook free of her. "Merrick would never marry a whore like yourself, Comtesse," he gritted out.

Barlow lifted to his feet, stretching the ache in his back from sitting so long. The waiting part, this was difficult.

Merrick awakened that evening to a circle of grave faces. It hurt to smile and his neck pained him when he moved. He stared first at his hugely bandaged hands, trying to remember.

"Which of you will be kind enough to explain this to me?" he husked, lifting one of his hands.

"How do you feel, Merrick?" Barlow asked intensely.

"Like I have been hung," Merrick winced.

"Are you quite rational enough now to understand what we tell you?"

"Quite, Mr. Barlow." He tried a smile and groaned instead.

"Do you remember where you have been for the past few weeks? Can you remember what provoked you into this state?" Barlow asked quietly.

Emory Marsh squeezed between Barlow and Ditwell and sat down on the edge of Merrick's bed. He grinned at Merrick's discomfort when he jostled the bed.

"Good God, Merrick. This conversation sounds like something from the Inn of Courts. Just tell us how in the bloody hell all this happened."

Merrick was thoughtful for a long while. "That afternoon when I saw you in Godstow, the day after my audience with Her Majesty, I should have told you then. They 'nationalized' my ship. They're going to make a floating museum out of it. She said, my sea tactics while flying the British flag were in violation of some policy with the Union States. And, she was right. They were."

Ditwell shuffled his feet. Barlow turned and paced to the window. Emory was silent.

"I thought at first it was a mistake, a threat of some sort. I expected to get off with some type of reprimand, the recall of my captain's papers for a given period of time, something that could be redeemed in time. Padiah used some legal tact to reach Lord Derby for an explanation. Then, bit by bit, the truth began to surface."

"I need some air," Emory said suddenly, his eyes humid. "You don't need to tell us the rest, Merrick. We already know."

"Then you know about Cara's part in all of this." Merrick laughed strangely and shook his head. "She gave the ship away to the Crown. The price was its captain."

"What are your plans now, sir?" Ditwell asked guardedly.

Merrick allowed Barlow to help him with a drink of ice water. He settled back on the pillows, staring up at the ceiling.

"I'm going home to Aylesmere, to Adria. I'm going to be the country squire Padiah has always wanted me to be. I'll raise sheep and send for Sancho Pelagra to tend them for me. I'll build a stable for blooded horses, some Andalusians like Seth Holmes has. We'll re-design the gatehouse into a cottage home. Adria likes those stacked Roman stones and half-timbered walls."

Emory Marsh started for the door. Barlow halted him.

"You tell him. You tell him *now*," he said sternly.

Emory walked defeatedly back over to Merrick's bedside. He untied a canvas portfolio and drew a tattered sketch from it. He handed it to Merrick.

Merrick glanced at it, seeing an unknown face, a seaman with coarse features, a woolen cap pulled low over his ears. Emory pointed to Adria's initials in the lower right hand corner of the sketch.

"This one," he choked, laying another sketch before Merrick, "she signed her full name on, 'Adria Kelly'."

"Where did you get these?" Merrick demanded weakly.

"At the docks where she sketched them for her passage money," Emory managed to say.

"Passage money to *where*? She's at Aylesmere with Padiah."

"No, Merrick. I wish to God she were. She came to London with me to find you after some woman named Eunice Blanchard wrote to her telling her that her husband, John Kelly, was alive. She was waiting in the Clarence while I went to see Cara Breaux. When I came back, she was gone. We traced her to the docks. All that took a week. It was too late to stop her."

"Oh, Christ," Merrick groaned, covering his eyes with bandaged hands.

"She was distraught enough as it was. I

shouldn't have left her alone to wait. It's my fault, Merrick. I'm sorry as hell."

"Are you sure, very sure she sailed?"

"She used the name 'Sommerfield,' but the clerk at the Port of Clearance remembered her when I described her to him. The dockmen all remembered her, one Russian in particular who bragged of being her cheapjack. The sketch I showed you was of him."

Merrick struggled to a sitting position, not certain of what to do with his cumbersome hands. He paled noticeably when he swung both legs over the edge of the bed.

"I think this is unwise, sir," Barlow said with a nod to Ditwell. "It is best you regain some strength first."

Merrick had to agree when he tried to stand. "When did she sail and on what ship?"

"The *Laverstroke* out of Hamburg bound for New Orleans," Emory offered lamely, "on Wednesday last."

"That's a rusted out windjammer that was wrecked by calf ice on the Horn. Laeisz towed it to Valparaiso for salvage. The British Registry condemned it. It's not fit to sail," Merrick said with agitation.

"A man named Thorson Luhder bought it from the German firm. It was reclassified and outfitted for coastal trade," Barlow said solemnly.

"He was her captain when she went down at Cape Horn. His crew mutinied in the thick of it all. He was a crimp in Bristol because no one would trust him with a command. I know this man. He's demented. Are you certain it was the

Laverstroke?"

Barlow showed Merrick a copy of the cargo manifests, port of destination, and the one name on the passenger list—Adria's. Merrick scanned over it, searching for the captain's signature and the Port of Clearance stamp. They were both there. He folded the paper and handed it over to Barlow.

"That was an expensive bribe to get a copy of this," Merrick said tiredly. "He was nicknamed 'Whoreson Luhder' when he was crimping for a living. Adria always runs away when she's frightened. I wonder where she will go when she meets the end of the deck."

Adria laid her pair of sunstone earrings on the patch of frayed velvet and stood back while the shopkeeper raised a jeweler's glass to his eye and examined the stone. He blew his breath on it and polished it clean.

"Aventurine has only the value of common glass, nothing more," he said dryly. "Your set is worthless here in New Orleans, except perhaps for the value of the sentiment."

Why, you mealy skinflint, Adria thought stubbornly. He wanted to play at bargaining, just like the man in Matanzas had done when she purchased them. She knew, or thought she knew, what price they would command.

"And how would you value 'sentiment,' sir?" she asked sweetly.

"The war has eliminated the price of sentiment here, madam. Even a family's most treasured heirlooms have found their way to my shop for the price of a sack of flour."

And you sold their treasured heirlooms to the Yankees at twice their worth, Adria seethed. She reached to retrieve the earrings, and as she did, her White Chapel shawl slipped from one shoulder exposing the ugly crisscross bruises along her throat and upper breast. The shopkeeper was gaping at them, at her.

Well, let him look. Let him see them. Everyone else has, Adria thought, staring back at him, daring him to comment. She turned to leave.

"A moment, madam," he called after her. "Your set does have an unusual oval design. I may have a buyer in mind for them, I could offer, perhaps, say a quarter dollar for the pair."

"I had in mind a gold dollar for them," Adria said coolly, stretching an obvious advantage.

The man sucked in a breath and laboriously began counting through coins he kept in a cigar box. He fished out a three-dollar gold piece which he held tantalizingly in front of her.

"When did you have a meal last, girl?"

"I don't remember, sir."

"You don't appear a common woman of the streets," he said testingly. "I can generally recognize one in my business. Those bruises you carry tell me life has been hard for you of late. I pray my generosity will prevent any further harm to you."

He watched with a strong curiousity while Adria opened her worn reticule and carefully placed the coin in a zippered pocket. Adria dropped the earrings in his palm, wrenching her hand free when his fingers closed over hers. She glared coldly at him.

"I have never been that hungry yet, sir."

"You will be. You will be," he said trailing after her as she made her way to the door and slammed it closed.

An hour later with the strength of a decent meal inside her, Adria wandered down Canal Street, caught in the bustle of people, jostled suddenly to one side by an enormous black man. She shoved at him. He didn't budge. Adria moved to step around him and he moved with her. He pointed then to his tongueless mouth while he pantomimed the motions of a boxer. He glanced desperately back over his shoulder, trying to tell her something.

"Are you in trouble? Is someone chasing you? What is it you want from me, is it money?"

He was nodding to all her questions.

"Well, I haven't any money for you, and I certainly don't intend . . . step out of my way at once."

The Negro shook his head. Something in his huge liquid eyes touched her, a small honest moment of need. She didn't know why she was about to do what she did.

A thickset man in a Bowler hat approached them, swinging a cane he carried like a weapon. He tipped his hat to Adria and pointed his cane at the black man's chest.

"How'dy do, ma'am." he oozed forth a smile, taking time to draw a soiled handkerchief from his vest pocket and mop it over his face. "The Brute is fast, I'll give him that," he grinned. "Gave me quite a run here from the docks. I'll thank you proper for slowin' him a mite. He never run from a fight before, don't know what spooked him lessen' it were that Oriental. But, we gotta' remember that niggers ain't no normal breed of man."

Adria stiffened her back. She couldn't look at the man, he reminded her too much of Thorson Luhder, the way he used his hands to punish, the pasty flesh oiled and smooth. He sweated in the same way, too, and his eyes were just as piggish and cruel.

"And why, sir, would you be pursuing a man in my employ?" she asked loftily. The words were said. There was no going back on them now.

The man smacked his tongue over his lips, eyeing Adria with new interest. He removed his hat and held it between his beefy hands.

"Well now, missy, them blacks sometime looks alike, 'specially the bucks. This here one was brought to New Orleans for his known speciality which is usin' his fists for a livin'. Bets is already laid on him. A little mistake of look-alike, I reckon."

"The mistake is your own, sir. This man is employed by me as a bodyguard."

The man nodded politely, unconvinced. "An interestin' fact, ma'am. Appears this same nigger standing here is a pugilist who come from a slaver down Jamaica 'afore the War. Had his tongue took out by a white lady what claimed he was, well, a mite on the friendly side. Looks to be he ain't learned his lesson yet what with him hangin' still behind a white girl's dress tail." His smile faded then to a threat. "You'd have to show me some papers on him."

Adria gathered herself for battle. "Truly, sir!

And why would I need to show you any proof? Are you an emancipation official?"

"Well, no, but—"

"If you wish to continue this senseless discussion, there is a Yankee settlement office near River Street. My servant, uh, Marsh will accompany us there. I can assure you now that you have no case. Marsh is a free black in my employ. I brought him with me from Savannah."

Well, by damn, Prouty Bawden almost said aloud. Here was one of them 'quality gals' from the coastal Old South. She spoke with the sweet airs of quality but her clothes looked more like poor trash. But there was a lot of Southern women these days lookin' downright shabby. It was as close as he, an upriver Yankee, had ever been to a real Southern lady. Sure, she was lyin' through those pretty teeth, but she sure wasn't givin' an inch. He glanced at the interested crowd that had gathered behind him, overhearing a few remarks that leaned in favor of this uppity little gal with white-yellow hair who was defendin' a poor nigger bastard. The boys down at the docks wouldn't believe this story.

She was starin' him to size with those glass-hard yellow eyes of hers in a way that made him want to crawl back down the street. Colonel Cawthorne's bets were the heaviest on this nigger, but that thievin' dullard could wager just as profitable on the Oriental when he told him about the way that slanty-eyed, yellow-skinned animal could use his hands in a whole mess of tricky ways that would kill a man. This nigger brute was too hard to manage anyhow.

All those years of usin' a whip on him and starvin' him had made him brainsick. It was just as well, he decided. At any rate, he was backin' off from this one.

"As you say, little lady," Prouty Bawden conceded. He snugged his Bowler back on his head, expecting her to smile at him, but she didn't. No, her kind wouldn't smile at his kind. It wasn't proper.

Adria smiled dizzily up at this hulking black man, seeing the gratitude in his eyes as Prouty Bawden elbowed his way through the crowd that had gathered to watch. She waited until the man had disappeared down Canal Street.

"I can't explain why I lied for you. You are free if you want to be," Adria spoke softly to him. "You do understand what I'm telling you, don't you?" She watched him slowly nod his head that he did. "I had a friend named Marsh in London. It was the only name that came quickly enough to me. You are free to go."

The man didn't move. Without any order from her, he took her reticule from her and secured it beneath his powerful arm, clearing a wide path for her down along Canal Street. He stayed a step behind her, their shadows on the aged brickwork walls a strange contrast of frailty and strength.

CHAPTER 27

Merrick lifted his eyes to the *Warlock's* topgallants. Clew rings jangled against buntlines, stirred to sound by the rasping motion of steadfast anchor chains.

The workmen had gone for the day, leaving behind grainy footprints in the sawdust that lay about in powdery heaps across the deck. He was prepared for this, Merrick told himself, looking up at the dead smokestack where the sooty track of her burn still ringed the white steel. He couldn't count the times he had glanced there in the past.

The steps to the dock bridge were gummed now with rust and chipped at the corners. A new type of off-loading ramp had been constructed, one strung with paper lanterns; walkropes had been replaced by blue and red banners. Near the helm ladder a ticket cage with the price of admission stenciled in bold numbers advertised in slanted letters, "*The Swiftest Ship in the World.*"

"You can't board her, mate," a voice from behind him said.

Merrick turned slowly around to face a small, wiry man with his sea cap rolled low over one eye. He grinned wofishly at Merrick before pulling a bottle of rum from beneath his sweater.

"Join me, mate?" He swallowed.

"Another time, perhaps." Merrick smiled, turning back to look again at the ship.

"I tried to bunk aboard her last night but they routed me off. Ah, but she was a pride in her day, a glory ship."

"Aye, that she was," Merrick said quietly.

"I saw her drive into the Strait of Le Maire with her sails at blast and smoke fuming from that smokestack during a snow squall. She nosed into a tide rip, bore up, crossed and was gone before a clipper alongside her port could reef out. I was mating on the *Pigeon* out of Boston for San Francisco when we crossed her on the tail of barrier easterlies. We fell into the doldrums and were making only backway when she crossed the Equator. We figured her at twenty knots that day. Some of the mates swore her captain hoisted a salute when he passed our bow leaving Cape Horn."

Merrick remembered the day very well. He had given the order of salute to the clippers.

"She was fleet without her engines," he said, remembering.

The man, a dockside rummy, agreed with a healthy pull from his coveted bottle. "I saw it done, the engines, when she was in the ways at Liverpool. Most scoffed at the idea of mixing sails and steam. She's proved them wrong until her iron was caved with carcass shells. She's finished now."

Merrick started to argue otherwise and caught himself. So that was the reason given to the public, that the *Warlock* was damaged beyond repair by Federal artillery. It no longer mattered, he thought, what people believed about his ship. He knew what was true. He watched the man saunter off along the Victoria Embankment, turn and touch his cap to Merrick and skip away in stride.

Merrick swung his leg over the dock bridge and climbed the ramp, ignoring the "No Admittance" sign. The mercury lamp near the up-deck ladder had been smashed inside its cage, the same lamp Adria had unwittingly ignited that long dark night in the Savannah River, the night he had been furious enough with her to strangle her with his bare hands.

Thinking back on that moment, he stared down at his newly healed hands, at the scars that would always remind him, scars he could see. The other ones, no one would ever see.

His chartroom and quarters had been stripped clean of all their furnishings, even down to the linen curtains at the porthole. An upended crate stood in one corner, supporting a sled-basket of carpenter's tools and a round tin of nails. The one bleached plank on the floor of the cabin, one he had familiarly paced during the long hours at sea, was still there. He paced its length again just to soothe a memory.

Waterloo Bridge, Blackfriar's, Southwark, Tower Bridge, The Pool, Millwall Docks, East

India Docks; he could navigate the Thames by himself, blindfolded. But he'd need an engine room crew, firemen, stokers, he'd need Broly who knew the *Warlock's* engines, and one other man with him at the helm. Two on deck could manage the mooring cables. He could sail her out with a fair wind, without tugs or a pilot.

"What you are thinking to do is wrong."

Merrick spun on heel at the sound of Barlow's crisp voice.

"And tell me just how in the hell you know what I'm thinking?" Merrick asked sullenly.

"It's quite evident, sir, by the way you are pacing that plank."

"I could do it. I just may do it," Merrick shrugged, unaware that he had been pacing so strenuously. "Where would you approximate a sump-class windjammer to be now that sailed from Ramsgate three weeks past?"

"I would have to say in the track of northeast trades, between 32 and 31 north latitude."

Merrick nodded shortly. "If Luhder hasn't committed his usual navigational blunders, or driven his crew to mutiny, he should bring to dock in New Orleans in a forthnight. Adria will go from there to Matamoros to join Kelly; overland will require at least another week, by packet, five, perhaps six days."

"McKay's four-master, the *Great Republic* has off-loaded her cargo and will sail in ballast to New York. She'll make the crossing in 19 days with fair seas," Barlow spoke thoughtfully.

"That's too god-damned long," Merrick fumed. "If I could get the *Warlock* coaled and crewed-on we could port in New Orleans before then."

"And you could hang for stealing a 'national trust,' Barlow remarked dryly. "The *Warlock* is no longer yours, Merrick. Even should you succeed in this madness, which in all probability is quite likely, it would be a criminal act against the country and flag you have sailed under."

Barlow was right, and when he used Merrick's surname, it was in all seriousness that he spoke. It all just seemed like a huge waste of precious time.

"I'm going to find Adria and resolve this matter with Kelly. She doesn't love him. She never loved him."

"You are presuming that, perhaps. I am reminded that she left you to go to him," Barlow said tightly.

"Did I ever tell you how we first met? It was on an abandoned stairwell beneath the attic room at old City Hotel in Savannah. She was coming down and I was climbing up. Neither of us could see, we could only touch. I never did get around to asking her why she was there in the first place."

Barlow frowned against a wash of pity. Merrick was well now, in spirit and in body. His hands were nearly healed from the self-inflicted cuts and no longer resembled bandaged clubs. He had been living in his lodgings in Godstow. He hadn't seen Cara Breaux again, despite all her wheedlings, and he had been sober, entirely so since the day he and Emory Marsh had found Merrick at the Comtesse's home. This trip, this last agonizing look at his former ship, was testing his cure.

"It's a vast land to search for someone," Barlow said finally.

"No more vast than the sea. I *will* find her," Merrick said determinedly, taking one last look around him before he freed his thoughts in a new direction across the Atlantic miles.

Admittedly, Juan Cortina was fascinated by her. She was thinner than he remembered, with a jolting maturity he had not expected. The molten flicker from the kerosene lamp reflected Adria's neatly coiffured hair, setting it to a wild shimmer. Her pert, delicately-boned features were shadowed in mystique. Only her eyes, topaz and cool with the same defiant glitter he remembered, told him this was the same woman, Kelly's woman.

"Ah, and so, Senora Kelly, you have conquered Europe, *esta bien*?" he said, refilling her wine glass. He drew a wedge of lemon from the fruit bowl and sucked gently at it.

Adria shrugged, watching him toss down his tequila, then dab at his moustache with a napkin before reaching for a fresh lemon. He smiled curiously at her.

"Tequila is but a poor man's drink, raw like the cactus that spawns it. It is said to hold a worm of conscience."

Adria smiled bravely at him, trying to hide her impatience. The questions were still unanswered. Kelly was *not* in Matamoros waiting for her. He had left without a word to anyone. The shock of learning this had stayed with her long after she had appeared at the door of the Wellman's house, after Elizabeth Wellman had starchily directed her to Eunice and Dickson's modest home, still unforgiving of Adria's behavior. She had frowned censuringly up at Marsh, who waited a few obedient paces behind Adria, his eyes wholly distrustful of everyone Adria spoke to.

Eunice sank into a porch chair, clutching at her breast and fanning her face with her apron.

"Adria, my dear! I never thought to see you again," she gasped. She wept forth a few surprised tears and pulled Adria down into a chair next to her.

"He's gone, my dear. He was gone last week when I sent James to invite him for supper. James went the next day, too, and Major Kelly never returned to the hotel. That clerk, Mister Hewitt who replaced that dreadful Mexican man who used to be there, told James that Major Kelly had bought two horses and pack supplies a few days before. He didn't say where he was going, he just left. I told Major Kelly where you were, I even gave him the English address of Captain Ryland's home in Aylesbury. I told him everything I could remember about China Grove and the people who came for the gold. He seemed to be understanding. I tried, I honestly did try to do what was right."

Adria found herself consoling Eunice while the sickness inside her mounted. She had come so far alone to find Kelly, across an ocean, surviving rape by Thorson Luhder, the price of her passage with its accompaniment of degradation and punishing bruises, the hideous endless nights of just surviving until the next dawn. The scene she had witnessed of Merrick making love to the Comtesse Breaux played over and over in her thoughts all the while the *Laverstroke's* captain brutalized her. Nothing remained then except hate. And later, the thought of finding Kelly and learning to love again.

The bone-jarring overland trip with an immigrant train to San Antonio had been won by her wits. She sketched portraits and landscapes, exchanging them for one meager meal a day taken with the buyer's family, usually a poor lot who begrudged her and Marsh a few spoonfuls of beans and a slice of cornbread. She had spent one night with the wagon master in his wagon, another one with the trail scout which bought her a dress and a pair of shoes when the wagon train arrived in San Antonio. They were kind, lusty and grateful men who didn't make her hate herself for it. Marsh had earned his own way by taking odd jobs, carrying and toting for some of the women, and once even lifting a wagon-gate while the wheel was replaced. He did nothing in the way of work for others without her consent. She had tried to explain very simply to him, without much success, the need to bargain her body for their wants. The disapproval was strong in his eyes.

The visit with Eunice had devastated her. Dickson sat in his rocking chair, a frayed and faded Rebel flag spread over his thin knees, his lips moving in whispers in rhythm with his aimless rocking.

"We have so little now," Eunice was complaining. "I wrote to the bank in Savannah where Dickson had some funds, and they replied that the Yankees had confiscated all Confederate monies under the laws of reconstruction. Why, it was nothing more than outright theft. I don't understand how Dickson could have been so careless to leave it behind." She paused to consume a mouthful of apple cake.

"I do take a little work for the church on Sundays, playing for the services and some of the church events. It all pays so little, hardly enough for flour and molasses these days. Lordy, I don't know *when* I've had a spoonful of clean white sugar. Oh yes, I do remember now, it was at Elizabeth's tea for one of the King girls. They were twins, you know, and I think Elizabeth has one of them in mind for young James. I do so detest asking Elizabeth for any kind of charity, but sometimes—"

"When you saw Kelly last," Adria interrupted, "how was he? How did he look?"

Eunice set her teacup down and lifted puffy eyes to Adria.

"Why, he looked just *fine*! Well, maybe he did look a little savage, but that's to be expected after what the Yankees did to him. But, he was still handsome. He does have such unusual eyes for a man."

Dickson ceased his rocking and leaned over the arm of his chair towards Adria. "The azaleas are in bloom all along Abercorn Street. Did you notice, Colly dear, whether our purple ones blossomed among the white ones?"

Adria rose to leave, seeing through the

window that Marsh was already on his feet near the door waiting for her. She patted Dickson's shoulder and rearranged the Rebel flag over his knees.

"The white ones bloomed early this year before the lavender ones," she said softly to him. "The lions on the posterns will have a perfect setting for autumn."

Woodenly, Eunice followed her to the door. "I shouldn't pry I know, but I have had cause to wonder how Captain Ryland accepted the news about Major Kelly. When the two of you were at China Grove you did seem so affectionate."

"There was never an opportunity to tell him about Kelly," Adria said coldly. "The last time I chanced to see him he was, how did you phrase it, 'taking liberties' with his French mistress."

She heard Eunice's horrified gasp as she closed the door, and smiled grimly. That little morsel of gossip should keep all the staid ladies in Brownsville entertained at their next garden tea.

Adria drifted back to the moment, feeling General Cortina's heavy eyes on her. He settled into the settee next to her and took her hand between his.

"There was a day, *senora,* a day much like this one. The air was warm like today. I told you then that day at the Banco de Federacion that you would come to me, soon or late. Do you remember?"

"I want to find Kelly," Adria said stubbornly.

"And Kelly does not want to be found."

"You do know where he is then, don't you, General?"

"Kelly, he comes to see me. We play a little poker. He wins, I win. And while we play, he talks."

"I'm his wife. I have a right to know where he is," Adria insisted.

"Kelly tells me different. He goes to see Father Amyas to have the marriage forgotten."

"Kelly wouldn't do that," Adria said indignantly.

Juan Cortina threw back his head and laughed. "Kelly, he say the same of you, *senora*. 'She would not go to London with the Englishman captain. She would wait for me.' "

"Oh," Adria groaned miserably. "I *must* find him and explain. We thought the Yankees had killed him. It was all a mistake, a horrible mistake."

"To me, little one, you do not explain this thing. I take two wives by the laws of the Church, and other women I find 'interesting' for a little time. For all this, I learn nothing of love."

"Please," Adria was pleading now, "if you do know where he is. . ."

Somehow, Juan Cortina was stroking her hair, urging her head to rest on his shoulder, brushing at her tears with a handkerchief that smelled strongly of lemons. Adria felt limp with weariness, with the struggle that reached mile after endless mile. Kelly was out there somewhere in those bitter, unseen miles, waiting for her. Juan was comforting her with soft Spanish words, with a tenderness that disarmed her. She opened her mouth to speak and he kissed her, parting her lips expertly, his tongue like a weapon that gently wounded.

She was slightly drunk, she knew, when the effort to escape his hands became too exhausting.

"You have not had a man, any man, for a long time," he murmured, his lips sorting over the lace ruffle that kept her nipple from him. His fingers slipped inside her bodice and drew it apart. The suckling sounds, heavy and contented, reached across the numbness of emotion. The need flamed through her, fed by the awesome desire Merrick had once inspired within her, a bittersweet symphony of touch, of scents, of violent gentleness that she could try to imagine again when Juan Cortina lifted her in his arms and carried her to an upstairs room.

Restlessly, Adria turned onto her side, feeling Juan's arms slacken with sleep. His lovemaking had proved ardent and practiced, a worshipful possession of her body that forced at last a hellish release. His mouth wandered her body with a peculiar hunger that one moment took her that way, the next with a piercing drive inside her that made her hate him.

When it was over, when exhaustion brought the calmer moments, they spoke of Kelly. He told her, promised her, he would help her find Kelly.

She felt strangely at peace with herself as she stared up at the low-beamed ceiling, watching a macambre duel of liquid moonlight play over the walls. The weariness had left her. She wrestled now with her familiar demon, almost ready to conquer it. Merrick's face, his jade-green eyes taunting and amused, haunted through the waltz of shadows, reminding her all too well again of defeat.

CHAPTER 28

Juan kept his word which surprised her, a promise made in the throes of passion when neither of them was rational. He did demand one more night with her while the wagons and mules were being readied for the trip to Fort Davis. His dubious army, some clad as *campesinos*, others in the sand-drab uniforms Adria remembered from the day she and Kelly visited the bank in Matamoros, were mounted in slipshod formation, watching as the mules, some of them still bearing questionable *US* brands, were wrestled into their traces.

"Did you steal the mules, Juan?" Adria asked tongue in cheek, knowing she had touched a sensitive point with him when his caressing hand at the small of her back paused.

"They are in Mexico which makes them mine," he snapped. As quickly then, his mood softened. He smiled down at her and added, "Mules are the devil's own beast, so they needed a little persuasion to swim the river."

Adria laughed with him, seeing a different man in the sunlight than the one who had devoured her with his lovemaking in the upstairs room above his headquarters. His moods were like quicksilver, affecting all reason, all decision. Kelly must have somehow learned how to equalize Juan's moods, whether from necessity or from friendship, Adria couldn't know. Now, when Juan looked at her, his dark eyes sharp and cruel, he frightened her a little. He smiled, but his eyes did not.

"I worry for you," he said softly, pressing her hand against his cheek.

"Marsh will be with me when I take the stagecoach to Fort Union."

"That man is imbecile!" Juan erupted. "How will he protect you? By breaking each man in pieces? That takes too long against rifles."

"Perhaps there will be no need," Adria said hopefully.

"You do not know what you say!" Juan stormed at her, his dark face tight with anger. "This country is bad, bad for me; for a woman to travel alone out there is stupidity. I lied to you a little." Juan paused when he saw the flare of amber in her steady eyes. "Not so much for you to hate me. I know where Kelly is, where Kelly says he goes, but whether he is still there, or no—"

"I will find him," Adria said with conviction, wondering at the sudden warning throb in her breast.

"I would take you to Kelly myself, but for me to cross the border there, to maybe meet some Union cavalry would be death for me, a pain I will risk for you if you but ask it, *mi chica*."

Adria shook her head. "No, Juan, I will not ask it. I came to you penniless and worn, looking for Kelly. You were my last hope. You are keeping your promise to take me part of the way. That was all of our bargain."

Juan traced her cheekbones with his palms before cupping her mouth to his. "I think I will not keep this promise. I think I want you to stay with me. I think I want a son from you, no, many sons all with hair the color of sunlight."

There was a sudden, odd thrumming in her ears that blanked out everything. Juan brushed her lips lightly with his.

"I play with words, that is all," he said, shrugging, taking her by the arm. "Come, I want you to meet someone. You will like him because he will take you where you want to go. His name is Chato."

El Chato was indeed, by all appearances, everything that Juan Cortina promised in a horse. A cunning breed of Arabian strain and tidewater mustang, sired, Juan swore, by one of Maximiliano's own stallions.

"A prize Kelly missed, or he would have won the horse from me at cards," Juan smiled, nodding toward the gate where El Chato pranced through, his dark nostrils testing the cool dawn air.

"He is magnificent," Adria breathed, coaxing the stallion to nuzzle her outstretched hand, noting the arrogant glint in his eyes. He pawed at the ground, setting a curious tremble along his tightly bunched muscles, a performance, Adria was to later learn, of pure defiance.

"He is yours, *chica*, if you can convince him," Juan said with a hint of challenge.

Juan's style, Adria thought furiously—a gift in name only until it was somehow won from him, like all the other gifts he promised, but never entirely.

"Saddle him, please," Adria said between clenched teeth, ignoring the jeering howls from Juan's men. Juan, himself, paled some when he saw her determination, then snapped the order in Spanish, hooding his dark expression of concern for her.

The dismal terrain sprawled monotonously in every direction. A brazen sun leaned across the horizon. The wind, hot, fickle and relentless blew eternally, salting the air with a fine dust that invaded everything with subtle vengeance. Adria breathed it, ate it in her food, slept in it each night. Naked vegetation and wind-barren land and white hot sky. As for water, there was none.

Juan Cortina watched Adria dismount, swerving his horse quickly aside as El Chato didoed in his habitual arrogance. Adria jerked at the ring-bit, bringing him to heel. Chato snorted a playful apology, nuzzling along her arm as she reached for her canteen. The water was tepid with the strong metallic taste of trapped water. She took a long swallow, then cupped her hand and poured a careful amount for the horse.

"You pamper Chato," Juan glowered down at her. "A good horse must learn severity."

"A good horse needs water in this oven of

hell," Adria snapped back, feeling a sword-like pain in her side when she straightened.

"A thirsty horse will sniff the land for water," Juan needled her, admiring her trim backside when she bent to adjust her stirrup. "Better that the horse is thirsty than you, *chica*."

Adria looked up at him, shielding her face from the sun and studying the low horizon to the west. Juan had already strayed far inside the river border from Ojinaga, whether out of concern for her or from a sense of daring, she didn't know. Fort Davis, where the Butterfield stage road crossed from San Angelo, lay a brief twenty miles north of the place where they had camped last night. The grim silhouette of Sleepy Lion Mountain was grayish, blurred in the distance, and yesterday Adria heard, or imagined that she did, the bugle report for assembly at the fort. Tonight, when the fort's sunset cannon sounded its protection, it would be close enough to include her.

The fevered ride from Matamoros zigzagged the muddy Rio Grande, a bone-wrenching ride from the first bleak whisper of daybreak, until the greedy desert sun lazed just above the horizon. The nights, star-strewn and cold, Adria bedded among Juan's men, her body protesting the jarring abuse, her mind too numbed with exhaustion to question the madness in her heart.

She lapsed into a dreamy confusion, lost in the vastness of the land with nothing to weight her thoughts except survival. She rode to escape, an escape to nowhere, to no one, only to the flattened horizon that rolled endlessly beyond her.

Marsh had developed a gnawing dislike for the land, his face stoney, his glances backward more frequent as the miles unraveled. He sat as an enormous figurehead in the wagon seat, his eyes dull with misery. Each night he left the campsite and none of Cortina's men stopped him. Juan shrugged at Adria's concern, remarking only that if the Negro became lost they would not waste time searching for him.

"He wanders in his own hell," was Juan's final word on Marsh's brainsick behavior.

Marsh carried his Sharps carbine like a club as he stalked his way towards Adria. His eyes shifted heavily when Juan barked an order to bring a mule for him.

With a disgusted grunt, Juan swung down from his horse, jerking his head in Marsh's direction.

"I tell you again, a man who speaks only to himself in his mind is a danger, *chica*. Who knows when the devil will call his soul to hell? Who protects you then, eh?"

Adria shrugged a reply, refusing to be drawn into another argument with Juan over Marsh's dependability. Juan spat an oath in Spanish and took her roughly by the arm, leading her away from the others.

"For you I risk *gringo* cavalry and death if they take me. For you, I come this far. Not even for gold would I do this. I think you drive me to agony. I hurt here," Juan said, thumping his fist against his heart, "for you." At Adria's ready protest, he pressed a finger to her lips.

"No, let me say. I watch you all the days we

ride. The nights I see you alone in the cold and that should not be. I say, 'eh, Juan, you warm her, you love her a little. Then I think, no, she rides to find Kelly. For Kelly you do this, you say. But it is not for Kelly you search for in your heart. It is for another man, *verdad, mi chica*?"

Juan bent down and kissed her fully on the mouth. When he raised his eyes to hers, they were shadowed and moist with emotion.

"Tell Kelly I give him his woman and a good horse, but like the *Indios*, I can take them back in a day. Kelly is not the same man as you remember him. You will find this is so. There is still time to go back to Mexico with me."

"No, Juan," Adria whispered tremulously, shaking her head.

"*Vaya con Dios*, then," Juan murmured against her cheek, his arm already lifted above his head, summoning his men to remount.

El Chato lifted his head to the wind, sensing Adria's shudder of uncertainty, his hooves working the sand while she mounted. Adria swung him about, remembering the few steady moments the stallion tolerated while his rider mounted. She motioned to Marsh to follow her, refusing a last glance at Juan.

She knew what she would see. Juan, his silhouette chiseled against the bright horizon, a swarthy figure clad in dark leather, looking every bit the part of a wild *revolutionario*. He would wave farewell in a wide sweeping gesture. He wouldn't smile, not this time, but would hold his pose, waiting for her to turn back. She couldn't look back. She might change her mind if she did.

Riding alone with Marsh was restful, a contented time that renewed the strange bond between them. Whether he listened to what she was saying or not didn't matter. It felt good to talk to someone, to free the thoughts that tormented her. She found herself telling him about Savannah, reaching far back to a time when she was simply Adria Sommerfield. She described the terrifying run through the Yankee blockade, exaggerating the danger, or perhaps it had been as real as she made it sound now. Somehow, Merrick's presence became entangled in her ramblings until she spoke more of him than herself. Merrick found her when she was lost in Matanzas, he stood off a Confederate mutiny after disciplining Kendall Chase, he cared for her when she was ill from shock. He agreed to take the gold to China Grove when the Yankees came to Brownsville. He tried to go back for Kelly when he fell wounded. Merrick took her to London with him, to his magnificent home in the Chiltern hills when she had no place else to go.

Her eyes misted then, the words began to choke her and the pauses between speech grew longer.

Marsh was looking at her in his strange, brooding way. His deep eyes flickered once with pity before he glanced again back over the miles they had ridden since leaving Juan Cortina. He pressed his lips tightly together and pointed to his mouth, telling her without words not to voice a past for which there was no cure.

Adria touched her heels to Chato, freeing his lead. Chato loosened his stride in swallowing speed, tossing his head as he ran. Adria felt his tremendous strength surge free and laughed into the wind. She was free. They were both free, finally.

The way station was part adobe, part soddy, set well within the compound of Fort Davis. It felt cool and safe inside, enough to offset the scent of unwashed bodies and the trailing aroma of fire-blackened meat that sizzled over an oven-pit. A thickset man with greasy unkempt hair introduced himself to her as Ebe. He drew a chair for her at the table, then motioned Marsh outside the door.

"Some of us Southern Texans take offense at eatin' at the same table with niggers," he grinned.

"Do you indeed, sir," Adria said warningly. "Then would you be so kind as to set my place for me outside the door? I tend to take offense at eating at the same table with Southern Texans."

The room fell suddenly quiet. Ebe eyed this girl who stood as tall as her defiant height would allow. Her hair was long, slipping from the pins that held it beneath her wide-brimmed hat, a golden color whitened by the sun. Her skin was dark from exposure, her slender hands roughened by a long ride. Yet, it was her eyes that fascinated him, a topaz glitter set in thickly-fringed lashes, eyes that sparked with determination. The thick lamb's wool jacket, cavalry shirt, the leather breeches she wore could almost pass her off as a boy until he could see closer to the pert thrust of her breasts. He wished then he had never opened his damn mouth.

"I'm right sorry, ma'am, seein' as how you're an abolitionist and all. The war dies hard out here."

"The war died hard everywhere, especially in Savannah," Adria said tritely, seating herself at the table.

The meal was without ceremony, more of a controlled stampede to fill thick platters with a suspicious looking meat that floated in a reddish, greasy sauce. Adria declined all but a slice of cornbread smeared with currant jam and dill seed. The scene surrounding her was enough to quell her appetite and make her wish she *had* taken her meal on the porch outside.

Marsh sat at a small corner table away from the men, eating slowly and fillingly, his eyes vacant. Ebe, the waymaster, singled out a driver and a guard for conversation, taking his own plate and edging in between them. His muchly recited remarks were obviously for the benefit of the stage passengers.

"Yessir, 'ole John Butterfield has got him a million dollars invested in these here runs. That's includin' 700 horses at corrals all along the route. Heard Ben Dowell over in El Paso say that some stagemaker in the east, think it was New Hampshire, takes him a thousand dollars off Butterfield for each new coach."

"He could fancy 'em down some," the stage driver said, licking at his fingers. "Them side lamps ain't needed, and that forty pound freight boot ain't never been filled up full. Them brass doorhandles jes' rattle off over by Eagle Springs."

"I heard old Espejo is kickin' up with his braves down by El Muerto. He raided a settler's train last Thursday week before the troops from Fort Quitman ran him to the Guadalupes."

"Aw, them Apach', they was only lookin' for salt."

The men snorted at some joke of their own and fell to eating with sounds that reminded Adria of wild hogs. Her nerves were as taut as a bowstring, as though she had been holding her breath, afraid to let it go. She glanced to Marsh for reassurance, but he stared past her, chewing at his food in quiet tolerance. She left the table intending to make certain that Chato was properly fed and stabled for the night before she retired. Marsh met her at the door and shook his head, telling her that he would see to the chore.

She slept in a loft room without windows, hearing throughout the night the restive sounds of the horses, of far off animal cries, snoring sounds from the men bedded below in the way house. She peered once down the ladder shaft to see Marsh propped against the wall by the ladder. He wasn't asleep. He was watching, listening.

She pulled her saddle blanket over her and forced her eyes shut. A stray memory, the one of meeting Merrick on the stairwell that December night at the hotel in Savannah brought a smile to her lips. She thought he was a Yankee. She thought he was many things he proved in time to be.

CHAPTER 29

Another man named Marsh, slight of build and of fairer complexion, slouched against a brick storefront on Canal Street in New Orleans, smiling at what he saw. New Orleans hadn't changed, the people still laughed at simple things, fevered music still blared from riverfront doorways, the renowned brothels with their watered bourbon could still make a man feel at home. The crude blue uniforms that prowled the streets couldn't change the fabric of a city much older than their war. No one could ever conquer the charm of this city.

Emory Marsh sprung his watchcase open and glanced at the time again. Where the devil was Merrick? How long did it take to check the whorehouses in the French Quarter? Maybe he had stopped to sample the merchandise, but they had both had a fill of that last night, him with an octoroon, or was it a quadroon? Her name had been Dahlia, that much he did remember. What the hell difference was there in fractions anyway? Fractions didn't matter in bed, on that he and Merrick agreed. But Merrick had been in poor humor last night, and waited downstairs for him, questioning everyone in the place for news about Adria. They had argued again this morning about Adria's means of supporting herself.

"How do you *think* she would get the money to take her to Matamoros," Merrick asked him.

"She didn't strike me as the type for this," Emory insisted.

"She didn't strike mas the type to barter herself off to that madman Luhder for her passage either."

"She could have sold some more of her sketches," Emory argued lamely.

"She'd need more money than that, and people aren't going to buy some schoolgirl sketch of themselves when their bellies are hungry," had been Merrick's final word on the matter.

Emory moved a few steps out of the sun, pausing beneath a jeweler's sign. The perspective of the whole sign was wrong, he decided, studying the diamond-shaped sign that hung above the Worchester plate, a set of Lowestroft servers, one silver porringer, and an *epergnes* engraved with coronets. He glanced away, then looked again, drawn to a set of earrings laid in the corner on a patch of emerald velvet.

There couldn't be two pair exactly the same. The stones were oval like teardrops, sunstones with a milky hue, and one stone had a small imperfection in the center. One of them he knew would be slightly off its setting. Adria had shown it to him.

The shopkeeper removed his jeweler's glass and frowned over the counter at him.

Emory wanted to blurt out the question to him, but managed to contain himself. "I would like you to show me the pair of sunstone earrings in your window," he said matter-of-factly.

The man eyed Emory's expensive Harris-tweed coat, the small diamond signet ring Emory wore on his little finger and grumbled over to the window.

"I had to take the pair out of the window for a Yankee colonel and his companion yesterday," he complained, setting the earrings on the counter in front of Emory. "As it was, they didn't buy them."

Emory lifted them reverently and studied them. The one, as he expected, was darker in the middle and slightly off-centered with its setting. They were Adria's, there was no doubt in his mind.

"What can you tell me about the lady you purchased them from?" he asked carefully, making a show of drawing his wallet from his vest with an intention to buy them and bribe the man for information.

The shopkeeper warmed at the opportunity. "I overpaid her for them, that's for sure. When I saw those bruises all over her pretty little self, I just went soft-hearted. I see a lot of need pass in and out of my shop and I'm conditioned to most of it, but this little lady. . ."

"How long ago was it that she was in your shop?" Emory asked quickly, seeing Merrick pass by the window outside. He motioned to the man to wait while he went to get Merrick.

With deliberate pleasure, Emory dropped Adria's pair of sunstone earrings in Merrick's palm. Merrick turned the stones over in his hand almost with a caress.

"What is your price for them?" he asked the shopkeeper.

"Are you buying them back for *her*?" he leered at Merrick.

"I don't see that that is any of your concern," Merrick said, suddenly short-tempered. He didn't like the man and wondered just how much advantage the man had taken of Adria.

The man scratched his neck and took up his jeweler's glass again. "The gentlemen yesterday were interested in the pair and made me a sizeable offer of twenty dollars in gold. They seemed to know something of the lady's husband and were anxious to find her. They mentioned something in regard to some big to-do over a shipment of Confederate gold that was lost down on the Sabine. They said they'd be back today with the money."

Merrick counted out four half-eagle gold pieces and matched another stack alongside it. "You can tell them you had a better offer, and you can tell me who these men were."

The shopkeeper's eyes glittered with greed. "Gladly, sir, most gladly," he said, raking the coins into his cigar box. "There were two gentlemen, one was a Yankee colonel by the name of Cawthorne, I think the other man called him. His friend, a promoter of some type, by the name of Bawden came in first and described the lady to me, said she had chiseled him out of a buck 'nigger' who ran from a prize-fight at the docks. The girl told him that the black was her bodyguard. That, of course, was after I bought the stones from her."

"You mentioned that these men were acquaintances of the girl's husband," Emory prompted, seeing the stormy glint in Merrick's eyes.

The man shook his head. "That part I overheard when they were talking among themselves. Seems there was an agent of some repute, a friend of theirs they referred to as a 'Virginian,' who was at odds with the cause and told them about the gold. The lady's husband, if he was such, was someway involved in it. They were arguing about sending a telegraph to this 'Virginian' when they left. I told them the girl had said nothing to me about her plans. New Orleans is a very big city for someone like her."

Merrick wrapped the pair of stones in his handkerchief and pocketed them. He left Emory to thank the man, afraid his temper wouldn't hold much longer.

"That muckworm bastard," Emory gritted, falling into stride with Merrick. "He turned quite a profit for Adria's earrings, as much as a Romney will bring in Devon Alley. He wouldn't tell me what he gave Adria for them."

"I should have known it was Kendall Chase. I suspected everyone but him," Merrick said heavily.

"I say, Merrick, there is something that needs

explaining here. I confess to being somewhat in the dark about what happened *before* Adria came to London with you. This thing about the gold, for instance."

"It's too long a story, and it's finished now anyway," Merrick said shortly. He walked a few paces and remarked, "She wasn't at any of the 'houses' and hadn't been there."

"Did you honestly think she would resort to that?" Emory said with disgust.

"I know what women do when they're desperate for money. It always involves a man. And it appears that Adria is very desperate for money by now," Merrick said, patting his coat pocket to assure himself that her sunstone earrings were still safely in his possession.

Adria was, in fact, very desperate at the moment for the long ride to end. The Concord stage hurdled over another rockshelf in the road, bringing a screech of wood against iron and stone. The driver swore at the team, laying his belly-whip across the lead horses. The coach leaped almost midair before slide-rolling its way back onto the prong of road.

The gentleman passenger inside the coach with her fetched his hat from the floor and offered his hand to Adria, lifting her back into the seat.

"It always rocks like this near Fort Quitman," he said encouragingly, settling himself back in the seat of the coach. He hadn't prompted any conversation before now, and Adria hadn't either. By his attire, Adria judged him to be a speculator of some sort, carrying his usual curious-looking briefcase. He tolerated the ride with a casual acceptance that told her he was a regular traveler on this stage route, or that his bones were made of pure iron.

Adria gripped the brace strap and glanced out the window, craning her head around to see that Chato still trotted from his lead rope at the rear of the stagecoach, and that Marsh, who refused to ride inside with her, was still positioned in the mail boot. Marsh nodded to her, folding his enormous arms across his chest, pulling his hat back down over his eyes. Chato was fighting the rope, didoing in halting strides with its ease length, off-pace with the team horses.

Soon, Chato, soon, she promised, gritting her teeth against another jolt. Two more days to Mesilla where Kelly would be waiting.

A blistered cottonwood tree, the only tree Adria remembered seeing since leaving Barrel Springs, loomed ahead in the rusted twilight. Its gaunt winter branches fanned out over the road like charred fingers against the sunken sky. Adria snugged her coat closer about her, warding off the sudden seeping chill that always preceded a desert sunset. She was bone weary and hungry. Marsh must be hungry, too. There had been no way station since leaving Fort Davis, and they hadn't had the money to purchase extra food for the day.

Chato's warning snorts brought her upright in the seat. They were moving faster now, and seemingly uphill. The first sounds, thudding sounds, rolled against the coach like a rock-slide. The sounds were louder, pelting and cracking from all directions. They sounded like rifle shots.

The man with her hunkered to his knees on the floor of the coach, jerking Adria down with him.

"*Give 'em their heads*!" he shouted above the thundering sounds.

Adria freed herself from his restraining arm. "My horse!" she cried, "I've got to untie him, I've got to get out—"

He pulled her back down beside him. "No, you ain't! You ain't goin' to do nothin', little miss. Lute can outrun 'em."

"Outrun who?" Adria gasped, thrown suddenly against the seat when the stagecoach veered off the road.

The man swallowed his breath. "It's likely old Espejo or one of his war captains, Nicholas or Antonio. Lute's a good one. We'll make it to Hueco tanks."

"But what do they want?"

"The chase mostly, if it's tame Indians," her companion said, risking a look out the window. "I don't think it's Victorio, he's too superstitious about attacking near a mission. He's more 'Mex' than Apache, at least he has some Christian in him. He won't—"

The words strangled in his throat, lost in a gurgling sound that continued to suck at the air long after his body shuddered and was still. A blood-red arrow quivered innocently through his throat, trapped in the thick flesh that held it. He slumped heavily across Adria, his sightless eyes gaping up at her.

Adria stared down at him in fixed horror,

unable to move. She was going to die like this, the same way, alone, without—

"*Merrick*!" She screamed his name, a scream that became lost in a sob until she was screaming again.

The broken red-paneled door of the coach swung open against the side of overturned stage. How quiet it was, quiet enough now to hear the gathering of wind. Adria tried to move and couldn't, so she sat staring stupidly up at the figure crouched in the doorframe. She didn't feel anything, not even afraid.

His features were flattened against wide-set cheekbones in a square, coppery face with gashes of white and yellow paint smeared below his eyes. His mouth was a grunting slash when he reached down for her, wrenching aside the body of the man inside the coach with her whose weight trapped her. He paused to wipe at bloodstains with the man's coat, all the while watching Adria closely.

"*Nuest-chee-shee*," he snarled at her with jerky and powerful movements when he pulled her from the coach. His fingers clawed through her hair, snapping her head back until she cried with pain.

"*Ink-tah*," he spat, flinging her to the ground. He stood straddling her, cleaning the blade of his knife on his leg.

"Adria rubbed the sand grit from her eyes, tasting the mercury taste of blood in her mouth. It wasn't over, it was beginning all over again.

"*To-dah*," the Apache growled, reaching down suddenly for her coat and ripping it off of her. He leaned close over her, so close she could feel the tickle of his lashes. The animal scent of him when his matted hair fell across her face made her retch. She moved then, but not fast enough to keep him from falling on top of her. He tore at her clothes, working her breasts in his hands, stretching himself over her, smothering her. It was useless to fight him, he was so strong.

A lone rifle shot sung over them, scarring the wood in the overturned coach. In a single movement, almost too quick for the eye, the Apache leaped to his feet and moved silently away from her, answering some command from across the moonless desert.

They were going to leave her here to die, she thought numbly, waiting and listening for sounds. The wind soothed over her, cool and faithful, the last thing she remembered before a slithering darkness overcame her.

Gutteral sounds with long distrustful pauses between words drifted from the shadowed ruins of an adobe bell tower. Adria had long since given up trying to understand what was being said and she was too exhausted anyway to care. Her horse, the one they had set her on, was lathered and spent, his head drooped wearily, long past feeling the nick of insolent grass flies that swarmed his haunches. For a full day and a night, Adria had ridden with them, the five Jacarilla Apaches who had attacked the stagecoach.

Watching them cut the coat pockets from her traveling companion, watching the glint of their greedy knives, seeing the enjoyment in their eyes as they hacked the seats inside the coach to shreds, had left her strangely unmoved. She was oddly immune to the carnage around her, no longer wondering what had become of Marsh and the others, feeling only a vague twinge of sorrow at losing the stallion Juan Cortina had given her. She seemed to see things from some great distance with a curtain of shock in between. It was all that saved her from losing her mind. She knew what they were doing to the dead man, and when. She heard the grunting argument that followed. And when she saw the hideous bloody thing they dangled in front of her, she didn't flinch, and she didn't faint.

Brutal stupidity, that's what it was. Their sum effort had gained them six horses, two mail pouches, a bundle of St. Louis newspapers, which one of the Apaches promptly relieved himself on, and one white woman who didn't count as value. Their treatment of her told her as much.

After one staggering blow that sent her sprawling and senseless, she no longer spoke or begged for *tu*, for water, the only word she understood. Kernels of white corn and a gristly strip of meat were swallowed gratefully without water. She fared much better than her horse whose rattling, exhausted breaths were torture to her ears.

During the ride away from the wrecked stagecoach she lost all sense of direction. The Rio Grande flowed south of Fort Quitman, if she remembered correctly from the Butterfield map tacked on the door of the way station at

Fort Davis. Sometime before dawn they had crossed the sand shallows of a wide sluggish river. By noonday, there was no trace of any river. The ragged, sprawling country had resumed its hostile scene.

With her wrists still bound, Adria lifted her hands to her face, brushing away matted tendrils of her hair that clung to the bloodied welt on her cheek. Pain brought her head up with a sharp gasp.

The one Apache, the one who had come within inches of raping her, jerked her hair through his dirty fingers, kneeing his horse close to her. She must be still, very still, and not cry out. Courage to withstand pain was all that brought any measure of respect with these animals that called themselves Indians.

The voices inside the bell tower ceased. The tall Apache, the one Adria had named to herself, the Straight One, ducked beneath the blunted archway, his seamed, coppery face a mask of fury. He squinted up at the sun, then pointed to Adria.

"*Anah-zont-tee,*" he grunted with contempt.

With a show of dignity, Adria straightened in the stirrups. They were ready to do to her now what they had been planning. They were testing her, waiting for her to beg and scream for mercy. She wouldn't, she'd die first. Dying couldn't be worse than what had already happened to her.

She kicked a command to her horse and he bolted forward. He caught only one full stride before a rifle shot dropped him. He spraddled in the sand and fell, his hooves upraised and pawing desperately at the air. Adria rolled with him, her wrist cords hopelessly tangled in the reins. She tried to squirm free and couldn't. A new pain surged through her, rousing her from a near faint.

The horse was still now and rigid. Dizzily, she could see a gathering of horses around her. She was going to be trampled and she didn't have the strength to care.

A flash of butternut gray uniform, so clear she knew she was delirious crossed her vision. The yellow stripe sewn along the leg moved in a line that stretched upward to a voice that laughed in a flat tone.

Why was it taking so long for someone to help her? She floated back to life and left it again, still feeling the burden of weight crushing her. She was being pulled and lifted in too many directions. She screamed to make them stop.

"You must be very still, Miss Sommerfield," the same voice said. "We didn't know."

They were wrenching something from her, something she was unwilling to give. She felt it leave her body and shuddered at the relief from the pain. Someone held her head and forced her to drink something that tasted like blood. She vomited without caring who saw her.

A face loomed over her, harsh eyes above a full-grown beard that partially hid a disfigurement which caused one cheekbone to sag.

"I am known among them as the Scarred One," Kendall Chase said, honing each word carefully. "Do you remember who I am?"

"Yes," Adria nodded with a whisper, no longer able to see him.

"You are bleeding very much. We have an herb we are going to give you. You must not fight the medicine. It will help you."

His words, soothing and distant, were reaching her through the layers of pain. He wasn't going to harm her. He wasn't going to let anyone harm her. She swallowed the bitter tasting paste he spooned into her mouth. She knew when he covered her with his Confederate longcoat. She knew when it was dawn, and when the night came again. Beyond that, there was nothing.

CHAPTER 30

The air was thinner and crisper now as they turned their horses north toward the hazy cathedral peaks of the San Andreas mountains. Adria wakened and slept in the bed of a splintered corn wagon, no longer tortured by the steady pull of the wheels over uneven ground. The patterns on her blanket, the ones of thundergods and angled mountains, swam before her eyes, and no amount of will power could bring it into even focus.

Kendall Chase rested the pace, reining alongside the wagon and glancing over the sagging wooden side at Adria. Pain was etched on her face, a beautiful face despite the pallor. There had been a few anxious moments for him back at the border sandbanks when she had unexpectedly miscarried the child he didn't know she was carrying. It would have to be Ryland's bastard, he guessed. She hadn't been Adria

Kelly long enough unless that hot-tempered killer she had married for God knew what reason, had been more debonair than he looked.

What a stroke of luck it all was. The telegraph message from El Paso, relayed to him in Mesilla, brought the news he had been waiting for. Prouty Bawden in his loutish verse told him that Adria was in New Orleans, which meant that Merrick Ryland would be close behind on her heels. Colonel Cawthorne was still interested in knowing the exact location of the gold which was supposedly buried somewhere at China Grove, and was willing to pay handsomely for the information. The cost of all this, thus far, was a dozen Sharps carbines, three horses, and a case of 'Taos lightning.' Espejo, that old renegade, wouldn't chance another attack on the Fort Davis stage road, but Nicholas had been thirsty enough to agree. They hadn't violated her at his orders, but had argued for her price. That had taken the better part of a day. She had to believe he had rescued her from them. From the look of her now as she lay so quietly in the wagon bed, she would be ready to believe anything he told her.

The dried mescal which looked like hardtack, with a fibery pulp that tasted like burnt molasses, the chewing of which was deathless, Adria was forced to spit out. The *tornillos*, screw beans counted out to her, were equally as unpalatable, a nut-like pod with the flavor of sweet mud.

Kendall Chase smiled at her from over a mesquite fire. He unstoppered his canteen, listed to his feet and walked slowly over to where she was sitting.

"The food at my camp will be more to your liking," he said, offering her his canteen. "I seem to recall your fondness for wine. I can't offer you wine at the moment, but this will refresh you."

Adria took a sip. It was the same pasty liquid that she had been given that miserable day at the site of the bell tower. She coughed and swallowed it.

"Do you as a rule carry medicine in your canteen?" she sputtered.

"It's called *tiswin*." He smiled down at her. "It is a cure for many annoying things."

"Like hunger, I suppose," Adria said tiredly.

"For hunger and loneliness, oftentimes for despair," Chase frowned thoughtfully. He settled to his heels beside her, scooping up a handful of sand and letting it trickle slowly through his fingers.

"There is no time out here, and no hourglass for the sand. There is no forgiveness for mistakes."

Adria shivered suddenly and reached for her blanket. Chase snugged it over her shoulders for her and leaned back on his elbow.

"It was all a long time ago, Lieutenant Chase," Adria said carefully, watching his eyes. He was remembering, just as she was.

"No one has called me that for a long while," he sighed. "I left the Confederate ranks, you know, in Matamoros. I joined for a time with General Juan Cortina's so-called army. I didn't approve of his style, so I came here."

"So you live here, among these—*savages?*" Adria asked him.

"I command these 'savages' as you call them. The Indian Bureau promises them beef and rifles, blankets and horses, and grain for the winter. They tell them to bring their squaws and children to some wretched land the Yankees have given them to live on. It is starved land, hopeless land, so they become beggars, or they steal to survive. For those who choose to ride with me, I provide for them. I think for them. I protect them from their own ignorance."

The firelight was swimming in circles before her eyes. Adria shook her head to clear it. What he was telling her sounded almost benevolent. Then the nausea began building again inside her. She needed to go for a walk by herself, but didn't trust herself to stand for any length of time.

"I'm feeling ill again, Lieutenant Chase," she said weakly, struggling to her feet.

He seemed to understand. He took her arm and growled an order to one of the men. He held her head while she retched, bathed her face with his handkerchief when she was finished. When she crumpled he lifted her in his arms.

Adria wakened to the scent of cool earth and rusted leaves. They swirled to the ground from the cottonwood tree overhead, roused to life by a freshening wind. It was almost dawn, the stars were tarnished in a whitening sky. A sickle of moon still held behind the curtains of the peaks. It was another beginning. She felt Chase stir beside her, not alarmed that he was there.

He folded her against him and sighed.

Chase's armed camp lay among the crude ruins of a Spanish *bastion*, with a stack-stoned watchtower still intact. At first look the camp resembled a temporary Rebel entrenchment commanded by an ambitious officer: boundaries for the remuda, an enclosed headquarters area beyond the ruined *bastion* walls, and a neat line of darktents for supplies. There the similarity ended.

The Apaches stood in sullen groups, watching while the man known to them as the Scarred One rode past, followed by a wagon with a white woman in it, and the other five, outcasts like themselves. A straggly collection of dogs and small children trailed behind the procession, past all the vacant eyes that watched, past a scattering of camp fires.

Manchito, the one Adria had labeled the Straight One, dismounted first. He circled the wagon and pulled Adria from it. He led her across to one group of them, pointed to her and said something to them in Apache. Hostile and dispassionate eyes stared back at her. One of the women, cowering in a dirty blanket, spit at her; the others only looked.

Adria glanced around for Kendall Chase and saw him walking towards a three-sided building with a roof sagging with brush. She started to follow him, but the man, Manchito, gripped hold of her arm. He said that filthy word to her again, "*To-dah,*" and it sounded no less threatening this time when he said it than it had all the other times.

It was useless to argue with this savage ignorance, so Adria followed where he pointed. She found herself inside a dirt-roofed, clay-chinked cabin with a wagonsheet for a floor. The wall near an extinct fireplace crumbled with broken stones that were kicked into a pile and covered with mesquite brush. A pair of antlers dangled over the collapsed doorway, and one horn held a human skull. Tailings of white shale were everywhere.

Her cell, where the miles had ended, Adria thought desperately, glancing about her. The misgivings she had felt all along, particularly after Chase's display of kindness in bartering her away from the Indians who had attacked the stagecoach, were surfacing to reason. She hadn't been rescued, she was a captive here. She had been paid for with horses and rifles, a poor bounty for people who were starving, people whom Chase had told her he was befriending.

Perhaps she was wrong. Perhaps she was just weary and confused after the ordeal of the last few days. There was no one to pay ransom for her, if that is what Chase intended, and the only other thing she had ever heard of that Indians did with white women was to trade them to other tribes of Indians for slaves. They never lived very long, she had heard; they either died of starvation or maltreatment.

What in God's name was she thinking? Chase was a gentleman, a Virginian, who respected women of his own kind. Hadn't he always proved himself to be a gentleman? Then she *had* to make herself remember it—that long ago night in Matanzas when he had come very close to raping her. It was the strain of war, and the horrendous circumstances of that voyage. It had affected all of them. She had even believed she was in love with an Englishman. She had believed it long enough, foolishly enough, to have his child, or nearly have it. That part of her life was finished. The search for Kelly had finished it.

Adria crawled into a corner by the wall where the sun still warmed the stones. She cradled her head in her arms, closed her eyes, and fell into an exhausted sleep.

The sound, a high wailing scream, brought her to her feet. From the doorway she could see nothing in the darkness outside. Bluish smoke from a gathering fire trailed like fog around the whole camp. There were other sounds now, like animals in pain, sickening sounds followed by a dull drumbeat. She heard Kendall Chase's voice above the others. He was speaking to them in their own tongue with words that sounded like a speech of some kind. She tried to listen, but could make no sense of anything he was saying.

When Adria tried to leave, she was met at the doorway by Manchito. He motioned someone else inside, a woman, tall, strong and slender who moved with a rhythmic grace. She was carrying a plate and cup in her dark, sinewy hands. She was young, as young perhaps as Adria was, yet her eyes were dark with hardness and hate.

"I do this because Chase, he orders it. But I do not serve a *puta* like you," she spat at Adria.

Adria blinked up at her, startled at the English spoken with a heavy Spanish slur.

Somehow, she was staring down at the woman's bare feet when one of them came up hard, almost kicking her full in the face. She caught at the foot and twisted it hard, tripping the woman backwards.

The woman flew at her. "*Puta*, Yankee *puta*!" she screeched. Her fingers clawed for a hold on Adria, raking over her cheek, bringing the first blood. She was stronger, much stronger, and her weight pinioned Adria to the ground.

"You think I do not know? You think Kelly does not tell me?" she rasped in Adria's face. "I know why he marries you. Kelly, he does not want a *puta* like you. Kelly wants the *gringo* gold you have for him. Did he tell you that?" She tightened her hold on Adria's hair and pulled with both hands. "Did he, eh, *did he*?"

"*Callate*!" Chase snarled from the doorway. He gripped Erlinda Mateos by the blouse and ripped it from her. He kicked her off of Adria and sent her sprawling into a corner with one hard blow across the mouth. He was about to strike her again when Adria got to her feet and clutched at his arm.

"Please, no, you must stop this. We are no better than savages ourselves," she gasped, brushing at the tears that streamed her face.

Chase let his fists swing at his sides. He barked an order to Manchito while Erlinda crawled to the door. He stood for a moment looking dazedly at Adria.

"To rule savages, you must be one yourself," he said calmly, helping Adria to a broken-down stone bench near the wall. "She came here with me from Matamoros, she and her brother,

Ignacio. The boy was thrown from his horse during one of our forays and died a few days later. She hides her grief in hate."

"She was Kelly's mistress. He told me about her," Adria choked out,

"She was, shall we say, 'accommodating' to many men besides John Kelly. When the Yankees came they mistreated her, so she says. That is why she came with me." Chase turned irritably on heel then towards the door, towards a whimpering, infant sound that seemed to be following him.

He nudged at the crawling infant with his boot, toppling it over. The child began to cry.

"*No*!" Erlinda screamed at him, snatching the child up in her arms. "You do not kick this one!" She wrapped the child to her breast and coaxed a huge dark nipple between his tiny lips. She glared at Adria and her mouth twisted in a cruel smile.

"Now you tell me who is John Kelly's wife," she hissed, thrusting the child close to Adria's face. "See him and tell me."

The child whimpered again, a sound that would forever haunt Adria. She stared down at the small, strongly handsome features of a child with dusky skin and curling hair whose silvered eyes, Kelly's eyes, blinked innocently up at her.

Chase watched Adria drink the last of the *mescal* in her cup. He poured some of his own into her cup and smiled at her.

"You are restless again. Why don't you ride out with us tomorrow? It won't be a punishing ride like some of the others. You might even enjoy it."

"I can't quite picture myself as a marauder, however much you try to justify the need for this sort of life you lead," she said with bitterness.

"This is not a vicious life, only the business of life," Chase defended. "Apaches are born thieves. If not stealing from their enemies, they steal from each other. It is a mere game with them. I simply harvest their talents, and the harvest feeds and clothes them."

The strangeness she kept feeling, mostly when she joined Chase in the nightly ritual of drinking this peculiar concoction made from a desert plant, the effect that made her stumble when she walked straight, limbless except for one slender thread that kept her together, was seeping through her again. It made her forget everything save the nebulous horizon that she knew was waiting there. The nights when she didn't drink the *mescal* were worse. On those nights, she remembered too much.

"Are you certain that you inquired everywhere in Mesilla for Kelly?" she asked dizzily. "General Cortina said he would be there, or at Fort Seldon. He was to become a scout of some sort for the army."

Chase laughed shortly. "Juan Cortina lies for his own convenience, which is one of the many reasons I could not serve with him. The man I sent to look for him was entirely reliable. He told me what I have told you. John Kelly had passed through there a month or so past. Word was left for him at the fort that you were safe and searching for him. He was instructed to leave word where he could be found," Chase said smoothly, watching Adria's reaction.

She believed him. The *mescal* was working its magic on her. She believed him, trusted what he told her. The rest would be easier now. The distance was shortening.

Adria rode out with the raiding party the next morning at dawn. The spoilage they committed seemed innocent enough, almost like child's play. The defenseless *honyockers* with their few pitiful cattle and a harness-galled field horse. The nester woman in faded calico rags who clung to a worthless brooch, an unsuspecting farmer with a wagonload of his precious grain. They gave over easily, too much so, Adria thought, already hardened to the playful rules of the game. She was even given a name now, a Spanish one, not an Indian one, "La Tigra," the tigress because, Chase had told her, her eyes were like the night eyes of a mountain cat. To be someone else at these times excited her.

The raids along the Jornada del Muerto were more serious. The swooping attacks on several wagons at once, scouted in advance with each position reinforced in the event a cavalry escort appeared, required more of Chase's men. Chase was cautious, and the yield from these raids was considerably more than he had expected. Only once had he misjudged innocent looking prey. It turned out to be an armed payroll wagon from the mines at Pinos Altos.

Adria watched from a distance. The assault was quick and cunning. The Mescaleros moved swiftly and soundlessly, appearing and disappearing while Chase ordered a constant rifle fire. The splintered payroll chest was left behind, its contents flung into cowhide pouches that the Mescaleros carried on their ponies.

Adria swung her horse around, glancing at the grisly sprawl of bodies strewn like discarded dolls over the flat road. She felt suddenly, violently sick.

This was wrong, it had always been wrong. Chase wasn't a savior to these wretched people, he was a murderer and a robber, parading as their general. This wasn't a game, it was murder, and she was just as guilty as they were.

She had to get away, somehow she had to find a way. They watched her, true, but trusted her now. She was given the freedom of the camp, her own horse to ride, one that Manchito had brought to her. She had her own place to sleep, such as it was. Chase confided in her and they often talked of a future while they drank the questionable *mescal.* She would pick a time and simply ride away, through the formidable trails down from the San Andreas peaks, trails she had come to know well. She could find her way to Fort Seldon, and—

She couldn't do any of these things. She was a thief and murderess. She would be hung.

"*Ugashe*!" Chase snapped at her, catching at her bridle. With a long grim smile, he handed a thick piece of paper to her.

It was a sketch of herself, a wanted poster with neat black letters that bore her name, "La Tigra."

CHAPTER 31

They called themselves the California Column, a roughshod, mule-tempered, glory hungry, Yankee-bred militia that rode north to the morose land of the Navajos. After picking over the bones of a starved Confederate cause, after chewing at the heels of its army, they found a new war, one conveniently slanted in their favor. The Arapahoes and Navajos fled before their sophisticated cannon and Sharps repeaters, stunned by the encroachment of civilized man in their land—if one could consider the California Volunteers civilized.

A line of adobe and log buildings, looking even smaller against the awesome backdrop of rock-faced cliffs and sandstone monoliths, formed an off-centered square, home to the California Column, and formally known as Fort Defiance.

Just who or what they defied was never very clear in Kelly's mind. Maybe it was the hungry squaws with their hordes of bawling children, or the drunken and crippled warriors who begged at the gates of the fort. At any rate, for twenty Yankee dollars a month, a bed and food and a good horse, he could 'defy' with the best of them. It had taken some time, but he could move among the blue uniforms now that crowded the fort without feeling, even when their burring accents needled like a piece of iron in his gut. There were no Rebel stockades here, no goddam Yankee colonel named Cawthorne who punished and threatened in turn with questions Kelly never would answer. There was no one here who knew him, and he didn't know anyone. It was better this way. He did his job, what the Yankee army paid him to do. They didn't pay him to make friends or discuss his past. It was better all around.

He slammed the stove grate shut and kicked a chair beneath him. Yesterday, there had been another empty skirmish with the usual job of reforming scattered troop columns that he ended up herding like cattle back to the gates of the fort. He wondered at times during the long ride back how in hell the California Volunteers had ever found their way to this borderless territory in the first place. They couldn't read trail signs or follow their own tracks back. They had to be led by the hand or told. Maybe that was why the Navajos held out against them. Maybe they thought that these ignorant blue soldiers would get themselves lost one day and disappear for good.

It was colder now and some days they didn't ride out at all. Days like this one when the enemy was boredom.

Sergeant Vance Templeton propped his boots against the stove and squinted over at Kelly. Templeton was a down-east Yankee who wore his army blue like armor, ill-fitted and cumbersome with a huge frame slightly stooped, a penetrating stare, and, as befitted a Yankee sergeant, a mouth that opened and closed like a rat trap.

"Feel like some cards?" he growled at Kelly.

Kelly looked at him with his stone-hard eyes, colder and meaner every time he looked at Templeton.

"I want your squaw for tonight, all night," Kelly said.

"Well, she's all 'appointmented' up. Them troopers from over at Fort Canby has already paid me," Templeton snuffled.

"Tell them I paid first." Kelly lifted out of his chair and strolled to the window, looking out at a hellish twilight reflecting off the red sandstone monoliths.

"Now I can't do that, it ain't businesslike. Besides, she's all wore out anyway. You'd get a better piece of ass from one of them redstone pillars you're starin' at."

"I said I wanted her for tonight," Kelly repeated, turning around to face Templeton. Templeton stiffened in his chair, feeling a nervous sweat pop out along his brow. He had heard someone call this man Kelly, but most of them, like himself, never called the broody Rebel scout anything.

He used his finger to wipe his nose. "Squaws ain't real wordy if it's some talkin' you want to do. If it's just plain fornicatin', she ain't bad.

Seein' as you're so fire-tailed eager, I can maybe see to puttin' you at the front of the line."

Kelly spun a liberty gold piece on the stove lid. "Tell her to wash," he said, striding to the door.

Templeton struggled to his feet, reaching for the branded coin, then dropping it when it singed his fingers.

"Been forgettin' to tell you something," he called after Kelly. "There was some Mex lookin' for you, or for someone that sounded like it might be you. He said you knew him from down in Texas. He come in with them supply wagons from Santa Fe, the ones what was attacked by Apache scum while they were crossin' the Jornada Muerto." Templeton tossed the coin in his palm to cool it, watching Kelly while he had his attention.

"Them miners thereabouts is pesterin' the army to action since losin' that big paymaster's wagon. They killed off the guard too, only one fella' lived long enough to say what happened. He says there's some white woman ridin' with them, if that ain't more of them Apache lies."

Kelly shrugged and started through the door.

"Don't you want to know who's doggin' you?" Templeton baited him while he pocketed Kelly's coin. "Said his name was Reyes—"

The harness room reeked of sour leather. Kelly kicked apart a stack of saddle blankets and spread them out. Warm, patterned wool scratched the bare skin on his back when he stretched out on top of them. He lay listening to the padded whisper of her *n'deh-b'-keh* boots across the clapboard floor when she came inside the room. The beaded deerskin dress she wore jangled briefly as she stripped out of it. He didn't want to see her face. He was glad for the darkness of the room. Breeds like Templeton's squaw, like Erlinda had been, were better in the dark, away from the light of conscience.

She smelled faintly of sheep and sweat, but her flesh was clean and cool beneath his hands. He felt her shudder as his hand closed over one breast. When he drew it away, it was wet with a sticky milky residue.

"Oh, Christ," he swore, pushing her away. That bastard Templeton, pawning off a suckle squaw on him, on all of the horny misfists in this god-forsaken place. Some of them probably wouldn't even notice, or mind it if they did. They wanted a fast go at her just like he did. But he sure as hell needed to be drunk for this one.

"Keel-lee," she said, bewildered. Her coarse fingers marveled over the ridge of scar on his chest, over the knot of broken bones in his right arm that had left it near useless for a long time.

"Just feel all you want to," Kelly gritted, knowing she didn't understand a word he was saying to her. The flash of memory never lasted long anymore. It was hard to even remember how the pieces fitted, like the smile of sun on her hair, or the hot golden glint in her eyes, the liquid feel of her, and her scent, like wheatfields after a fragrant rain.

Aroused now, Kelly mounted her, letting the sensations take over. He humped at her, hearing the hot clasp of his flesh to hers, groaning through a short-lived climax. He withdrew and let her knead him to hardness again, but she didn't know how. Finally, he moved her hand aside.

He wiped dry the seep of maleness and reached for his pants. He heard the door creak open and fumbled for his Dancer. Someone was moving through the pegged snarl of harnesses. An arm reached through the tangle and separated them.

"Eh, Kelly, why you hide in here?" Delano grinned down at him. His eyes flicked innocently over the naked squaw beside Kelly and he shook his head, slowly.

"Welcome to the whorehouse. This one's name is *Gaage-ish-tia-nay.* It means something like little woman-bird." Kelly smiled, nodding in her direction.

Delano started to laugh, and for the first time in many months Kelly was laughing with him.

Delano took a hard swallow from the bottle of 'Shoshone black,' then handed the bottle over to Kelly. Kelly was the same, only changed a little. His face was coin-hard and the bitter lines around his mouth still tugged it down. His eyes were clearer gray and still flashed like knife-steel when he looked at you. His one arm was lumped and swung at an angle. The one the Yankees had broken for him at Fort Brown.

Kelly turned the wanted poster over and stared at the blank side, then turned it back up. This "La Tigra," or whoever the hell she was, *did* look like Adria. But then, a lot of women looked alike, especially from a distance. It couldn't be Adria.

"She's in London with Merrick," Kelly said at length.

"I think the same like you, Kelly, so I wait and I listen around. Then Juan, he come back and tell me he take her to Ojinaga. I think maybeso Juan does a little *cayote* and fool me, but he swears, no, and says she goes to find you."

"*Jesus Christ*!" Kelly erupted. "So he just turned her loose in that land of nowhere all by herself."

"She wasn't so much alone. Juan say he gives her a horse, a good horse, and that there is a black *hombre* with her to protect her. She wants to take the stagecoach to Mesilla and come to where you are."

"Where did you get this," Kelly asked, slapping the poster in his hand.

"They come in a big bundle to Fort Brown. I go and see Juan again and show it to him. He still a little mad with you for killing Rocco, but he thinks like me, to tell you this. All the way when I come here I see more posters of the *senora*, and I hear more things."

"Such as what?" Kelly demanded to know.

"I hear what the *soldadoes* say. I listen everywhere. They say she speaks s-l-o-w, and she rides with a man Juan says he knows. The man comes from the same Rebel place with her on the ship. Then he deserts and rides a little time with Juan. Then he goes away."

"I remember him," Kelly nodded. "His name was Chase."

"Maybeso he is the same one," Delano shrugged. "Juan says the British captain breaks the man's face so he grows a beard to cover. He talks slow like the *senora*, and he speaks Apache."

Kelly smiled dryly. "Could be he's just an Apache with a beard."

"You maybe joke, Kelly, but this is bad. These *ladronos* kill the payroll guards from the mines at Santa Rita and steal all the gold. It causes much big trouble in the Muerto. The army at Fort Seldon, they go to hunt down this man Chase."

"They might just get lucky and find him," Kelly frowned. "Where are they going to look?"

"They will track some north, then go south and west to the border, I don't know for certain. They don't know either. They just ride and look."

"That's trackless country for someone who doesn't know it. There are hundreds of trails in and out of those washes and the sand keeps covering them up," Kelly said, rubbing his fist along his jaw.

"You know the land, Kelly. I think maybeso you like to leave here and ride south where it is warm. What you do here anyway with all these Yankee devils?"

"I nursemaid them into thinking they're soldiers," Kelly laughed. "I bring them home when they're lost."

"She is lost, too, Kelly," Delano said quietly, watching the flicker of decision on Kelly's face.

With a bloated screech the locomotive panted to a stop, suffocating itself in steam. The wooden cars behind it jolted to a standstill bringing forth angry, braying sounds from the shipment of army mules inside.

Merrick swung down to the ground, shrugging his collar up and stamping his feet to warm them. The sky was villainous and to the north black woolpack clouds promised snow. He drew off his gloves, his breath a cold halo as he signaled to the engineer.

The railhead had ended abruptly with the unfinished sections stacked like black coffins along both sides of the tracks. Merrick stood closer to the hissing steam that billowed from between the wheels to warm himself. He studied the pale violet peaks in the distance and wondered if Adria was warm out there, somewhere.

It had been more than six months now. He had stopped counting the weeks of frustration since leaving New Orleans, weeks when the enormity of finding Adria at all was clearly overwhelming. He tried to think as she would as to the places, the people, the routes she would use in searching for Kelly. He had made only one wrong guess, a costly one in time; he had gone to China Grove.

The *chenier* was just as they had left it, haunting and still echoing in its remote, liquid emptiness, still sheltered in tottering determination, the foundation of the once grand house now a moss-swarmed gravestone.

In Brownsville, Charles Wellman was stiffly cordial over a glass of brandy with Merrick, his answers to Merrick's questions reserved.

"I can't say as how I ever approved of John Kelly, though I knew that Adrian Sommerfield had brought him up through the ranks during the Mexican War. I knew something of the nature of his dealings with Juan Cortina, not that I approved of the association, mind you, though I realize now the necessity for them. Men like John Kelly are an unlikable sort. They play a role of decency for awhile, then revert back to themselves. In his case, the need to prove himself with his inborn killer instinct set him apart from decent people. He killed one of General Cortina's officers shortly before the Yankees arrived here. Did you know of it?"

"No, sir," Merrick replied absently, trying to veer the conversation away from Kelly's shortcomings. This wasn't what he had come here to discuss.

"I thought perhaps when he became acquainted with Adria, she might reform him to some degree. I think now that we were wrong to encourage the friendship. One of the King twins was rather smitten with John Kelly for a time until Elizabeth spoke with Eustacia King, the girl's mother. After that, the girl was never permitted to see Kelly again. He took up with some Mexican girl over in Matamoros. There was some talk about it, of course, but people do tire of gossip, fortunately."

"Do you know where Kelly went when he left here?" Merrick pressed.

"Adria went to see Eunice and asked her the same question," Charles Wellman said. "It was a bitter thing for him, the way the Yankees mistreated him. When I heard about it, Paul Kenedy and I went to see the Post Commander to appeal for his release. He refused, saying the orders were from higher up. A Colonel Cawthorne from New Orleans arrived shortly thereafter. The rumor went that he knew about the gold shipment to China Grove and was determined to lay hold on it. It was much worse for Kelly after that. They kept him chained to a post, most of the time in one of the cellar rooms by himself. His right arm was broken during one of their 'questionings'."

"How did this man Cawthorne know about the gold?" Merrick asked, nearly certain he knew the answer.

"It seems there was an informer among the Rebels who sailed from Savannah with you, some man who later deserted and rode with Juan Cortina for a time. You would remember him. His jaw was broken while he was on your ship."

Merrick shifted in his chair. "I broke it," he said. "The man lied to me and endangered my passengers and my crew because he disobeyed an order. He deliberately allowed contamined water to be stored aboard my ship."

Charles Wellman paced the edge of the room, deep in thought. He fumbled in his vest for his pocket watch and checked the time with a mantle clock.

"Will you stay for dinner with us, Merrick?"

"No, sir. I thank you for the invitation, but I have some other calls to make."

"Are you alone in this search for Adria?" he asked seriously.

"A friend came with me to New Orleans. He balked at coming this far out into the frontier. He wasn't seasoned to it, and I persuaded him to wait in New Orleans. He's an artist by choice and somewhat on the more delicate side of nature."

Charles Wellman was frowning over his brandy. "I could arrange a contact with Al Sieber to find a scout for you."

"I appreciate the offer, sir, but I prefer to find my own way," Merrick spoke heavily, finding himself in the same hallway that he had left one stormy evening with Adria Sommerfield on his arm.

The wind was colder now and crinkling the territorial map Merrick had spread out on the ground beside him. The wanted poster, the one of a woman called "La Tigra" who fiercely resembled Adria, was laid out alongside the map. Thick lines showed hardened features, with cheekbones too wide, the tilt of her eyes viciously pronounced. Following the posters was like following fenceposts. They had appeared all along a neat trail from General Cortina's headquarters north to the Rio Salado to Ojinaga. There had even been one pegged to a ferry crossing post on the Rio Bravo del Norte. He wasn't fooled. Someone was laying a track for him.

The engineer of the train was walking back towards him, pulling a heavier coat on over the one he wore.

"That bossy Arabian horse of yours is kicking up again, Captain Ryland," he said between steamy breaths.

"He's probably insulted in the company of mules," Merrick smiled, rolling up the map and poster sketch and tucking them under his arm. He glanced at the loading plank where the arrogant stallion was stepping gingerly down.

Here was an animal he had never expected to find in this country, a breed of sinewy mustang and powerful Arabian, a difficult and intelligent animal.

The station agent at Fort Davis had been only too glad to sell the horse to Merrick.

"Well, he weren't broke in right," the man told him. "Them Mexes don't never do it right. They use them spade-bits that are worse than mean on a young horse. This one come hobblin' in one day through that canyon over there with an Apache arrow stuck in his left haunch. There's the scar where I taken it out," he said, pointing to it.

"He's a contrary son of a bitch, always stirrin' up the other horses. He broke through two fences to get at some mares. He looks kinda' like a horse what belonged to some lady passenger a while back. She acted all uppity over somethin' I said about the stud nigger she had with her. They called the horse some Mexican name. Damned if I can remember what, but I sure do remember that little gal. I thought she was a boy when I first seen her, dressed all rough like she was. She had cyes like little gold nuggets with fire in them. And them tits of hers could sure set a man to wantin'."

Merrick had thanked the man named Ebe. "I want him fed your best corn grain," he told him.

"None of them other horses get it," Ebe grumbled back.

"I don't ride any of the other horses," Merrick said impatiently, counting out the agreed price and watching El Chato display his usual contempt for anyone courageous enough to try to ride him.

The train whistle blew forlornly in the emptiness, a sound swallowed by the wind. The giant wheels reversed, spurting billows of hot steam across the dull-gleamed tracks. The engineer thrust out his hand to Merrick.

"I hope you find them people you're lookin' for. It's mean country to be lost in. Fort Seldon is twelve miles straight on up the track bed there. You might be better off gettin' one of them army scouts to ride with you. For a good price, they'll trail anywheres, and where you're goin' is a long cold distance."

"It's a close distance now," Merrick shrugged, grasping El Chato's reins and waiting while the horse calmed enough for him to mount.

CHAPTER 32

The barracks room at Fort Seldon where Merrick waited was deserted. A row of boney, unused cots stretched along the length of the room, a room soundless now except for the moaning of the wind outside.

Kelly stood easy. Only his eyes, stale with disgust, betrayed any emotion. He had never knowingly shot a man in the back before, but the broad, straight target Merrick Ryland was presenting to him was tempting at the moment.

"What the devil do you want, Ryland," Kelly spat out.

Merrick lifted his wide shoulders in a deliberate shrug and slowly turned to face him.

"I need you to scout a trail for me into the San Andreas mountains," he said quietly.

Kelly squared his arms across his chest and leaned back against the door. "That Yankee bastard, Cawthorne, knew three names—Adria's, mine and yours. He said you told him."

Merrick's eyes hardened. "Kendall Chase told him."

Kelly moved to open the door. "Find yourself another scout. Mickey Free, 'Peaches,' or any one of Sieber's men can trail for you."

"I don't think they would have the same interest as you in this particular job," Merrick said steadily.

"I don't have *any* interest in it," Kelly said flatly.

"Adria is with Chase. He's somewhere in those mountains."

"Well now, you've been listenin' to too much Indian talk washed down at the saloons," Kelly drawled, his eyes as cold and hard as steel.

"You callous son of a bitch!" Merrick exploded. "Don't you care what happens to her? She *is* your wife, or was that just talk, too?"

"I seem to remember after that day at Port Isabel *she* forgot that and so did you. Now I'm forgetting it," Kelly gritted. "Get the hell out of here, Ryland, before I forget the *one* favor you did for me that day."

Merrick unfolded the poster sketch of Adria and turned it face down on the table. He took a pencil from his coat and drew four intersecting lines across a relief of the Jornado del Muerto that met in a circle.

"Chase's attack perimeters form a complete arc that follows south along the Rio Grande," Merrick said, pointing with the pencil to the spot on the map. "They never outreach too far from their main camp which I calculate to be about here. They've left a clear break for the border through the maze of ravines, here.

There's a lava flow to the west that no one can track over. The army here at Fort Seldon is wasting time in the basin below the mountains. It's too accessible."

Kelly studied over the map while the moments trembled past. When he was finished, he looked hard at Merrick from across the table.

"You think you can just walk in here like you were still in command of a ship and start snapping orders to everyone with this blue sky idea of yours, don't you? Well now, I think different. For one thing, you're forgetting that I said I won't track for you. For another, you don't even know *who* it is you're hunting. You think *maybe* this white woman on the poster is Adria, but you're not sure. You think Chase is in the San Andreas and she's with him. You think to just ride into his camp with his hundred-strong jackals and tell him you're taking her."

"Something like that, yes," Merrick said.

Kelly shook his head. "That's one thing I *did* admire about you, Ryland, you were always good for the gamble."

"Three weeks ago before the snows, Adria was seen near La Union where they ransacked an arsenal and headed for the river. Carleton sent a company after them, but they never found their tracks," Merrick said, frowning over the map again. "I figure they didn't go all the way to the river."

"They didn't. That was just a diversion skirmish while Chase was attacking the freight wagons at Engle. They were needing blankets and food."

They looked steadily at each other for a few more moments. Merrick softened first and managed a tight smile.

"That's why you're here, instead of at Fort Defiance like I was told," he said finally.

"It could be," Kelly shrugged, feeling exposed. "But I won't track for you. What I do, I do on my own."

"She left me to find you when she knew you were alive," Merrick admitted. "If I could have stopped her, I would have, just so we understand each other."

Kelly stalked out then, leaving the door to creak on its hinges in the bitter wind.

Four days later, with a tremulous sun creasing the clouds, two men rode through the snow-crusted gates of Fort Seldon, their faces grim against the cold as they reined east toward the San Andreas mountains.

With a show of determination Adria crushed the satin pulp of a yucca bloom between her hands, working it into a lather that smelled of weeds and salt. It was the nearest thing to soap that she could find, and she was going to bathe regardless of the cold.

She glanced cautiously about her, then unfastened her *serape*, taking great care to place it within reach along with her Henry repeater rifle. The rifle was long and weighty, cumbersome to carry when she went to the lava pool to bathe, but she always took it—that and her 'Green River' knife that Manchito had given her.

She shuddered again when she thought of last night with Manchito. Last night he had come very close to doing what he had threatened to do countless times before: to gash a 'V' across her nose with his knife, the mutilation for unfaithfulness among Apache squaws. How he judged this so-called adultery she couldn't even begin to guess. The Apache mind defied all reason.

Kendall Chase was afflicted now with this same savage reasoning. He was touchy and cruel, chewing more of the peyote buttons and drinking the mescal with a relish that bordered on habit. He never sought her out for conversation any more; in truth, he avoided her. The wandering conversations, the promises he had made to her about helping her find Kelly were a thing of the past. He counseled with Manchito and a few outcast war captains from other tribes, and he spent his nights with Erlinda Mateos.

She, "La Tigra," had been given to Manchito as his squaw. Pleading with Chase had been useless, appealing to his sense of decency, or what remained of it, had provoked brutal laughter.

"You will toughen with use, like all Apache possessions," he had told her.

And, she had. Her weapons were as much a part of her now as the *n'deh-b'-kehs*, the deerskin boots soled with mescal fiber that she wore on her feet. She refused to wear squaw's dress, the newly cured buckskin half-dress that hampered her movements. She clung to the muchly patched cavalry shirt and corded breeches that Juan Cortina had given her. Only the *serape*, a cape woven in Santa Fe of warm Navajo fleece, was worn with any degree of pleasure.

How simple her habits had become. She bathed when she could in the lava pool where on warmer days she could shed her clothing and rub it clean over the rocks. She ate their food: *mesquite* beans, juniper and sumac berries, cattail and tumbleweed roots, and once, before Chase perfected his raids along the freight routes, she had even eaten the inner bark of a yellow pine. Today, there had been sunflower bread. She had eaten her ration and still felt hungry.

Chase and the others would return today with plunder. The lean, leathery faces would smile over their cooking pots, the squaws would bicker over the division of the spoils, and Erlinda would snatch away from them the coveted bolts of cloth while Chase approved. They would paw like jackals over what remained. Manchito would ravish her again tonight as he did each night, and with dawn, she would seek the refuge of her lava pool well hidden below a ridge of fire-blackened lava rock.

She broke the slush in the pool and washed quickly, gritting her teeth against the chill. She dried herself with her *serape*, hating the scent of wet wool but thankful for its warmth. She tossed her cartridge belt over one shoulder, then froze motionless, listening to what had alerted her.

She studied the craggy ridge above her, seeing a silent, telltale trickle of sand spill between the rocks. Something, or someone, had disturbed it.

Cavalry would make noise, even faint noise—the jangle of harness or creak of leather. She had memorized these sounds, the difference between horse and mule sounds: a horse breathed in snorts, a mule with more resonance.

Adria reached soundlessly for her rifle and backed slowly along the edge of the pool. Something moved above the ridge; she caught its brief reflected motion in the pool. Her mouth dry, her own breath singing in her ears, she inched slowly toward the madrona tree, the only point of shelter between the pool and the fringes of the camp.

She saw the shadow first, a shape that grew to the form of a horse, riderless and unsaddled, appear over the lip of the ridge. He began a careful descent down, picking his way among the smoother stones. He was unbranded, except for a moon-shaped scar on his left haunch. She kept watching him, struck by his familiar motions, almost able to predict them as he craned his neck to drink from the pool.

"*Chato*!" she called, her breath tight in her throat. The horse lifted his head in her direction and perked his ears. He swung his head and plodded slowly towards her.

"How have you come to be here," Adria wept, caressing over his muzzle and flinging her arms about his powerful neck. "How did you get away from them? Did you run very far and very fast?" she crooned. Her fingers tested over his coat; no scratches from *torete prieto, vino ramo*, or other desert brambles, no alkalai bloat from drinking poisoned water, no leanness from winter forage. There were no knife scars or whip burns on his flanks, telling her that no Indian had ever owned Chato. This was the miracle she had been praying for, coming in the way miracles appeared, wholly unexpected.

Chato tensed then and jerked his head free. He paraded away from her and began his arrogant pacing and pawing at the ground. Adria laughed at his antics, thinking how strange her laughter sounded after so long a time. She moved toward the horse, stopping in stride to prop her rifle against the madrona tree. She chased him, then commanded him to come to her. She was quiet then, listening again to the hushed silence.

She was quick to think of it, but the hand that reached for her rifle and snatched it aside was much quicker.

"No Apache will ever steal that horse," a voice said from a few feet behind her. She could only see a shadow of a man, tall and menacing, who was going to take El Chato away from her again.

She stood very still waiting for him to move closer behind her. She could feel the blade of her "Green River" knife snug inside her *n-deh-b'-keh*. When she turned to face him, she would be ready with it.

Chato was pawing furiously at the ground, snorting his fear. He reared once close to the man, the distraction she had been waiting for. The seconds were time enough.

She brought the knife up and around in a wide, quick slash the way Manchito had taught her, finding the low, lean, muscled target she sought. She twisted and stabbed with it, until it sunk deep.

Merrick lunged in close to her, averting the fatal downward stroke, grappling the knife from her fingers while a bloody furrow spurted across his ribs. He knocked her to the ground before Adria could reach for his Spencer. Its barrel was pinning her to the ground and he was holding the rifle.

"If you move again I will kill you."

"Merrick." She tasted his name. He staggered slightly. His free hand was inside his coat and when he withdrew it, it was red with his own blood. Adria held her breath, afraid that when she moved or spoke, the rifle would discharge. He might even drop it and it would fire.

"You savage little bitch," he grated at her. "Kelly. . .said," Merrick fought for breath, "he said you would be this way now. I didn't. . .believe him." He tried to catch at Chato's mane and missed.

"Chase and the others are close by. They know this place, they know that I come here," Adria said in a whisper.

"I know where the camp is," Merrick struggled to say. "Chato broke his hobble and I came after him. I thought you were—"

He never finished. His hand was fixed in Chato's mane in a near death-grip. He motioned to Adria with the rifle to mount ahead of him. He pulled her *serape* off her and clumsily tried to wrap it around his ribs.

"There is a way out of here through the *quebrada*. I can show you, but I must go back to them," Adria said desperately.

"Get on the damn horse," Merrick choked out.

It took a long time for Merrick to mount behind her. For once, Chato was patient. Merrick's breaths came ragged and pained when he slumped against her, still holding the Spencer firmly between them. He was telling her in broken words where Chato's saddle was and where his camp pack was buried.

Adria hurried Chato through a maze of *ocotillos*, through clumps of saltbrush and creosote, widening the distance from Chase's camp through a backtrail over lava rocks. Not even Manchito could find tracks here.

She knew when Merrick's rifle loosened in his hands and started to slip from his grasp. She grabbed for it seconds before it touched the ground. Stunned, she began to wipe his blood from the stock with her shirt. She was doing him a kindness; she was saving his life. He stood a much better chance of surviving the knife wound than he ever would with Chase. For her, for "La Tigra," it was too late. There was no going back.

CHAPTER 33

Adria nudged Merrick's outflung arm with the toe of her *n'deh-b'-keh*. He didn't stir. He just lay there stretched face down with one hand beneath him, gripping his ribs.

Tomorrow she would decide. Or, she worried, perhaps Merrick would die during the night and decide for her. None of this was her fault anyway. She hadn't asked him to come looking for her. How could she have known he wasn't just another bounty hunter like the others who had come near the camp? There had been five within the last month and Chase had killed each of them in a different way.

She had Chato again and Merrick's new Spencer rifle. She had found Merrick's camp pack and the horse's saddle where he told her they were buried. That had been the first time Merrick had slid unconscious from Chato's back. The effort to help him remount had almost made her decide at that point to leave him where he fell. But something had made her try again. She owed him this much for finding Chato for her.

Adria flung the camp pack across the floor of the ice cave, watching Chato to make certain he didn't break his picket. She had put Merrick's *jaquima* bridle on him a few miles back, more for convenience than discipline. The saddle, weighted with silver that Merrick must have paid some outrageous price for, would have to wait. It was too much of a prize for her to fight Chase for. Keeping Chato from him was going to be difficult enough.

Merrick groaned deeply and said something she couldn't understand. She knelt down on her heels beside him, debating what to do. How could he still look so strong when he was so helpless? Well, she would do what she could for him, treat the knife wound the way she had seen Manchito and the others do, and leave him to find his way back. By the time he did, she, Chase and the rest would be across the river in Mexico.

She touched his hair, leaving a gentle imprint in the dark sculptured wave that caressed his neckline. Merrick's hand came up suddenly, catching at hers as he rolled onto his side, his jade eyes fever-bright when they found her.

"Who taught you to use a blade that way?"

Adria let his hand drop. She squirmed away from him and reached again for the rifle.

"*They* taught me," Adria spat.

"Do you know how to use that Spencer?" Merrick winced in pain.

"They taught me that, too."

Merrick watched the amber ice flash in her

eyes. "Are you going to shoot me, or stab me again, or just leave me here for the *zopilotes*?" He tried to smile.

Adria swung to her feet. "They would *choke* on your arrogant flesh," she sneered. "I will dress your wound, but that is all I will do for you. You came here alone. You can find your way back the same way."

Merrick was beyond argument. Through a throbbing maze he watched Adria begin to scrape ice from the seeping walls of the cave. She gathered up the shards into a pile near him. He heard the clatter of tinware as she searched through the contents of his pack, her movements mirrored on the pristine whiteness of the cave walls.

The knife gash was horrific, but clean, a deep, neat slash from rib to rib above the lean hardness of his belly. At first, Merrick didn't seem to feel the woolen ice packs she applied to the wound, careful to only touch the severed places lest it adhere. Then the pain was feeding through him, brilliant and colored with fire.

"*God dammit, Adria*!" He writhed, slapping her hands away. He fought his way back to consciousness and lay there, panting.

"There's some whiskey in one of the canteens. Bring it," he gasped.

"No, I need it to cleanse the gash. And you mustn't drink anything yet."

"Like hell you're going to pour whiskey over that," Merrick groaned. "Is this some of your Apache medicine, or is it the way you learned to torture before you kill?"

Adria scooped a new handful of ice slivers

and repacked the wound, deliberately less gentle than before.

"Knife wounds are routine with the Apache. They take a favored warrior many miles for snow or ice to pack his wounds. But they never allow him water to drink until the flesh heals over."

"So he dies of thirst instead." Merrick winced when Adria peeled away the last strip of wool from his wound.

Adria rose angrily to her feet and kicked the camp pack far to the other side of the cave. She struggled to control the sudden ridiculous tears that were stinging her eyes. She turned calmly then back to Merrick.

"I am taking Chato," she said steadily. "I will try to get a camp pony for you when it is safe and leave him near the mesa. Chato is mine. Juan Cortina gave him to me."

Merrick's eyes touched over the length of her and lifted to meet the confusion in her own. "Knowing General Cortina, you undoubtedly earned that horse," he said.

"Words and lies." She shrugged, gathering up the spilled clutter she had kicked across the cave.

"I never lied to you, Adria." He could see it now, the soft flash of emotion in her humid topaz eyes. How small and defiant she was in her ugly, raw attire. She was almost beautiful beneath the layers of filth.

"All men lie," she spat at him. "I believe nothing of what you or any of them say. I have learned."

"Why did you leave Aylesmere? You knew I

was coming back, you knew there were reasons that kept me in London."

"I saw you with one of the 'reasons,' in a room that smelled of oranges," Adria said with disgust.

"So it was *that* day," Merrick nodded painfully.

Adria tossed her head. "That day, another day, the same lies," she shrugged, ready now to confront him. She was moments too late. Merrick was past hearing her now. He had quietly fainted again.

The twig fire had wasted to ashes when Merrick opened his eyes. A powdery dawn was swelling over the fringes of cold sky. He lay there a moment, listening to Chato crop the lush stand of grama grass near the entrance of the cave. He felt over the neatly bound bandage covering his ribs and waited for the weakness to spend itself before he tried to get up. With some measure of relief he realized that Adria hadn't taken the horse.

The camp pack was on the other side of the cave where Adria had kicked it. He dragged himself along the floor of the cave, pausing between thrusts to rest. He reached far for it and fumbled through the tins of salt beef and coffee to find the canteen of whiskey. His hands closed over it. When he unstoppered it, it was empty.

Merrick pulled himself up against the ice-slick wall, needing longer breaths now, sweating despite the gnawing chill against his back. He came fully awake then and saw her, wondering just how long she had been watching him, settled as she was Indian-style on her heels against the far wall of the cave, hugging her knees to her.

"I want that whiskey. Where is it?" he demanded.

"I hid it away where you won't find it," Adria said sullenly. "Your pain is your own doing. When you move it tears the wound."

Merrick broke off a chip of ice and sucked thirstily at it. He used what was left of it to wipe it across his face. His hand located the empty rifle sling and inside of it he found the second canteen with the whiskey in it. He drank half of it and let it burn slowly through him.

"You didn't hide it well enough," he shuddered, wiping his mouth with his hand. "Why did you stay the night?"

"They came, three of them. Manchito, I knew because his horse drags a shoe."

"Is he the one who set your leg so that you still limp?" Merrick asked brutally.

The words found their mark. She had tried to walk to correct the limp. She hadn't known what they had done to her that hideous day at the bell tower when Chase shot her horse out from beneath her. She only knew she still limped and always would. And Merrick would know, and laugh at her.

"*Tagoon-ya-dah*!" she spat, rustling to her feet past him with salty strides.

Merrick lunged for her and tripped her backwards. She bit at the mouth that closed over hers, hot and angry, and left a taste of blood. Her nails clawed viciously over his back until he forced her wrists above her head. His flesh was hot and savage against her own and his mouth was suffocating her.

"All right, by God," he spit at her when he brought his hand up hard across her mouth. She whimpered and he struck her again.

"Since this is all you understand, we'll do it *your* way," he husked before his fingers ripped away her cavalry shirt. He kneaded her breasts to hardness, hurting her and forcing a cry from her. He slapped her across the nipple and this time she fought him with all her strength.

"*Heshkes, bastarde,*" she hissed, choking on her tears. She felt it then, the hot, dreaded thrust and knew she was losing.

"Do they do this to you?" Merrick heaved, taking her nipple between his palms and kissing away the burn of pain. He began to suckle it with great gentleness, still holding her firm beneath him while he moved within her. He felt the stir of response and cupped her mouth to his, tasting the flavor of her tears and his. His mouth slackened and he thrust himself deeper and more roughly into her until she surrendered with a soft moan.

Still holding her wrists, he pulled free and flung her legs apart. He burrowed into her, his mouth touching and tasting, the lash of his tongue searching out each place where she was vulnerable. She writhed against the mouth that was assaulting her, losing the moments when Merrick freed her hands and let them guide his mouth.

The little death came like hunger, then in budding ripples, so fragile she feared to shatter it. She held it as long as she could when it shattered of its own accord, leaving her to grasp over the summit to the utter softness where it dissolved.

"Merrick. . ." Breathing his name hurt. He re-entered her and convulsed quickly, still kissing her, his hands warm, smoothing over her hair.

Adria laid her cheek against Merrick's chest, alarmed at the bright seeping rush of blood through his bandage. She stroked the crisp furring on his chest, hearing the soft exhausted breaths that told her he was asleep. She traced the scowl that brought his dark brows together in a dream of pain, or perhaps, rapture. For this small time, she was at peace with herself and him.

Merrick stood in the entrance to the cave, watching the desolate wash of long shadows over the convulsed rocks. The pain had drawn to a throbbing ache now. He had changed the dressing himself and knotted it as tight as he could stand it. He had slept too long, confident that he had tamed Adria.

Only he hadn't. 'Squaw man,' wasn't that the name for his kind of fool? Kelly had warned him, they all had told him about what happened to a white woman who lived any length of time with Indians. What he had done, what they had done, was instinct with her, not affection. She could no longer differentiate between the two.

The hulk of mesa gleamed brilliantly in fiery hues of sunset. He needed to find Kelly, to warn him and the cavalry off before they positioned to attack Chase's camp. There was no purpose for it all now. Adria had made her decision. She was one of them.

He should have told her that Kelly was with him. It might have made a difference. But it was too late for that now, too. She had been gone when he wakened. And, she had taken Chato and his Spencer rifle, just as she told him she would.

CHAPTER 34

He was here because of Adria. It sounded right, it just didn't *feel* right, Kelly told himself. He swept the dawn-gilt mesa with his field glasses, tracing an invisible line from the craggy rocks to the lone madrona tree still planted firmly in place.

Where in the blazes was Merrick? He should have axed that tree by now, telling him that he had found the escape trail to the river from Chase's camp. The pointed end of the 'V' attack would position there to trap any survivors. It should have been done two days ago when Merrick went out on his own reconnaissance of the complicated terrain.

Something was wrong, he could feel it low in his gut. He never should have listened to Merrick in the first place. What in hell did a British sailor know about Apaches? Sure, he and Merrick shared a vengeance for Chase, only *he* could wait. Chase's kind made mistakes of one sort or another, sooner or later. And when he did, he, John Kelly, would be there waiting for him to show himself. It would take only one shot.

Neither of them had been positive that the woman they had seen from a long distance in the camp, the only one who wasn't Indian, who walked different and lived in the ruined soddy by herself, was Adria. She looked too tall to be Adria, and she had been carrying an infant in her arms. But, a year could change a lot of things with someone, especially a year living with Indians.

If by chance they *could* take Adria out alive, if she was willing to go, and he had laid odds with Merrick that she would't be, there would be some explaining to do on his part. She probably still thought herself married to him, if being with the Indians hadn't blanked out that part, too. He had seen it happen too many times, seen too many "white squaws" after the braves had finished with them. They weren't "white" anymore, and they weren't all Indian. They were just some kind of animal with pale skin.

Kelly hadn't thought about *how* to tell Adria until now. Maybe he wouldn't have to tell her. She could just keep right on believing that they had been married all neat and proper that night in Matamoros, that the few meaningless words in the church he had paid Father Amyas to say, with his own solemn promise that he would marry Erlinda, had been binding.

Well, Christ, he had planned to marry Adria sometime. There was the mission to think of then, the god-damned gold that Hardee wanted delivered to China Grove. He couldn't remember now just *what* he had been thinking then, except that he had to have Adria that night. She had needed a lot of persuasion so he did it her way, and lied to her. He may have loved her, he didn't even know. One night with her was a sorry yardstick for measuring love.

The sun, blood-red and growing, yawned over the slump of mesa, firing the saw-toothed lava rocks with light. It was the battle light he needed over chosen ground, the same cruel sun that soured the dead and afterwards dried the blood-soaked earth. God, how many times he had waited for that light.

"They have the Henry repeaters, Mister Kelly. I counted a rifle apiece for every savage, stolen, no doubt."

"No doubt," Kelly said. Ignoring this green-ass boy lieutenant from Fort Fillmore hadn't worked, and agreeing with him only encouraged him to quote more military text. It was another aggravation he didn't need at the moment.

"Just what do you estimate the strength of our enemy to be, sir?"

Goddam, that was the last straw. Kelly rounded on the young lieutenant and backed him a step.

"I'll say this once, Lieutenant whatever-the-hell-your-name-is, so listen real hard. What you call the 'enemy' is Apache which makes it all different. They don't fight by any rules, they fight by instinct. You don't parley with them, and you don't make textbook cavalry charges. You just kill them before they kill you. Hell yes, they have those Henrys. That rifle you load on Sunday and fire it all week. Now I need just one thing from you—one long artillery diversion, just long enough to snatch the girl and ride hell for leather out of here."

"I believe I understand the order, sir," the lieutenant said, flushing a quick salute, his eyes watery with humiliation.

"Just make damn-fire sure that howitzer is positioned," Kelly growled, focusing again on the madrona tree in the distance.

The sun blazed above the mesa, spilling a golden hue over the aged lava flow. One of the horses snorted his impatience. Kelly turned murderously to the black mute who leaped to muzzle the horse. This peculiar nigger had appeared out of the blue one day and attached himself to the men of Company B at Fort Fillmore. He sure as hell wasn't a soldier, a cowhand, or much of anything but a work-brute whose movements were quick and reliable considering his size. He stayed apart in the corrals with the horses and carried a picture of Adria's face that he had torn from one of the wanted posters in his breast pocket. Kelly had seen him looking at it. He wouldn't trust the Negro in battle, though. He had seen too many of their kind take to their heels under fire.

The drumfire in his gut reached slowly to his brain. He couldn't wait any longer for Merrick. The cavalry was poised and ready, breathing hot and deep in their positions. They would make a clean two-pronged attack and close the 'V' after he had Adria. There wasn't any more time to consider.

Kelly mounted and rode along the ranks. He touched his spurs to his horse and dropped his hand. The order was said.

The howitzer thundered above a clash of bugles. His horse was running headlong with the others through blue-smoked dust, jolting and leaping over a fallen horse that screamed its pain. Brush huts exploded like matchwood, showering the air with debris. The boy lieutenant was outpacing him, his Colt drawn, pointing with it towards the soddy cabin. He smiled frozenly and dropped from his saddle sill clutching the Colt in a death-grip.

Kelly's horse reared, nearly unseating him before he shot dead the Apache that grabbed at his bridle. He brought a fan-round up with his Dancer, halting four of them. He swung his rifle butt around the horse to clear space to advance. He spurred hard when he felt the horse start to buckle beneath him. He rolled clear of him seconds before the horse toppled.

The door of the soddy was just a few yards to his right. He needed to reload the Smith carbine; the Dancer was empty save for one reserve cartridge. He crawled low against the adobe wall and caught the swift motion of a shadow behind him. He almost fired, then recognized the nigger brute who was strangling to death two Apaches he had locked between his enormous black hands.

"God damn, no—not that way!" Kelly shouted to him. The Negro froze in motion and smiled at Kelly moments before he slumped, fisting at his belly, his mouth working in agony. He fell near Kelly, gritting out Adria's name.

Kelly reached for the door to the soddy. He dropped a cartridge in the chamber of his Dancer and nudged the door open. He stumbled over one body, a big, well-muscled Apache whose head was half blown off. Behind him, something hit the floor—a pair of elk antlers. He searched around the room quickly. Adria wasn't in it.

"*Kelly*!" He dropped at the sound, trying to put a name to the voice. He heard her moan from somewhere near a pile of stones. It struck him then, the voice, the accent.

"Erlinda?" It was a few seconds before she spoke.

"*Si*, Kelly." This time her voice sounded weaker.

Kelly struggled among the debris over to the mass of stones, clearing enough of them away to find her. When he tried to touch her, she pushed his hands away.

"No, Kelly, do not touch me. I am broken much."

Kelly sat back on his heels. "Dear Christ, Erlinda," he choked. "How in the name of God did you get *here* in all this?"

She laughed, coughed at the same instant. "You say once you come back for me when it is your son," she rasped. "So you come."

Kelly could see her now. "So I came," he swallowed.

"I hide him, Kelly, when Manchito say there are soldiers. I hide him from them."

Kelly peeled her *camisa* down from her shoulders, seeing what he knew he would find. He pulled the *camisa* back up over her.

"I want my son, Erlinda. Tell me where he is."

"You want much, Kelly, like I want much," she whispered now. "Chase, he say all the time he give me much, but he lies." She smiled wanly at him. "I think I go back to Mexico. You take me there. You take *kay-nay* and me there."

Touching her now couldn't hurt her, Kelly thought, lifting her gently against him and smoothing the dark tangle of her hair from her face. He covered her as best he could with what was left of a wagonsheet on the floor. Stupidly, he began to slip pinfire cartridges into his gun until he heard the snap of cold metal lock the chamber. He stared down at his hands which were trembling furiously. The ground was shuddering beneath him, dislodging more of the chimney stones.

Why hadn't someone given the cease order on that howitzer before it blew them all to kingdom come? Schoolboy soldiers, that's what they were. One plus one was two, but not here, dammit, not when you fought Apaches.

Kelly got to his feet. He *would* take Erlinda back to Mexico. That's what she had asked of him. Father Amyas could read over her and it would be decent and proper. It was too late for anything else decent between them. Adria would know where Erlinda had taken the boy. He might even be with her.

Artillery shock trembled the soddy, buckling the overhead timbers. Kelly plunged for the doorway, kicking the door from its hinges and shielding his face from splintering wood when he ran through it. A brush fire was licking through the camp, torched by a lone cavalryman with a ravaged guidon snapping from his saddle.

"Damn you!" Kelly shouted at him. "Who gave you that order?"

"A massacre, sir! We trapped all of them!" the trooper shouted back, swooping low with his torch to fire a still-standing hut.

"Shit," Kelly gritted, combing his way through the smoke to where a battle-dazed pony stood. He started to shuck out of Merrick's borrowed sea coat when something made him stop.

"You didn't find her, did you?" a voice said.

"Just who am I supposed to be looking for?" Kelly paused, his fingers near the butt of his Dancer. He started to turn slowly around to the voice. He wasn't fast enough.

Kendall Chase fired point-blank at the tall blue target. The shot was perfectly centered and controlled. It pleased him.

Kelly stumbled forward in a half-crouch in time to bring his gun around, squeezing off one shot before his fingers went numb. The Dancer dangled in his hand, refusing to obey the screaming command from his brain. Another bullet kicked through him, caving him to his knees. He had only a glimpse of beard and scar, of eyes fired with hate. A blurry warmth seeped over him, cushioning his fall. He was floating then, spread-eagled across some dark chasm.

"*Gentleman, the day is ours*!" Colonel Adrian Sommerfield's words rung out clear, as clear as the moment they were spoken. What made a man so damn honorable, unless he was just born to it?

"*Eh, Kelly, you know with war or women a man has pain.*" Delano Reyes' words of simple compassion. They could still make him smile. He wanted to climb and reach that voice that was fading from him. It was too far over the ledge of pain.

"*We runnin' or fightin', Major?*" Kelly shuffled directions, leaning towards Clarence Lietman's voice. Then, it too, was gone.

"*You say once you come back for me when it is your son. So you come, Kelly.*" Erlinda's words punished him and made him regret too much. . .too much.

He started to tremble, somersaulting over himself, facing and leaving himself. He grappled for the ledge that crumbled to nothingness in his hands. Then there was a new-old face that grew to shape, contorted and ugly with hate.

Oh, Christ, not him. Not that man, his father, with his 'justice strap.' He wouldn't do that to him ever again, not in the eternal ever.

"*My name is John Christopher Kelly. Major John Christopher Kelly, Texas Mounted Volunteers. . .*" He was saying the words over and over again to someone.

Kendall Chase nudged Kelly's arm away from his face, expecting to see Merrick Ryland's face closed in death. The mistake glared up at him from sightless silvered eyes. He hadn't shot Ryland, he had shot this gunfighter who claimed to be married to Adria. But the man had been wearing that hated blue coat of Ryland's, and walked with the same fast stride of arrogance.

Chase pulled Kelly's body behind the frame of the soddy and began searching over his clothes. Cartridges and a tobacco pouch, a key and one liberty gold piece. He hadn't been worth killing. Through the smoke, he could see the cavalry reforming their ranks. He must hurry.

Merrick found the pony tethered to a saltbush near the mesa where Adria had said she would leave him. The starved horse blinked sullenly at Merrick and lowered his head when Merrick unfastened the rawhide hobbles between his forefeet. Merrick leaned hurtfully over the pony's back, waiting until the stitch of pain in his ribs lessened. The rifle sling made of fibers held Adria's rusted Henry rifle and seven cartridges. A tobacco canteen full of slushy water was tied beside it. There wasn't any food pack.

The trail of smoke on the other side of the mesa was darker and thicker now. It hung above the lava spill in gathering clouds and smelled of woodsmoke. Kelly must have fired the camp, in spite of his intentions otherwise, which could mean one of several things. He could have Adria and the cavalry had decided to destroy Chase's camp; or the cavalry had been overeager and decided on a full-scale attack beyond Kelly's plan to just rescue Adria. He needed to find out just what had happened.

Merrick threw his leg over the pony's back and moaned with pain. He tried to straighten and couldn't. The ground swam before his eyes and when he opened them, he was lying on it. The pony had grazed over near the mouth of the cave. He didn't know how much more time had passed while he lay there.

The smoke from the direction of the camp was thinner and trailing now. There should be someone riding up here through the 'V' to look for him, if he could just hold until they got here.

Merrick brushed away a swarm of gnats drawn to the scent of blood on him. The wound was a brighter, uglier red now and oozing through the layers of cloth that bound it. He glanced toward the cave then, in time to notice that the pony had flattened his ears, and perked one in the direction of the snow pool. Merrick reached painfully for the Henry and shouldered it.

The rider was moving recklessly across the sharp lava rocks, whipping his horse when it stumbled. He wasn't staying to the shadows either, he was riding in bold sunlight which meant that he wasn't running from anyone.

Merrick kept watching the careless approach of horse and rider. From this distance the rider looked like Kelly, wearing the sea coat he had lent to him when Kelly left his own coat back at Fort Fillmore. The Dine stripe identifying Kelly as an army scout was still tied on the left arm of the coat. The man wore a Stetson like Kelly's with the two eagle feathers across the brim. But he didn't sit a horse the way Kelly did.

Merrick wiped his mouth with the back of his hand, spitting out the taste of stale sweat. He focused hard on the horse the man was riding, sickened at the whip slash wounds on the animal, the worst of them across the horse's face. He was tossing blood as he ran. And the way the horse canted to one side—there was only one horse he knew of that ran like that.

Merrick struggled to his feet. He wanted a nearer look at the bastard who had somehow managed to take Adria's horse away from her. Adria would never part with Chato unless—

Chase reined the stallion taut. He'd have to stop at the lava pool and wipe the blood that was streaming down the horse's face, blinding him and making him stagger. It had taken countless blows to bring this animal to obedience, the kind Manchito used on his ponies. If they survived the beatings, they were good ponies. If they didn't, he would simply steal a new horse.

Adria would never say where she got the animal. Even Manchito could not force it from her, and he knew all the ugly little ways to hurt a woman the most. Chase hadn't watched all of it. Even he, as toughened as he was now to the Apache way, had to walk away. She belonged to Manchito now, she was his squaw. He could do with her whatever he wanted. It was Apache law.

Chase tied the lathered horse away from the pool to further torment him. He watched the horse strain at his leather, needing that long drink of snow water.

"So now you learn," he laughed at him. He unknotted the wind-kerchief that hid his beard and leaned across the rocks to the pool. It had been much easier than he had thought it would be. No one questioned the ripe appearance of another white Indian scout in the chaotic aftermath of a massacre. He spoke enough Apache to confuse an already flustered sergeant new to his command. He calmly saluted the burial detail and rode out of his own camp. At times, even his own ingenuity amazed him.

Chase lapped at the water, then lifted his head suddenly when he heard a scramble of rocks above him. He slowly unleathered the Smith carbine that had belonged to the Texan.

"Chase!" Merrick gritted from behind the blued barrel of the Henry. "Lay your hands out flat on the rocks where I can see them. Leave that carbine where it is."

Chato stomped the ground nervously at the sound of Merrick's voice. He arched his neck furiously and pulled at his tether. Chase didn't move.

"Where did you get that horse and that uniform?" Merrick shouted down at him.

Chase squinted up at the voice in the sunlight. "I bought them," he said clearly. He could only see Ryland's boottops, which meant that Ryland couldn't see his fingers inching ever so slowly toward the carbine.

"Where is Adria?"

"She's dead. They are all dead."

"And John Kelly, where is he?" Merrick demanded.

"He took longer to die," Chase sneered back. The words echoed a moment in the wind.

Merrick picked his way between the rocks toward the pool. His heel snagged a rock and he stumbled. It was the moment Chase had been needing. He brought his carbine up and fired in a scatter. Merrick tumbled sideways between tall pleated rocks at the same moment Chato broke free from his tether, dragging the roots of the madrona tree behind him.

Merrick shouted him aside. The fifth shot from Chase's carbine twanged above his head against the rocks. He cocked his Henry rifle and sighted.

"I count five, Chase. You have one left," he said, his voice hollow in the windswept stillness.

"It will give us time to talk before I kill you," Chase shouted back. "She's dead, Ryland, but she served her purpose well. She was beginning to enjoy the life I introduced her to while we waited for you. I knew you would come for her. I was certain of it the day we pulled what was left of your son from her body. He didn't look at all human, nothing more than a crushed, bloody mass of soft bones. We strung it in the sun for the *zopilotes* to feast on."

"What in hell are you saying?" Merrick choked roughly.

"She didn't tell you? How thoughtless of her," Chase laughed. "Women are like that with their little secrets they keep from men. Ah, well, no matter. Frail as Miss Sommerfield was, she probably wouldn't have survived childbirth anyway."

"You're lying to me about this," Merrick said unsteadily, "the same way you lied about the water casks that were contaminated."

"The truth can be interpreted in many ways, depending on the believer," Chase said above the nest of rock. Ryland was nearly in range now, just a few more feet.

"God damn you, Chase," Merrick said suddenly, standing up. The Henry was shouldered and ready. Merrick started to walk towards him.

"I told you—I told you that day on the ship I would kill you for what you did to me!" Chase screamed at him.

"I watched her die. She died beautifully. She was mine. She was never yours!" Chase bellowed.

Merrick judged the shot and slanted out. The sound thundered among the rocks, swallowed in its own echo. He fired the Henry and kept on firing until the chamber clicked empty.

CHAPTER 35

A death stench hung over the still smouldering rubble of what had been Chase's camp. Merrick rode Chato through the carnage, past the grim-faced troopers who paused over their shovels to stare up at him. He reined up before the only Sibley tent and dismounted. There was no orderly on duty, no need for one.

Slowly, he untwisted the top on his canteen. The water inside was still slushy and tasted of stale whiskey. He drank some, then cupped his hand and poured the rest for Chato.

Blood had caked over the awesome welts on Chato's face, muddying the stallion's fine markings. Merrick dabbed some water over them and stroked the horse's muzzle. There would be time now to treat them with soda and creosote ointment. He would have good forage and rest in the lush Chiltern pastures near Aylesmere for all his days.

The sergeant in command, haggard and

reeking of shortbit rye, shambled between the tent flaps, staring first at Merrick, then at Chato, lastly at the blanket-covered body strapped across Chato's flanks.

"Well, *sir*," he rasped, scratching beneath the dusty brim of his forage cap.

"The man was a Confederate officer. Bury him away from the others," Merrick said, turning on heel.

"And I bet *you* was a Yankee," the sergeant grinned.

Merrick looked coldly at him. "It was never my war, sergeant."

The sergeant lowered his eyes and paced a step with Merrick. He glanced back at Chato and said, "Where you and your horse get bloodied up like that?"

"It was a personal war," Merrick tossed off impatiently.

"That's what this here one was," the sergeant spit. "I'll be needin' a paper signed for that man you brought in. Maybe you could ride on back to the fort with the column."

"I'm riding in another direction," Merrick said.

The man stared down at his boots for a moment, then frowned up at Merrick. "You know any of these here people we're buryin'?"

"I knew the man who brought you here, and the one across my saddle."

"The Dine scout, that Kelly fella', he taken a bullet in the back. We buried him up front. All them others is ordinary Indians, what looked to count about eighty of them includin' the squaws and a handful of youngsters. Oh, yeah, there was a Mexican woman too, one of the boys up from Fort Brown chanced to know. Said she was a dancer in one them cantinas they got down there when she weren't whorin'."

"Where did you find *her*?" Merrick asked.

The sergeant nodded to where he pointed. "In that burnt out soddy over there. Ain't nothin' left but the chimney." He watched Merrick walk away and hollered after him, "You won't find nothin' there, mister. We already looked. There ain't nothin' but rocks."

He knew it was morbid to sit here like this beside a pile of charred rubble that had once served as a chimney for a much needed fire on bitter windswept nights like this one. It was ghoulish to keep sorting among the burned stones, finding here and there a broken bead or a fragment of decorated pottery. It seemed for the moment the only way to keep his sanity, to keep him from retching his guts out or run screaming out into the night. He was looking for something that might have belonged to Adria. He didn't know what it would be, perhaps something she had just touched.

He hadn't found her among the victims. No one had. And no one even remembered seeing a slender-limbed squaw with topaz eyes and hair the color of white honey. He should have forced the truth from Kendall Chase before he killed him, before Chase killed Kelly, before the cavalry killed Erlinda and the others, before the lust for killing made madmen of them all.

Merrick tossed the stones back on the pile. He studied the hollow wall where the fireplace had been. It had been a deep one, large enough to step inside. It could even have been a kiln, perhaps for the mud bricks that were stacked around the camp. A few of the cooking-hooks were still bolted to the rocks, twisted and rusted now with time. There was a sagging and rust-spotted oven door centered behind the fire wall, a door very much like the boiler doors on the *Warlock*.

Merrick leaned inside the hearth and touched the metal. The handle was cold, and free of cobwebs and dirt. The door snapped from its hinges when he opened it and clattered to the floor beside his foot.

It wasn't much of a sound, more movement than sound that made him look inside. It looked to be a long lump of leather attached to an oblong board. When he touched it, it squirmed. He drew it out towards him in the lantern light.

The child made no cry, but closed his eyes against the harsh brightness. His tiny fist doubled over Merrick's dark finger when Merrick unloosened the swatch of flannel cloth over the child's mouth. He whimpered once and sighed, following Merrick's hand with his curious, silvered eyes.

Merrick could only stare down at him through the hot mist of his own emotion. Here, thank God, was something alive, one who had survived this madness. There was no mistaking that this was Kelly's child, the one Father Amyas had told him about that empty day in Matamoros when Merrick went to the parish to see him. This much had been true—the rest no longer mattered.

* * *

Thunder drummed above the iced San Andreas peaks among bloated snow clouds that swirled from the north. One of the pack mules following on a lead rope behind Chato brayed his fear and balked. Chato strained forward, snapping taut the length of leather between them.

Damn that mule, damn all mules. Kelly was right, they wore their brains in their ass, and they only worked backwards, and only half of the time. You had to understand mules to work them, and at the moment he swore he would trade twenty mules for one good pack pony.

Merrick dismounted and walked back to the mule. The man-wise, trail-wise mule eyed him with contempt. Merrick tightened the spade-roll bit and gave it a jerk.

"It's my way or your way," he muttered. "We have a lot of miles to ride together so it will be *my* way." The mule snorted once then followed grudgingly on the lead rope behind Chato.

Merrick paced up to them and lifted the cradleboard from the saddle. "You're hungry, aren't you, *nino*." He smiled, shouldering the child to him. He couldn't just keep calling him, *nino*. The boy needed a name, a good Christian name, something like John Christopher Kelly, after his father. And he, Merrick Ryland, would have to find a woman to care for the child sooner or later. There were too many things about all this he didn't know yet. There were still these many miles to ride to Fort Seldon, and after that an ocean to cross. And, at the moment, they needed safe shelter for the night.

Chato halted suddenly, his nostrils flared, his head lifted to the wind, testing the scents around him. Merrick grabbed too late for Chato's reins. The stallion trotted a few paces, pulling the string of mules with him. He didoed in stride and stopped.

Puzzled, Merrick let him go. Chato grazed a few paces nearer the entrance to an ice cave where grama grass grew thick and black-seeded. It was as good a place as any for the night once a fire was set. It was well sheltered from the wind and commanded a good lookout over the terrain below. He remembered this all very well after spending two agonizing nights in it.

Chato was troubled. He had moved again, swinging his head now in the shadow of the cave opening. Merrick felt along his saddle pack and unholstered the Henry. He slipped the magazine cartridge beneath the barrel, lowered the trigger guard. It was probably an animal seeking the same refuge.

Shadows were longer now, slanting blue and cold over the top of the cave. The wind seemed to be chanting over the spread of rocks, the same sound the wind made at times in the top-gallants. Only there wasn't any wind all of a sudden. It was spent now, quiet like a dead spot on the sea. He could still hear the chanting.

The form inside the cave was huddled Apache-style on its heels, naked except for a tattered *serape* thrown over one shoulder. The chanting was monotone, unlike anything Merrick had ever heard before, repeating the same words, "*Yah-ik-tee, Yah-ik-tee,*" over and over again.

Merrick's heart locked in his throat. It was

Adria—broken and bruised, but alive. His hand trembled over the tangled spill of her hair and touched her shoulder. She began to sway on her heels in a trance. When he turned her face to him with one finger, her eyes were glazed and hooded. Ashes and paint slashes were smeared on her cheekbones and forehead. She was ice-cold to the touch.

"*Nuestche-shee*," he said gently, lifting her to him. She stood staring down at his hands, refusing to lift her eyes to him.

"Do you know me, Adria?" he said, swallowing down the need to crush her to him.

"*Mer-rick*," she counted out the syllables the way an Indian would.

Merrick wiped his mouth with the back of his hand. She was in shock of some kind. He needed to think of something, and quickly. He led her by the hand to the entrance of the cave where Chato was grazing. She didn't seem to see him. He shucked out of his sea coat and wrapped her in it, then drew her close against him, just holding her.

"I wanted to die. I tried to die. There was nothing left. They took Chato. They beat him. They made me watch," Adraia said in monotone.

"I have Chato," Merrick husked. "See, he's there. He knows you." Merrick tilted her face to where she could see the horse. "I brought you another present," he said, reaching in the coat pocket and dropping the pair of her sunstone earrings in her palm. Adria's fingers closed over him, and slowly, so slowly she lifted her eyes to him.

"Do you want to wear them?" He smiled, smoothing her hair away from her face. "They match your eyes." Adria nodded meekly and let Merrick help her put them on.

"I have a tin mirror in the camp pack. You can see how beautiful they look," he coaxed, his voice humid.

"No!" Adria cried suddenly. "I do not see myself!" The tears came then in a rush, streaming her face. She covered her face with her hands, this time letting Merrick fold her in his arms. She was still sobbing in gasps when Merrick lifted her and carried her outside the cave.

Chato had grazed over near the rock where Merrick had propped the cradleboard. He stood protectively over the now whimpering child.

"He's hungry. We need to feed him," Merrick said, looking about him for some firewood. He was reluctant to let Adria leave his arms.

Adria stared open-mouthed down at the cradleboard. "You have *kay-nay*!" she burst out. She slipped from Merrick's arms and dropped to her knees beside the child. She began to croon to him in Apache, the way she had heard his mother do.

"Speak English to him. He won't be raised an Apache," Merrick said shortly.

"He was born in the Apache camp. Erlinda told me so," Adria said, untying the leather trappings that held him.

"That does not make the boy an Apache."

Adria picked the boy up in her arms and comforted him, indifferent to what Merrick said. "Kelly will be proud when he sees his son, when we, when I take him to his father."

Merrick wanted to rage the truth at her, but hesitated. He walked over to Chato and unfastened the camp pack. He watched Adria comforting the child.

"You should have told me about *our* son," he said. "How long did you carry him before—"

Tears sprung to Adria's eyes, and for a moment, Merrick was afraid she would slip into shock again. He was pressing her too hard, with too much, but he couldn't help himself.

She held up three fingers, shook her head, and held up four of them.

"Say it to me," Merrick demanded. "Don't use sign."

Adria caught a breath to speak, but no words came. *Kay-nay* had discovered her sunstone earrings and was reaching for them, squealing with delight.

Merrick took the child from her and set him between his feet on the ground. He watched him crawl in a circle and sit up. Adria stood quietly beside Merrick, her head bowed, a trace of a smile on her lips.

Merrick took a hard breath and turned her to him. He had to tell her sooner or later, and now seemed as good a time as any.

"While we're having this rare moment of honesty, there is more you will have to know. There isn't any easy way to tell you."

Adria looked at him with her steady topaz eyes. She wet her tongue over her lips and seemed to brace herself. Merrick sensed a long shudder pulse through her.

"You know, don't you?" he swallowed. "You know Kelly is dead. He rode here with me to find you. He was at Fort Fillmore that day I happened on you at the lava pool. He didn't know I had already found you when he ordered the attack on the camp. I was scouting the back-trail to the river while he was arguing with the cavalry over tactics. Chase killed him at the camp."

Adria didn't flinch. She just kept searching his eyes for more truth.

"They all died, except Chase," she murmured. "I heard the cannons. I knew they would all die. Manchito, he brought me here to the cave. He thought he would find you. He thought he could beat the truth from me, but I wouldn't tell them where I got Chato. I was hurt and could not come back to you then. He saw me take the pony. They do things to women. . ." her voice broke, but her eyes were cool and steady.

"No one will ever touch you again, or hurt you," Merrick rasped out. He took her hand, seeing the livid burn marks on the palm. His mouth touched over it.

When he could find his voice again, the words came more gently. "There is this to tell you. I killed Kendall Chase."

"*You*?" Her mouth formed the word.

"He was riding Chato and wearing Kelly's clothes," Merrick said. "Given the same circumstances, I would kill him again." He turned on heel and started to walk away from her.

"Merrick," Adria said softly, touching his arm.

"You and Kelly were never married," he blurted out. "Kelly paid that priest, Father Amyas, to read a Spanish benediction over you.

Kelly gave his word to the priest that he would marry Erlinda Mateos if Father Amyas would perform this one 'favor' for him. I went to see this Father Amyas and he told me the truth. There was no record of any marriage. So all this was for nothing!"

Kelly's son began to cry and Adria ran to him. She lifted him in her arms and coldly turned her back to Merrick.

CHAPTER 36

Merrick collected enough mesquite bark and bramble from the uprooted madrona tree for an armful of firewood. He dropped it in the middle of the cave, arranged it, and set a match to it. The sudden light gave the icefall interior of the cave an awesome pristine glitter.

Adria had melted some snow water and washed herself and *kay-nay*. The child was happily chewing on a leathery strip of salted beef she had found among Merrick's rations. She had yet to find a way to open the curious tins of milk.

"I need your knife," she told Merrick, reaching along the loop of his belt for it.

"I don't trust you with knives yet," he said sullenly. He opened the tin and handed it to her.

Adria sat back on her heels. "I don't know how to feed him."

"All women know such things."

"But he wasn't weaned," Adria insisted. "Erlinda always—"

"He's hungry enough to take it from a spoon in small drops," Merrick shrugged irritably. "If we can ride ahead of that snowstorm above the peaks, we can be at Fort Seldon by midday tomorrow. The sutler there will have some of what we need for him."

Adria felt his eyes scald over her again. He wasn't being kind to her any longer, he was sullen and short-tempered and watching her every minute. She was beginning to feel more and more like someone's captive again. He looked drawn and haggard, like he hadn't slept in weeks. He was unshaven and his usually immaculate sea coat was salted with dust. She had offered to help him with the canvas shelter he made for Chato and the mules beneath the lee overhang of the cave. He had crudely ordered her back inside the cave to watch *kay-nay*.

At least now some of the apathy and the numbness that had been so much a part of her was thawing. Events were still hazy and muddled, and much too painful to sort as yet. She didn't speak in broken phrases so much any more, because each time she did, Merrick corrected her. She couldn't think very far beyond the moment. She was still too unsure of herself.

"I can't go to Fort Seldon with you, Merrick," she swallowed.

"And why is that?" he snapped at her.

"Because of who I am—or was."

Merrick swore to himself. She sure as hell *would* attract her share of attention looking the way she did, wearing his dark wool undress shirt that hung well to her knees. She had knotted it about her small waist with a braid of twine he had seen her work to shape in a matter of minutes. Her long shapely bronzed legs, her waist-long white-gold hair, her bare feet, and her riding stride saddle like she did, would probably cause a stampede among the ranks. But she wouldn't have to explain anything to anyone. He had already made certain of that.

He leaned back against the cave wall, his jade eyes searing the length of her.

"I have a paper signed by General Canby and a Major Lynde at Fort Fillmore that says you can—with certain conditions of pardon," he said slowly.

Adria pretended not to hear him. She set the coffeepot to boil on a hook over the fire and meticulously began arranging the tinware on a blanket, plates in the center, utensils on each side. She prayed Merrick wouldn't notice that she was trembling so.

"What are the 'conditions'," she said without looking up.

She felt him move to stand above her. She closed her eyes, dreading being sentenced. She heard *kay-nay* then, and glanced quickly to see him amusing himself with a ball of cloth she had rolled for him. His trusting crystal eyes smiled back at her. The moment was so fragile, so perfect.

There was a strange tightness in Merrick's voice when he spoke.

"That you agree to become the wife of a British citizen." He sounded like he was reading the words to her. "That you agree to become mistress of a gatehouse in the Chiltern hills, one with leaded-glass windows and Cotswold stones for the fireplace. That you agree to raise another man's son along with the ones he will insist on having when he makes love to you each night."

Adria quit following his words. She turned to him. Merrick reached out his hand to her and lifted her to her feet. He was smiling at her in that rare and wonderful teasing way of his. Merrick gathered her to him and kissed her searchingly, as though for the first time. Her mouth was hot and moist and eager against his demanding one. It was all the answer he needed.